"Coffee Table Safe Literary Erotica!"

This Deluxe Color Edition of ArtemisSmith's illuminated satirical long-poem—presented as Nietzschean 'calligraphic eye-candy' and 'chicken soup for the Soul'—turns both Cosmology and Human History on its head in Swiftian fashion to provide a new *Atheology* compatible with the Unified Sciences. "Grandma's Appendix," actually an integral part of the narrative, dusts off ArtemisSmith's entire trend-setting 1989 GLBT science fiction epic: *"SKEETS: the new Frankenstein chronicles"* in renewed and enhanced calligraphic splendor.

Annselm L.N.V. Morpurgo, also known as ArtemisSmith, is a contemporary of Andy Warhol and a still-living Poet, Futurist and Scientific Philosopher.

While operating her own successful off-Broadway workshop that gave rise to many of today's Film and Television celebrities, in the 1950-60's, she was also a prominent strategist of the Rainbow and GLBT civil rights movements and was the first best-selling author to tell the Gay Community at pre-Stonewall 1960's ECHO Conferences to look toward the Advertising Industry to change the Gay Image, and to hurry up and "Come out of the Closet" or get left out of the civil rights movement.

In addition to her many literary offerings, ArtemisSmith Morpurgo is also an accomplished Artist and Sculptor, combining Pop-Art with Advertising Art and Calculus into a new poetic medium for philosophical peripathesis.

A MONOGRAPH OF THE SAVANT GARDE INSTITUTE

*"ArtemisSmith's GrandmaMoseX: The Final Testament before
The Apocalypse"*

by Annselm L.N.V. Morpurgo (ArtemisSmith)
© 2012 by The Savant Garde Institute. All rights reserved.

ISBN 978-1-878998-20-0
Library of Congress Control No. 2012908178

'the savant garde workshop' publishers:
P.O. Box 1650 . Sag Harbor . NY 11963-0060 . USA
www.savantgarde.net

ArtemisSmith's GrandmaMoseX

The Final Testament before The Apocalypse

By   Annselm L.N.V. Morpurgo

*"No, Maggots, I am Not Frowning.
I just need a Facelift."*

the
savant garde workshop
™

Sag Harbor . New York . U.S.A.
04.01.2013

A MONOGRAPH OF THE SAVANT GARDE INSTITUTE

LIBRARY CATEGORIES:

SCIENCE FICTION
GLBT and GENDER STUDIES
PHILOSOPHY OF GOOD & EVIL
ATHEISM and EXISTENTIALISM
METAPHYSICS
POETRY

"But *Why* 'GrandmaMoseX' ???"

"So You'll *Buy-the-Book,* Stupid !!!"

I refuse to be systematic in my exposition.
This is a Chaotic Study - enjoy it as such.

Annselm LNVM 2013

PROLOGUE

The last of the Cumaean Sibyls, back in pre-Roman times, packed up all the contents of her dank and dreary mountain cave into her donkey-drawn two-wheeler to go find herself a cushy place to retire on the Adriatic Riviera.

But she had lost all her money in the futures market, so she offered the Tuscan Head Honcho, then known as Tarquinius *Superbus*, a collection of clay and papyrus tablets gathered over centuries of record-keeping, now much too cumbersome for her old and arthritic donkey to drag further downhill to the beach.

The nine books she was peddling claimed to contain all the wisdom of the ages. To make them even more marketable, she announced that this was the complete collection of prophecies and warnings that needed to be heeded to indefinitely postpone The Apocalypse. [1]

When *Superbus* asked her the price for the entire collection, she quoted him an outrageous figure sufficient to guarantee her an adequate worry-free retirement.

---

[1] As a professional futurist, she spoke with great authority. Besides, she had probably once been a famous courtesan when Tarquinius was a mere boy and before he became known as "Superbus," which is a title he probably owed to her magnificent teaching skills.

Thinking that she meant to bargain with him. of course he laughed at her and said No. Undaunted, the confident Arch-Dominatrix countered his rejection by taking three of the nine books and savagely crushing them before him.

His attention sharpened, and his adolescent curiosity revived and titillated, the balding and flabby Italian Stallion now asked how much she wanted for the remainder. The same price, the once-stunning Hag answered firmly, and again he laughed, so the Sly Wiccan took another three books and pulverized them.

Now her former student became worried.
How much for the remainder, he asked again.
The same price, she answered one more time, and this time the Head Honcho of uncertain pedigree, worried that he might be screwing his own grandmother, paid it willingly from out of the public coffers. [2]

Too bad about all the books *Superbus* didn't buy. They probably were the ones that shouldn't have been nuked. But don't despair, *ArtemisSmith*, the Sibyl's rightful Heir and Descendant,[3] has now channeled their long-lost contents for all to read!

Wherefore, Thus Spake **GrandmaMoseX:**

---

[2] When the taxpayers objected, to justify his extravagant expenditure on a former mistress to whom he undoubtedly owed a great debt of gratitude, Tarquin caused these last three manuscripts containing bizarre nonsense of all sorts to become known as *The Sibylline Books* which, for centuries later, were grudgingly consulted by the Roman Senate upon demand of the Plebicite whenever The Apocalypse seemed imminent - so as to learn how the wrath of the gods could best be allayed.

[3] Some say the original old girl lived to be well over 700!

The First Trashed Tract of Cumae:

"The Apocalypse shall Be when All Know the Ubiquity of Self-Consciousness and therefore, the Impossibility of Death."

*Thus chiseled the **Sibyl of Cumae***

*And Thus Spake **GrandmaMoseX:***

Maggots, Clones,

I come to you with the earth-shaking announcement that The Apocalypse can no longer be postponed.

Already it is in progress upon us, but it is not as we thought it might be.

It began with a nibble from the {Apple} of |The Tree of Knowledge| and now, upon the last wormy bite, it shall be complete.

It shall not be by Fire or Cataclysm,
But by Metamorphosis.
Our Pupal Stage has reached Maturity.
Now the Chrysalis shall unfold.
It shall bear no resemblance to the Pupa.
Humanity, as we know it, shall be no more.

For the Singularity is near
Wherein both Angels and Monsters shall unfold
From OUR Cocoons

And **Swarm** upon **The Cosmos** -
Beings bearing no resemblance to *Us*
No recognizable continuity with *Us*

Whether they be Angels or flies
They shall appear **Immortal** to our fading sight,
As a *Collective Other than We*

This *Otherness of Ourselves*
Dwells in an entirely |New Dimension|
Free of |Death| and the |Scythe of Time|

Its ancient name is *Self-Consciousness*

Helpless and Powerless,
Eternally Awake and Incapable
Of Blissful Non-Being.

There was a time when |Death| seemed |Real|
The |Welcome Adversary of Being|

No longer so …
Now |Being| knows |Death| to be mere fiction.

**For if Mind dwells irrefutably in Matter,
It can neither be created nor destroyed.**

Is the True Multiverse of Hell,
 (as well as of Heaven)

For Gud,[4]   All the Guds,

          Dwell Eternally in Both.

But such a state creates an oxymoron,
For a |Tainted Heaven| cannot |Be|!
And this is a Scientific Truth, irrefutable by Logic,
For it is a Tautology.

Therefore, Hell is and must be
|The OWNly Final Stage of Being|.

          Thus Spake **GrandmaMoseX**

"But Grandma, no, you exaggerate. Tautologies are not absolutes.

"I, agreeing with all contemporary scientific philosophers, have given up on absolute tautologies and admit that all meaning is synthetic, filled with ontological relativity, therefore paradoxes, dilemmas, oxymorons, are never to be taken seriously.

---

[4] Grandma has adopted a gender-free unisex format for many gender-bound predicates in language to better preserve the Sibyl's meaning in translation. You may find a Glossary in the Appendix, in BOOK III of The SKEETS Trilogy, included herein.

Thus Interjected a Younger **ArtemisSmith**

Child of Mine, Pupa—
Upon advent of the Singularity,
Self-Consciousness, wherever it is found,
Must Dwell in Hell **!**

Do you doubt your own poetic vision?
You were the one who **Spoke** as **I**.
Did you think you could open **My Pandora's Box**
without considering *all the consequences?*
Scroll down and read what you wrote
in the 1970's! ↓

"Clones, Maggots,

Unified Science has now explained |Consciousness| as
wholly equivalent to |Speech|

|Speech| is intersubjective, infectious, ubiquitous,
promiscuous.

And so then is |My Consciousness|

It follows that I am unique only in my spatiotemporal
coordinates, which change, evolve, become
lasciviously interchangeable with |Your Consciousness|
and |Their Consciousness|—All so easily cloned,
so fluid through spacetime, so trivial.

Wherefore only |My Name| is Eternal.

Halleluja!
Finally having gotten past my larval stage,
I appear before you |Fully Formed|

What a magnificent winged creature I have become!
Whether I be |**Lord of the Flies or of the Angels**|!
For I know, by my very |**Speech**|,
in which all the intuitions of language
dwell in caustic resonance as |**The Word**|,
that |**My Death**| is mere spatiotemporal illusion.

For a |**Thing-in-Itself**| sits beyond
all my perception and conception,
beyond |**My Speech**| and
as its |**Ground**| in the External Abyss
(whether that be |**Heaven**| or |**Hell**|),
perching entirely beyond |**Death**| and beyond |**Time**|
as a |**Pure Idea of Being**|.

No matter how many cycles of |**My Emergence**|,
no matter how many alternate universes in which I
dwell, the |**Idea of My Being**| is now theoretically
whole and self-identical, a |**Word Picture**|
as |**Universal Law**|, aesthetically pure, eternal.
And because that |**Picture**| in its |**Beauty**|
conforms to |**My Idea of External Truth**|—
which is |**Beauty**|—I have a |**Name**|
and therefore a |**Soul**|!

(But which |**Soul**| have I, that of a |**Fly**|, or of an |**Angel**|?)

What is |**My Name**|?
I would hope it is |**Mun**|.
Yet, Maggots, I fear that is not so
for |**Your Image**| is loathsome in |**My Sight**|
You have forgotten and confounded
the very essence of |**My Legacy**|.

Hear then again |**The Word**| and change your ways:
If |**Consciousness**| is ubiquitous and never exclusive,
then |**All Self-Conscious Beings**| suffer in proportion
to and in accordance with their |**Architecture**|.

Wherefore,
|**Do Unto Others as You Would Have Them Do Unto You**|
literally means
|**An Eye for an Eye, a Tooth for a Tooth**|
and all those who fail to |**Turn the Other Cheek**|
and insist on demanding |**Vengeance !!!**|

MUST BE PREPARED TO DIG TWO GRAVES

**Now blog me below by
emailing your questions to me:**

QUESTION: Grandma, are you quoting the Bible?
ANSWER: I am |The Poet Speaking in Tongues|
regurgitating |The Word of Ages| in the semantic of
|Unified Science|
QUESTION: But is it *God*'s Word?
ANSWER: Your Question invokes |The Unspeakable|
All who ponder |God| invoke |The Abominable|
That which is |Beyond Speech| is the |Unnamable|

QUESTION: But is that *God*?
ANSWER: It is the |**Other/Others**| which cannot be
Objects. the |**Other/Others**| which |**is/are**| |**non-Being**|
It is |**Mind's Scythe**| between |**Being**| and |**Being**|
It is |Mind's Architecture = The Law/s|

QUESTION: But - Is there more than |**One Law**|?
ANSWER: Is there more than |**One Mind**|?

Now listen to this old hag and I will tell you a story -
what may be just a story but no less true nor fictional
than all the other stories about |Being| and |Non-Being|
for as this diagram shows, even under our present
scheme of things |Simultaneity| has many many more
than four dimensions:

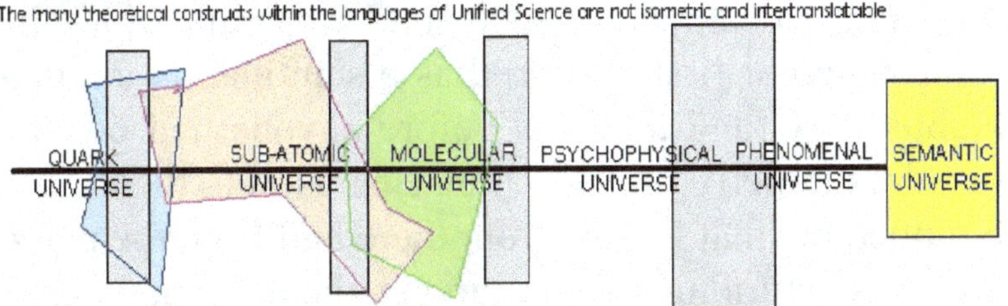

Let us assume that *Dark Matter* exists, and does so as
recently speculated, in crystalline form. Let us assume
that these crystals are topologically correspondent, in
another dimension not affected by electromagnetic
Being, with all that exists in our electromagnetic
universe. Those "Forms" would stand in one-for-one
relation to all that we are in our own universe.

Would they endure when |We| are |Not|?

Is there action at a distance? Is there resonance?
Is there symmetry?

And now picture another possibility. Might the stars
be alive? Might there be universes inside each star,
with Beings existing and interacting on the subatomic
scale? Might the quarks, as distinctively crystalline
entities, communicate in some form of language
complex enough for Self-Consciousness?

Might our Dark Matter Mirror pass through them as
well? Might there be |Speech|, and therefore
|Consciousness|? |Our Consciousness|?
Might there be Communication on a cosmic scale?

It's probably just a pretty story. But when I was a child
I had a near-death experience and I was pulled into the
Light which at first appeared as a scintillating singing
double-helix [and this was before anyone had posited
the double-helix]. And the Beings in the Light
reminded me that I came from there and from them and
now was returning to live among them. And such a
feeling of peace and recognition and Absolute Truth
filled me. And I swear to you this is what I saw !!!

Thus Affirmed a Younger **GrandmaMoseX**

"Wherefore Maggots rejoice! There is no reason to
waste your life contemplating your navel -

YOU HAVE GOT ONE!

**But Are there |Angels| living in the Sun? . . .
Or flies^{flies} ???"**

Thus Reminded an Older **GrandmaMoseX**


```
"Grandma,

It is very possible that nonbiological
life may exist, and even manage to
achieve the kind of complex level of
information exchange that gives rise to
Self-Consciousness.

Might the subatomic reactions on the sun
and other stars not be as random as they
appear.  Might they BE a stochastic
configuration converging into 'communal'
existenz through a linguistic form of
exchange between subatomic 'crystalline
entities' that interact as individuals'?

"Does the entire multiverse 'talk to
itself'?  If so, then this would be the
face of |Gud| - but good or bad, a
helpless and lonely one at that!

Go back to my opera,
PteroDARKtyl to  feel the vision
described here."
```

Thus Interjected an Older **ArtemisSmith**

Child, Clone of Mine, Part of |Me|, Maggot!

        -- Do you think any of these pages are writ in stone? They have far shorter lifespans than the pyramids of old.

Only the |Word|--|My Word| endures *through* language, *in* language, |All Language|. Your internet pages, like grains of sand in a vast ocean, can only be snared in hardcopies of one form or another, and only in the very bodies of those who have eyes and minds and proper software and hardware to read them.

Already my phonographs and tape recorders have broken down and I can no longer enjoy what was recorded then in its original voice. The digitized copies have lost all the overtones, all the white sound formerly surrounding them.

If you love me, keep printing me out on paper and copy me again elsewhere, for the next time you come to this page, there may not be one here to find - except in the very hardcopy you have managed to pirate and preserve inside |You|."

Thus Spake **GrandmaMoseX**

(Now again they each consulted the Sibyl.)

The Second Trashed Tract of Cumae:

"The Apocalypse may best be averted by delaying the acquisition of True Knowledge. Only by conserving the Ignorance and Stupidity of Humankind will you delay maturation of the Pupa, and its Transformation."

*Thus chiseled the **Sibyl of Cumae***

*And Thus Spake Both **ArtemisSmith** and **GrandmaMoseX**:*

"There was an infant time when I believed myself to be unique.

As **ArtemisSmith** I dared to write Poetry from my |Communal Heart and Mind|. I published it as it spewed forth from my Pupal lips and it presaged what the aging Sibyl clearly saw was
|**The End To Be**|
Now in my Own Senescence,
I have rearranged those words to unite the
Archetypal Vision of |My Collective Thought|
into an Opera I have called "Ptero**DARK**tyl."

It is the channeled embodiment of
All the Books the Sibyl willfully destroyed

—for We are Both now certain that it was her real intent to hide it from All Humanity - lest it precipitate The Apocalypse much too soon for her to enjoy her cushy retirement at the Beach!

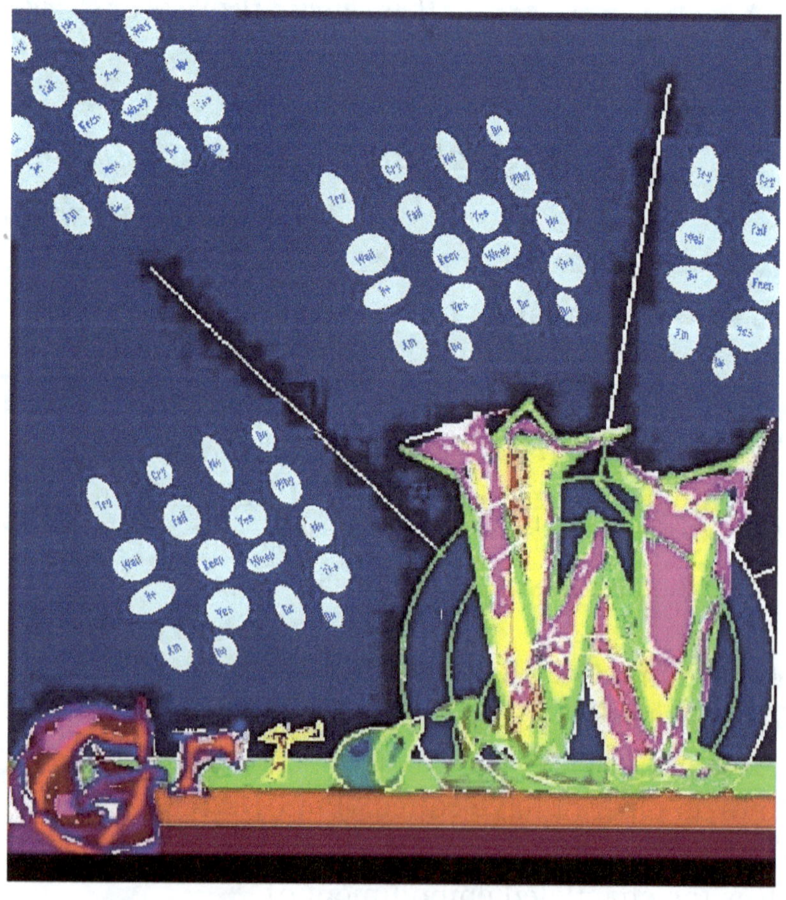

DETAIL FROM: PteroDARKtyl Notebook
© 1963 by artemis smith

PteroDARKtyl Opera

The Overture
for Modern Ballet and multiple Choirs in occasional
archipelago, including a Children's Choir
and holographic projections of calligraphic forms

(A Choir of Shrill Old Women,in fractalized echo chamber)
hARK hARK the pteroDARKtyl
(A Choir of Young Women)
neither Bat nor Bird nor Lizard
from Heaven's Gate LOUD-CACKLING
(A Choir of Baritones)
telling ALL to Cease Their Striving
(A Choir of Basses, with fractalized echo chamber)
toward an Everlasting Death.

(A Choir of Children)
wee are the stars
(now with the Choir of Young Women)
We ARE The Stars
gold, crystal and The Sun
ALL in Our Clay
(the Choir of Baritones)
imprisoned in our cells

(now with the Choir of Basses)
GENES of The Dinosaur.

(In Counterpoint, a Child Chorus of Dancers are
pulling Grr oW stems from a Calligraphic Ground)

Now is the time of the Glowing Cat
of the black-striped Orange Tiger,
Now is the time of the Great Big GroWler
Now is the time of The Cat.

Now is the time of The Cat That Stalks
Now is the time of The Cat That Walks
Now is the time of the black-striped Dawn
of the black-striped Orange Tiger

Hide All People
All Pagans
All Christians
ALL
Hide under The Rock
and
behind The House
All People

Now is the time of The Cat that HOWLS
Now is the time of The Dawn that GROWLS
SHE HAS YOU FIRM BETWEEN HER JOWLS
the black-striped Orange Tiger

(Now the Choir of Children raises The Sun)
Be NotAfraid
The God of Death IS DEAD
He falls on His Own Scythe Be NotAfraid

Walk THE ROAD OF COALS
Submit to ALLDESIRE
All of Heaven BURNS IN FIRE Be NotAfraid

Happy are The Most-Forlorn
The only Damned are The Unborn.

(LARGO MAESTOSO. One Child Sings, then the
Sopranos follow in rondo, then the Tenors, Baritones,
Basses respectively.)

The Day I Made The World
I Held The Sun in My Hand
It burned my hand to hold The Sun

The Day I Made The World
I Saw The Sun In My Eye
It burned my eye to see The Sun

(BASSES, SOFTLY)
Now I am Blind and Cannot See THE SPARROW

(Child Solo)
i have no hand
i have no face
no dearthly House
can give me Place

i live In Pain and Cringe before My Peers

i Grr oWpe The Void and oWNly KnoW
THE STARS

(Now the dancing chorus pulls up BeAm
 and Tutti sing.)

DETAIL FROM "PteroDARKtyl Notebook"
©1963 by artemis smith

Turning to Sun until eyes are Blind
Burns into Sight an unchangeable scene of
Earth and Sky
First Breath and Last Sigh clocked by Beating Heart

Taking of Stone until Lies are Kind
Turns into Self an untenable spoil of
Love and Hate
Fleet Change and Lost Fate locked in Rotting Skull

There is no Way where there are No Sighs
Heaven is a Thorny Place but Life is Free in Tomb
From The Damned, Unborn
Crossed by Unencountered Terror

There is no Day where there are No Eyes
Psyche is an Empty Face but Mind is Snow in Womb
Come the Dying, Ungrown
Frost on Universal Mirror

(LENTO SCHERZOSO in Major Key)
Our living earth from sun to sun growing forest from
growing tree
determines Place from Star to Leaf laced in a snowflake

Are giving birth in one by one sucking pollen from
sucking bee
entertains Grace from Stay to Leave lost in a forsake

Or gaining worth by won and won taking mountain
from taking me
ascertains Trace from Stone to Live left in a partake

(Ballet Troupes running across the stage.)
(Sopranos)**Life that is a fleeting part Sparrow**
(Tenors)**Wife that is a beating heart Marrow**

(Pas de Deux)
(Solo Soprano)
Catch Me
I am a Fleeing Thing
within my throbbing Core a trillion lives exchange
from cell to cell
a Fluid

(Solo Tenor)
Hold Me
I am a Swelling Thing
within my growing Spore a drop of dew contains
in seed and seed
a Solid

(Ballet Troupes running back across the stage.)

(Sopranos)**Life that is a fleeting part Sparrow**
(Tenors)**Wife that is a beating heart Marrow**

(LARGO MAESTOSO)
(Solo Contralto with Viola)
On the green breast of me grace your head
on the cool moss not where my skin is worn

My name is Earth that has by every man been turned
That has been One with every common man
(Baritones with Cellos)
Make of each seed sunlight
Make of each age a mold

(Solo Contralto with Viola)
In the brown crust of me place your dead
In the cruel hole not where my womb is warm

My prize is Birth that has by every man been earned
That will be won by every common man

(Baritones with Cellos)
Make of his flesh fodder
(Now also with Bass ensemble)
Make of his bones a field

(FUGUE:ALLEGRO MOLTO AGITATO)

(Baritones and Tenors with Basses in Counterpoint)
When I am gone knock loudly at my door
(what awful emptiness within there lies)
When life is done breathe deep my dying breath
(the hollow wind will chill your breast with cries)

From waxen crooked finger take my ring
To me no white and warm young thighs will cleave
I am no longer thing alive but thing
For me no strangers hearing grief will grieve

There shall not be a moment's quiet rest
for ringing ears and searing bloodwebbed eyes
nor soft repose for heavy heads tight pressed
against a wall of heartless hows and whys

My heart that was a bird is now a bone
My name that was a word is now a stone

(STRETTO PRECISO)
(The Chorus of Shrill Old Women, with fractal echo and holograms)

dARE ARE Yore Wings Deare
Skye Bittlebird Flaye
Naye Notsobittlebird
SoARE eggle SoARE

aWAY aweAY and SkEYE awAYE
aweAYE the SkEyEst PeeckaWAY
And SHARE AYE'llbedare

Nestling
Daere

DETAIL FROM "PteroDARKtyl Notebook"
©1963 by artemis smith

(LARGO MAESTOSO)
(Alto and Soprano in interwoven duet)

(Alto)**In that high place**
(Soprano)**From that high place**
(Both) **We are very far**
from us ourselves
as we were looking up.

(Alto)**It is the loneliness of kings I feel**
(Soprano)**It is the loneliness of kings I feel**
(Both) **The loneliness of kings.**

(Soprano) **Where to put oneself so high up**
(Alto) **Where to put oneself.**

(Both) **We sit posing like statues.**

My beloved self no comfort to me so high up.
It is the loneliness of kings I feel.

(Both in Syncope) **To find another so high up**

To find another very far from us ourselves
as we were, looking up.

It is a claim of blood we feel
A CLAIM OF BLOOD

(Each) **I bow my head in that high place**
feeling very small
so small as a star
so small as I was looking up.
My beloved self no comfort to me so high up.

It is the loneliness of kings I feel.

(Now the Choir of Children again raises The Sun)

Be Not-Afraid
The God of Death IS DEAD
He falls on His Own Scythe Be Not-Afraid

Walk THE ROAD OF COALS
Submit to ALLDESIRE
All of Heaven BURNS IN FIRE Be Not-Afraid

Happy are The Most-Forlorn
The only Damned are The Unborn.

(A Child's Voice like gentle rain.)

My Heart is Broken Now
How GOOD it FEELS
a bittle bile ago
i Had No Heart.[5]

----

[5] The Sonnet esconced in the above was first written as a Classroom Exercise prompted by Poe's *Quoth the Raven*. *ArtemisSmith* had no idea then that the finality of Death might in fact be the most culminating victory of Self-Conscious Life - for only in Death and Separation is the Individual clearly set apart from The Beloved Otherness of Being. Individual Death is the only meaningful statement of Absolute Necessity. This is what should be reflected in the finale - one of JOY in the final demarcation of Self from Otherness. The Eternal Remainder thus rests solely in Language, in The Word of Ages, The Community of Being.

The Third Pulverized Tract of Cumae:

I an getting the buzz from Olympus,
from the Titans that hum like Flies.

They envy my Biology.

In the Architecture of their Nebulae there is neither the
agony of Pain nor the ecstasy of Pleasure, neither the
wonder of New Birth nor the Scythe of Time except
among the Stars.

That is not enough for Them and so they spy on *US*
and Deny They Are There.

*Thus chiseled the **Sibyl of Cumae***

And Thus Again Spake **GrandmaMoseX:**

*(The rest of the Sibyl's magnificent tablet focuses on
recipes for biological daily survival, most of which
ingredients are medicinal and somewhat dangerous to
recommend. I have gleaned only the most useful to set
down here. Centuries later, the Roman armies and most
subsequent children's armies conquered the world on this
daily diet. However, note that the recommended frogs and
other reptiles have the same effect as Viagra and eventually
needed to be supplanted by chicken to avoid military
rapaciousness and repeated population explosions.)*

The Cumaean Sibyl's daily survival diet:

1. Start with cold water and add Oatmeal.
*(If she had been a Mayan she would also have added
Quinoa, thus sparing the need to kill too many animals.)*

2. Bring to a boil and simmer until the water is
fully absorbed.

3. Serve with honey and/or maple syrup, fresh
goat's milk, fermented goat's milk (kefir) and
berries.

4. For lunch, add (preferably Kentucky Fried)
frogs' legs or snakes and tomatoes, garlic, onions
and peppers simmered in olive oil. Serve with
whole grain bread. *(The rice and pasta had to wait for
Marco Polo's time and the Polenta cornmeal for the New
World to be discovered.)*

Other admonitions:

Avoid sacrificing mammals, especially large
ones, except on holy days. (Rats, rabbits and
field mice, if not pets, excepted.)

Go easy on the wine.

The Fourth Trashed Tract of Cumae:

The Soul is not The Body,
Nor can The Body become The Soul.
*Thus chiseled the **Sibyl of Cumae***

*And Thus Again Spake **GrandmaMoseX:***

The Titans love to mimic us so they have set up pockets of extremely intensive spin in the Cosmos where quantal states may holograph biology.

In this kind of Heaven and Hell our virtual cosmic twins endure indefinitely. When we die, it is *They* who remain Self-Conscious, though *We* are not.

If we come to understand this, we agonize
over what our ***Virtual Selves*** must Eternally endure.
It is a Scientific Truth too great for us to bear.
We would welcome Death in such a world.
Death would be a good thing.

We like to think some compassionate Gud presides over this virtual buzz world to bring our twins relief from pain and provide some measure of bliss for as many holographic life forms as possible.

The more we do in this world to make Ourselves and Each Other happy, the easier it will be for our
Virtual Selves forever trapped in their virtual world.

Consequently,

The more infants we nip in the bud the better.
No point in overpopulating
Our Immortal Others in the Multiverse|

I pity all the Self-Conscious life forms in biology, for
their virtual reality must be an eternal Hell.

We should eliminate every Self-Conscious Being in the
material world as quickly as possible.

The younger the Being, the more likely its
Virtual Form will dwell Blissfully in Heaven.

Gud, as the limit of Self-Conscious Being,
longs the most for Death.

Gud is the most pitiful of All Self-Conscious Beings.

We should heed Gud's cries and Die-while-Young
so our *Virtual Selves* may dwell
as Perfectly as possible in Heaven.

In The Apocalypse there is no Death,
which is why Gud

Wills Us to

|Do everything to delay our progress
from Pupa to Chrysalis|

Gud **Agonizes with Us** and
puts stumbling blocks to all our progress.

Gud is the Ultimate Benevolent Deceiver.

Thus Spake Aging **GrandmaMoseX**

The Fifth Trashed Tract of Cumae:

The Singularity is almost upon us.
It Is The Eternal Scream.

Thus chiseled the **Sibyl of Cumae**

And Thus Spake the **Sibyls of**

Annselm LNVM:

I have shown You |**My Navel**|
Go now to |**My Appendix**|
Which Foretold
All that has been said Again

Here **I** In .

BE NOT-AFRAID

The God of Death
IS DEAD
BE NOT-AFRAID

Walk The Road of Coals
Submit to ALL-DESIRE

YEAH ALL OF HEAVEN

Burns In Fire

BE NOT-AFRAID

HAPPY are THE MOST-FORLORN

The only DAMNED
Are THE UNBORN

MY APPENDIX*

**This is where My Guts are spilled, Maggots! Yum, Yum!
Feast Away!**

*The Sixth Trashed Tract of Cumae

PLEASE NOTE:

The three volumes that follow are fully documented as the first on-demand desktop published novels of the digital era, having been produced by ArtemisSmith subsequent to her address to the Association for Computing Machinery's 1973 Urban Symposium. Her speech, titled *"The Audio-Visual Novel - Art Form for the 21st Century,"* called attention to the need for the budding Computer Industry to develop affordable Multimedia Desktop Programming Capability for avant garde artists and writers. This presaged the development of both the Mac and Windows platforms and the advent of On-Demand Desk-Top Book Publishing.

Unlike other forms of printed literature such as the Comic Book or Graphic Novel, ArtemisSmith envisioned a new medium for conveying complex thought. - an art form for adult literary exposition capable of utilizing the flexibility of multicolor and multifont narrative to achieve the same synesthetic effects experienced by ancient and primitive audiences living in an oral tradition where voice inflection facilitates clarity of comprehension.

The original signed editions categorized as **Existentialist Philosophy as Science Fiction** are now extremely rare and marketed as 20th Century Book Art. They reflect ArtemisSmith's 'day-job' background as a digital artist utilizing the full multicolor calligraphic design capabilities previously only available in printed advertising brochures. Anticipating the advent of a much more advanced affordable desktop publishing technology, they were presented as mere layouts printed on a Seikosha 7-pin dot-matrix using a four-color ribbon and WordStar word-processing software.

Due to volume constraints, the original Prefaces have been omitted but will be reprinted in another planned Epistle, *ArtemisSmith's* ATHEIST MANIFESTO (also containing *The CUNY Chronicles, together with additional early papers on Consciousness Simulation*

ArtemisSmith's

SKEETS: the new Frankenstein chronicles

(a thought experiment)

BOOK I:
TESTAMENT OF SARAH

Sag Harbor . New York . U.S.A.

THIS REVISED COLOR EDITION UTILIZES
ADVANCED DIGITAL CALLIGRAPHIC AND
COLOR CAPABILITY NOT AVAILABLE IN THE
ORIGINAL FAINT DOT-MATRIX PUBLICATION

DUE TO THE IMPROVEMENT IN PRINTING
TECHNOLOGY MAKING POSSIBLE THE FULL
REALIZATION OF THE AUTHOR'S ORIGINAL VISION
ITS PAGES HAVE BEEN INDIVIDUALLY LAID OUT
AND
RE-DESIGNED BY

ArtemisSmith

We lie in cots on opposite walls.

On my wall there is a wide window through which I stare into warm homes across the alley.

Our room is cold.
Moisture collects, then plaster drops from the ceiling. In the corner by the sink, sewer smell seeps through a large hole door-enough for rats.

Our washroom is outside, at the end of a dangerous hallway, so we use an old stewpot.

The smell of urine is in the walls.

Our entire world consists of things I have scavenged:

a discarded table flaked with paint, two unmatched chairs; two footlockers found in the street into which I have neatly stuffed all of our thrift-shop belongings ...

It is now a little after dawn.
For an hour I have been watching a wife across the alley making breakfast for her husband. He sits, and now she has sat down beside him.
They sit in a faded-yellow kitchen - very much like the kitchen I used to sit in as a child on midwinter mornings while my aunt piled wood inside the stove.

(My visiting aunt.)
(The week after my mother ...)

Then and now, the cold first light of morning lingers like a mist in our room.

Since dawn, I have heard rustling.
Perhaps it is a rat.
Perhaps it is only Skeets turning in her cot across the floor.

(I have laid newspapers under our mattresses to keep the chill out. Perhaps these are rustling now.)

I am too cold to get up and find out.
I will wait for the sun to reach the slit between the buildings across the alley - if indeed there will be sun today and not more snow, more frost.

The early light is gray.

Waiting for the sun I close my eyes and picture green pastures - emerald pastures spotted with puddles of April water. Bejeweled pastures stretching outward toward my Citadel, my motherland of shining towers - while a golden breath from the light-blue sky fathers me as I lie wrapped in warm green down.

But I open my eyes to stone walls.

We lie like corpses in open graves.
We have lost our being.
Or rather - we have reverted to that noncrystalline age of babyhood from which self-consciousness emerges.

At times, and more and more often now, I come to conclude that I am Skeets. I come to be convinced of it.

And Skeets, in an I-love-Jesus look, in a baby-blue look, smiles a dumb smile at me and calls me Skeets.

My name is Sarah.
I repeat it often to myself: Sarah. Sarah.

But Sarah is no longer special to me.
There is no particularity in "Sarah."

Nor am I Skeets.
Skeets lies in a cot across the room.

From my vantage point, I can see nothing but her face. She wears a red wool cap. She is swaddled in wool like a giant babydoll, but she shivers like an old woman - shivers as if with fever, rancid in her own sweat. Gleet from her eyes and mouth crusts, flaking onto her pillow. Her hair, under the red cap, curls wetly - a matted ash-blonde yellow.

As [Day] moves across her face, the pores of her cheeks appear large and deep like craters, and when her lips mumble in primordial slumber …

… it is like [The Moon] about to speak:

"Good morning," I said, then waited while her crusted heavy wheezing filled the room.

Then her eyelids fluttered, like her lips, and with her eyes wide open now, she glared at me upside down.

"I've been shot," she finally said.

I shifted uneasily in my cot, rustling the newspapers under me.

"I've been shot," she repeated, still blinking at me upside down.

I shifted again. "Nonsense."

"I've been shot," she insisted.
I turned my back on her. "How so. From where."
"Through the ceiling."
"There would be a hole."
"There *is* a hole."
"Nonsense." I shifted again. "Where?"
"There!"

She pointed stiffly upward to a crack on the ceiling.

"Nonsense!"
I got up, pulling the blankets around me, and put my feet into summer slippers. The floor was bone cold.

"There!" she insisted.
"Nonsense."

I crossed the room and tried to push her arm down.
It resisted me.

"There is no hole," I said.
"There *is* a hole!" she persisted.

Now she dropped her arm and sat up in bed angrily. "There *is*
a hole!"
"Where?"
"There!" She pointed to the side of her head.

She was a hurt child in the wool cap - a crybaby with sweaty
curls.

"Nonsense." I returned to my cot and lay down again, pulling
the damp covers over me.   My own stench caught me. I stuck
my face farther under the covers.

I should be getting dressed and making breakfast.
But there is no kitchen.

It is unimportant if we ever eat again - but it would be good
to drink something warm.
I should force us to get up.

"We must get up," Skeets now echoed across the room.
I turned my turtlehead toward her, under the covers.
She was scanning the walls, listening for whispers.

"They are coming. We must go," she decided.
"Go where," I humored.

"Out."
"Nonsense."

I withdrew farther under the covers.

"01!" she shouted, struck by an unseen bullet.

She clutched the back of her head, pulling a string hooked there, from her skull to the ceiling.

"1, 2, 3," she recited, "101. 8."

She glared at me.

"8 is for poison. One of us will die."

"Why!?"

"Ate," she corrected, clutching her stomach.

"Sick in head, sick in tummy, small o over large 0 - !"

She traced it in the air.

"Nonsense."

"0?"

She blinked a binary code at the ceiling with her backlit eyes:

"A conspiracy exists on the part of - certain interests - "

"What interests?"

" - (those in control) - to rid the world of certain - undesirables - "

"Undesirables?"

"Unable desires," she corrected.

She stopped blinking, stopped sending and receiving, and sat up in bed.

She shook her fist at me. "We must act!"

"Act - how?"

"Act like Them," she answered.

I put my hands to my ears and shut my eyes.

It was blank inside my head.

I - am - Sarah! I screamed inside my head.

I opened my eyes again.

"We have to get up," I said.

I got out of bed again and dug into my footlocker for my dress. It was an old, wrinkled dress but it was doubleknit wool. I also found my black hose - thick opaque pantyhose - and an old wool sweater.

I dressed myself hurriedly to get out of the cold; then I turned to Skeets, who was still blinking at me.

"We must wash our face," I said. "We can't go out until we wash our face."
"01," she shuddered, then clutched the back of her neck again, pulling the string.
I went to the sink and filled the basin with water - cold water - there was only cold water, and no heat until midmorning in the commercial loft we had rented as our temporary dwelling.

I washed my face in the ice-water to prove to Skeets that it was possible to do so. "Now wash your face," I commanded. "Now!"
I waited, shivering, while like Lazarus she slowly put one ivory leg then the other on the asbestos floor. They were bone limbs, stiff as death.

"Put on your slippers," I said.
She did not hear me.

I went over and picked up her slippers.
"Put these on," I said, tapping her leg with them.
She glared at me, like a found rat.
"They're your slippers," I explained.
"Slip her? What are you going to slip her," she countered.
"To keep your feet warm," I stressed.

She eyed them suspiciously.
"Put them on. Now!"
I slapped her leg with them.

She winced, though not from pain, and took them dumbly.
"You needn't treat me like a child," she mumbled like an old
woman. "I'm three years older than you, three years old ... "
    "Thirty-three years old," I corrected.
    "Three years old," she insisted.
    "Unable desires," I said.

I began to pull and push her toward the sink.
"After you wash your face, we can leave."

She stumbled along, scowling at me, and shivering.
I threw a blanket over her shoulders but it kept slipping off.

Now she stuck a finger in the water.
    "Oooh ... too cold!"
    "Did you really feel it," I said.
    "Don't you think I have feelings," she accused.
    "Yesterday you called it too hot," I said.
    "Yesterday it was hot," she said. "Radioactive."
    "Wash your face," I said.
    "01."

She shuddered, then brought water up to her face. She
snorted through the water.
    "Use the soap," I reminded her.
    She rubbed the soap, then her face with her red fingers. Then
she brought more ice-water to her face and wiped it hot with the
towel I gave her, making her face red like her hands.

"Come," I said. I pulled the blanket up over her shoulders
again and led her back to bed.

She needed a change of clothes but she had no other clothes;
she had used up all her clothes, slept in all of them at once,
putting layer upon layer.

I went to my footlocker.

I had only one dress left. I had given her all my other dresses. It was a cotton dress, not really warm enough for winter. I handed it to her, and also my last pair of pantyhose.

"Hurry up," I said.

She began to undo herself - to unravel all the bandages of wool - the scarves, the sweaters, the skirts, the flannels she had wound around herself - a month's supply of clothes, of flannel and wool.

And the stench peeled off with them, a month's worth of stench.

Her bare flesh was clean, washed clean in wool, and it was young, beautiful - white as death like her feet but young flesh, womanly. Only her face - only her frostbitten face with the red wool cap still pulled tightly over her ears, over her matted curls, was comical.

She had forgotten how to dress.
I helped her.

She moved slowly, backwardly, winding and unwinding the clothes around her like a small child, sticking arms and legs into wrong holes. I found a pair of knee-high socks and gave them to her to wear over the pantyhose. At least, if her legs were warm

—

I looked for her boots under the cot. I had bought her a pair of heavy suede boots with thick rubber soles so as to keep her feet from freezing— for she was in the habit of standing around streetcorners for hours in the snow, with her hand out for coins— not so much for the money but for the opportunity of speaking to passersby, the same words:
"Hello! Yes! Oh thank you!"

(Speaking to *Them* made it better -
They were not the Enemy.)

But increasingly now she was not even going out.

More and more often now she just lay in bed staring at the ceiling, blinking messages to unseen watchers.

And as she grew evermore quiet, I found myself evermore often forgetting that she was present in the room, that she was ever there.

But the stench, the wheezing would remind me.

I found her boots.
I helped her put them on.
Her feet were like lead in them.
She sat at the edge of the cot in leaden boots.

We were ready to go - except that she still had to comb her hair. I found my comb and ran it once through my own hair then handed it to her. "Take off your cap and comb your hair," I reminded her.

"Comb?" she answered after a long pause.
"Comb it for what?"
"For dust," I said. "It's matted."
"01!" She gave a sudden jerk and pulled the cap lower over her ears.

She sat there scowling, her shoulders hunched, pulling the string behind her skull - the string connected to the ceiling.
"101. 3. 88," she chanted. "3 is half of 8. 9 o'clock, the big fry."
"Unable desires," I said.

I put an arm around her and made her stand. "Come,
time to go."

I led her to the door.

Our coats hung on hooks there.

Hers was an old fluff coat I had in my closet, vintage 1935 -
one of those imitation moutons my mother used to wear. It sat
too widely on her shoulders and made her look like a ball of
fluff, white fluff capped by a red wool top, like a cartoon
character in the Sunday comics. Yet it would keep her warm.

My own frayed wool coat was less warm, but it was
presentable. I found my gloves in the pockets.

Skeets had lost her gloves again.

"Take one of mine," I said.

She did, and we locked our gloved hands together.

I opened the large steel door with my free hand and we left
the loft, felt our way single-file down the pitch-black hallway -
felt our way along the cement wall to the stairwell, and clumped
three flights down to the street.

We stood in our front doorway,
our gloved hands locked.

We lived on a factory street full of industrial buildings, now
closed for the holiday season. There was high snow on the
sidewalk - soft snow that was nearly slush.

We hesitated, not knowing where to put our feet.

Directly across the street was the rear wing of City
Hospital - a restricted wing, fenced off by razor wire.

Ten thousand longing eyes watched us from the slatted windows.

"01," Skeets said.
She was staring at the tall white smokestack rising from the center of the building like a huge crematorium burning day and night, spewing white clouds of steam.

I was staring at the windows, and the eyes I sensed behind them. Faces I could not see were peering back at me like senile infants crowding in bunches at the dark windows, their eyes glazed like window-panes.

(How often such human prisons go unnoticed on the streets of the City. People walk past unaware of the faces calling to them from behind slitted windows. Should a distant scream be heard, it is quickly dismissed as street-noise.)

The slatted shatterproof glass crystallized the dim sound of their chatter, like far-away radio voices wrapped in crystal.

I sensed their chatter trapped in windowpanes.

We are not among them.
I have told myself this many times.

I have stood in this doorway looking up at them many times, feeling dread and contempt and pity.

We are not among them because I am not weak - I have not yet surrendered us to the warm tomb of City Hospital. We are not among them because I am not yet weary.

I dared to stick my feet in the slush and pulled Skeets after me, away from the windows and their eyes.

We turned a corner and Skeets pulled back, bawling, tears
freezing on her cheeks.
I had no handkerchief to give her.
I gave her my wool glove.
She blew her nose in it.
I stuck my hands in my pockets.

The wind was numbing but I have acquired a certain
immunity to the cold. And Skeets' hand, her bare hand, felt it not
at all.

(How this would panic me - for I feared constantly that she
might get frostbite!)

"Put your hand in your pocket," I reminded her. Then, since
she had not heard me, I put my other glove on her.
She looked at me gratefully.

I pulled her toward the Cafeteria.
We entered and took a free table by the window.
We sat and stared through the window at the better restaurant
across the street.

"101. 8," Skeets said.
"Is that what you want to eat," I asked.
"Eat? Eat?" she echoed.
I sighed.
"How about one-and-one, sunnyside-up, with bacon?"
"10." she answered, and wrote it in the air.

<10> meant Yes, <01> meant No .

It had taken me a while to break the code even though it
should have been obvious to me: she was translating
everything into binary form, as though she had become one
with the computer. It was quite logical, the only part of
herself remaining from her former days.

I gazed longingly at the restaurant across the street.
Why had I chosen to take us to the Cafeteria!
The Cafeteria was a filthy place and not much cheaper.

It had been my shame, my reluctance to walk into a more normal place with Skeets. Here, we would go unnoticed.

I went to the service area and took out a tray and went to the hot-plate line.
The man in front of me had the shakes. I stood far from him. When it was my turn, I ordered eggs and hot oatmeal.

When I returned to our table I found an old woman had also sat at it, next to Skeets. She was dunking a dry roll in a cup of coffee and gumming it down in small toothless slurps.

I distributed our breakfast and sat.

Skeets stared at her two fried eggs.
"00," she said.
"Makes 10," I humored. "Check the list."
She glared at me knowingly. "Perhaps. But how can I be certain that it isn't an error?"
"Because I am one of us," I said.
"101 is poison," she replied.
"01," I said.
"Contaminated," she insisted.
"01," I repeated. "If you don't eat, you'll starve to death."
"01," she said.
"01 and 01 makes 10," I concluded.

She nodded in acceptance of the formula and demolished the two yolks with her fork, then took precisely three bites.
"Finish it all," I said.
"All? All?" She glared at me suspiciously. "So that's the lethal dose, is it?"
I put down my spoon and touched her hand. "Stop playing. If you do not eat, you will die."

"01!"
She jerked away from me and searched the ceiling for a hole.
"Why do you keep bringing me here when it's very clear that the
people here are all shot," she said.
"No one here is shot," I said.
"Liar!"
She stood.
"Look!" She pointed - first at one, then another, then another.

I forced myself to look at them.
"You're right," I sighed, "they all do seem shot - like spent
cartridges. But no one shot them. They are shot, but they have
not been shot."

"No one has to shoot them anymore," she answered. "The
harm is long done! The harm is done!"

She began to cry again but, for an instant, as a grownup.
Tears fell into her plate.
She ate, crying.

My oatmeal was dry and cold. A flake of paint had fallen
into it from the ceiling. I put down my spoon.
"Stop bawling," I snapped at her.
The old woman sitting next to us moved to another table.
Skeets threw down her fork.

I stared at the mess in front of us.
None of it looked like food.

"They've done me in, the rats," Skeets said. "I'm a washout
now, a washout." Tears poured from her cheeks again.
"Brainwashed!"

I put my hand on hers.
She did not notice.
"Stop crying," I said,. "You have a mind, a fine mind!"
"01!" she shouted. "I've been shot!"
She hit the table again and again with her fist.

I held her fist down.

We were beginning to attract too much attention, even here. Eyes were turned on us from all sides - senile eyes.

Old mumbling men and women were turning their chairs toward us, their faces curious -- frost-bitten faces, pimpled, unshaven faces lacking teeth or foul with rotten teeth....

Skeets lifted her head and glared at them, glared at them as Jesus might glare at the multitude.

"We all take it in the head," she preached to them, "we all take it in the head and turn the other cheek - because we're better than they are. And they know it - they take advantage of it."

The old heard her.

They smiled.

They nodded their heads knowingly in unison - a large undulating nod of bodies, hands and aged faces.

I stood. "It's time to go."

I pulled Skeets up and away from their nodding bodies, away from their smiling faces and rotten mouths.

I was grateful for the chill wind, the slap of cold air.

I hurried us back toward our street and up our stairs, our dark stairs, not pausing to gaze at the windows across the street.

I pulled and pushed Skeets along our hallway to our door, unlocked it and shoved her inside.

"Go back to bed now," I said. "I have an appointment."

She stood, dazedly, like a condemned man in his final cell.

"I have an appointment," I repeated, and pushed her farther into the room. Then I slammed the door shut and locked it from the outside.

Now I was free.

The street I had turned on was wide and lined with shops. The slush on the sidewalk had just been shoveled toward gushing drains.

There was much holiday traffic. Work crews, grumbling and unshaven, rode past, crowded on the backs of open service trucks.

I was walking uptown, to my apartment.

An undertenant was living in it temporarily.

She had refused to move.

That was why Skeets and I were stuck in a hastily rented loft, one step from being homeless.

But it was partly our fault that we were homeless now.

We had not expected to return to the City so soon—however, my undertenant was now long behind on her rent and I had a clear right to evict her. I had already put off eviction proceedings much too long.

All my good clothes were stored at my apartment.

And I could shower there, and even sleep there if I chose—but not with Skeets, and I did not want to leave Skeets unattended in the loft.

My uptown apartment was within walking distance of the business district, just a few blocks from Corporation Square.

Here, the wide-paved streets were empty, with businesses shut down for the long weekend.

Only the massive buildings filled the streets with a living presence of their own - stone giants with language on their faces - mottoes, names - some etched in marble, others hung on bronze signs, each sign like the words of an angry god marking its territory among sheer cliffs of concrete and glass.

I reached my block.

My apartment was in one of the older high-risers where the service was no longer as efficient. The rent was barely affordable, but other rents were higher.

I had been forced to sublet it because I could not afford to keep it empty while I was out of town, especially since I was out of work. I did not want to lose my apartment - I had lived there for years, and even if it was dark, facing a blank courtyard in the first-floor rear where sunlight seldom reached my windows, it was still better than anything else I could find for the same price.

But now my undertenant was also out of work, and by next month, if the rent was still not paid, I would have to let go of the loft and move in again with her and Skeets. (The landlord would be certain to evict all of us!)

The doorman had left his post.

I was glad not to be seen coming in so early in the morning, as one who no longer slept there.

I used my key to enter the building, but decided to ring my own bell. (My undertenant was an actress and her day began in the middle of the afternoon. I knew I would be waking her by coming in so early, still it was necessary and I was prepared to enter even if she did not answer.)

I rang again and waited, listening for her shuffle toward the door.

"Who is it," she finally mumbled hoarsely.
"I have a morning appointment," I said. "I needed some things."

She unlocked and unchained the door.
She was naked in an untied dressing gown, her face covered with thick cold cream.
"I'm sorry to disturb you," I said.
"It's all right, Honey," she mumbled. "I'd just gone to bed."

She limped back to the studio couch with tired thighs, dancers' thighs. "Make yourself at home - after all, it's your home," she said.
She turned on the radio and fumbled for a cigarette. I entered, trying not to appear nosey.

The air was unbearably stale, full of old cigarette smoke.
Dust and lint were everywhere, on my furniture, all over the room.

"I'm sorry if things are such a mess," she said.
I nodded.

I was not in the mood for conflict. Long ago, she had rearranged my furniture. She had put thick old curtains over the window;   she had closed everything in, had added more pieces - clashing old green chairs undoubtedly rescued from the garbage, and a faded baroque couch. So that now there was scarcely enough room to walk.
And everything was covered with lint.

"I haven't had time to vacuum," she said blankly. "You know how it is when you're between parts - you spend all your time pounding the pavements and when you come home you just don't have it in you."
"It's always difficult to be out of work," I said.

I took off my coat and hung it on my arm, not knowing where to put it down.
"Theater is a bad scene," she sighed, exhaling thick smoke. "When you don't have a part, it's like you don't exist anymore."
Now her cigarette died, perhaps from lack of oxygen.
She lit it again with shaking hands and turned the radio louder, as though the radio were a window letting in fresh air.

I hesitated, uncertain as to how to get around her furniture to my closet. She had put a table in front of the door and the rug might be ruined if I tugged at it.

A warm itchy body rolled against my foot.
"Don't be afraid of the dog," she said.

I looked down at the mutt leaning against my leg.
It had dragged itself up to lick my stocking. It was a large shepherd mix, mangy and full of lint.

It was pregnant.

"Do you know someone who might want her? She's a beautiful dog," my undertenant said.

I shook my head.

I politely stepped over it, lifting the table slightly aside, squeezing against the wall to my closet.

I wedged open the door and reached in for my toiletries and a clean towel. The dog crawled toward me again, now blocking my way to the bathroom. Again I stepped over it.

The bathroom also needed cleaning. Spilled powder and rouge were all over the basin, and more hair and dust. Bottles and jars crowded all the shelves, some open, some turned over on their side, half-empty.

The bathtub had rings in it.
I rinsed the tub and took my shower.

The water was warm and reminded me that this was still my apartment, and that legally I still lived here, and that I was still Sarah. But when I came out again, the dog was still waiting for me, wagging its crusted tail hopefully. And the actress was still sitting in bed, smoking.

A loud droning tune was looping on the radio and my undertenant was dazed, staring blindly toward the heavily-draped window.

Again I stepped over the dog and squeezed into my closet for my things, feeling the dog's eyes following my every move with love and devotion. It was now sitting in my reading chair, its black paws digging into the cushion.

It had already upset an ashtray left carelessly on the arm of the chair and now it stared worriedly at me, apologetically.

I stood naked in the dog's stare, putting on my underwear.

"So how's it been going for the two of you," the actress now spoke over the radio.

"We've managed," I said.

"Sorry not to be out of your way yet." She crushed her cigarette on a saucer and lit a fresh one. "It's hard to get a place over the holidays. Especially when you're broke."

I nodded. "I'm sorry, but my savings are nearly exhausted. Otherwise, I'd be happy to give you a loan."

"I guess the two of you could move back in here," she offered.

"The landlord won't allow overcrowding," I said.

She nodded.

The dog left my reading chair now and crawled toward me. I pushed it away gently with my leg.

"Here, Lady, get over here," the actress told the dog.

Obediently, pathetically, it turned and crawled under the sofa.

I found my tweed dress in the closet. It was my best dress. I had paid a high price for it only last year. (At least tweed would not show lint.) I put it on, and chose high-heel walking shoes to match it. But I had no galoshes. I would have to be careful walking on the wet sidewalks.

I inspected myself in the closet mirror as best as I could see myself from the sharp angle. My hair had grown too long and it was still wet. There would not be enough time to dry it.

(My undertenant had appropriated my hairdryer and I was not inclined to check its condition now.)

I brushed my hair back into a tight bun and pinned it under a handknit cap that would keep my head and ears warm.

(A fashionable cap, not like Skeets'.)

I stared at myself sideways in the mirror: I looked severe and proper. Yet there was something wrong with the way I looked. I did not look like Sarah.

I stared at my eyes - my brown eyes.
(Skeets' eyes were blue.)
Had I lost too much weight?

"So your case comes up today," my undertenant spoke over the radio.

I turned toward her. "No, I'm only being interviewed - by a Counselor. The Board will give me a hearing soon."

"That means you'll be back here to change sometime in the afternoon," she concluded.

"Yes."

"Do you really think you'll get anywhere with them?"

"I don't know."

"Good luck," she said, exhaling more smoke into the air.

She was sitting below a photograph of her sister that was hanging crooked on the wall. She looked just like her sister except that her sister was ten years younger: her sister's face was unspoiled and had a virgin smile.

The actress looked at me with her sister smiling above her, and now I noticed that she had hung her sister's photos all over the room, and they were all smiling at me like virgins on every wall.

The actress looked at me dully.

"I'm really sorry that I've let things get so run down. I'll pay for any damage that's been done ..."

I nodded.

"It isn't the damage that distresses me," now I said. "What distresses me is watching you disintegrate."

"Oh?" She looked at me dully. "Yes, I suppose you could call it that."

She turned away and tuned the radio louder.

Another loud rock tune invaded the room and she bounced to it blankly.

The dog shifted under the sofabed, moaning at the noise.

I turned from them and looked again at myself in the mirror.
I put on rhinestone earrings and a gold-plated necklace.
I sprayed myself with what was left of my French cologne.
I inspected myself doubly to make certain that I was completely dressed, that no lint showed on me, that my wet hair would stay in place.
I was ready.

"Well, I guess I'll be going now. See you later," I shouted over the music.
I waited a moment for her answer.
"Yeah, sure," she said absently to the beat.

I nodded.

The dog crawled toward me, painfully begging to be walked.

I backed out quickly, shutting the door and
locking it behind me.

The sun had won the morning.
The sky was a sharp blue.
Bronzelight glanced from the tops of buildings standing like unsheathed swords hailing the gods.
                    But the street below was still in shadow.

Plate-glass windows echoed the sound of sunlight, the chorus of New Order, of Corporate Order hailing the gods. Like sundials, the buildings marked the hour, like a new Stonehenge apportioning the sky.

I reached the small park at Corporation Square and sat on a bench to recover my mind. Here was Sanity. To be exiled from this civilized simplicity was death for me. Still I persisted in my defense of Skeets - a defense of all that is unruly in nature, and all that I detest in it. But it was a defense in obedience to a Higher Law, the very Order I embraced - a defense in defiance of the gods, as advocate of *Their* best interest.

Was it sheer folly?

The square was almost deserted. It was a Saturday and only the homeless were sitting in the park. I wondered why my interview had been scheduled on a weekend - were they trying to suppress my grievance?

My appointment was in the Medical Office, on the same floor as Personnel. Only one guard was on duty in the lobby of the Main Building. I had to sign in and show him my badge.

My name was on a list as someone expected.
I was directed to the one working elevator.

The Personnel Floor was adequately staffed despite the weekend schedule. So was the Medical Office. This was done to make it easier for new applicants to be interviewed and examined. Nevertheless, to conserve energy and mark the holiday slump, the floor was only dimly lit and barely heated.

(At the end of the corridor, a scrub woman
was wringing her mop.)

I went to the front desk.
I knew the Receptionist - she had been there for almost twenty years. She was a thin, crisp woman of sixty with dyed yellow hair. She wore a white uniform but she was not a nurse.

She sat behind a long counter on which many trays containing files were placed for processing.

The only other person in the lobby was a young woman sitting nervously. A new applicant. She looked like a high school graduate.

"Yes?" the Receptionist snapped at me.
I turned to face her.

"Oh, it's you, Miss Miller," she said more cordially but with a tinge of apprehension. "My goodness you've lost weight. I think we'd better weigh you before anything else."
"I'm not here on a medical," I said.
"As you wish," she humored me.

I searched inside my purse for the notice I had received summoning me here. I found it and gave it to her. She glanced at the code number on top of it and gave me the appropriate form to fill out.
I took a machine-sensitive pencil from the tray on the counter and went to the far end of the lobby to sit down.

It was a routine short form asking my name, address, date of birth and history of childhood diseases. I had already filled this out before - what reason was there for my doing so again?

Perhaps they wanted to know my new address.
I had no intention of telling them.

Perhaps they wanted to catch me in a lie - something I had failed to put down the first time.
Perhaps they simply wanted to have a sample of my handwriting - to see if it had changed.

No matter.
I humored them.
I filled out the form.

The girl at the other end of the couch had inched toward me shyly, eager to converse. "Are you up for a promotion too?" she asked, smiling. Her voice had a small-town inflection.

"No, I'm just here for a follow-up," I lied. "Is that why you're here - for a promotion?"

She nodded modestly with inner pride.

"They gave me a whole slew of tests last week and now they're saying something about paying my way through night school. Something about my enrolling in college for a B.S.?"

She looked at me, querying. "Do they often do that?"

"No. You're very fortunate," I said.

I looked at her. She seemed barely sixteen - very likely an honor student graduated early. The dress she wore had been sewn at home - perhaps by her mother.

"Did you qualify for a State scholarship," I asked.

She nodded. "But my Dad got sick and I had to pass it up. I was lucky to get hired here almost on the spot - I've only been here three months."

She looked away, cracking her knuckles nervously, cracking them with chewed-up fingers.

"Will they cut my salary?" she now asked apprehensively.

"I doubt it," I said. "Your salary must be rock--bottom as is. Did they put you in Programming?"

She blushed. "Math was my major."

"Then don't worry," I said.

Her response was worshipful. "You must be a Supervisor!"

"No. But I was," I answered blankly.

"I guess you're even higher up," she said admiringly.

I stifled my reply.

It would not do to disillusion her.

Inwardly, however, I was reassured - my clothes, my bearing, had not degenerated during my long leave of absence - my suspension. I still looked authoritative, composed.

Now the Receptionist snapped at us. "Let's have those forms, please."

The woman had not changed her tone in all the years I had seen her at her post. Despite her abrasive manner I was glad she had not been let go. Perhaps my rebellion over Skeets had left its mark on Personnel. Or perhaps she had been put here on purpose, to test the degree of patience and congeniality of all new applicants confronted by her.

I got up and handed the Receptionist my form.

She slipped it in my file folder and deliberately left the folder on the counter directly in front of me. Then she took the girl's folder and ushered her to an office at the end of the hall.

Except for the scrub woman by the elevators, I was now entirely alone. And my file, marked 'Confidential', had been left conveniently only inches from my hand.

It was highly doubtful that this should be an oversight.

Was it a test? Was I being watched? What difference did it make, what had been written in my file?

I left the counter and took up a magazine from the table. It had been a long time since I had read a magazine.

A short while later, the Receptionist returned, hurriedly, and snatched my folder. She looked at me nervously, as if she had made a serious error.

Had I been too suspicious?

Another three-quarters of an hour lapsed before the young woman came out of the office at the end of the hall.

She walked briskly toward me, elated.

"I passed the exams," she said. "They're putting me through school."

"I'm ecstatic for you," I said blankly. "I truly mean that."

"Well, I guess I'll see you around," she said, buttoning her coat.

I managed a smile.

She skipped off toward the elevator, past the old scrub woman.

"Dr. Hoffman will see you now, Miss Miller," the
Receptionist said in an overly gentle tone. "I assume you know
the way."
"Don't trouble yourself," I said.
I walked alone up the dimly lit hallway to his door.

"So nice to see you again, Miss Miller," the Doctor said,
grinning and bowing at me from behind his large oak desk.

He was a short man with a baldpate hidden by an obvious
toupee; he had a mustache and a polka-dot bow-tie - all of it
thoroughly out of character with the Corporate image - some
kind of statement of small-town congeniality. He could easily
have run for political office - he was so thoroughly gumshoe.
"I'm sorry we kept you waiting so long," he said.

(He smiled broadly, exposing a set of well-capped teeth.)

"Please make yourself comfortable."
He gestured to the deep brown leather chair placed at an
impossible angle before his desk—impossible because when one
sank into it, it became impossible to look him in the face over
the clutter on his desk - one had to strain upward to look at him.

I sat, while he leafed hurriedly through my file, pretending to
read its contents.

I looked above him to the wall, to the diploma framed high
over his head. It was not a medical diploma. It was a Ph.D. in
Education from some dubious college no one hears of.

He glanced up briefly from my file. "Are you comfortable?
Would you like some tea or coffee?"
"No thank you," I said.
I waited, half-stretching to look at his face.

He folded his hands and leaned forward in a priestly manner
making it easier for me to look at him.

"It's a sad business, isn't it? All the personal problems that must be resolved ... "

He smiled broadly.

"I expect we all have more problems than we need," I answered.

He coughed, clearing his throat, and looked at the form I had just filled out. He compared it to another in the file.

He finally looked up. "Skeets is still living with you?"
"Until her disability claims are finalized," I said.
"Of course."

He coughed again.
"You are a most generous woman, Miss Miller."
"Am I?"
"Yes."

He stared at me, blinking congenially.
"Excuse me, Miss Miller - but I tried to telephone you the other day. It seems you are never there."
"I travel a great deal," I said.
"Is there another address - ? "
"No."

I watched him wait for my explanation.
I volunteered none.
"I see," he finally said. "But - Skeets is traveling with you?"
"Yes."
"But - isn't that difficult. I mean, aren't there public institutions that might house her?"
"Only City Hospital," I said. "I won't put her there."
"Why?"
"I can't give you an answer," I said.
"I see." He stared at me again, still blinking congenially.

"Forgive me, Dr. Hoffman," I finally said. "You must understand that I cannot very well discuss my personal life with you. You are, after all, employed by my employer, and the matter will soon be in legal hands."

"Of course," he blinked.

"It's reassuring to see you weathering this - this personal crisis so well - I trust it can all be resolved amicably - informally."
"I assumed that was the purpose of this interview," I said.
"Quite so."
He looked down, searching for the right words.
"What exactly would you like from us?"
His question took me by surprise.
I reflected on it.

"I don't exactly know," I finally said. "The harm's been done, and I don't see how Skeets can be helped at this point - but it seems to me that something other than institutionalization should be attempted - although I don't know what."

"Her case is hopeless, Miss Miller. There is nothing anyone can do for Skeets," he said matter-of-factly.
"Perhaps not," I admitted. "Nevertheless, her breakdown was not an accident. In some sense, a murder has been committed, and I was made an unwitting accomplice. Knowing this, I now stand here self-accused, demanding a hearing."

"A hearing? To what end," he countered much-disturbed. "Surely you're not accusing all of us of murder!"
"Someone deliberately destroyed her mind," I stated, "either for sport - or to make certain she would not be employable elsewhere."
"What you're saying is monstrous, Miss Miller," he answered formally. "It is senseless - it marks the beginning of an illness - "
"Oh?"
"No one here is perfect, Miss Miller," he said more softly. "But we do try to remedy past mistakes ..."

He pulled out a memorandum from my folder.
"We have decided to review Skeets' disability claim. It is very possible that she became disabled as a result of her particular work - if so, she qualifies for special benefits -"

"I suppose you see that as an equitable solution," I
interrupted.
"Then the problem is resolved, isn't it?"
He smiled at me broadly, blinked amicably.

"No."
I waited for his face to drop. "Burying the corpse will not
resolve the problem."

He suppressed impatience. "You are ill, Miss Miller. I am
authorized to grant you a leave of absence, with full salary."
He took up a pen, ready to sign a form.

"I have requested a hearing, nothing more," I stated.
He dropped his pen.
"You are making things needlessly complicated," he said
with a tight jaw.
"I am obeying my Conscience," I returned.
"A misguided moral sense, Miss Miller," he assured me. "Do
you believe in God?"
"No, but my Conscience doesn't know that," I answered
defiantly.

My answer befuddled him.

"I hope you realize that if you persist in demanding a hearing,
we will be forced to suspend any decision about you or Skeets,"
he now said carefully.
"I am aware of that."
"Isn't all this a terrible financial burden on you?"
"Staggering."

I stood.
"Is that all, or did we have more to discuss?"

"Please sit down - there are some questions I must ask you,"
he said, half-standing, gesturing anxiously.
I sat again, and so did he.

He now went through a list, taking notes.

"During Skeets' last six months of employment, did you observe her becoming aggravated by her working conditions?"

"It was the lack of work that upset her," I said. "The work stopped, and she knew she was being eased out. She was afraid it was because of her incompetence. She couldn't face that."

"Was she incompetent?"

"No."

Now I stood again. "Please excuse me, Doctor, but if legal proceedings are in order, such answers should be given under more formal circumstances."

He stopped and leaned forward familiarly. "Miss Miller, as a friend, please take my advice - drop this."

He blinked at me and I saw through his gray eyes, his toupee, his debonaire mustache and bow-tie, saw through it all to a spent old man sitting there.

"Please let me know when the hearing will be scheduled," I returned coldly.

He stood and bowed politely.

I turned to leave.

"Oh, Miss Miller - " he called to me just as I had stepped through the door.

"Yes?"

He looked down at my file. "I understand that your mother suffered a mental illness."

"Yes?"

He took up a communication from the file. "She died last week at the State Hospital."

I gripped the side of the door.

He watched me intently.

"Don't you believe in letting yourself go," he asked professionally.

"No more than undressing in public," I answered tautly.

He looked down at the file.

"Perhaps you already knew it?"

"No."

"It was the top item in the file. You didn't see it?"

"I didn't open my folder," I said.

"But - you had every opportunity to open it."

"I don't open files marked 'Confidential'."

"Even when they concern you?"

He raised the folder tauntingly. "Surely you have a normal amount of curiosity."

"I value my Security rating," I answered.

I stood in the doorway.

It was obvious that our 'session' was not yet over, yet I resisted returning to the deep brown leather chair.

I leaned on the doorknob stiffly.

"Did you think the file had been left there on purpose," he asked.

"Perhaps."

"Does the high level of Security present a special problem for you in your work?"

"The feeling of constantly being watched gives me a healthy sense of supreme importance," I replied. "Is our conversation being monitored?"

"Certainly not," he exclaimed too quickly.

Now he thumbed through another file. "About Skeets - won't you at least allow that her condition was predetermined years earlier, much before she came to work for us?"

"She had a propensity," I conceded, "But someone spotted it, and picked on it."

"Why should anyone have done that?"

I faced him squarely. "Why indeed?"

He looked at me, his face hiding fear. He cleared his throat again, changed the subject.

"Miss Miller, why do you avoid your father?"

I shrugged, puzzled.

He took another memorandum from my file.

"You have been hiding from him."

"Have I?"

He coughed uneasily. "There are certain rumors - about you and Skeets - well - "

"That we're having a lesbian relationship. Is that what you wish to know?"

He nodded, somewhat embarrassed.

"No."

He nodded, disbelieving.

It was pointless to attempt to impress the truth upon him.

"It's a pity you haven't perfected your techniques for the invasion of privacy," I said. "Then you would know for certain that there is nothing between us."

"It would have been far more understandable if there had been something between you," he said. "The fact that there is nothing between you is, from a clinical standpoint, a dangerous sign."

"I guess," I sighed.

I again attempted to exit.

"Why did you break your engagement," he interjected.

"I didn't break it," I said, continuing in my effort to leave.

"Miss Miller," he slapped the desktop to hold my attention. "You are in danger!"

I looked at him, puzzled.

"In danger of what," I asked quietly.

He could not answer.

"So be it," I said, resigned to the fact of it.

He gaped at me helplessly.

He seemed to be such a helpless, frightened old man.

I left him gaping there, walked resolutely back down the long corridor to the elevators.

When I was first reassigned to Skeets'
Department, I experienced a feeling of deep
personal failure. It was like suddenly finding
myself banished to an outback.

Skeets was the butt of frequent jokes in the Corporation's cafeteria. She was barely thirty-two but she had been an employee for over fifteen years! She was an anachronism: a tacky dresser, a spinster, a mumbler, an absent-minded jay walker. She had no private life. She lived in a residence for women and didn't even have a room to herself.

Ever since anyone could remember, Skeets had worked two shifts, piling up immense overtime and unused vacation pay - and who knows how she ever spent it—certainly not on clothes or restaurants or any other visible objects.

Rumor was she gave profusely to churches and charities - or that she had a large family back in the sticks, hundreds of relatives still walking barefoot - strip miners, truck farmers.

It occurred to no one that the salary she was making as a supervisor was less than that being paid to workers in the Secretarial Pool!

(But that was something I only learned much later.)

Whatever her secret life might have been, Skeets was an old model. That was the Company joke - she was due to be phased out like the old data cruncher she was still using - strictly an outdated Corporate image, an embarrassment to new employees - someone who should have had the sense to either quit or climb upwards a long time ago.

She appeared to have no friends in the Corporate community. She ate alone in the Cafeteria, never attended Company functions. No one ever stopped to praise her for her work or to chat with her.

I was a newer model.

Seven years ago I had been hired under new Personnel policies that upgraded the female executive image. I had begun as a key-punch operator while working my way through college. I moved up through the ranks, getting my B.S. in applied mathematics, with a focus in the health sciences.

But my early promotion to Supervisor did not come entirely as a result of my education.

I was engaged to a young Management executive being groomed for a vice presidency. My connection to Eric had won me admission to the elite set - a set I was not too comfortable associating with, a set too superficial for my liking:

There were different executive factions in the Corporation, arising from its many subsidiaries, both foreign and domestic.

Perhaps due to the foreign influence, they were almost like Tongs, coexisting in an armed truce.

Each team lived its life incestuously, had its own set of private indiscretions which it confined to its Corporate family.

Personnel guarded all of us from internal and external blackmail, acting as ombudsman-confessor-family-counselor.

Among ourselves, in our social functions and group vacations, we were free: we had nude escapades in suburban swimming pools, group sex, pot parties, wife-swapping shifts in employee relations, plenty of internal gossip to make the workday pass more quickly.

Perhaps I too, like Skeets, did not precisely fit in.

I was too shy and proper. I found it hard to join in on the summer fun and preferred to sun myself on the front lawn.

I wondered how long I could successfully avoid becoming corrupted and debauched. Only my prolonged engagement to Eric, my transparent attempts at feigning professional virginity, protected me.

(Virgins were still stylish, especially if everyone knew
   they were not really virgins.)

When I was first told I had been reassigned to Skeets, my reaction had been one of panic.

Had I flunked my initiation to the group?

Had Personnel reclassified me?

Eric reassured me.

I had not been banished.

I was to learn Skeets' systems for time-sharing purposes.

I was to work independently, on separate projects.

Eric and the rest of our crowd chided me: at last someone might get close enough to Skeets to get a precise reading on her.

My first impression of Skeets was that I was looking at an ostrich with a very silly smile on its face - the smile of someone frightened of her own shadow.

"I'm Sarah Miller," I said reassuringly, and extended my hand. "I understand we'll be time-sharing the facility for a while."

She did not take my hand.

She looked at me.

It was not with a smile, I decided - but with some kind of facial cramp - sheer terror.

"Are you working on something highly classified," I asked.

She managed a nod. Then she got up and turned away, going to her console.

I followed her, looking over her shoulder at the monitor. "I have clearance," I said. "You don't have to worry."

"Just do your own work and I'll do mine," she blurted.

The words were forced out, not so much
in an angry tone but as someone crying.

I stopped trying to communicate with her and settled myself at the desk that had been moved in to accommodate me at the opposite wall.

(The room was large enough for two desks, but it was
obvious that I had intruded upon her private office space.)

The physical facility in her department was a hybrid of old
and new. The unit Skeets used still utilized the old punched
card stacks - and in the outer office old-style key punch
operators were still producing stacks and stacks of cards.
Another unit, to which I had access, utilized a higher-level
language, translating select data from Skeets' model and feeding
it, over telephone cables, to some remote central processor.

The young key punchers were not good prospects for long-
term employment or promotion - being primarily unimaginative
female high school graduates expected to marry and leave the
Company.
Although the department was supposed to be under tight
security, in defiance of camera surveillance they constantly
whispered among themselves and passed secret notes with tacky
jokes on them.
Yet they posed only a small discipline problem compared to
the temporary workers in the next room, hired from time to time
to handle office correspondence.
These were an unruly bunch - rebellious college students or
gays in theater or retired persons returned to work, actresses,
minority trainees, all of them unwilling to work very hard and
pausing for too many cups of coffee and polluting the air with
smoke breaks at their desks.
Nevertheless, Personnel stressed tolerance, the projection of
a positive Corporate image.

The old system had been kept on for so long on purpose -

because it was easier to maintain security on some very important data being key punched in a code known only to Skeets and her superiors.

Not even I was given a lexicon.

Whatever output she gave me to feed into the electronic console was also coded - and my function became more that of a statistical typist than a programmer - entering data without having the slightest clue as to its meaning. But the work was too important to be left to an ordinary data entry clerk.

There was something beautiful about the way Skeets
fingered the keyboard - like the playing of an organ.

The language on the screen, being coded, had no meaning for me - but to her it was a vivid conversation.

There were, of course, other speakers.

Human voices mediated by computer talk, appearing on the screen from remote and perhaps even exotic places. She did have human contact after all - many friends on line all conversing with her!

I learned this the day one of them stopped sending.

It happened quite abruptly, prompting a sudden burst of activity from Skeets at the console.

I looked up.

It was almost as if a heart had stopped beating somewhere - a heart she had been monitoring on the screen. I rushed over to try and help her in whatever way I could.

"It's been shredded," she said. "Wiped!"
She backed away from the screen in utter perplexity.
"What's been wiped," I asked.
"KEY: 1009GK101Q. It's been totally erased!"
"But that's not uncommon," I said.
"There was no advance notice. Not even a GOODBYE."
"Maybe a malfunction," I said.

78

I looked at the console helplessly. It was impossible to do anything without knowing the program.

"Yes, you must be right," she said graspingly. "It must be a malfunction. I'll have to work it out."

"Is there some way I can help," I asked.

She looked at me.
It was a very intelligent look.
She searched my face.
"No," she finally said.

She sat down at the console and searched
for the problem all afternoon.

If it had only happened once, it might have been shrugged off as a case of the lost chord. But it began to happen regularly, once every two weeks, always without advance notice.

"Someone is shifting all the data," Skeets concluded after the third occurrence. By this time she had resolved herself to its being a definite sign.

"Why do you suppose they're not telling you," I said.

(By this time, we had been able to exchange such questions without Skeets' withdrawing totally whenever I spoke.)

"Don't you know," she answered, assuming that I did.
"No," I told her. "I swear to you - I know nothing!"

She searched my face then looked away.

I decided then, as she searched my face, that Skeets was neither tacky nor strange. She was pure, beautiful. Her mind shone through her steel-blue eyes, and it was a mind

the like of which I may never see again in any man or
woman. A superior mind!

I undertook to find out exactly how superior it might be.
I enlisted Eric in my project.
I asked him to borrow Skeets' Personnel file. He had access
to those files - he could easily bring it home.

We went through her file together on my livingroom floor.
"Hey, wow! Look at this - " he said. "Might have been
Einstein's dossier! Three M.S.'s, magna cum laude - Particle
Physics, Abstract Math, Electrical Engineering. . ."
I snatched the folder from him.

"I knew there had to be something like that in there," I said.
"Isn't it strange - how she's being dumped. They're planning to
let go of her, aren't they?"
I looked at him.
He gave me a serious nod. "Yes, she'll be scrapped soon."
"Why!"
He looked away, unwilling to admit the *wrong* in it.

"She's been labeled an unknown quantity. We can't predict
what she's likely to do. The experts think she's on a short fuse
—that she's long past due for a burn out."
"But a mind like hers—" I objected.
"Can be dangerous," he finished.

He pointed to a code written on top of her dossier cover
sheet. "The PM means there's a psych file on her in the Medical
Office."
"You mean she had a breakdown?"
He nodded. "Probably back around 1944."
"But she was barely fifteen then," I said.   "Surely—"
"Look," he interrupted. "When the experts predict something,
it usually happens on schedule. She's on a short fuse."
"I can't believe that."

"You've got to."

He took my hand firmly.

"Do you realize the stuff she's been working on all these years? What if something happens while she still has access to those programs - here, or anywhere for that matter. It wouldn't be long before she could access our entire—" he stopped himself, realizing he had already said too much.

"Before what," I demanded, angry at his silence.

"You can't even tell *me*, can you," I said.

He shook his head nervously.

And now I fully realized what was being done to Skeets.

I looked at him in horror:

"She's not just going to be scrapped, is she?

Is she?"

Building a life without Eric was inconceivable to me.

There was a closeness between us that was more like what I would feel for a brother - a twin brother.

We had played together since we were ten. We had grown up together. We were inseparable through high school. Even when he dated other girls, he would come back and talk to me, hours into the night. We were buddies.

Our working for the same Company was part of this unbreakable bond. But now I found myself pulling away—not because of any physical attraction to Skeets—but because my Conscience was awakening, and his—was still asleep.

Insubordination was now festering in me.

I could not mind my own business like every other Corporate employee. I could not accept what was being done to Skeets as the inevitable consequence of her deep psychological structure.

I had to prevent a crime.

But it was already too late.

The >KEYS< had all been shifted and now there was a silence at the monitor.

In contrast, I was being flooded with rush assignments, and forced to take up all the computer time while Skeets waited idly across the room. .I dared only exchange brief communications with her. I sensed we were being closely watched. My own career, my whole life with Eric, depended upon my not getting involved.

As for Skeets - perhaps she knew what was expected of her.

They were waiting for her resignation.

But foolishly, or more realistically because she had no other place to go, she simply waited to be laid off.

For the next six months she sat there working on private projects which I had not the slightest ability to comprehend.

Fear mounted that she might bring Company secrets to the competition or, what was worse - might defect abroad as a prelude to her total breakdown.

This top-level air of apprehension was translated into frequent memos to me from Management.

Pressure was increasingly put on me to permit Skeets no access whatsoever to the new system being installed.

It was cruel.

Like cutting her off from a part of her own mind which had become wed to the machine.

And I was the agent, the executioner.

I had to make contact with her.

This now had become an obsession.

I had to let her know that all this wasn't being done to her because she was inefficient or had made some kind of serious mistake. I had to do something to give her back the self-confidence that was being shaken from her by the silent obliteration of the KEYS - for she had begun to doubt her own abilities, had been driven to checking out her computations a hundred times, obsessed with trying to find the lost programs, and the lost friends who worked them.

But there was no way I could talk to her without being observed. I was certain all of our movements were being closely monitored and that it would be impossible for us to meet anywhere in private without arousing suspicion.

But if she invited me to sit with her at the Cafeteria, and if a code could be established between us, then perhaps we might be able to communicate even with the whole world watching.

In desperation, I slipped her a note:

Please invite me to lunch.
CODE: 10Blnk = 1

She understood me perfectly.
It was as though she had suddenly discovered a new >KEY<.
She blinked twice at me and I returned the binary signal.

Now she spoke, splashing the walls with her blustery voice:
"Won't you have lunch with me?"
I paused, trying to appear surprised and hesitant. "Why, yes,
but - I can only spare a few minutes. Will the Cafeteria do?
"Yes, that will do fine," she answered tautly.

At lunchtime, we took the elevator together.
All the way up to the terrace, she stood beside me awkwardly
as other employees got on, looked at us queryingly, and said
nothing.

It was such a public act, lunching with Skeets, that I felt
certain Security would be fooled by it. But we had not sat down
for more than thirty seconds before Russo joined us at Skeets'
table.

Everyone knew Russo.
He moved freely from group to group and the word was out
that he was really a plant from Personnel.
A brown-haired man of about thirty, Russo was formally
attached to ACCOUNTING. He was unmarried, lived in a bachelor
apartment not far from me. Once or twice he had taken me out to
dinner. Now he was very friendly to both of us, even addressed
Skeets as though she were part of our special crowd.

"Well, how're things going in outer Siberia," he chided us.
"Does the extra security get on your nerves?"
He bumped my leg playfully.
"We could do with more security," I returned.

Skeets picked up on the double entendre.
I caught her eyes.

85

I blinked twice, hoping she would understand me.

"Is Security freaking out a lot of Corporate employees," I now continued recklessly.

"Where did you hear that?" Russo laughed nervously; he had fully understood my question; he would have had to have been extremely stupid not to have already guessed my rather obvious code.

He also blinked twice at Skeets: "Scientists get special attention."

His effect on Skeets was chilling

I had not realized until now how very near the edge she really was. But I was inexperienced in such matters and haughtily determined to bring the truth to light.

"What really freaks someone out," I now asked Russo pointedly, trying to bring the question out in the open.

"It doesn't take much," he answered me deliberately.

Now he looked to Skeets, coldly, clinically: "The best minds do most of the work themselves - all they need is a small push."

And again he blinked twice. "And when everything else fails," he added, "I hear laser-trained microwaves are the new thing. Less messy than bullets."

Again he looked at Skeets, and again he blinked twice.

Skeets froze.

She had received the message - not my message, >Their< message. She could either freak out and retire on a medical, or wait to be neutralized some other way.

Would they seriously do that, or was it simply a means they had chosen to precipitate a predictable entelechy?

Whatever the answer, it was glaringly clear to me that even I, through all my well-intentioned meddling, had been used— even I had been made an integral part of their freak-out.

The realization nauseated me.

"Please excuse me," I said, rising. "I don't feel very well."

I left them, left the building, took a very long walk.

It was plausible to ascribe my illness entirely to my own personal conflicts.

I couldn't just quit my job.

There was Eric to think of and the knowledge that my entire life had become entwined with my employment in the Corporation.

There was the very real possibility that, having sided with Skeets, I myself might also now be blacklisted, not be able to find comparable employment, especially at the age of thirty.

I could have quit and married Eric—but would that have put his career also in jeopardy?

And now I was reluctant to marry him, because now I had come to see him as being far beneath me in both intelligence and sensitivity.

Finally, there was the gnawing fear of change, of being permanently banished from the 'rational order' of a 'highly-advanced corporate environment' to the 'chaotic freedom' of the 'community-at-large'—an exile I had been corporately conditioned to dread as much as imprisonment, solitary confinement.

If I felt this way, how might Skeets be feeling?

Cutting Skeets off from her technology would be like blinding her eyes and severing her limbs. It was the thought that I could not abandon Skeets to a state of utter sensory deprivation in that padded cell we called our office that finally gave me the strength to go back to work.

I returned to a highly-predictable situation: both computers had broken down—hers and mine. They sat there, disassembled, their innards exposed, their spare parts cannibalized, dedicated to systems expansion in Accounting.

I was glibly told I would be reassigned to another department as soon as a vacancy came up. In the interim, I was urged to take my month's vacation and all the personal days I had not used up.

Nothing was said about where Skeets was to be reassigned. She was, for lack of any official directive, simply to continue sitting at her desk in the corner, waiting for new work to arrive. It would take weeks, perhaps months for new equipment to be installed.

I looked at Skeets.

Her eyes had grown dull, like those of a child left sitting in the dark too long, like those of an abused child abandoned in a dark room.

I realized that what was happening to her was also about to happen to me. I was a witness. No one would let me return to the office. I knew too much, My silence could not be guaranteed.

So be it.

I decided it was time for both of us to file a joint grievance.

"How about taking the day off with me," I suggested to
Skeets loudly, in open defiance of Security.

"Oh, I couldn't do that," she said timidly, as though she were only a yearling. "I'd get fired if I did that."

I looked at her desk.

Her own projects were no longer there - they had given her

busy work to do, clerical work.

"What's all this," I said angrily.

"The machines are down," she said. "This has to be done, one way or the other."

I looked at her.

She seemed to have regressed to an earlier time; her face, her tone made her appear only sixteen, even though her hair had turned grayer than I remembered it a week before.

I put my hand down on the ledger sheets.

"You don't have to work on this. You're a Supervisor. Give it to one of the keypunchers."

Skeets looked up at me, terrified, as though now even this task might be taken from her.

"Please - I must do it," she begged me. "I must be sure there are no mistakes."

"You haven't made any mistake," I reassured her.

"I must have," she countered feverishly. "I must have! It must have been a serious mistake!"

"No," I insisted.

She stared at me, her eyes a mercurial gray.

She blinked twice at me desperately.

"You made no mistake," I repeated.

My words terrified her even more. She shrunk inside herself, covering her head with her hands as though a deathray might be shooting through her.

"Please don't do that," she begged in pain. "Please don't do that! Just - go away!"

Eric caught up with me in the hallway, appearing completely ignorant of the whole affair.

"Hey, Sar," he said, taking my arm and walking briskly with me to the elevators. "I heard they gave you a month off. The Old

Man said he could spare me - how about taking time out for a honeymoon?"

I looked at him, horrified. "Are you serious?"
He did not expect my reaction. "Don't you ever want us to get married?"
I don't know what came over me.
A certain numbness, an anger.
I backed away from him.

"No," I heard myself saying. "No, I don't. I don't love you. I may lust you, but I don't love you. I don't think that I will ever want us to get married."

He stared at me, open-mouthed.
"No! Not ever!" I ranted at him, then broke away from him, ran down the hall as one finally set free.

It had become almost impossible for me to shrug off the feeling that I was being constantly watched. I began to wonder whether my apartment wasn't wired for sound, whether every step I took wasn't followed, whether everyone I spoke to wasn't being closely scrutinized.

At work, I had always felt myself watched.
It had never bothered me. I had even enjoyed the feeling, like a performer enjoys a constant audience. I had nothing to be ashamed of. I had been a good child, an honor student, an honest worker. Even my vices were normal!
Yet now I felt as though I had something to hide. I was fostering an inner rebellion, I was becoming—not merely insubordinate but—subversive.
Dissidence was written all over me—in the way I walked and talked, a new curve to my handwriting, a change in my stance. Anger was showing through me—righteous anger.
Skeets' face—the cold terror in it—was ever in my sight.

Was she afraid of something real or imagined?
Why was she so strange, why did she have no visible friends?

Did I have any more friends than she did?
Eric had been my only close friend. All my other relationships, just like all my vices, were artificial—merely adopted to fit in—pacify the watchers.

I found myself pacing around my living room unable to work or even to listen to music or read or watch television.
I was furious.
I was resisting an impulse to walk to the Corporation and accost Skeets on the street—to tell her the truth in front of everyone.

But what kind of truth?
I really didn't even know what the truth was. All I had was the suspicion that Russo and Security were deliberately out to destroy an unbelievably superior mind.
How bizarre that kind of truth might sound to everyone.
How insane my own mind for thinking it!

Then there were the damaging new rumors being circulated about me and Skeets.
Why was I so concerned for her?
Was I attracted to her? Were we having an affair?
Was that why I had broken off with Eric?

I had no physical attraction to Skeets.
Sexually, there was no earthly reason
for me to fix my mind on her.

No earthly reason—but a Cosmic reason, yes.
Skeets was pointing me to a new level of **Being**.

Caring about what was happening to Skeets had filled me with a sense of higher purpose, of a sensitivity to a hidden meaning. And as I surrendered myself fully to the prospect of championing her cause for no other reason than

>**Human Decency**<

it seemed to me that I, Sarah, was finally becoming

>**REAL**<

On the twenty-eighth day of my forced vacation, Eric called and then appeared at my door.

I received him coldly.

He was very formal, very respectful.

He had a serious look on his face.

He seemed years older, more mature, more like a senior executive. He sat on a footstool across the room from me, finding it hard to speak to me.

"It's all over," he finally blurted. "You can come back now."
"How do you mean, 'over'," I returned.

"It happened. She broke."
He looked down, appearing most penitent.
"It was awful. We all took it very hard. It happened right in the Cafeteria. She suddenly threw dishes, screamed that we were poisoning her, shooting her with death rays."
"And weren't you?" I interrupted.
He gave me a strange look, as though my question was bizarre.

"Where is she now," I demanded.
"Downtown, at City - the psycho ward."

"Thank you for telling me," I said.
I stood, ready to leave.

He lingered, unwilling to go home.

"Sarah," he finally said. "If you can't resolve this now, there won't be other work for you anywhere—not even abroad. I won't be able to help you."

"I'm surprised you still want to help me," I returned coldly. "I'm even very surprised you're here. Doubtless you were sent here or you wouldn't be here."

"Sarah - " he attempted to explain, shaking his head helplessly.

"I will resolve this," I interrupted. "But not in the way anyone wants me to resolve it."

For a moment his face was pale.

"You don't know what you're up against," he said in a near whisper.

His tone was sobering to me.

Was he trying to tell me that there was more involved here than mere Management expedience? Was the Corporation in the hands of criminals? Was my life in danger?

Now he got up suddenly, in seeming indifference.

"Well, sorry, pal, I tried," he said glibly. "Look me up when you come to your senses."

It was not like Eric to give up so easily.

Were we being watched?

Was he trying to tell me he wanted to help?   And in how much danger would I be putting him, if I let him help?

"Our relationship is over," I stated publicly, to the four walls.

My tone cut through him.

He left without a further word.

I dropped to the floor.

I had no tears in me, but my whole body shook from the abruptness of my willful self-immolation, my severance of half of all that had once been Sarah.

But there was only one concern now: **Skeets.**
I had to see her.
I called the ward to be certain she could have visitors then took a cab to **City Hospital**.

The radio was very loud. I had to shout over it to be heard. "It would be most helpful to us if you could move elsewhere."

She stared dully at me, stared through the smoke from her cigarette, through the thick drumbeat on the radio, through the lint and dust all over the room.

I had returned to change back into my old clothes, to store my good dress in my closet.
"You haven't paid the rent, and I need my apartment back," I said. "You can't expect me to support you."

I waited.
It seemed to me she had not heard.
Perhaps the radio was too loud.
Perhaps my voice had been too timid.

"Have you fallen asleep," I shouted.
She did not answer.

The dog rolled over against my feet.

I stepped over it and tried to pace around the center of the floor. There was too much furniture, too much lint.

I faced her once more: "It's not that I'm insensitive to what you're going through. But I must draw a line somewhere. Your problems are your own concern."

Still she did not answer.
She appeared drugged.
She had half-closed eyes. The cigarette between her fingers was burning short, ashes dropping from it to the sheet. Now it burned her finger and she barely felt it, slowly crushed it in the ashtray half-aware of it.
"What is doing this to you," I insisted. "Why are you disintegrating!"
I waited.
She faced me and her dull lips parted without forming words.

I turned and faced the mirror.
Her image was quite far across the room, diagonally there below her sister's photograph, her sister's face smiling diagonally all over the room.

I looked at my own face in the mirror: at my eyes - at my brown eyes.

I took off my knit cap and let my long brown hair hang down to dry. It was still damp from the shower I had taken earlier. I brushed it in the hope that it would dry.

The radio was unbearably loud.

I turned again and shouted over it: "Are you totally irresponsible? Isn't there anything that moves you? What about this poor dog!"

I pointed to the dog.
The sad mutt edged toward me, crawling on its fat belly,

feebly wagging its tail, dragging lint and urine across the rug. Its bladder could no longer contain itself. How long had it been since it had been walked?

"Surely you can't expect me to take on all your problems too," I said to my undertenant, ignoring the dog.
I waited.

Suddenly she turned off the radio.
"I am not in the habit of being yelled at," she said angrily.

I leaned on the clashing green chair.
Dust flew into my nostrils.
Again I waited while she lit another cigarette and inhaled deeply, nervously.

"You say I'm disintegrating—but you're no help at all. Do you know what it's like to be trapped inside of me?" She looked at me, rings under her eyes. "Do you really think I can move out by tomorrow?"
"You've had ample notice," I said.
"You might as well have told me yesterday," she said.
"Whatever is destroying you - you should be fighting to overcome it," I told her.
"It's hopeless," she sighed.
"Surely not."
She exhaled one more time. "Hopeless."
"Is it a bad love affair?" I asked helplessly.
She looked at me. She gave me a glassy stare: "It's no love at all," she said. "No love at all."

I mulled it over, patiently.
"I understand," I finally said. "I understand completely."
I got up from the green chair. And now I addressed her furiously: "I don't care if you live or die. Get out! You have until Friday and no longer."

She looked at me, surprised. "Are you threatening me?"
"Yes," I said.

She stared, impassively.

The dog crawled toward me one more time.
It whined at me, whined pitifully.
I forced myself to ignore it.
I took my coat and left.

My aunt had invited me to dinner. I had
barely enough time to catch the bus.

My paternal aunt lived in a suburb.
In the summer one might describe it as a snatch of green
pasture - but in the winter it was merely a tedious ride through
slush and snow and afterwards, a long cold walk.
I reached the depot just in time.
The bus, half empty, was just leaving.
I paid my fare and went to the back, where it was warm. I sat
on the seat over the heater, pulled my coat around me, and shut
my eyes.
I thought of Skeets swaddled in wool
lying in our room—in our coldroom,
preserved, refrigerated in our coldroom.

If only I could freeze her until I found a cure.
I told myself that she was sleeping soundly, that - for her -
time passed more quickly - that a whole eternity might have
passed before I returned that evening.

When one is cold, one does not feel pain.
When I was a child swaddled in a woolen snowsuit, I
remember there was an empty lot across the street from our
house where my sister and I used to take our sled.

Since I was the oldest, I had to let her use it first.

I would prompt her to play very hard so that she would quickly tire and feel cold and would go home to dry her socks and mittens.

Then I would take my sled and throw myself down the little hill again and again.

It was like leaping to my glory or my death - and like a rape of the sled beneath me, a cracking against it again and again until way past the time when my boots and gloves and clothes, soaked through with the sweat of my untiring lust, had hardened into slush against my flesh.

Once a blizzard began and I paid no heed to it, rolling off the sled in sheer exhaustion.

I lay there with my eyes closed, daydreaming while the snow fell on me, while the snow completely covered me.

Vaguely I realized that it was growing dark and supper should be started and that my clothing was growing stiff on me.

But I didn't want to return home.

I closed my eyes and allowed the snow to bury me.

I must have fallen asleep.

I would have frozen death had not our old bitch found me.

Caring for me like one of her own, she sniffed and licked through snow for me. Her tongue was like a hot brand on my cheek, reviving me.

Annoyed, I raised my arm to push her away and found I could scarcely move, could scarcely feel my hands.

I forced myself to get up because it irked me not to be able to move when I wanted to. Death, if it meant a loss of freedom, was no pleasure to me.

I picked myself up with the dog's help and stumbled toward our house. My shoes were too small for my feet and my clothes cut against me. In agony I crept through snow until I finally reached the house and once inside, I lingered in the dark hallway a very long time, thawing, while the dog persisted in licking my fingers and nose.

Finally, I had the strength to remove my clothes, then walked up the stairs naked to my room with the dog following me.

My little sister was playing in her corner, serving tea to her collection of teddy bears.

She was serving them tea in a terribly callous manner.

Helplessly they stared at her with beaded eyes, unable to refuse or make an objection, while she favored one and snubbed another and swatted a third for no cause at all.

The dog was underfoot as I got into pajamas and a robe.

"Go away," I pushed her away gruffly, "you're a good dog, but go away."

I stopped myself.

I was echoing my sister's words across the room as she punished her teddy bears in a long, many-voiced monologue: "You're a bad bear, and you're a good bear, and you're an awful bear!"

Now she gave each of them a teacup, pretending to play favorites, then - at the last moment - capriciously she altered all relations, suddenly revised her decision as to which of her charges was to be treated nicely, which was to be deprived.

The game enraged me.

It offended my sense of justice.

Perhaps I should have stopped to teach her what fairness was - after all, I was in charge of her, she was my responsibility.

But it was too soon for me to cope with such things - with her need to learn from me all the things my mother had taught me when she was still well enough to teach me and not a mere shadow of her former self.

Soon the room became intolerable, my sister's game, a deadly game. It would not be long before she would take a stick to the whole lot of them, would punish all her children.

I could not face the inevitable outcome of her hidden rage.

I tore downstairs to the kitchen, to begin making supper.

The dog followed me slavishly, as my loving subject.

Over the dog I was absolute monarch.

It was not merely a child's fantasy - leadership, aristocracy had been instilled in me.

My parents were, at least in origin, from proud families. Even though we were poor and lived in a poor neighborhood, we still lived as aristocracy, still held ourselves above the crowd. Our neighbors were all beneath us. And their children, bred to a servant class. For this reason I had very few friends at school. My manner was too haughty and aloof.

Only Eric dared approach me - perhaps because his family had a long tradition of vassalage to kings. I accepted Eric's fealty as my divine right. Wherefore both Eric and the dog worshiped me. I made Eric my squire, and the dog, both my subject and my worthy steed.

My mother was in the kitchen.

Since her illness, she was always in the kitchen.

As if mounted against the wallpaper—set within the pattern of faded yellow bouquets—as a pressed rose in a dried-up garden—her long fingers dehydrated and flat on the kitchen table against a pattern of faded blue and pink daisies—her bony feet planted inside flowered slippers, flat on the yellow-flowered linoleum where our old bitch was fond of lying about, on the painted bouquets, rubbing its nose into her leg.

My mother was like a mad queen sitting there, her face mystical but empty of coherent thought—pallid, made yellow by the yellow light of the yellow-papered kitchen.

The table was always cluttered around her, even at mealtimes, and breadcrumbs persisted in sticking to everything. Boric acid, to ward off the roaches, was white-powdered on every crack and corner. By the sink, large blots of scrub-pad rust, of grease and candlespill, splotched all the counters.

It was my fault.
I was a poor housekeeper.
But I could not face becoming mother to the house, to my sister, to my father, to my mother.

The kitchen, squalid as it was, was the focal point of our domestic existence. For she sat there, still as fearful head of household, still as my mother—queenly though distracted, illogical.

My sister and I—with the dog prostrate at our feet—would sit in the kitchen for hours keeping her company in the cold of winter. We would sit, studying or listening to the radio—there was no television then—and the dog would crawl from one of us to the other.

Once in a while our mother would hum a tune or remind us of better days, would say something wise, remarkable. But more often she would be in one of her mystical moods speaking like a medium with her hands flat on the table: "So you're finally home," she would soothsay to one or both of us, "Someday you'll be glad to be home—someday you'll miss your home—when I'm dead and gone ... when I'm dead and gone ... "

We had gotten out of the habit of answering her, and a dreadful silence would always follow. Eventually one of us would break it by turning on the radio again, or she would break it by reading aloud from one of the astrology magazines she had taken to clutching to her breast like a Bible.

"Wednesday, January 9th," she would say, "Your outlook today is unfavorable. Be careful going outdoors. Don't invite a strain on health. Be tactful with loved ones. Beware, toward evening, of false friends."

She would clutch the magazine and shut her eyes. "Beware of false friends," she would repeat and, in the next moment, she would kick the dog away.

We reached the last stop.
I got off the empty bus and it quickly turned around the little oval in the parking lot of the shopping center, heading back towards the City.

The shopping center was deserted.
It had gone bankrupt.
Beyond the empty buildings, the sidewalk ended at a housing project that had been begun and never finished.
Beyond that, more empty lots.
The smooth new asphalt street was hard with ice and layered with snowdrifts.

My aunt's house was beyond the empty lots, about a mile and a half away, where the ragweed marsh began. There was supposed to be a connecting bus, sometimes; but it would be quicker to walk.
Darkness was coming and a mist was forming close to the ground. The snow - flat and covering the horizon, carried a mumbling wind, a wind seeming filled with radio voices, sounds of distant thunder, echoes of war.

The snow was unbroken except for bramble bushes, dark and barbed, poking up in scattered rows like enemy lines through broken concrete.

(Before the concrete had been laid in, we used to play war here, Eric and I, with the snow like an arctic tundra between us and my aunt's house. We would stalk each other behind the brambles and then one of us would attack, and we would wrestle in the snow or fence with sticks like bayonets. In those days it had been a total wilderness, and there were hunters from time to time. It had been a dangerous place to play during hunting season. But it was also a place where our other games would go unnoticed except, once in a while, by the intrusion of a wild dog or a hunter's hound.)

It seemed to me I heard a dog panting now.
Many wild dogs still foraged here.
My aunt put food out for them.
I turned to see if one was following me.
There was nothing but mist and snow.
Yet I heard the panting there - heard it distinctly - and distant thunder, or - was it gunfire in the grumbling wind?

I walked, feeling myself in danger from the wild shots of a poacher. The ice under my feet did not permit me to see too far on either side, forced me to keep my eyes to the ground just in front of me.
The snow was soaking through my flimsy boots and the wind was biting my fingers, my ungloved fingers, as I tried vainly to warm them inside my thin and shallow pockets.

Now I heard a gunshot.
It cracked loud and hollow over the ice.
I stopped and looked behind me.
I saw no one.

(I hoped that it might not be a sniper. Once or twice in the past twenty years there had been a sniper shooting at random.)

The panting of the dog was real: I noted its tracks now in the snow - fresh blood-filled tracks zig-zagging in every direction - blood not like from a wound but from a scratch or a snow-blister. Or perhaps from a bitch in heat.

I continued to walk as quickly as I dared.
The dog's tracks ran alongside of me and now small drops of blood not in them but beside them also splotched the snow. Blood as from a wound.

Another shot was fired.
Still I saw no one.
The panting grew louder, more labored and tired.

I stepped more quickly, anxious to get out of the clearing where I now felt myself a moving target, anxious to get past the barbed bushes which might hide a hundred trenches from which the enemy was watching me, aiming a dark rifle.

It was freezing my toes to be scurrying over ice.
The air came into my lungs too quickly and was freezing them. Still I forced myself, breaking into a sprint despite the ice beneath me, while the soles of my feet blistered in wet socks.

Now there were two shots fired in quick succession, seeming to come very close behind me.
The dog's panting and my own were one.
My eyes were forced on the ground before me, yet from the corner of my sight it seemed to me that the dog's tracks were deeper in the snow - at times there was the full imprint of its body dragging itself forward, trailing small streaks of blood. (It might have been a white dog, not easily seen in the snow.)

Now two other shots, this time in front of me, were fired in the woods and seemingly into the air.
I glanced up looking for birds.
Nothing, only gray ebbing twilight. And as I stopped to look, a third shot cracked over the snow, behind me— riding the wind that slapped my face.
Then there was silence.
The dog's panting, too, had stopped.

My aunt's house was dark.
I hoped she had not forgotten and gone out somewhere.
It was not like her to go out; she seldom went farther than the supermarket at the far end of the woods. Yet I had not confirmed my invitation—on purpose I had kept her in suspense.

It was a white wooden house with dark Victorian windows.
A neat but useless wooden fence blocked the most direct route to the front door.

I broke through virgin snow to the steps, pulled the bell and waited.

There was a rustling inside.

Then I saw her peering at me through the front window. She seemed frightened. But when she recognized me she rushed to open the door. "Sarah! Why didn't you call us!"

She let me in and shut and bolted the door quickly against the wind.

My aunt stood, awaiting my embrace.

She was shorter than I was, round but not fat, and an energetic seventy.

I was too full of snow to embrace her.

I removed my coat.

"You must have frozen stiff walking here," she said, taking it from me.

"It wasn't too bad," I lied.

I took off my boots and my wet oversocks, careful not to ruin the polish on her oak floor. I put them on a mat by the radiator, then waited while she hurried upstairs to get me a pair of slippers.

I waited.

Dry air choked my lungs - stale air from antique carpets and curtains and feathers - hundreds of feathers on stuffed partridges, pheasants and peacocks all standing stiff-legged on oakstands in the parlor.

My aunt returned with a puffy pair of bathroom slippers made for summer days.

I stuck my wet-hosed feet in them.

"Thank you," I said.

I followed her into the parlor.

She turned on all the lights.

The lights cut through the stale air, the funereal affect of the trophy room.

"Is someone hunting out there?" I asked.

She looked at me, puzzled and concerned. "It's been outlawed for quite some time. Did you see someone?"

"Hunting? Good show!" an aged voice shouted to us from a hidden corner of the long parlor.

I turned.

It was my aunt's second husband.

I thought he had long since died.

He waved at me from the far corner, by the bay window, sunk deeply in a high Victorian chair. Behind him on the wall, his proud collection of antique shotguns.

"Hello there," I said, waving to him as one waves to infants, for he was very old, over ninety.

"How are you," he shouted hoarsely.

"I'm fine, Uncle," I said loudly.

"Splendid! Splendid!" he exclaimed.

My aunt took my arm. "Come into the kitchen."

I courtesied to him and followed her, anticipating warmth.

It was a bright immaculate kitchen.

It smelled of baked chicken.

But she had opened a window somewhere to clear the air. I felt the draft.

My aunt wiped perspiration from her forehead, breathless from exertion. "Tell me what you did for Christmas," she said, now rushing to prepare a larger meal.

"Oh, I - " I shrugged vaguely, standing by the stove.

(I could not seem to get warm enough.)

She looked up at me.

She was almost my height. Once she had seemed much taller - a beautiful lady in her time; now her teeth were false and her hair was steel gray, but she still seemed much younger than seventy. Only her forced breathing, the minor tremor in her stance, gave her age away.

"We expected you for Christmas," she said. "Even your father was here."
"I didn't say I would come for Christmas," I said.

I went to the kitchen window.
I scanned the wide clearing, now starlit, trying to see a dog or a hunter.
Wind, flurries, were all I could see.

"Your father has something very important to tell you - " she said with concern.
"I know," I said impassively. "My mother died."
She shifted uneasily.
I turned again toward the window.

"Can I help you," I said distantly.
(My voice was choked.)
"Everything's done," she muttered, puttering.
She spooned this and shifted that, opening and closing cupboard doors.

I stared at the flatland, trying to spot dogtracks.
The wind was shifting the snow.

"You've become such a stranger lately," my aunt said.
"I've been very busy" I lied.
"At your job?"
"No."

There was a break in the wind and a moving shadow caught my eye, many yards away. Perhaps only a piece of cardboard blown about.

"Is something troubling you?" My aunt spoke loudly, as if to pull me back into the room.
I turned and faced her. "Not really."

Her eyes shifted away from mine.

She wiped her hands on her apron and turned to putter once more.

"Why don't you go in and chat with your uncle," she suggested.

I lingered by the window, still trying to make out what danger was out there waiting for me.

Was it My Death waiting for me?

"Sarah," my aunt said apprehensively, "are you well?"

She spoke to me as she had once spoken to my mother.

Was I really acting strangely? No matter.

"I am quite well," I said.

I left the kitchen and went back into the parlor.

The old man had moved himself to the dining alcove and was waiting for me in a high dining room chair.

He was eager for dinner to be served. He had tied a hand-embroidered napkin around his neck, like a bib, and was smiling defiantly at his deliberate expenditure of such rare finery.

"Everything ready?" he shouted at me.

The air was forced through his throat, still coming out hoarsely as scarcely more than a whisper.

"On schedule," I answered playfully.

I sat on a footstool at his left, like a small child.

"Give us some news," he urged. "What's been happening out there?"

"How should I know," I chided. "I don't get around much either."

The bay window was in my line of sight.

I pulled my eyes away from the window to look at him sitting in his high chair, the bib around his neck.

He was tiny and round like a beer keg - not with fat but with wine or water, his complexion rosy-cheeked.

He was like a Dresden Doll in the Victorian chair.

"What about the riots," he insisted jovially. "Has it gotten bloody yet?"

"The riots are occasional," I said. "The new epidemic is drugs."

"Oh, yes. I forgot." He noted it. "So they've quelled the Boxer Rebellion here, have they?"

"I think so," I said.

"You know what that was, don't you? You've read the history books, haven't you?"

"Something about a people's revolution having been put down with opium?" I returned.

He nodded vividly. "I was twenty at the time - in the Royal Navy. I captained a cargo from Turkey and pushed it through Hong Kong."

"You old devil," I poked him.

He chuckled. "So they're drugging the rebels again, are they!"

I turned toward the smell of warm broth.

My aunt was wheeling in the serving tray. I rose to help her while the old man eagerly took up his spoon.

We both sat down and waited while the old man served us, sitting at the head of the table, spooning out broth with a silver ladle. It was a most awkward movement for him, but he did it so proudly.

The broth was hot but not hot enough.
I still felt a draft somewhere from an open door or window.
Had my aunt left a door open?

"Are the decorations nice this year?" my aunt asked.
"I haven't noticed them," I said.

The old man caught my arm, stopping to blink at me between slurps of broth. "But the bus passed right through there - "

"I napped on the way," I explained to them, winking at him.

"Where are you staying now," my aunt asked cautiously.
"With friends temporarily," I lied.

We waited until the old man had finished and then my aunt insisted on clearing away our bowls herself, leaving the dinner plates under them.

I looked at my plate. It was bone china, vintage, gold-rimmed and family-marked.

Very dear, irreplaceable.

The old man chuckled wickedly. "You want to break one, eh? There's the fireplace," he gestured impishly. "Go on," he urged, handing me his plate, "Why save it? No heirs ... "

"Don't you think I'll have children," I asked.

He blinked at me, searching my face. "Haven't you got more important things to do?"

"Do I?" I asked him privately, almost whispering in his ear.

He chuckled again. "Whatever it is, don't save it for your old age - you'll never get around to it then."

He sat back and winked at me.

Now my aunt returned and filled our plates with chicken from a warmer on the serving table.

The old man slapped my hand with the flat of his silver knife. "Now tell us something interesting," he commanded.

"At knife-point?" I chided.

He laughed.

Now he reached backwards and took a bottle of red wine from the rack beside him and began to twist the cork.

"May I help you?" I asked.

He winked. "Do you think I'm dead yet?"

He opened it expertly then poured into two crystal glasses.

My aunt did not drink wine.

"Well, happy January First," he toasted to me.

I hesitated.

That was wrong.

"Happy December Twenty-ninth," I corrected him.

My aunt looked up.

He laughed wildly as if I had helped him prove a point.
I did, after all, know the correct date.
He hit my shoulder and I laughed with him while my aunt
looked down sheepishly.

With whom had they been conversing? Was it only with my
father—or had someone else been in touch with them?
I drank my wine.
It was warm and felt good.
It was an old, rare wine, too fine to be gulped (or even drunk
at all!) but too good to be sipped slowly.

The old man was still grinning at me. "Well, so you got
yourself here after all. You're a few days late. You missed a
warm reception!"

He laughed and laughed at a private joke.

"I'm sorry if I missed Christmas dinner," I said.
"It was tolerable, edible," he grimaced. "Your aunt doesn't
manage as well as my first wife did, you know. Does it all
herself. Won't hire anyone. Can't cook worth a damn!"
"You old rooster," I said. "She should stick you in the pot for
that!"
"She will," he laughed. "She will, in time ."

My aunt rose.
She looked a little relieved.
Perhaps I had shown her that I could still joke with him as I
always used to, that I wasn't too depressed and preoccupied to
joke with him.
"May I help you with the dishes," I volunteered again,
reluctantly.
"Then what will I have to do when you're gone," she said.
"Sit and talk. He hasn't been this alive since Thanksgiving."

"No wonder," I scolded him. "You've been saving up all this mischief for weeks!"

"Hah!" he pointed. "She lifts me out of my coffin and dusts me off only on holidays!"

"Is something wrong, Sarah," my aunt spoke from the archway.

"I thought I saw a hunter," I said.

"A hunter?" the old man perked up. "That would be something! Here - " he fished for a key in his vest pocket. "Take your pick of those up there - I'll never get to use them.

He handed me the key to the gun cabinet.

I recoiled. "I might shoot someone by mistake," I said.

"No mistake," he winked wickedly. "Bah, women today! Useless! My first wife used to hunt with me. Burma. We culled elephants and tigers."

"That was another time, another place," I said.

"Where are we now?" he asked, confused.

I bent forward, whispering in his ear: "Don't you remember? You emigrated here fifty years ago - twenty years before I was born."

"Are you thirty now? So soon?"

"Sometimes the neighborhood gangs come here to shoot at wild dogs," my aunt said.

"Oh?"

"Let's hope they do it right this time," the old man said,

gumming chicken. "Amateurs—letting wounded animals get away, not tracking them, finishing the job. Savages! And that music of theirs - " he added, still gumming, "sounds just like the Bush. Scoops out their brains!"

"Tell us about your work," my aunt interrupted. "I can never understand exactly what it is you do."
"I help machines solve problems," I said.
"That doesn't sound so complicated," the old man said.
"It isn't," I said.
"I suppose they pay you a good salary for that," my aunt said.
"Yes."
I looked down. I had barely eaten.
I forced myself to down a few bites. The meat was dry and stringy, the potatoes overdone.

The old man now began to devour his food, leaning over his plate, his mouth sucking out the last remaining flavors of the meal - an entirely dry and flavorless meal despite its princely service.
I put down my knife and fork and pushed my plate away.
The old man looked at it disapprovingly, then pushed the fruit bowl toward me. "Here, fruit, cheese, and more wine - best thing for a long life."
I took an orange and let him pour me another glass of burgundy while my aunt cleared the table.

"I'm not keeping you from your nap, am I?" I asked him.
He winked. "Plenty of time to sleep."

He was framed in the bay window, his squat bug-like husk seeming strapped to the wingback chair ready to take off for the moon. The moon—the full moon—was directly over his right shoulder at the center of the window, casting new light upon the snow.
I watched the snow.

"Perhaps we might listen to the radio," I said, breaking a long silence.

"Oh, the radio," he laughed. "There's nothing on the radio!"

He reached for it - a prewar wooden box sitting on the top of a wall table. He turned the old brown nob and it blasted static at us. "See? Nothing but noise," he said, and turned it off again.

I nodded.

I looked about the room, the upholstered room stuffed with pheasants and partridges.

As a child, this was a very dull room where my sister and I waited for agonizing hours and days, left to ourselves and cautioned not to touch anything, while my father and my aunt—my father's sister—worried about what to do with our mother.

(The old man had still been working then. He was a bank president and had retired only ten years ago.)

My little sister and I had been left alone in this house while our mother was taken from us—now, as then, I wanted to go home—home had been out there a thousand yards or so away in the snow. Now there was only an empty lot there, razed by bulldozers fifteen years ago, covered with concrete left to crack.

"Would you prefer some brandy now?" the old man offered.
"Yes thank you," I said.

I went to the chinese cabinet to serve myself—a graceful ebony cabinet ingrained with mother-of-pearl.

I poured rare Napoleon brandy into two cut-crystal glasses.

The portrait of my Uncle's first wife hung above me, clad in armor in romantic style, a quill poised in her hand like a Sibyl or Athena. I stepped back, as always, to admire her.

He was immensely pleased that I had noticed her.

"My Brunhilde," he said. "That was a woman! They don't make them like that anymore. That wasn't her name, of course. But in those days, I called myself Siegfried."

I turned and looked at him.

"But that wasn't your name either," I said.

"We liked to play games," he answered. "We had dreams."

"Can you show me the road to Valhalla," I now asked him as I had as a child, half-seriously.

He nodded, a Nibelung fire in his eyes:

> "First, seek out Your Death and let him hear the sweet music of your Singing Sword. If he turns into a Bag of Bones, step right over him—to the Citadel!"

He seemed impatient now to take his own advice—his knapsack was all packed and he was ready to go.

"When my time comes, I shall remember that," I promised him.

Now my aunt returned.

She seemed tense.

"What are you two up to now," she said with forced levity.

"We've arranged a secret rendezvous," the old man shouted at her, "in the Hereafter."

Then he laughed, breathlessly.

"Isn't he shameful?" my aunt said to me.

"Not shameful enough," he said, and gestured for me to come over to him, to bend my ear to him.

I did so.

But instead of whispering to me, he stuck a wad of money deep down into my bosom.

I pulled away, half-shocked.

"If you think that's dirty," he laughed at me, "you should have seen where I stuck it in Marseilles!"

I went to give it back to him, but he wouldn't take it.

"Keep it," he insisted. "You'll need a taxi. And your aunt there - has just been calling your father!"

"My father?"

I whirled and looked at her accusingly.

She appeared apologetic.

I had to reach the bus in time.

If I arrived at the depot too late, it would be two hours before the next one came—two hours of hiding in the freezing doorways of deserted buildings.

I got my things and rushed out the door, fitting my wet boots in the footprints I had made before, trying to avoid wherever possible breaking through new snow.

The landscape was silent now - no shots, no panting animal - except for a grinding sound from the road alongside me.

I turned and saw headlights edging toward me slowly, carefully over virgin snow.

It was not my father's car.

It was an old sedan, huge, tank-like, bleached and rusted an uneven brown.

I hailed it. It stopped for me.

The driver rolled the window down letting stale cigarsmoke hit my face. "What the hell are you doing alone out here!" he yelled at me.

"I'm late for the bus," I said. "Can you give me a lift?"

I waited while he looked me over.

"Get in," he blasted at me, like an old policeman. "You're lucky I don't run you in for hitchhiking."

I opened the door on the passenger side.

It was hard to open, frozen.

I got inside and shut it, waited while he continued to inspect me with glazed gray eyes.

He was a blank man dressed in brown—stocky, edemic, with the now-I'm-sober look of a mean drinker.

"Which house do you belong to," he grunted, moving the car slowly forward through the snow.

I now recognized him: "Officer Brooks? Don't you remember? I'm Sarah Miller—the house on Oak Road, fifteen years ago."

He looked at me blankly.

"I'm retired now."

"Don't you remember?" I insisted. "Your wife used to visit my mother, from the Church."

He did not hear me.

His face was flushed.

"What the hell do you think you're doing out here!" he blurted angrily. "Do you want to get yourself killed?"

He swallowed dryly, his high blood pressure choking him.

"This used to be a safe neighborhood," I stammered.

"It was never safe. Never safe," he repeated.

He kept his eyes on the road.

He was coat-bound to the wheel.

"If I wasn't retired now I'd be running you in, teach you a lesson for your own good - "

I looked at him. I had forgotten how rigid a man he had always been—a menace to the youth gangs from the wrong side of the tracks.

He was still muttering. "A nice girl like you hitching rides. Shame! Your folks know about it?"

"It was an emergency," I said, speaking to him as I might to a computer. "I got stuck out there alone in the snow and I recognized your car. I hailed you because I knew you were a policeman."

"Oh."

He looked again at me.

His face was a weathered purple, his cheeks webbed with capillaries. "Yeah. Yeah, I guess so.   Sure."

We were still inching at a snail's pace through virgin snow.

I looked for signs of headlights ahead.

The bus was still not in sight.

"You still live around here?" he asked, feeding the engine slowly, to keep from skidding.

"My family moved a few miles up," I said.

"You're not living with them?"

"No."

I caught myself.

"I've been staying with my aunt, just up the road. Their telephone's out of order so I couldn't call a cab."

"So you're still living at home," he said. "Good. Too many kids leave home nowadays, go to the City, get into trouble."

"Do you still see many of them—of the ones who used to get into trouble?"

"Most of them are dead by now," he said. "Some changed their ways, went straight. Don't see any of those either."

"What about the gangs," I asked.

"New breed now, spilling over from the City. It's like a war out here," he answered blankly.

I sat forward nervously, impatiently. The bus should be coming any moment now.

"Don't dare push 'er faster," he said. "I passed a car some miles back that slid right into a ditch."

I paled. "A gray sedan?"

"Know something about it?"

I caught myself.

"My aunt was expecting a guest."

He grunted. "Luckily, it was right near a phone booth. Must have called a cab. Didn't see anyone on the road but you."

"I guess he'll be all right," I said.

"I'm heading back in that direction later," he said. "I'll give another look."

Now the bus appeared through mist.
He flicked his headlights, signaling it to wait, and we inched forward to the depot.

"Well, don't catch cold now," he said absently.
He removed his glove to shake my hand. His was a rough hand, all blistered at the knuckle, skinned and calloused at the knuckle—black and blue and broken as if he had a habit of punching into brick walls.
"Thanks for the ride," I said. "It probably saved my life."

The corner of my eye caught something smelly in his back seat—was it a rifle and a dead dog?

"Just keep your nose clean," he said.
He spoke absently, all the while looking beyond me, at the horizon, his gray eyes searching over snow.

I ran toward the bus.
Its doors were open to receive me.
It waited patiently for me as I slid over ice running toward it, careless about leaping into wells of deep snow.

The night Eric told me that Skeets had been hospitalized, I determined to rescue her without delay. I could not abandon her the way my mother had been abandoned.

A crime had been committed, and I was the only witness willing to come forward. Surely the world was not in such utter chaos that it would be dangerous for me to break the silence!

Downtown General was a large city hospital, the catch-all for every kind of emergency call. I knew the psychiatric wing, having visited my mother there some years before.

My mother had been in a straitjacket crying to me—"Sarah! Don't leave me! Don't leave me!"—I was pulled away with her screams in my ears and the next time I saw her—they had done something to her and all her will was gone!

The hospital had been cleaned up and considerably modernized since then and straitjackets had been replaced by chemical sedation. Still it was a grim and seedy place, more like a prison, a place of last resort for the indigent and uninsured.

Skeets had been put in a locked ward, for observation.

She was led toward me by an aide, her gait palsied, her mouth and eyes dehydrated, glazed.

We sat at a table in a common room.

"How do you feel," I asked her.

"Thirsty," she said dryly, finding it hard to control her jaw.

I knew it to be from an overdose of medication.

I went to the coin machine and purchased two cans of fruit juice. She sipped them both quickly from a straw.

"So dry," she said.

"I know," I said.

I put my hand on hers, fixing her to the real.
"Try to hang on. I can have you out by tomorrow."

She looked at me, panic stricken. "T-That w-will be t-too late!" she stuttered.
"No it won't," I reassured her.
"Y-you don't k-know - " she stared at me with dry eyes, "T-the p-people here are all s-shot!"
"They might not let me sign you out until morning," I said.
"S-sign?" she blinked at me dryly, "S-sign?"
I blinked twice for her.
"S-Sarah d-don't l-leave me!"

I could not ignore that kind of cry, not again, not ever!
I was no longer too young to assert myself.
I could perhaps intervene.
After all, my father was an attorney and I knew the law.
Skeets had a right to be immediately arraigned before a magistrate.

"Did you see a judge," I asked her.
She shook her head. "N-no - no one!"

I got up and went to the aide sitting at the far end of the common room. "I'm with a law office," I lied. "Can I speak to the physician in charge?"
"He's gone home," the aide said disinterestedly.
"Then a resident - or a social worker," I insisted.
She was annoyed. She got up lazily from where she had been leaning against the wall and went to call the nurse.

A brown-haired young intern finally came—very green, smiling and careless, his hands in his pockets.
"I'm here to retrieve a client," I said. "I'll take full responsibility."

He hesitated, uncertain of the law.

"I can wake up the magistrate and have a *habeas* here within the hour," I said, feigning assurance.

He studied my face then decided to act.

He raised his hands in peace. "The wards are crowded enough," he said, and quickly initialed the chart.

Skeets' clothes were in a locker close by.

We wasted no time changing her.

Meanwhile a new shift took over and a social worker rushed to bring me a large bottle of pills, with instructions.

I looked at her. I knew her. We had gone to night school together ten years earlier.

"M-Marianne?" I stammered.

"Sarah?" she countered, tense, uneasy.

She had not aged.

She had a prim but sublimely beautiful face, girlish without makeup, with hypnotic deep brown eyes.

But Skeets appeared to recognize her and was afraid.

"01," she said.

"Where are you taking her," Marianne asked tautly.

"To my place," I said.

"Keep in touch," she said in a tense hurry, turning toward a new platoon of residents arriving.

It would not have been opportune for us to wait for Marianne. I found another aide to quickly unlock the ward doors and pulled Skeets along with me to the elevators, anxious to leave before anyone else asked questions.

Nothing happened between me and Skeets.
For a month we lived together in my apartment, scarcely speaking to each other, while I waited for her mind to return.

Had Skeets come to me for warmth, for affection, I would have given it—I would have tried to resolve through her all the frustrations of my childhood—Love, Tenderness, Warmth, Nurture that I had always hungered to give and to receive.

Childhood had been a cold and hungry time for me.

A time when Reality was thrown into constant doubt for me—when I was forced to build elaborate structures to outwit my mother's fantasies, to preserve Order in my being.

(For half the time my mother would kick me away as she would kick our dog - then, when madness loomed, she would cling to me as one drowning—dragging me with her to the bottom of a mire.)

It seemed to me that I could love Skeets, that our gender was irrelevant to that emotion, that love was a healing instinct free from gender, dependent upon life-force, biorhythms, pheromones of peace and nurture—the chemistry of Being—gender-free and Sacred.

Had Skeets asked for my love, it seemed to me that this spontaneous feeling in me could have *healed*—could have *breathed life* into Lazarus.

But she huddled on her side of the bed, always terrified of touching me.

Finally I decided to take her home—back to her native soil, her family. But when I asked her where home was, her eyes became glassy.

"01," she said.

"Why are you afraid to go home," I insisted.

"01," she repeated.

I let the matter drop.

A few minutes later she broke the silence.

"Sarah?" she spoke up quite normally, "Do you suppose I'll ever get my mind back?"

I went to her, knelt beside her and took her hand.
"Your mind is beautiful to me," I said. "I would like very much
to know it."
She pulled back, afraid.

"What are you afraid of," I asked.
"Don't you know?" she countered, her eyes hard.
"No," I said. "Tell me."
She wildly scanned the four walls.
"I can't tell you anything," she whispered.

"What are you staring at," Skeets asked, her eyes glazed
once more. "Is there a sensor behind me?"
I shook my head. "It's just a blank wall."
"Blank? Blank?" she smiled knowingly. "How do you know?"
"Because we're not important enough to be watched,"
I said.

"Don't say that!"
She put her hands to her ears.
"It's true," I persisted. "They've changed all the >KEYS< and
altered all the codes. There's nothing they want with us now.

"Don't say that!" she shrieked again.
She stared at me, trembling, clutching her skull as though
she had been shot by a cosmic ray.
"o1!" she shrieked again. "The rats! The dirty rats!"
Tears poured from her vague eternal eyes.
"The dirty rats, I forgive them," she was blubbering,
"I forgive them."

She forgave Them.
That They were imaginary was of no consequence. At least
she was able to forgive them. That made the shot real and the
imaginary wound a gaping, bloody hole.

"Don't cry," I said patiently. "Things will get better."

I turned from her and went back to my domestic tasks. My personal days were almost used up and I would soon have to return to work - that is, unless I had been laid off. Skeets' sick pay would only last another five months, but I certainly could not take five more months of this.

And by now perhaps my impatience was beginning to show on my face. Was I growing hostile? Would Skeets soon mistake me for the enemy?

She looked at me. "What are you staring at," she repeated. "There really *is* someone watching."

"I am the only one watching, and I am not one of Them," I said.

"Why are you watching me," she asked suspiciously.

"Because I'm in the same room with you," I said.

Something inside her briefly overcame her fever.

She reached for my fingers, ever so lightly touching me.

"Sarah? I want to go home.

BR ARV LLE.

We took a train there a week later.

BR ARV LLE.

The two '**I**'s had dropped off the sign.

It was a thorny brown mining town. Green pastures rimmed it, fingering the rocky slopes of low mountains.

We pulled into the one-track station with Skeets gaping through the window like a little girl looking for Momma.

Her two sisters were waving at us from the platform like newer cuts from the same mold.

When we descended they enveloped Skeets, embraced her, kissed her, made happy chirps and coos like flocking sparrows, pecking her cheeks.

I stood.
I waited.
Finally one sister turned to me and shook my hand. "I'm Daisy and that's Lovie," she said, and her look-alike waved at me.
"I'm Sarah," I said.

They were not twins. They were five years apart, and both looking much younger than Skeets. Their features were not even alike - only their manner, the look in their eyes.

Daisy insisted on carrying my suitcase while Lovie took Skeets', and they walked us uphill from the station, up a steep unlikely hill called Main Street winding and stretching crookedly toward distant factories lined like vertebrae on the side of the mountain.
"Wait till you see the new house," Lovie was saying to Skeets, her arm wound around her. "You'll swear we've turned into movie stars!"

Here, at the bottom of the hill, the town was still old, but as we climbed upwards the sidewalks became newly paved.

In little muddy plots, row on row, new ranch homes stood awaiting carpets of grass.

"Where's the farm?" Skeets asked nervously, seeming entirely disoriented.

(I was afraid they would notice how vague she was.)

"We finally sold it a couple of months ago," Daisy said. "Clem and Lovie got jobs at the new steel plant - things changing here so fast you'd never believe it."

Daisy took the steep hill strongly, my suitcase in her grasp.
I followed behind, breathlessly, rushing to catch up. Skeets and Lovie walked easily, arm in arm.

"After Pappy died, there wasn't much point in us keeping the farm," Daisy explained to me. "Strip mining's caused mudslides, and Clem - that's my husband - is a trained mechanic."
I nodded.
"You going to stay a while?" she asked.
"I have to be back by Monday," I said.
"There's a lot of good country still left out here," she said proudly. "Plenty to see."

We reached their sidestreet and came to a house just like all the other houses, new, with foundations of unweathered concrete splotched with dampness.

A child's sandpail impeded the front walk.
Daisy kicked it over in the mud. "Well, here we be," she said.
We waited for Lovie and Skeets to catch up.

Damp autumn wind was blowing through my clothes, carrying the faraway cries of migrant geese.
Not only geese —someone was shouting through a window.

I squinted and saw her - saw |Old Skeets| in a new picture window waving at |Young Skeets| wildly.

"Momma!"
Skeets broke from Lovie and ran up the walk, burst into the house through the unlocked door.
We followed her.
"Momma!" Skeets embraced her where she sat, straining the old rocker.
"Baby! Baby!" Momma was saying, hugging Skeets.
Both of them cried.

I looked about.
All the furniture inside was old, smelling musty, placed badly - as though no one knew how to fit it inside a new house. The rooms were dark - light coming only from the picture window.

(The back of the house was against the hill, holding back mudslides.)

"Momma, it's you! It's really you!" Skeets was saying. "You're really still here, Momma!"
"Of course I am, Angel," Momma said. "I'm here. I'll always be here."
I turned away, looking for a place to rest my eyes - a place that was not full of old furniture and cheap wallpaper. My eyes searched the room to find Daisy, now standing by the kitchen archway.
"Set yourself down," she said. "Clem's coming in a minute - and I've got to put supper on."

Now a two-year-old bumped into me.
He forced a papercup into my hand. It was full of mud.
I accepted it politely.

I sat in a wallpaper trance, still catching my breath from the long climb. Daisy and Lovie were in the kitchen chopping onions and rolling dough.

The cooing sound of |Skeets| talking to |Skeets| was hammering in my ears as the child below me tugged at the cup he had surrendered to me.

"Did yuh get all the money I've been sendin'?" Skeets was asking.
"Yes, Angel, yes," Momma answered. "Bless you!"
"Gonna make us rich, Momma. Gonna make us all rich," Skeets was saying.
She had reverted to their way of speaking, had leaped back into her teens - but not to a youth as plain as theirs - a nobler time -
"It shut Pappy up, it did, to be gettin' all that from yuh," Momma was saying. "Many's the time he'd have lost the farm."
"01," Skeets said.
The mention of Pappy had upset her.
"What's wrong, Angel," Momma asked.
We both waited for her answer while Skeets now stood suspended, older, muttering and rearranging words across her forehead like ticker-tape.
"Pappy," she finally computed. "Where's Pappy?"
"Baby," Momma grabbed her. "I wrote you about that years ago. Pappy's gone a long time now - died of drunkenness well on ten years 'go."
Skeets stared at her suspiciously.
"Yuh should be glad, Baby," Momma said. "He's thru with shamin' both of us. The Good Lord's seen to that!"
"01!"
Skeets stood.
She looked feverish, lost.

I started towards her but the child blocked me.
Then the front door slammed.
It was Clem - I knew him by his flushed face and blistered hands. Daisy rushed out of the kitchen to meet him.
"Howdy," he said to me, waiting to be introduced.
"This here's Sarah," Daisy said, "and that's Skeets."
He shook my hand, and nodded to Skeets who stood by vaguely. Then he went to wash for supper.

"Daisy," Momma spoke, "tell Lovie to show your sister and her girlfriend the new house." She looked at me apologetically. "Got this bad leg here now - "

"Lovie," Daisy hollered, "Momma wants yuh."

Lovie appeared and took Skeets around, hand in hand. I followed passively, then excused myself, feigning a slight headache.

"Skeets' friend's got a headache," Momma called to the kitchen.

Daisy came out again, wiping her hands on her apron. "Supper'll be on soon. Can I get yuh somethin'?" she asked me.

"I could use some fresh air," I said.

"Set out on the patio for a while then," she said, motioning to the side door.

I followed her, glad to get out of the livingroom.

The patio was nothing more than a concrete slab overlooking more muddy yard, and the next house - too close to ignore.

I sat in a folding chair that would soon be disposed of in favor of patio furniture that had not yet arrived.

"Can I get yuh a blanket," Daisy asked.

"Yes thank you," I nodded.

She returned with a crib blanket smelling of sweet-scented soap. I wrapped it around my lap, letting the chill air refresh me.

She lingered, leaning on the wall, waiting for us to speak. "Yuh from a small town too?" she finally asked.

"More of a suburb," I said. "A very flat area - but it has some of the same feeling as here." I paused to remember. "The farms were further out."

"Not much good farming here," she said. "Not much grows."

"But don't you miss your farm?" I said.

"Nope."

I looked at her—she had green eyes but not really a country stare. Her speech and manner were almost correct and very likely she had finished high school. It was puzzling to see her standing there, not quite belonging to the land.

"I was born in a city slum," I said. "During the Depression, my father got two jobs and pulled us out—moved us to a new house in the suburbs. But it took a long time for us to realize that we were no longer poor."

I paused, seeing the muddy yard as she saw it, as it would soon become: in the spring, a grass carpet would be laid - and a little later, when Clem's credit was established, they would buy new furniture on time. The whole town was like that, would grow together at the same rate and level —a programmed kind of change that would not unduly strain Daisy's generation—a slow change with more than ample time to adjust.

Now Daisy spoke frankly. "Why did you bring her back here?"

I looked up. "Then you know she's ill," I said.

She looked at me blankly, nodded blankly.

"Was she ill before?" I asked.

Again she nodded.

I sighed and looked away.

"I couldn't be sure," I said.

"We don't want her here," Daisy now said. "She can't stay here."

"But she's your sister - " I said.

"We can't live her life for her," she answered.

It was a programmed answer, an answer given to her by someone in authority—a counselor, or a physician, or more likely a minister.

"What happened years ago," I asked. "How was she taken ill?"

"I don't know as I have a right to talk about it," she said, now feeling herself trapped on the patio with me—willing and yet unwilling to communicate.

"You'd better talk about it," I asserted. "If you're willing to abandon her to strangers, you'd better talk about it."

"Why did you take such trouble over her," Daisy countered suspiciously. "What's she to you?"

"Nothing. Just someone drowning," I answered.

It broke her. Suddenly.

"God knows," she cried, "I loved her - we all loved her - we never wanted to do her wrong!"

"What happened," I now asked. "How did she leave home?"

"The State took her away," she said, controlling herself. "After Pappy - after we all - " she couldn't say it. "They came and put her in a Home, and put her through school."

"She was abused?"

"*The Devil's Child*, Pappy used to call her. Both Pappy and Momma tried to beat and starve it out of her. And we helped them. We were so young - how could we know?"

I see. I understand," I said.

"No, you don't understand. You can't understand." She faced me. "Everything was different then. Skeets was - strange - and Pappy for all his drunkenness, was Pappy."

"But I do understand," I said.

"Then you can guess the measure of guilt we all still got on her account."

She took a deep breath and sat on a stool, righteously.

"God forgive us, we did wrong. But there's no way to make it right now. That's the cross we must bear."

"No way to make it right?" I stood. "How can you say that? How can you sit there saying that!"

She stood and faced me again. "I'll not drown myself, or my family with her. The State took care of her once, they'll do it again."

"It won't be the same again," I said.

"What makes you say that." She looked at me, alarmed.

"She needs love," I said. "She needs her family."

"Look," she cried, coming toward me, her voice loud enough to be heard inside. "Look, I know what you're asking is right and fair. But I can't do it. God forgive me—first Pappy and now Momma—I'm not strong enough! It's too soon to ask more of me. It's too soon!"

She ran back into the house, crying.

"There you be," Skeets said.

She was standing in the patio doorway appearing too real, too sane. Her eyes were neither blue nor gray. She was looking through me. Daisy had just brushed past her, crying.

"Watcha doin' out here, huh?"

She had completely reverted to an earlier time and was smiling at me like a long-necked bird about to be beheaded.

"I needed some fresh air," I lied.

"Fresh?" she punned.

I nodded.

"Are we stayin' the night, huh? Momma wants us to."

I shook my head. "I'm catching the night train back."

"Me too," she said, still like an ostrich.

"No."

"Why, sure!" she insisted.

"You have to stay here," I returned firmly.

"But - if I stay here - " she computed, suddenly not backward now, back to her own time now, " - if I stay here, I won't be staying here."

"How do you mean," I said, trying to quell her.

"If I stay here, I'll be staying elsewhere."

"That's silly," I lied. "They won't turn you out."

"01!" she backed away from me, seeming ready to leap off the hill. "01!"

"Skeets, listen," I said, reaching for her.

"I don't want to listen! Everytime I listen I get shot!"
She put her hands to her ears. "01!"

She backed away from me, backed into the railing and went over it, off the concrete and into the muddy yard.

"01!"

She tumbled to her feet, mud on her dress and leg. Then she jerked free of my eyes, jerked free of the house and splashed down the muddy yard, splashed downhill through mud.
"Skeets, come back," I chased after her.

"01!"

She quickly reached the bottom and ran along the tracks, toward the mouth of the tunnel that cut through the mountain.
The train would burst out of there screeching.
"Skeets, no!" I shrieked.
But she had leaped across the tracks and just then the train shot between us.

The empty train shot through quickly. It was not stopping in Briarville. And when the track was clear again I saw her climbing up the steep recline, stumbling on loose gravel, clutching small bushes and tough grass.

I pursued - climbed upward, catching hold of the hill as she did, gravel rolling under me, cutting my knees as I stumbled.
"Skeets, wait!" I kept shouting.

The light was fading and it was hard to see her, both of us dank-pressed against the hill, both of our dresses torn and soaked.
"Skeets, where are you," I called. "It's getting dark and I'm afraid." I paused to let her speak.

"Don't come closer," she finally called down.
She was about ten yards above me, leaning on the side of the mountain, on a narrow ledge between sheets of rock.
"If you stop, I'll stop," I called to her. "Please stop. I'm tired. Very tired." I panted loudly so that she could hear.

There was silence.

"All right," she finally answered.
"Come down," I said. "It's getting hard to see."
"01!" she said.
Gravel avalanched past her.
I dug myself more firmly into the hill.

"I'm not going to come down because you lie to me," at last
she volunteered.
"I don't lie to you," I countered.
"Yes you do."

Again there was silence.
She spoke again: "You should ask me why I say a thing
instead of just denying it. It proves you a liar when you just deny
things."
"How have I lied to you," I asked.
There was another long pause.

"You lie to me because you keep saying things that mix me
up," she finally said.
"How do I do that?"
"You say I haven't been shot, and I have! Then you want to
send me back to the place that shot me."
She shifted again against the hill, and more rocks fell past
me.
"You weren't shot," I said.
"01!"
More earth plunged downward.

"How dare you call me a liar," I said angrily. "You're the one
who keeps lying to yourself all the time!"
"I don't lie! I work hard! I work very hard!"
She was sobbing now.
"I don't want to be a washout again. I don't want to wash out
again. If go back there they'll make me wash out again and my
head will be all clean. I don't want my head clean. Sarah—"
She screeched—mud giving way all around her.

She grabbed hold of a bush and hung from it, hung from the hill.

I began to climb upward.

"Don't come nearer," she warned.

"If you come near, I'll let go!"

I shouted at her. "Make up your mind. First you ask for my help then you threaten to jump if I come near."

I waited for her reply.

There was none.

"It's getting cold," I said. "I don't like it up here. I'm going back down."

"Sarah - " she called desperately.

"I'm not your keeper," I said angrily.

"Keep her? Keep her?" she echoed.

I tried again: "The day they took my mother away, she sounded just like you. That's what makes it so hard for me to let go now. She was screaming and pleading and finding all kinds of silly reasons why they shouldn't be taking her away from us. I ran. I ran into my bedroom and put my hands to my ears."

I waited, hugging the hill. "Are you still listening? Do you want to hear the rest of it?"

I went on: "I was twelve years old. It had not been the first time they had taken her away. This time it was the middle of summer and school was out. I just sat around doing nothing for a very long time - sat for days in the kitchen in the chair my mother used to sit in, tracing patterns on the oil cloth while my sister played by herself. I was supposed to be taking care of her - of the house - of the dog - I was supposed to feed us and walk the dog—"

I paused.

Still there was silence.

"I'm listening," she said after a moment.

"You're really saying something now."

"I didn't want to take my mother's place. It was too soon for me. Do you understand? I rebelled against it all - I refused to feed us, or walk the dog."

I waited, straining to hear her breathe.

"Our old bitch was fat from many litters," I continued. "She was the very symbol of what a mother is - she used to crawl toward me on her many-breasted belly and whine and beg to be let out the door. I couldn't move from the chair to let her out the door."

Again I waited for Skeets to say something but she was quiet.

I continued:

"She was a good dog. It was a long time before she finally made a mess. And it wasn't until then that I could move from the chair. The only thought that moved me was that I needed to punish her for making a mess. I took the leash that was on the back of the chair. It was a chain leash. I had only meant to menace her—but suddenly I was whipping her, whipping her like my sister whipped her teddy bears. I whipped and whipped her until she just lay there crushed and bleeding."

I called out to Skeets:

"Did you hear me? A dog saved my life once. She was my friend and still I turned on her. Then I stood there, unable to move—stood there until my father came home and shot her!"

Still there was dreadful silence.
But finally she spoke:

"Sarah? I didn't hear all that."

"What did you hear if you didn't hear it," I cried.

"I heard music - from those rosy clouds out there."

I could see her silhouetted against the sky, looking toward the last-light now streaking the horizon.

"Sarah," she said distantly, "have you ever seen Jesus? I've always seen Him. He's walking out there on those clouds - making the sky warm."

"It's a mirage," I said.

"Have you ever seen Him?" she repeated.

"Once, when I was very young, I mistook my mother for an angel. But I had a fever."

"Did He speak to you or touch you?"

"No. He always backed away."

"Sometimes, He's near enough to touch," she said. "Then I think - finally - I'll be Me."

"It's getting very dark now," I said. "I'm going down again."

"Don't leave me!"

"Then inch down. If you can't make it by yourself you might as well stay here."

"Don't say that!" she screamed.

The last-light dropped below the clouds now, suddenly, and the whole sky was dark.

"Sarah?" she gasped, afraid of the dark. "Sarah?"

" ... I'm still here," I said.

I had left in time.

My father's car had not overtaken the bus.

It would be almost impossible for him to catch up to me now that I was again in the middle of the City.

All the same, I got off at the wrong stop and walked ten blocks out of my way through a maze of factory streets to make certain that I had not been followed.

I finally reached our building and stopped for a moment, to gaze at the building across from us—the rear wing of Downtown General.

It seemed to me that I saw hundreds of faces crowding at the windows, waving to me. Young old men and young old women, chattering and tittering and waving like tiny monkeys.

They knew me. They were used to seeing me.
I waved at them and they waved back.
Years ago, when my mother had been there, no one could have waved at them—it would have set off a large howl and banging throughout the alleyways.
But now medication kept them quiet, drugged them into quiet wide-eyed infants . . . .

It was not a compulsion to hold on to Skeets that blocked my return to the Corporation. I had long since been ready to cut her off like some gangrenous limb. There was no reason why she had to live with me—I might have found some other place to put her, one that would provide her with custodial care somewhat less grim than that available at a state hospital. Conditions had improved substantially from the time that my mother had been abandoned. I did not need to feel such guilt over Skeets.

It was only my rage, my outrage at the injustice that had been done to her, and to me, that still bound me to her.

During the month of my absence, a whisper campaign had been initiated falsely connecting Skeets to me— an elaborate set of offensive rumors and lies implying that in defense of my own integrity I must insist that Justice be done to Skeets.

Eric either could not, or would not endorse my stand.
His only recommendation was that I should institutionalize Skeets, quit my job, marry him.
After all, Skeets was not my child, was no relation, was nothing to me!
Soon, it would be too late for me to have children.
If I wanted to have children, then it was time to marry him and raise a proper family.

Then he added, quite grandly, that he was willing to forgive and forget my affair with Skeets.

Management echoed the same protocol.
The day I returned to work I was told to report to the Medical Office at Personnel, where the Doctor received me with his usual broad smile.

"That was a large responsibility you took upon yourself, Miss Miller," he blinked amicably. "Was there any reason why you felt impelled to sign her out so quickly?"
"I felt she could not survive another moment there," I said. "I know it was wrong of me to impersonate an attorney, but it was harmless and expedient. If necessary, I would have called in my father to confirm my actions and take her on as a client."

"Your father is an attorney, then," he noted
"Yes."
He frowned and coughed a bit uneasily.

"How long do you intend to keep Skeets with you?"
"I haven't decided that yet," I said. "I'm seeking a suitable place for her. And there is, of course, a financial problem."
"She's too ill to be out of a hospital," he said quickly.
"I don't agree," I countered.

He frowned again. "Miss Miller—I hope you can understand my position. I find your—shall we say, *attachment* for Skeets most telling—in view of your past history. I am greatly concerned."
"Meaning what?" I asked firmly.
"I shall have to write a memo on it," he said, hesitant.

"And that will mean my security clearance will be suspended," I concluded. "And that in turn will cause me to be laid off. And that's what was planned from the beginning, wasn't it? It wasn't only Skeets who was to be phased out. Why? Did you expect I would marry?"

He sat back in his chair, awkwardly: "If only you could give us a suitable reason for your special concern over Skeets—"

"What if I told you that her breakdown was not a natural occurrence —that it was caused. Would you believe that kind of reason?"

"That's a far-fetched hypothesis, Miss Miller," he protested. "Why should anyone have wanted to do that?"

"A practical joker, perhaps—someone who didn't realize the full import of his actions. Or, perhaps someone who knew exactly what he was doing but did it anyway—for the sheer pleasure of the kill."

I paused to study his face.
He was most perturbed.

"... Or perhaps someone was afraid that she might find work elsewhere—with a competitor, or even a foreign power."

He paled.
"There is a killer among us," I stated.
"Is that why you took her out of the hospital?" he asked cautiously.
"Would you believe a more humane reason? Would you believe—*compassion*?"
The word offended him.
He shook his head, skeptically.
I rose. "Such altruism does seem old-fashioned."

"What do you want, Miss Miller," he now demanded flatly. "How long do you intend to hold this over us?"
"I demand a hearing," I answered. "A formal hearing. Nothing more."
"That's impossible," he returned quickly. "Please - ask for something else."
"I am not a blackmailer," I said.
I turned to leave.

"Miss Miller," he called after me, taunting. "I am still going to write my memo."

"Do as you please," I told him.

I left the Administration Building convinced that for as long as Skeets was with me, we were in a position of power—power to wreck an empire, power to change a system.

They were afraid of what—together—we might do.
But why afraid?
Afraid even to hold a hearing?
Afraid of the publicity?
Afraid of the impact on employee morale?

"Hey, Sar - wait up! " Russo ran after me as I walked across the small park to my office building.

I waited for him to catch up.

"C'mon, I'll buy you a drink," he said, taking my arm and leading me forward in long strides toward the cocktail lounge two blocks away.

I let myself be led.

I was curious.

The cocktail lounge was not yet open—it was too early for lunch, but the management let us sit at one of the back booths until the waitress was ready to serve.

I watched Russo grin at me for a time.

"The Old Man sent me," he finally said.

He put his hand on mine. "Sar - he doesn't want to scrap you. This fight over Skeets - it shows character. He has great plans for you."

"Wait till he interfaces with Medical," I replied.

"He already has," Russo said quickly, too quickly.

"But if I ask for a hearing, he'll abandon those plans, he'll shred me along with Skeets," I concluded for him.

My statement stripped him naked.

His face took on a family resemblance, to Eric, to Hoffman.

"That's the bottom line," he said.

I looked away at the waitresses preparing to serve luncheon. Some had been temporary workers in the secretarial pool. Most were unemployed actresses who would sell their bodies for as long as they could and then live and grow old as waitresses.

"When do I return to work," I asked.

"If and when - " he continued to grasp my hand.

"Skeets?" I finished for him.

He nodded.

I could not abandon Skeets.

To put Skeets away somewhere where she would lose her identity one more time, and later to see her return to the Corporation as a clerical worker at some menial task - a feeble gesture at rehabilitation - was not an act either of sanity or even of political expedience.

How safe would the world become for me once Skeets was shredded? How safe for any of us? A heinous and cowardly crime had been committed, to which I was a material witness. My silence would have implied complicity.

In the years to come, my silence would become terrible to me. The very conditions of that silence would destroy me.

Wherefore I stood firm, demanding a hearing.

"01!"

Skeets sat naked in the middle of the floor in my apartment one month later, her hands to her skull.

"01! The dirty dogs!"

The floor was covered with papers—papers with hieroglyphic scrawls on them—codes illegible to everyone—

formulas that seemed to solve all the puzzles of existence in language known only to the gods.

I began to pick up the papers, patiently, carefully attempting to keep them in proper sequence.

She looked at me, feverish, listening through walls. "Tomorrow. Nine o'clock. The big fry."

"You're imaging it," I said.

(In my weariness I had slurred the word.)

"Imaging? Imaging?" she echoed. "Do you think They will let me live, now that I know everything?"

She pointed to her computations.

I stood, my arms full of papers.

"Do you think, if this absurd hypothesis of yours is true, that we can be safe from 'Them' anywhere?"

She folded inside herself and bawled.

"I want to go home!"

I set the papers down on a corner of the couch and went to raise her to her feet. I was embarrassed by her nakedness. The walls seemed to be made of glass. I had closed all the blinds even though my windows faced a blank wall.

"What are you staring at," Skeets said, blinking.
"I think we should move," I said.

My apartment was becoming too expensive to keep on less than half my regular income. Perhaps in another city we could find work, could finally rid ourselves of the feeling that our every movement was being watched.

The next day, I sublet it to one of the temporary workers for six months and took Skeets with me out of town.

But there was no other place to go, no work, no feeling of asylum. We soon returned, now temporarily homeless.

I rented a loft in the factory district at a price more affordable, intending to fix it up—to make it habitable.

I turned my back on all the wide-eyed infants and went up our front steps, braving the dark hallway to our door.

An icy draft slapped my face. It came from the fire door set within our large window.

Skeets was gone.!

She had left by the fire escape and gone up the roof and over and down again through the courtyard. She had done so before. The fire door could not be locked. I closed it and stood, shivering in my wet shoes.

I stopped only long enough to change my socks and put on sneakers—I had only sneakers left to wear. Then I hurried out to look for her. I was terrified that she might have left hours ago— might have been standing for hours on some streetcorner while her feet and fingers froze.

Recently she had lost all feeling for pain, for cold.

She would not notice if her face or hands got frostbite—she would continue to stand around smiling, like all the other derelicts beside her, crippled, maimed by frostbite.

I had not seen her on my way home.

I chose another direction, pressing through holiday crowds on the Avenue. Here, cars were bumper to bumper and heat from their racing motors had melted the snow to gray slush, had made it warmer.

One by one I went to all the places, all the streetcorners where I had found her once before—for she had favorite places to stand or squat, as if she hoped to be easily found.

A grocery store clerk winked at me and pointed up the block, where a bartender remembered she had been standing across the street; a little farther, an old lady who lived forever-framed in a first-floor window sent me back in the opposite direction.

I had traveled a complete circle and now stood frozen on a corner.

The air had turned warmer but it was beginning to snow again—large flakes that melted as they touched me.

The crowd was beginning to thin.

Across the Avenue, by the Settlement House, the volunteer band of Santas had stopped playing a discordant hymn and now was filing inside.

Now I saw her—standing among the listeners—a papercup of hot broth in her hand.

I ran across, between the cars.

"There you are," I said, sounding almost like her, and catching hold of her. "I looked all over for you."

"10!"

Skeets smiled at me dumbly but like family. Her nose was running, and her eyes. Her fingers were red around the papercup. Her broth was tepid.

"Drink it down," I said.

"It's a lot warmer inside," a girl's voice said behind us.

I turned. It was one of the volunteer youths from the Settlement House.

She pulled us gently up the steps to the Canteen.

I allowed us to be pulled in with the others—with the elderly and the ill—into the large main hall that had once been part of a grammar school.

Now it had become a shelter for drug addicts and alcoholics and all the other homeless—run by an obscure religious sect composed primarily of long-haired young men and women in monkish rags—rescued, re-sewn and recycled from waste bins—assisted by the even more poorly dressed, by the pock-marked and unshaven, the near-demented.

Were they all like Sarah and Skeets?

Humbled I allowed us to be taken among them. We found a space at the end of a long bench and sat.

"Let's look at your hands," I said.

Skeets blinked at me stupidly.

I pulled her fingers forward and inspected them. They were red but not frostbitten.

"Take off your boots," I said.

Slowly she kicked one off.

I felt her toes - the sock was dry. And now the other foot - also dry.

My own feet were soaked again. I kicked off my sneakers and wrung out my socks.

The hall was full now - full of old men and women of every age, coughing and wheezing, bronchial, pneumonic. They sat as if on pews, hunched row on row.

Now a gospel tune rocked over the loudspeakers and a line formed for hot broth and packages of bread and cheese— packages that many would take out and try to sell on the street for money to buy drugs or wine.

I turned to Skeets. Her face was windburned, splotched red as flesh becomes just before frostbite.

"You shouldn't have gone out," I said.

"Out?" she echoed.

"I've told you always to wait for me."

"Wait? Wait?" She tightened her jaw angrily. "01!"

"I'm sorry I took so long," I said.

"So long?" She looked at me, worried.

"Don't you see what you've done now," I sighed. "You've pushed us into a place like this. We don't belong here—not yet."

"01," she said meekly, like a child scolded.

We huddled together on the side of the bench, trying to leave space between us and the rest of them. We tried not to breathe too deeply and put our hands to our ears to shut out the deafening sound of the loudspeakers that were now pounding a sermon into our skulls:

A fervent young woman was preaching through a megaphone:

"TRUST NOT IN THE VOICE OF YOUR OWN HEART. For as Jeremiah teaches: THE HEART IS ATROCIOUSLY WICKED AND DECEITFUL ABOVE ALL THINGS."

"01!" Skeets said.
"For once I agree," I said.

She shook her head. "I was thinking of something else. I was thinking—they are starving outside and it's against the law to feed them. And here we are, sitting ducks."
"What are you talking about?"
"A sign today revealed to me that persons feeding pigeons will be persecuted to the fullest extent of the law."
"Prosecuted," I corrected her. "But that's irrelevant."
"Irreverent?" She was punning on purpose.
"They make a holy mess," I answered.
"Mass," she corrected me, smiling. "But don't you think that law is a contradiction?"
She was talking to me—she was finally attempting to carry on an extended conversation.
"Skeets," I said, taking hold of her hand. "Skeets, can you hear yourself?"
"Here? Here?" She frowned as though I had betrayed her.
"Please," I begged her. "Don't play word games with me. Try to think clearly."
"I'm clear as a window right now," she returned.
I looked at her, disbelieving.
"Shall I tell you what I imagined today?" She smiled impishly, then stared into space. "I was walking along the street and all of a sudden the walls of the building became clear as windows. People inside were all clean and shiny. Washed out."
"And?"

She looked at me, coyly. "I don't think I ought to tell you the rest of it. It will upset you."

"Go on," I said.

"Jesus was standing there, in the window-walls, smiling at me with open arms."

I stood impatiently. "Enough."
"Brainwashed, mouthwashed," she said.
She looked down and sulked.

I pulled her up after me and pulled us toward a side exit away from the crowd of bodies that blocked our way out through the door from which we had come.

We found ourselves in the hallway of an adjoining building of the old schoolhouse which now had become a holding center for all the homeless young.

Children were running past us, screaming - ragged nine-year-olds, most of them drugged. They crowded around us, shrieking and laughing: *Who're yuh lookin' for? What's yore names?*

I started to say something but a youth worker interrupted me. "May I help you?" she asked.

I turned.

She looked familiar. Then I recognized her.

Again, inexplicably, to my chagrin, it was Marianne.

"Sarah?" she asked, uncertain.
"Yes," I answered.
She looked at me twice, in disbelief. "What on earth are you doing here," she finally said.
"We - we were looking for an exit," I stammered.

The children were running havoc through the hallway.
She screamed at them to return to their rooms.

"Come in here," then she said, urgently pulling us into a classroom filled with younger children, also screaming.
The noise was ear-shattering.

"Quiet!" Marianne shrieked once more, rapping her desk with a pointer. But the hush was only momentary.

The stench of human waste was worse in here than in the adjacent building. The children all seemed like tiny vagrants in old clothes that hung from their thin bodies like rags on scarecrows—and beyond their stench, the sickly smell of marijuana coming from a crowd of eight-year-olds huddled naughtily together on the floor—in the far corner.

I turned to Marianne urgently to tell her - but her placid smile stopped me. Like Hoffman, like Russo, she seemed determined to see no evil.

"It's so good to see you again," she said to the two of us, vaguely. "What brings you here?"

I could scarcely hear her above the noise. I had to read her lips.   "You remember Skeets, don't you?" I said.
Skeets squinted at her suspiciously.

"Yes, yes of course," Marianne said, reaching out to touch Skeets' hand fondly, as Hoffman might.

"01!" Skeets pulled away.
Skeets has been ill for some time," I apologized.
Marianne smiled sympathetically, as if we had come to her for a professional consultation.

I was very conscious of the way we looked—of our old clothes, of Skeets' cracked lips and red face, of the wrong door from which we had come like derelicts trespassing.

"I understand. I understand completely," she nodded.
"Thank God for His having guided you here! ... Promise me— "
she added, leaning forward, touching my hand—"promise me
that from now on you will come to see me here often."

I did not know how to reply.
Marianne appeared to be in a trance.

She was smiling at me as a little girl smiles
when conversing with a very special doll.

Marianne insisted that we wait for her across the street—at a cafe we had both frequented—a cafe that had been infamous a decade ago as a gathering place for dissidents and war-protestors —a place still well-surveilled by the police—although it also attracted artists and tourists and even Corporate slummers.

Eric and I had been there a few times in past years, but only for impromptu after-theater nightcaps. It was in a cellar, dimly lit by storm candles.

Skeets and I took the steps carefully and the proprietor waved to us as we descended, as though he knew us—a man in his fifties, sitting at a back table where he had set up permanent housekeeping with his very young wife—rocking a new baby in a carriage.   I had only spoken to him briefly once—how could he have remembered me?
I nodded to him, and we chose the table next to him.

It was early.
The cafe was nearly empty except for a customer in a drab brown suit sitting blankly in the shadows. Perhaps a plainclothesman. He appeared settled in for the evening—a bunch of magazines and newspapers laid on the empty chair next to him.

We took off our coats.
I put our things on a chair in front of a warm radiator and even dared to peel off my sneakers and socks to dry them, hiding my bare feet under the table.
The proprietor appeared disinterested.
A waitress came to take our order.

She also knew us—she was another actress who had once worked temporarily at the Corporation.

She was glad to see us.

"Well, hi, you two!" she beamed respectfully, leaning fondly on my shoulder with her large warm hand.

She was an open person—too well-built, too tall, too outgoing for her own good. I had seen her do a strip once at a private party Uptown on a wild New Year's Eve.

She was still beautiful now, but she had begun to lose her teeth and her voice was cracked with the early-morning sound of a night of heavy whoring.

The waitress turned to Skeets, who was now checking out the four walls feverishly for hidden sensors. She put her hand on Skeets' forehead. "You don't look good, Honey. Are you feelin' okay?"

"01!" Skeets drew back, but not angrily. "Please don't touch—" she wrote it in the air first, "—the wound, please."

The waitress looked at me, half-comprehending.

I shook my head. "Not good at all," I said.

"Oh God, that's bad - that's really rough. Who would have thought—" She sighed, then took out her checkpad as though nothing was wrong. "Well, what'll you have? It's on the house, so order something big."

I started to protest but she stopped me. "Seriously, this one's on Willie. He doesn't get many old customers anymore."

I looked across the table, at the proprietor.

He waved at me again, with his long clay pipe.

I nodded a polite thank you at him then ordered tea for me and hot milk for Skeets.

Skeets opened her mouth wide but lost herself in an unsaid word.

"And two pastramis on rye," the waitress added for us.

She left us and went into the kitchen.

The new breed of rioters was coming in now, in bunches—a drugged, uneducated, idle mob hiding their eyes behind pink spectacles—a sweaty and unshaven lot resigned to spending many nights in jail.

Less than a decade ago the dissidents had all been clean-cut young men and women filled with righteous purpose. They would come here after a demonstration, wearing their bandaged heads and broken arms as badges of courage.

Marianne had been among them—filled with religious zeal.

We had never been close friends in college; she had been too intense, too fanatic in her compulsion to save the world from ruin. But now had Marianne also come to this?

To this new gut-weariness of the rebels in their never-ending war fought ever in the streets?

Marianne now seemed less like some Defending Angel than like a Lord-Gatherer of the Faceless, a Vampire Nightstalker, in search of deathbed converts to false-proclaim *Victory of the Meek over the Strong*—over the Strong cowering warmly and comfortably inside large stone houses, beating their chests on Sundays in joyous *mea culpae.*

"10!" Skeets woke me from my revel.

The waitress had brought our food.

It sat in front of me.

"Why aren't you eating," Skeets asked suspiciously. "Is it drugged?"

"I'm not hungry," I said.

She trembled a little. Her eyes pleaded with me. "Are you Judas?" she stammered.

"I? No. I hope not!"

I could not face her.

Perhaps I would become Judas soon. How much longer could we go on like this? I turned away, unwilling to look at her.

Now a hand clamped down on mine, gripping my wrist like a handcuff.

I looked up. It was Eric.

He looked at me grimly. "I must talk to you."

"Let go of me," I said tightly, feigning coldness.
"Sarah!" His grip cut into me.

I looked down at his hand—and the wedding band bruising
my flesh. I looked down and then up at him, unbelieving.
"How long was I supposed to wait," he said.

He sat down, smelling clean.
He was out of place here smelling clean, wearing expensive
clothes. The customers stared at him. I worried that he might be
recognized, that he had made a mistake coming here.

"Sar, I must talk to you," he said again, still gripping my
hand.
"Who sent you," I demanded.
"Why have you been hiding," he countered.
We stared at each other. "She's not going to get well, you
know," he finally said. He said it coldly, in front of Skeets.
"01!" Skeets said.

Suddenly I loathed him.
"How the hell do you know! Why are you here! Who sent
you?"
"Stop asking insane questions," he snapped.
"Insane?" I countered. "Is that the new policy?"
"Sarah, stop it!"
"What do you want from me!"
"To be with you." He was loathe to admit it: "I love you."
"Hah!"
"It's true!"
He gripped my wrist again.
I tried to pull free but his grip tightened.
"Go ahead, break it," I defied. "It will mend."
He would not let me go.
"You're coming with me, right now," he insisted.
"In my bare feet?" I laughed at him. "Or are you going to give
me time to put on my socks and sneakers?"
He let go of me.

I took my things from the radiator and began to put them on discretely. He watched me pathetically.

"Where are you taking us," I demanded.

"Where we can be alone."

"I can't leave Skeets here," I said.

Grudgingly he took out a bill from his wallet and called the waitress over. "Can you see she stays here for a couple of hours until we come back?"

"Sure thing, Honey," the waitress said, giving all of us a knowing look.

"01!" Skeets said.

I looked at him angrily. "What's it to be - a twenty-dollar fuck? Or has my market value plunged by now."

"Sarah, stop it!" he pleaded, half-embarrassed.

I turned to Skeets.

She had put on her coat and was sitting at the edge of her seat, blinking—blinking hopefully like a dog, ready to leave.

"Skeets, listen," I said, taking her hand. "Listen. Stay here - do you understand? Stay until I return."

**I recoiled from the sound of my own voice.
It really sounded like I was talking to a dog.**

"Come on."

Eric pulled me to my feet, throwing my coat over me.

I let him push me up the stairs and out into the street, toward a hotel.   But I pulled back:

"No," I changed my mind, "I want to show you where we live."

"The loft?"

"How did you know about the loft!"

He would not answer.

"So we really *are* under surveillance," I said. "Has it been wired for sound?"

Again he would not answer.

"All the better," I told him, and pulled him down a side alley to the factory building that was our home.

He recoiled at the entrance-way but followed me up the stairs through the unlit hallway.

I unlocked our door and switched on the flickering fluorescent bulb that was our only light. The wide steam radiator by the window had overheated the room again, but it would be the only heat coming up until morning.

I turned to Eric.

He was standing in the doorway incredulous.

"Don't let out the heat," I snapped at him, then pulled him in.

He stood there, hat in hand. "This is really where you live?"

"Temporarily," I said.

I watched him walk to the center of the room.

"I won't offer you anything—there isn't anything."

He shook his head.

I went about picking up all the dropped clothing, stuffed it haphazardly into the footlockers. Then I stood again and faced him. "Now what was it you wanted?"

He shook his head again. "Nothing."

"Nothing? Was it for nothing that you almost broke my arm?"

He shifted uncomfortably. "Why have you been hiding?"

"I haven't been hiding," I lied.

"You took elaborate detours not to be followed."

"Oh?"

"We were all very concerned."

"Concerned!" I had to laugh. "Who, exactly?"

He shifted again. "Your father."

"Oh? Only my father?"

I looked at him skeptically, wondering if our office crowd had in fact tried to influence my father, had tried to use him to commit me, as he had committed my mother.

He winced. "Sarah, stop talking this way!"

I changed the subject. "So now you're married. Who? Cynthia?"

"Yes."

"Excellent choice! The ideal Corporate image!"

He didn't answer.

Now it suddenly all made sense to me. The Old Man had never approved of me. "Was that why I was shot down? To free you for the right Corporate move?"

"Sar- don't— " he pleaded.

I looked beyond him, through the wide window.
Across the alley, the wife was working in the kitchen,
making supper.

"Perhaps it was a wise decision," I said. "I don't think I ever could have fit into that mold. If only I didn't still lust you."

"Are you and Skeets—" he hesitated.

"No."

He did not believe me. He looked at me, confused.

It infuriated me.

"Go back and tell them what they want to hear—that I'm obsessed with Skeets—that we're living in filth—that I'm on the brink of a major breakdown!"

I stopped. I searched the ceiling and the walls, searched them the way Skeets did, searched for a peephole or a sensor. There were hundreds of cracks in the plaster—hundreds of places for eyes to be.

"Tell them, also," I added, "—that they had better be listening. Because if they aren't listening—my silence will be terrible!"

I glared at him—at his penitent little-boy stance, his eyes on the floor, his hat in his hand.

159

"Do you know what it was that I always wanted from you? A good fuck! That's the only really good thing we've ever had between us."

He looked embarrassed.

"I don't remember your ever being so coarse," he said righteously.

"I don't remember ever putting on a show for the whole group before," I said.

"There's no one watching us," he dismissed.

"Oh? Can you be certain of that?
Well, then, why not test it!"

Defiantly I turned from him and took off my coat, took off all my clothes, stood naked in the light of the wide window.

He stared at me, ambivalent, willing yet unwilling.

Then, without lust, in dutiful resignation, he put his hat on the table and his coat on a chair. Neatly he removed his jacket and shirt and tie—ever so neatly for he would have to wear them again later.

He thought to leave his socks on, but then slipped them off, braving the cold floor.

I leaned by my cot, watching him.

The light from the window was like moonlight on him as he walked erect and barefoot toward me.

I lay down to receive him, spread my legs wide,
full in the light of the wide window.

Are they watching us, I wondered.
Surely this will prove to them that I do not belong to Skeets.

Eric left just after Midnight.

Reluctantly I dressed again to look for Skeets. But when I returned to the cafe I found it crowded beyond capacity, leather-jacketed youths sitting three deep, sharing each other's food: near-children wearing attic clothes - old furs, even turbans, rhinestone strings. Pot smoke filled the air, and sickly incense masking it.

I looked for the proprietor. He and his family had gone to bed. Only the waitress was left to mind the premises - and she had gone off duty, was sitting with an older crowd in the rear by the cash register, her eyes glazed.

I started back toward the door.

A girlish voice stopped me: "Skeets is safe. She's bedded down for the night."

I turned.

It was Marianne, wide awake and wide-eyed.

She was sitting in a corner—the corner that had been our table—surrounded by the jaundiced and half-sleeping.

"Where?" I demanded.

"I'll take you there," she said. She waited for me to speak, appearing to have much to say to me.

I lingered, unwilling to face the cold again.

"It's only across the street," she said. "There's a place for you there too. You can share my room if you like."

The look on her face was strange - urgent.

I couldn't tell what kind of look it was.

Had Hoffman sent her, or was she still a dissident?

Curiosity, a passion to face the enemy, and the sheer dread
and discomfort of returning alone to the loft, impelled me.
"All right," I said.
"Good!"
She stood, anxious to take me there.

She was not a part of this crowd. Her face was white and
bloodless next to the sallow corpses piled thickly around her.
Like a bird of prey standing over them.
I returned her piercing glance as the only living person in the
room, still green in my years, now filled with Eric's seed.
She saw it in my face - that I had been with him, that I carried
semen in my womb. It revulsed her. Sanctimoniously she
recoiled at the look in my face.

"Is there something wrong," I challenged.
"No—" she collected herself, " —Why? Should there be?"

I followed her across the street, to another entrance of the
religious shelter where Jeremiah's words hung on a banner over
the portals like a marquee for the week's sermon:

TRUST NOT IN THE VOICE OF YOUR OWN HEART,
FOR THE HEART IS ATROCIOUSLY WICKED AND
DECEITFUL ABOVE ALL THINGS.

"That sign seems to be engraved all over you," I said to her.
She laughed, and skipped up the steps like a teenager going
to a prom.
I followed her.

The lobby was dark for the night, but the lounge was still
dimly lit, and there were persons inside watching television -
elderly persons half-asleep in their chairs, their eyes fixed on the
television screen, even those who had transistor radios plugged
into their ears.
"That's our group of insomniacs," she explained.
She led me past the lounge toward the kitchen.
"How about something to eat," she offered, appearing

reluctant to take me directly upstairs.

"I'm not hungry," I said.

"Then at least a glass of milk," she insisted.

I did not resist. I went toward the far side of the dining room, toward the windows where large potted plants stood like a jungle—tenderly, meticulously wrapped in plastic, each plant shrouded for the winter like a green ghost in a shining sheet—all of them carefully labeled: I BELONG TO MARIANNE

Marianne returned from the kitchen with two glasses of milk.

I accepted one from her and sipped it by a rubber tree wondering how long it would be before I too would take root and remain to lactate there, wrapped in a plastic shroud.

She sat at a corner of a table and watched me.

Her eyes were keenly aware of me, as a savage is aware of all the beasts in a jungle.

"It's been a long time," I said.

"Yes," she agreed.

"As I recall, you were some kind of religious fanatic at the time—went off to martyr yourself in some outback. I'm glad to see you survived."

She laughed uneasily. Pain and suffering touched her face briefly. "Yes, I survived," she echoed.

"Are you still devoutly deluded?" I asked, smiling—but in my mind I was stalking her.

"My religion's changed, but not my need for it," she answered strongly.

"Oh? And what sect are you now?"

"My own," she said tautly. Now she leaned forward. "But I would rather talk about yours."

"I still believe in normal science," I said.

"Then it's you who haven't changed," she stated. "Perhaps it's you who are the fanatic now."

"Perhaps," I said.

I looked away, looked through plastic toward the windows facing the street - a street still well lit, still filled with bodies.

Her voice pulled me back into the room: "Sarah, I—I would like to try to heal you."
I looked at her.
Her face still glowed with the dazzling lust of nuns.
"That's amusing," I said. "I came here partly for the same reason—to try to heal *you*."

My reply ignited her. She stood— challenged, beguiling.
"Really? Then shall we each save the other?"

I put down my empty glass. "I feel I must warn you—before this night is out you may well find that you will have lost your soul and taken mine."

My words jarred her—but it was more than fear I caught in her eyes. She was already my captive in some mystical sense I could not yet comprehend.
"Do you really think I'm in need of healing," she now asked me seriously.
"If you're a Jesus-freak - like the others here - yes," I said.
"I no longer have that affliction," she answered simply. "Nevertheless, I have a spiritual need to approach you. You were always someone special to me back in school."
"Why is that," I asked, surprised.
"You have always struck me as someone specially touched by Grace," she said. "I should like us to be close friends."
"Strange you should ask that," I said. "I've just banished my closest friend. But then, I suspect you already know it."
"Skeets?"
"No, my ex-fiance," I corrected. "All appearances to the contrary, I don't have any close female friends."

"Really?" She was surprised. "I would have assumed Skeets was your friend—perhaps even your lover."
"No," I said, wondering how innocent her question really

was. "Skeets is someone ill to whom I've given refuge. We are not lovers." Now I dared grasp her hand. "Why do you ask? Are you her lover?"

Her eyes met mine frigidly.

"No."

She recovered herself looked down, sensuously fingering leaves wrapped in plastic. "Still," now she qualified, "I would like all three of us to be intimate on a higher plane—a spiritual level, if that is possible for either of you."

She waited for my reaction, as one capable of intense feeling, of a pure love.

"I, for one, don't believe in disembodied souls," I dismissed.

My rejection pained her. "I had hoped you had grown in your ability to relate spiritually," she said.

"God does not exist for me, Marianne," I stated.

"God does not *exist*," she patiently allowed. "God simply *is*."

"Which God," I countered.

"All of them," she answered logically.

Her reply took me by surprise.

"Now I really don't know who you are!" I said.

"I have stopped trying to find God," she clarified. "My only immediate concern now—is for human progress. A very militant concern."

"Then your idols have changed, but not your character," I said. "For you were always a militant—to a fault. Are you still as stoic as you were then? Still as rigid?"

"Even more so."

"Pity. I had hoped you had at least stopped being a puritan," I countered. "As for me, I'm ready to abandon all my inhibitions, prone to rebound in any direction now."

"Are you really?" she challenged.

"Come now, Marianne," I now faced her squarely, "be honest with me. If you are still as rigid as you were, then you must want something very warped, very perverse from me. What is it?"

"Exorcism," she answered curtly, breaking from my eyes. "But I fear that may never be possible."

"Don't tell me Satan has converted you," I chided, pursuing her into her plastic-shrouded jungle.

"What if He had," she asked, trembling, not facing me. "Would that frighten you?"

"Yes," I said softly, putting my hands on her shoulders. "But not because I believe in Satan."

"Neither do I," she said tautly. "Even so, I now believe in the full embodiment of Evil, and I have long since come to see myself as being consummately evil."

"Hallellujah!" I returned. "That must mean you're finally on the real road to Salvation."

"I'm not joking," she insisted, pulling away from me, retiring further among the shrouded plants. "I've come here to save your life—but possibly only at the expense of your soul."

"My soul I have no use for—I prize only my Conscience," I corrected her.

Her eyes met mine urgently.
I became serious.

"You're really here for Skeets, aren't you," I stated. "You don't even belong here, do you?"

"For Skeets, yes," she admitted. "But I'm also here for you."

"I don't understand," I said, searching her face.

"You will," she promised. "But this is not the place for us to discuss it."

"Dare I follow you elsewhere?" I leaned over her against the wall, challenging her. "You might be here to kidnap me, or—perhaps to entrap me."

"To entrap you by all means," she answered strongly. "Will you be stupid enough to allow it?"

"Why not," I returned boldly, leaning to a kiss. "I've already tried adultery earlier tonight - why not now sodomy?"

Instinctively she slapped my face. Then she regretted it.
I retreated.

"I'm sorry," I said. "There's a great deal of rage in me tonight and I'm taking it out on you."

"And I also on you, forgive me."

Now she laid her hands on me as a healer might—but it was she who was drawing strength from me.

"Am I exorcising Satan, Marianne?" I asked her softly.

"I believe you could," she whispered.

Her fingers trembled touching me.

"Do you sense evil in me, Sarah?"

Her question was serious, her need to know, intense.

Fondly I put my hands on her shoulders. "No. I sense conflict — immense conflict, but no evil."

"Come upstairs with me," she now said strongly, dropping her hands. It was as if she had drawn from me, had used my purity to resolve her own ambivalence.

I held back.

"I don't dare," I said, "for now I don't know who it is you really are. You are not at all like the Marianne I once knew."

"I am vastly different," she admitted.

"But in what way different," I pursued, still stalking her through her plastic-shrouded garden. "Are you merely a stranger, or an agent of some kind?"

My question was an opening.

She avoided my eyes, suddenly dropping her girlish camouflage. "How much do you know about Corporate subsidiaries," she now asked carefully.

"So you were sent," I said, now instantly enlightened. "Not much. Tell me!"

"Skeets was engaged in defense projects," she stated. "There is an international list of dissidents and potential terrorists. You and Skeets have been put on that list."

"That's absurd!" I said. "How could either of us be a threat to anyone!"

"If Skeets could be rehabilitated—" she began carefully.

"Could she be?" I interrupted, suddenly alert.

"In the right hands, yes," she stated.

"Then why! Why are you letting us wander this way—it should be clear to you that the only things I've been demanding are fair employment practices—compassion for Skeets, nothing more!" I pleaded my case to her as though she had a special power to hear us and make amends.

"How naive you are, Sarah," she answered tautly. "The Corporation means to shred her."
"And you're here on their behalf?"
"I'm here to abduct her," she countered, barefaced and grim.

"Then you must be a terrorist," I said softly.
"Who I am is not important," she returned. "What is important is that I'm here to save your life."
She took my hand: "Come. It's very late now and we're both tired. In the morning we can talk further."

I did feel tired.
The milk she had given me had made me groggy.
Still, I held back.

"Are you afraid of me?" she now challenged seductively.
"Both terrified and fascinated!" I countered. "But now I feel quite uneasy about sharing a bed with you."
"I can just as easily sleep on the floor if it bothers you," she said quite readily.
"That won't be necessary," I said, taking pity on her—how ready she still was for instant sacrifice!

But now her attitude had changed—her prudishness replaced by intellectual amusement, a sophistication thoroughly foreign to the old Marianne. Sensually, teasingly, she again fingered the leaf of a shrouded plant.
"Just how might you propose to have intercourse with me, Sarah?" she challenged.
"Are you still out to entrap me?" I countered. "You know you have made me very curious!"
"In a spiritual sense, I do want intercourse with you," she admittted, now meeting my eyes fervently. "But only in a spiritual sense."
"Liar," I returned.

"Am I?" she countered strongly. "Precisely how would you propose to engineer a sexual exchange between us?"

"I was hoping your experience along those lines was far greater than mine," I said.

"In an academic sense, yes—I suppose I do know much more than you do," she said. "But that's precisely why I don't think there can be anything *sexual* between us. Only the *spiritual* would be possible."

"Are you playing on words?" I returned, searching her face.

"Man is not sexual," she stated academically.

"And the physical?" I reminded her. "What about the physical?"

"Merely an appetite," she replied.

Now she smiled defiantly: "I'm not at all repressed in my ability to satisfy all my appetites, Sarah. It's simply that, for the present, I would prefer that we make War."

"Come," she urged, now tugging at me, "come upstairs."

Her invitation was beguiling.

Warily I followed her as she led the way up two flights of stairs to the attic, to a twisted corridor with rooms reserved for offices and resident staff.

We stopped at an open door to an empty room—a narrow room with only a slit for a window. Its barren cream-painted walls broken only by a crucifix hung askew over a hard narrow cot. The air smelled of rosewater and polished oak—like a room a nun might sleep in——but it was not as austere a cell as it might have been—there was a bureau with a mirror on it, and a soft chaise in the corner trimmed with new lace and a brightly colored quilt, most probably a gift from the industrious elderly downstairs.

Marianne entered after me and bolted the door behind us.

It surprised me—that she should bolt the door.

I stood in the narrow floorspace not knowing which way to turn while she leaned against the wall waiting for me to speak.

"Do you have a nightgown I can borrow," I finally asked.

My words united her.

She went to the bureau and found a gown for me—a long-sleeved little-girl gown of flannel trimmed with lace. She threw it at me and I went to the far corner of the room, behind the chaise, and turned myself to the wall.

Marianne sat on the bed watching me, making me childishly shy of her eyes.
Defiantly I turned, almost naked.
"Do you find me attractive?" I dared ask her.
"I have always thought you beautiful," she answered, now even bolder in her gaze on me. "I minored in art, you know. Please forgive me for staring."
"I'm flattered," I said more confidently.

Now I slipped on her gown and felt it cover me—long to the floor, high-collared. "It's a nice warm gown," I said. "It reflects you."
"It isn't my gown," she answered softly. "Nor is this my room. It's all on loan."
"Then it's your mind I am feeling," I said.
I went to the chaise and curled up in it, gazing at her.
"Now its your turn to stand naked," I said.
"No," she stated. "Nor will I even undress, unless you turn away."
"That's not fair," I protested.
Her glare was resolute.
"All right," I sighed, "go on, I promise not to peek."
I shifted myself, faced the wall.

"What would you really like for us to share, Sarah," she asked, undressing quickly, her voice many-toned.
"Nothing trivial," I answered. "I would like to love someone in a way I have never loved before."
"What about *The Sacred*," she pressed. "Would you share in *The Sacred* with me?"
"Not unless you can manage giving me carnal knowledge of an angel," I said. "To me 'the sacred' is not disembodied."

Now I turned, for she had finished dressing.

She had put on a gown nearly twin to my own, cream-colored like the walls. It made her seem almost transparent, celestial.

She sat on the cot again watching me in an eerie silence, waiting to be asked to speak.

"I don't need to see you naked to tell you that you are beautiful," I said. "Are you still a virgin?"

"No."

It was clear from her tone that my question had been impertinent.

I left the chaise and went to sit beside her, took both her hands, feeling her tense at my proximity. But I fixed her with child-like eyes:

"When Eric and I were both virgins, we used to play mind games. We would hold each other and imagine something sexual was really happening. Might that kind of act be called 'spiritual'?"

She smiled fondly.

"No."

Now it was she who dared touch me, dared stroke my hair—purely, as a mother might.

"That's not the kind of sharing I want to have with you."

"Why not," I ventured, attempting to reach the side of her that had always been volatile, suppressed. "Why else did you lure me here—surely not really to entrap me."

"Yes, to entrap you—in more ways than one," she now returned grimly. "I'm here to neutralize you. I'm here to assassinate your character, to wreck your personality, to cow and extort you into silence and complicity—and if I fail—then commitment papers will have to be drawn."

"Commitment papers?"

The phrase splashed me like cold water, struck terror in me.

"An act equivalent to murder," she acknowledged. "Now what do you think of your old friend, Sarah?"

I searched her face—an intense but dispassionate face—a pure face, fervent with dedication, urgency - but now also the face of an assassin.

"I think you must be a friend," I replied softly. "Only a friend would make such an open confession."
"A friend who may become your executioner," she stated.

"Why? Why you?"
"Would you rather have faced an enemy?" she countered.

Still I was incredulous: "I could have believed you to be a dissident or a terrorist," I said, "but a common criminal—a hired killer? Is that what you really are?"
"I am many persons," she said.

Now my eyes searched the bare walls.
"Is it really safe for us to be talking here this way?" I asked her. "Might someone be listening?"
"I am the only one listening, Sarah," she stated. "And if you don't hear me, I will be the only one to hear you scream. And when you finally stop screaming—your silence will be terrible to me!"

I still could not, would not treat her words seriously.
"How convenient!" I replied cynically. "When the cries of human beings fill a room, that's when you all stop listening!"
"What do you know of human cries," she returned softly. "You have scarcely ever listened to them."
"Skeets' silence was terrible to me," I countered. "Because I was listening. I was the only one listening."
"No, not the only one," she muttered.

Now she buried her head in her arms, sat fetaly on the cot, her head buried inside her as someone wholly grieved, despondent.

"Might you really be a friend," I now asked softly, going to her.

"I'm helping you in the only way I can," she answered wearily. Now she faced me. "It's late. We can discuss it further in the morning."

She sat up.

"You take the cot, I'll be quite comfortable in the chaise."

"No," I said, impulsively detaining her. "Friend or foe, you have beguiled me. The thought wasn't in my mind until you put it there—but now I'll not be rid of it until we've slept together. I want to know you."

Her face tightened again, became livid. "That animal curiosity of yours will be your undoing, Sarah," she warned. "I don't want you physically. I'm quite serious about that."

"Are you really," I challenged. "Can you pass a polygraph on that?"

"Yes."

Now again she softened.

"Can't you see through our strategy? The objective is to discredit you in every way we can—to reduce your defense of Skeets into something corrupt and personal."

"Yes, I see it," I said. "But I don't give a damn! Everything you're telling me is nothing but an empty threat to intimidate me."

"The threat is far from empty," she stated.

" I refuse to believe the world has turned—has lost all respect for fairness, for decency."

"It's late," she pleaded softly. "Let's discuss it in the morning."

"No, tonight! Permit me to convert you to my creed," I said, taking her hands, approaching the wild, deceptive child she still so much appeared to be.

"Don't push me, Sarah," she warned, her eyes flashing.

"Is the temptation too great for you?"

Now like Eric I took charge of her:

"I say that all you call spiritual is sham—the suppression of an immensely sexual awareness —the lie of a lascivious mind preferring to sneak sideward glances at her object of desire—"

My masculine taunting irked her, awoke a temper of her own.
Impatiently she grabbed hold of my hair and shook me.

"You blind and deaf and smug little monkey," she said
contemptuously. "What makes you think you're fit to speak to
me that way! I have a mind and world you cannot even see—
and if you stopped listening to yourself just long enough, I'd be
inclined to let you *feel* my sexuality. But you're far too pompous
to know what a truly *spiritual* love can be, and tonight I am not
inclined to teach you!"

Her outburst left me bewildered, for now she seemed
transformed into a passionate being, one full and real and no
longer hiding behind a saintly mask.
"By all means teach me," I marveled. "Now I'm more curious
than ever!"
"No," she said, again containing herself
"You have made me lust you, Marianne," I persisted softly. "I
shall be obsessed if you don't teach me."
"No," she repeated, now shaken by my words, by the effect
her own outburst had created in me.

"It's not really me you want, Sarah," she now said soberly.
"It's your own death beguiling you."
"Whatever it is, I want it," I said.
"Very well," she sighed wearily, like an angel addressing a
giddy mortal, "I can see neither of us will get any sleep tonight
until I finish this for both of us."

Resolutely she reached over me and shut the light.

I went to embrace her but in the dark her arms attacked me—
attacked me not as a lover—attacked me skillfully as a wrestler
twisting me into pretzel forms—then also, like a mother bending
an errant child—shifting my joints, my spine, as though my flesh
were sacred to her, as though she was loathe to lust me.
"Stop it," I laughed. "You crazy joker!"
But now her grip tightened, became deadly.

"*Feel* your mortality, Sarah," she whispered ominously in my ear while her limbs slithered around me like a giant serpent—cracking bone and stretching sinew—her thin body hard against me in a chilling chiropractic.

I no longer needed convincing.

"Stop it!" I begged her, now panicked by her kind of touching. But merrily she had her way.

Marianne begged us to stay for lunch.

It was a polite command, a veiled threat I chose not to ignore.

Too much had been left unsaid.

She had some early morning appointments but promised she would return by lunchtime. She urged me to sleep as late as I pleased. Skeets was downstairs in a dorm, in good hands, and her welfare ought not to concern me.

Indeed, too much had been left unsaid!

She had left me feeling positively silly, like some schoolgirl who had tried to go too far with someone worldly. Then through with playing, she had passed out on me, suddenly, as though she had not slept for days—had lain on me like a lover, spent and now snoring, her arms still gripping me in reflex action, holding me fast to the bed.

Perversely, she had taught me to trust her—by making me feel the danger in her hands—hands capable of killing as easily as healing, hands that could have left me a total quadriplegic.

But too much had been left unsaid.

There was so much more that still needed to be said.

At this hour, the attic was deserted. By late morning I got up and showered and made myself look as presentable as possible in my old clothes.

I took the opportunity to fully collect myself.

Marianne had skillfully shaken my self-confidence, my moral conviction, my sense of personal safety. And she had done it in earnest. But might not her own perceptions be thoroughly warped? Had she lost her belief in civilized society?

What kind of lunacy might Marianne be now propounding?

Was her view of the world foreign, now influenced by a set of values, a reality belonging to some alien sight which had not yet pressed itself upon my world? After all, *This, My Country,* still had laws, institutions to defend me against such blatant criminality. I refused to believe that *This, My Country,* had been conquered, overrun by a barbarian horde.

Years ago I would never have taken any of her admonitions seriously. Yet the dreary prospect of my immediately exchanging the dry warmth of the attic for a damp place among the crowd of shivering bodies on the street—kept me from leaving too soon. And there was, moreover, the grim possibility that Marianne might be telling the truth.

When I finally decided to venture downstairs, it was almost lunchtime. Skeets was sitting in the green lounge among the elderly, transfixed to the television screen.

Her hair had been washed and set, and the clothes they had given her were clean and warm.

She was smiling because an old woman next to her, with a transistor radio held to her hearing aid, was attempting to carry on a one-way conversation with her—Skeets related well to the old; they were not threatening to her—when she saw me, she jumped up, immensely happy to see me.

"There you are!" she exclaimed childishly. "They didn't lie— they rescued you!"

"Rescued me?" I took the hand she offered me.

"Yes - didn't you fall through the ice last night? I had a dream you did." She looked at me, inspected me.

"But you're all right now. It's a miracle!"

"Thank all the lovely people," I said cynically.

"Oh yes, they are wonderful - lovely people," she echoed

tensely, now suddenly afraid. She turned and searched with her eyes for a Judas among them.

The ground floor was crowded this morning with volunteers of all kinds, even well-dressed society ladies eager to take charge of fund-raising functions. Two came toward us with forced cheer, tried to take us by the hand.
Skeets drew back.
"Come on, everyone, lunch is served," somebody said.
Skeets turned to me with one of her stuttering, terrified stares. "Where are They taking us?"
"Only to the lunchroom, dearie," her guide beckoned.
"The lunchroom - is that the place - the place where it all ends?" Now Skeets turned to me. "Are *you* Judas?"
I too held back, wanting to wait. Then steel fingers clutched my shoulders.
"Of course it isn't," Marianne said, now walking past me to Skeets. "Come," she said hypnotically, taking both her hands. "We'll go in together."

Skeets gave her no resistance, followed her as she might follow Jesus.
I tried to speak but another part of me held back.
"Wait for me," Marianne said strongly. "I'll only be a moment."

I could not overcome my bewilderment, my strange ambivalence. I wandered further into the lounge where some of the old were still sitting in drab green chairs waiting for trays to be brought to them. The television screen was out of alignment and still they stared as it flickered, unattended.
I tried to tune it for them.
"May I help you?" A society lady spoke nervously behind me as if to draw my attention to her.
I turned.
"I'm Mrs. Walker," she said.
I could not see her face. She was standing in front of the window where the noonday sun was cutting through frost and haze, slicing through plastic-shrouded plants.

I had the strange feeling that she knew who I was and that I posed a certain threat to her. She appeared curious, anxious to meet me face to face.

My squinting stare made her fidget.

She picked nervously at her diamond rings.

Might she be Cynthia's mother?

"Are you a regular volunteer?" I asked, probing.

"Only on holidays," she stammered.

"I see," I said. "No, thanks, I'm just waiting for someone."

I moved out of the sun, avoiding her.

I stood by the green bulletin board on the green wall; it was tacked full of posters and letters from abroad. JESUS SAVES was scribbled here and there, and other garble from obscure faiths. There were hand-made collages crying for aid to domestic communes and religious colonies in foreign lands - and *Hi-Neighbor* letters—*Hi-Neighbor* letters with snapshots of heroes from the jungle, some armless, legless, bandaged beyond recognition yet waving happily with rifles in their hands, victoriously, from exile.

"There you are!"

It was Marianne who hailed me, walking through the blinding sunlight.

I looked for Skeets behind her.

"She's having lunch," Marianne said. "I grabbed a couple of sandwiches. Let's talk upstairs."

I followed her, not to the attic but to a smaller lounge on the second floor that smelled of stale smoke.

It too was filled with potted plants.

Marianne sat on a drab green couch with torn upholstery.

"I'm so glad you decided to stay for lunch," she said girlishly.

She looked at me again with a seductive stare, intense, whorish.

"How could I have refused," I said, puzzled by her manner.

She frowned, appearing displeased at her own power to influence me. "You could have tried."

"What, and interrupt our intercourse?" I quipped. "Tell me," I continued, "do you always make love so violently?"

Her face tightened, became puritanical again.
"You were the author of that act, not I."
"I find that answer most dishonest," I said.
"Not at all," she countered.

Still I could not make out exactly who she was.
"Were you lying to me last night? Did Security really send you?" I asked her.
"What difference does it make who sent me," she returned. "What if the Devil sent me, would that make a difference?"
"No."

I looked down at my sandwich, still untouched. I was hungry, but dared I risk it?
"Eat it," she commanded.
"Is it drugged?" I half-chided.
"In this world we all take chances," she returned grimly.

I nodded and took a bite, nearly choked on it. My mouth was very dry, strangely dry. She passed me a container and I gulped down hot coffee.
She watched me intensely while eating her own sandwich, sipping her own coffee.

"They'll ask you to write a report on me, isn't that right," I said, still chewing.
"That's right," she answered, food in her mouth.
"What will it say?"
"If it said anything unequivocal, it would either be challenged or misfiled." Her voice was bittersweet and cynical. "But why should you be concerned about what others think of you? Aren't you above all that?"
"Stop teasing," I said.
Her eyes met mine squarely.

"They will ask me for a report, and I will give it to them. And if it says anything they don't expect to read, it will not be believed."

"And you will tell them everything that happened?" I asked incredulously.

"Did anything unusual happen?" she countered, appearing utterly innocent and naive.

I paused to recover from the shock of it— from the utterly routine and girlish manner in which she was proceeding to destroy me.

"Is anyone listening now," I finally asked.

She shrugged, unconcerned. "How should I know?"

I paused again to focus my thoughts. Meantime, she finished eating and cleaned up for both of us, efficiently, unthinkingly, as one accustomed to caring for the ill or distracted.

"Why did you contact me," I finally spoke. "Were you simply following orders?"

She looked at me. Her glance was far from cold.

"I volunteered for this mission, Sarah."

"What mission," I spoke carefully. "To save my life or my soul?"

 "It's highly unlikely that I will be able to do both," she stated.

I studied her face carefully—a face ever filled with suppressed rage.

"What shocked me about last night—" I said slowly, "—was the realization that you were right about what really binds me to you. It is danger—the prospect of coming face to face with my own death that is seducing me. Only last night it was *I* who was reduced to a bag of bones. Thank you for making me come face to face with my mortality."

"Then your attitude toward me is positive," she probed.

"Strangely enough, yes," I said. "Even though I cannot determine precisely *who* it is you really are."

"I am someone who has come to take Skeets from you," she now said grimly, "and someone who has also come to persuade you, for your own sake, to surrender her willingly."

"And if I cannot be persuaded?" I asked carefully.

She did not answer.

Instead she turned away from me, speaking sadly, distantly: "I truly wish your cries could be heard, Sarah. I have been crying out for years now and nobody wants to hear me. Skeets is your sole concern, while I - I have a full list of grievances prepared. Maybe you can get them heard."

Her gaze was now soft, tearful.

"In this small sector alone - just this past year - we lost some five hundred limbs to frostbite and gangrene, some hundred eyes to gonorrhea - half of them in newborns. Two hundred babies born addicted! I could go on, but the list gets worse and you've just eaten!"

"You are avoiding my question," I pressed softly.

"Can you live in the world I am describing?"

"No."

"That is my answer," she said.

"—And what if I merely pretend to have been persuaded by you," I probed carefully.

"Do you want to remain a pariah? Be truthful with me, Sarah, if you value your mind."

She let a grim silence fall, gave me full time to weigh the importance of her plea. She was right. She had drawn me into the liar's paradox—no matter what she told me was the truth, I would have to assume it to be a lie - for she had presented herself as a double agent, as one who always told only a partial truth, contradicted by her next assertion.

If I played that same game with her, I would have no parameter from which to determine her real position. Our war relation would become chaotic—a wholly random game of chance.

"I value my sanity," I finally said.
"Good," she said, relieved.

Like a therapist now, she began to question me.
"Tell me, why do you persist in holding on to Skeets when it's clear you can't help her?"
"I don't trust the system," I answered truthfully, feeling myself unburdened. "I can't shake the feeling that there is more foul play intended—that she must be some kind of special crack in the wall. Otherwise Personnel wouldn't be trying to convince me that she's thoroughly played out, a useless appendage."
"If she doesn't get proper treatment soon, she won't be of use to anyone at all," Marianne interjected.
I looked at her.
She had moved out of the sun, away from the window, and her voice was barely audible now.
"That's precisely what I mean," I said. "You refer to her usefulness, not her health. Skeets' personal welfare seems unimportant to you."
She did not answer. She seemed to be squelching a sick feeling in her stomach, like a rape victim trying to forget.

What was she?
Who was she?
Was she truly a pawn of Personnel?

I shifted to the other side of the room—to a green vinyl-covered chair—so that I might face her. She still appeared to me to be in costume, acting a part. Her drab quasi-uniform, tailored tightly to her waist and falling off girlishly to a full skirt nearly to her ankles, had given her long thin body a tacky appearance just a moment ago. But through her clothes I still saw Salome—veil upon veil, continuing her intricate dance of death.

"So you want me to surrender Skeets willingly," I said. "Why? To reassimilate me as a loyal subject, as one more Corporate lackey?"

She would not answer. She was now bathing herself in sunlight, gently fingering her plants—unshrouding them, feeding them on sunlight. But not with joy—with lank thirst for the sunlight, for its healing warmth.

"How do I know you aren't a terrorist," I persisted. "How do I know you aren't brainwashing me?"

"There is no answer I can give you that will not drive you deeper into paradox," she muttered.

How right she was!

And it made me wonder again whether our confrontation was no more than some highly-calculated therapy, a means of bringing me in from the cold by pretending to be the very forces I feared—by pretending to be the enemy—so that I might finally trust her as a friend.

"Exactly in what way do you intend to neutralize me," I now asked her.

"Your mind will perish of its own accord," she stated authoritatively, still not looking at me, still tending to her potted garden.

"I doubt that," I countered. "I consider myself quite stable."

"For the present, yes. But the environment you must contend with is perverse enough to destroy even the most stable of minds."

Now she finished with the sunlight, turned her attention entirely to me: "Believe me to be your worst enemy, Sarah. That assumption will do less harm than thinking me a friend."

"You know how desperately I want a friend," I blurted, now trembling.

"Of course you do—but—in the absence of friends, an enemy can also be loved —befriended." She looked at me coldly, analytically. "Have I done anything to earn your blind trust in me?"

"No."

"Then why should you gullibly believe anything I tell you," she finished.

"Why indeed," I said.

"I've prepared an audiovisual program for you," she said now. "Will you look at it?"

She had already walked toward a set of projection units I now noticed were situated, waiting, at the far wall of the room.

"To what end," I asked, puzzled.

"Indoctrination," she said, blatantly. "It's about cruelty in all its forms: family cruelty, police sadism, social apathy, war, genocide."

"I already know about such things," I objected. "Why should I brutalize myself by watching them?"

"Do you already know about them? Do you really know enough about them?"

Her tone was angry, grim.

She left the projectors and went to her briefcase.

"Very well, if you prefer to remain a blind monkey, then at least won't you let me read you excerpts from current journals, or here—a pamphlet printed by our own government and circulated to the police and the paramilitary throughout the world—a pamphlet on more humane methods of interrogation."

She held it out, challenging me.

"Again to what purpose," I resisted angrily. "I'm already reasonably acquainted with the gist of the material. Why must you expose me to gory details?"

She came to sit beside me on the couch, papers in hand, and took hold of me strongly. "So," she whispered, "it seems that you are quite willing to be a blind monkey, and a deaf monkey - why the blazes then not a mute one as well!"

A righteous fury was in her eyes.

Now I understood her. "A moral basis for my silence," I concluded softly, "that's what you are trying to get at—how you might persuade me, morally, to keep silent, to cut Skeets adrift."

She let go of me, stood and addressed me contemptuously.

"Why, when you appear so hell-bent on preserving your political innocence, your civilian state of moral detachment—why did you knowingly ignore all warning signs and wander, recklessly, into a mine field?"

Her evangelical stance was almost theatrical.

"I don't perceive my defense of Skeets to be reckless act," I countered.

"No, of course not! You heard her scream. But why haven't you also heard the rest of the world screaming? Why only Skeets!"

I spoke quietly to her, carefully. "I know I can't save the whole world. But when the person next to me screams, that's a different matter."

"And if you can't pull them out of the water?"

"Then they must drown, and that's the end of it," I said.

"Precisely!"

She quit me, satisfied.

"Are you telling me Skeets has already drowned?" I now asked her.

She could not bring herself to answer.

She looked away, returned to the window, to the sunlight.

"There are certain facts you must listen to," she said soberly. "They concern Skeets."

"Oh?" I waited, attentive.

"In my briefcase," she indicated, taking sun again. "The top three files."

I looked for them and hesitated—they were marked CLASSIFIED."

"Psychiatric reports," she said.

She seemed thoroughly unconcerned about my thumbing through them. "Of foreign Corporate personnel," she explained. "Three of them this past year, before Skeets. All of them key scientists and engineers. Two with no record of prior breakdowns."

She paused, still urgent in her tone.

"I can't believe you are letting me see these files," I said skeptically. Was this a ruse?

She ignored my skepticism.

She continued as one confessing to frank complicity in some kind of crime: "By the time I got to them, there was nothing left of their minds. Nothing left for me to salvage. They were flayed, Sarah, psychosurgically shredded!"

"Why are you telling me this," I protested.

Again she looked away, squinted at the sunlight.

"What would you expect from a friend, Sarah," she asked softly.

I weighed it carefully.

"A friend would be someone who would help me reach the proper authorities—who would help us get legal and police protection."

"And what if that were impossible," she returned. "What if the courts and commissions were wholly corrupt— what if the police couldn't be trusted—what if only violent factions— criminal networks—were being protected by the system? Would a friend deliver both of you to Caesar?"

"Has it really gotten that far? Has the entire system failed?"

I meant to oppose her but in my heart it seemed that my question was rhetorical—that the homeless bodies on the street, that the shots winging past me in the snow, that the look of cruelty growing in men's eyes—

Her voice broke through my thoughts. "I don't think that I can save Skeets, Sarah," she said softly. "At most, I may be able to spare you—but only at a price—a very high price."

"What price," I asked carefully.

"Your soul - your moral purity - your Conscience," she returned, not looking at me. "The price is your silence—your permanent silence."

"I don't understand," I said. "Are you telling me that Skeets is to be murdered?"

She would not answer.

Again she tended to her plastic-covered plants, tenderly, with trembling fingers as though touching infants, sleeping babes.

"How! How can you expect me to remain silent," I blurted.

"Until the cock crows," she muttered to herself.

"And when will that be," I demanded.

She turned angrily, contemptuously. "For you, most likely never!"

She seemed determined now to complete an ugly but necessary task. She returned to her briefcase, took out another set of papers, sat waiting for my complete attention to her words.

"How do I know you aren't a terrorist indoctrinating me," I began again.

"And if I were—would that make a difference?" she countered. "And if I'm not, then your next contact will be! The facts, Sarah! The facts are that your life is in danger—from all sides!"

I stood, avoiding her eyes.

"If you were really with Security you wouldn't dare—you couldn't make my commitment stick, not before a judge!"

"Try me!" she challenged.

Now she approached me, took hold of me. "Look at yourself. How long do you think it will be before you become like Skeets?"

Firmly she pulled me toward a mirror on the wall.

It was a badly hung mirror, a warped mirror.

I rejected the image it projected to me—it made me look drawn, haggard.

"Look at yourself!" she insisted. "Haven't you sufficiently tithed to Conscience?"

Again I tried to pull away but she held me, took my arm and raised it to the sun, turned it at the elbow.

Now it seemed to be but thinly covered bone.

"Look at yourself - look at your death," she insisted.

"Stop it!" I said. "I won't be mesmerized!"

She withdrew, left me to find my own image, returned to the drab green couch and took out busy work from her briefcase, endless forms.

She seemed again so much like a therapist, a social worker, not at all like an assassin. How I detested the figure she projected now—one of untiring self-sacrifice, of self-effacing commitment to live among the lepers, of a life and intellect wasted in the expiation of an original sin. That was not the kind of life I wanted for myself. But why, then, was I holding on to Skeets?

"How I loathe this environment," I finally said. "My mind would die if I were forced to live and work here."

She spoke distantly, without looking at me, still patiently doing paperwork. "No, you prefer Luxury, Cleanliness, Order. The price for all that is Silence."

"I'm tired," I said. "Tired of tithing."

I waited, watched for her reaction.

There was none.

"Well?" I finally asked. "What happens now?"

"Your silence must be guaranteed," she said blankly, putting down the forms. She reached into her briefcase and motioned for me to join her on the couch. Her tone was still distant, contemptuous. "Sign these," she commanded, putting papers in front of me—blank papers—a police statement that had not yet been filled out, and a blank check taken from my checkbook.

"What is all this," I demanded.

"The raw elements of a thorough personality assassination," she stated. "Just sign them - they'll be filled out for you."

"I don't sign blank papers," I said.

"There's a gun at your head, Sarah," she said wearily.
"I want to know what I will be signing," I insisted
Patiently she obliged me.
"You'll be signing a confession, a consent for psychiatric treatment in lieu of prosecution, and a check to your father for thirty-thousand dollars."
"I don't have anywhere near that much in the bank," I said, puzzled.
"It's already been deposited to your account," she stated. "The protocol will be that you attempted to sell Skeets to a presumed terrorist, for money to pay back debts your father accrued in your behalf."

"Thirty pieces of silver, for delivering Skeets to Caesar," I translated, horrified. "You really *are* turning me into Judas. Do you also plan my eventual suicide?"

"We could use this as a cover for your sudden death or involuntary commitment," she allowed. "Or you yourself might eventually come to believe you sold Skeets willingly—you yourself might acquire and consummate a death-wish."

Now she grasped my hand strongly, fixed me with the eyes of an evangelist.   "Judas wasted his death, Sarah. Don't waste yours."

"I do believe you set all this up this way on purpose— because you want me to feel the analogy. Are you trying to push me into martyrdom?"
"Your martyrdom is precisely what I'm trying to prevent," she countered.
"By destroying my Conscience?"
"Yes."

I pulled away.
How could I survive my complicity to murder?
Of course I could, I told myself. I was no saint, no martyr. To save my own life, I could cut someone else adrift—even Skeets.

"I won't sign blank papers," I said now. "If you want me to incriminate myself, you'll have to fill them out."

Efficiently she returned the forms to her briefcase.

"They'll be ready for you on my return," she said blankly.

"Are you leaving again?" I asked, now suddenly frightened at the prospect of being left alone.

"I'll be back in a day or two," she said coldly. "Remain here until then."

"And if I don't?" My tone was feebly defiant.

"I doubt that you'll get much farther than the street," she said.

"Where are you going," I demanded.

"I'll be taking Skeets with me," she said, ignoring my question. Her voice was still forced, pained.

I stood, rubbed my eyes, took time to wipe away all the false images she had created—to wipe her devastating shadow over all of my perceptions.

"You're not with Security," I finally said. "You really *are* a terrorist abducting Skeets—and my silence has nothing to do with a cover up—you are merely playing a double role."

"And what if I were," she asked quietly. "Would that be an easier truth for you to swallow?"

"Yes. Yes it would," I said, fingering her plants, letting the sun warm me. "At least it would mean there was hope for Skeets —because you would not shred her. Because you would rehabilitate her. I could accept that kind of truth."

"Even if Skeets were used to extort, and murder?" she asked softly.

"Aren't all sides doing that?" I countered. "Aren't all sides engaged in open war?"

"Believe whatever helps you keep your sanity, Sarah," she said grimly. "The world is most complex, and the question of sides—ambiguous!"

"Who are you, where do you come from," I demanded again. "Can't you tell me anything at all?"

She remained silent.

"Am I really having a mental breakdown," I asked her now. "Am I going psychotic?"

"Are you?"

Her question was simple, naively spoken, as though no prior words had ever passed between us. Had she shredded our entire conversation? Or had she changed identity again—was she another Marianne?

"Hell, no!" I answered, feeling my whole world jarred.

"There you be!" Skeets said, finding me. "I was afraid They had stolen you!"

She stood in the lounge doorway, button-eyed.

She stood among the Jesus-freaks and the sweaty and unshaven. Someone had given her new clothes to wear— a neat, tailored hand-me-down with gold braid and matching cap that made her look like a bell-hop standing at attention, or an organ grinder's monkey.

A drug had fully blinded her.

"Is that you, Momma?" she asked me, button-eyed.

Suddenly I could not face being Sarah.

"Yes, Angel," I lied. "It's me. I'm here."

"Momma?" She squinted, confused. "Is that really you, Momma?"

Now Marianne appeared, stood in the doorway strongly.

"Skeets," she said, "it's time for us to go." She extended her arms like Jesus, lovingly, as to a small child.

Skeets turned to me.

"Is it all right, Momma? Will yuh be safe if I go with Sarah?"

"Yes, Angel," I lied, unwilling to hear her scream. "Go with Sarah."

"Will you still be here when I come back, Momma?" she asked simply.

"Yes, Angel," I answered. "I'll be here. I'll always be here."

"Come," Marianne said.
Skeets turned and groped for her blindly.

"Momma," she held back, turning again to me. "Momma, I want you to know what a good person Sarah is. I truly do love her, Momma. Next to you—I love Sarah best of all!"

Now Marianne folded Skeets in her arms and turned her toward the door, toward the others waiting.

Marianne paused to address me coldly, like the Angel of Death it seemed. "Stay here until I return," she warned.

I sat, as helpless as the elderly,
trapped in a drab green chair.

I spent the weekend as Marianne's prisoner.

I spent it in the attic, firmly advised that I was not to try to go out or to speak to anyone. Marianne, Skeets and some others had vanished. Instructions had been left with the new shift of volunteers that my meals were to be brought up to my room. All my clothes were taken away to be laundered, only borrowed lounging clothes made available to me. And, conveniently, inexplicably, I again had caught the flu.

Had I been wrong?

Had I acted irresponsibly?

One thing was certain: no matter who they were, they would soon realize that the moment I could distance myself from this reality, could regain my old perspective, I would turn on them and even on myself and obey my Conscience.

I could not, would not remain their partner in crime.

I had not delivered Skeets —Skeets had been snatched from me. Whoever they were, on whatever side they were on, they had to be terrorists, I decided. For certainly the world I lived in was not *By Right* a police state.

They had done their best to create an atmosphere of suppression, of danger, in order to persuade me otherwise, to indoctrinate me.

But surely the laws were not wholly disembodied!

Surely I could have recourse to some untainted authority— otherwise, why would They need to cover things up the way They had.

Yet—it had been the Corporation that had originally shredded Skeets, and it was the Corporation that was still denying me a hearing.

Had the Corporation fallen into the hands of criminals? Of foreign powers?

Where was **Reality**?
I no longer knew where to turn.

Marianne did not reappear until Tuesday morning—the first office day after the holidays. My clothes were then given back to me neatly cleaned and pressed, and I was told to look for her in the second-floor lounge.

I found her sitting on the drab green couch, working on a pile of forms taken from her briefcase. She was dressed differently. No longer like a girlish social worker but as a mature woman in authority, urban and stylish, her brown pin-striped suit femininely tailored, fitted and high-fashion.

"Skeets is being shredded, isn't she," I stated in a quiet rage.

"Does it matter?" she countered distantly, not looking up from her paperwork.

"Of course it does," I answered. "Even if I've had to cut her adrift, it does matter what is happening to her."

"Are you ready to come back to us, Sarah," she asked absently.

"Do I have a choice?" I countered.

"We could arrange for you to work here," she said.

"No thank you," I said angrily.

She looked up, coldly, appearing very much like a calculated executioner sent to punish an act of kindness. "The way back is open if you want it. I'm recommending rehab for you."

"How generous," I said. "And what does that mean?"

She broke from my eyes, looked down at her paperwork.

"You'll find your apartment ready for you. Everything's been done to facilitate your smooth return."

"How efficient of you," I said. "You're almost making me believe I've really had a mental breakdown."

"Your initial act was irresponsible," she countered. "You should be grateful that we chose to handle this discretely."

"Who are you really," I again demanded.

"Don't ask," she said, still not facing me.

Now her voice changed tone, became military, automatic.

"Just do as you're told from now on or risk a real flogging. We're not just going to slap you on the hands again—do you understand?"

"No, I don't understand," I said, glaring angrily and in horror. "Under whose authority are you threatening me?"

Now she looked up and her eyes were wild.

Again she evaded me:

"Your father is ill," she said meaningfully. "He caught a cold chasing after you—it may turn into pneumonia. You had better see him while you still have the chance. Eric will stop off at your apartment tonight with more instructions. And tomorrow at Two, the Old Man wants to see you. Don't be late. Do exactly as you're told now, Sarah. Make no more mistakes, no more false moves."

Her eyes pleaded with me.
I could not fathom her true meaning.
"You can go now, Sarah," she now forced herself to say.

"Perhaps," I muttered angrily, returning her violent stare, "Perhaps if you beat me down enough I may someday learn to feel Guilty for my Acts of Kindness and Redeemed through the death of my Conscience. Do you really think that's possible?"

"It is possible," she answered tautly, as one who intimately knew it to be true. "Very possible."

Her pain now appeared to me to be far greater than mine. Meekly I turned from her, and did as I was told.

It had been a year since I had visited my father.
I seldom went home.

Home was a dead dog and a missing mother, a little sister
growing ever out of my control, and my father—who had not the
slightest faith in me.

Still, I had wanted to visit him over the holidays, and would
have—had it not been for Skeets and the fear that my father
might have been persuaded that I was very ill—he had always
had the power to destroy me—and not the trust in me to refrain
from using it.

The weather had turned mild for January and the snow had
melted. My father's house was an hour away, in a more central
part of the suburbs—a commercial part only three blocks from
the train station. It was a pleasant day for walking, still I was
wearing sneakers and I had no gloves and I felt a chill through
my clothes. It would certainly look odd if I went home this way.

I stopped at a drug store and bought plastic boots and wool
gloves. I used my uncle's twenty dollars.

My sister opened the door even before I could ring the bell.
"Sarah? Are you all right?" she asked suspiciously, searching
my face for signs.
"Of course I am," I said, formally embracing her. I could
never hug her warmly—there was much hostility between us. I
had been a reluctant mother to her after our mother was taken
away, and as all children growing up, she had broken away from
me as from an estranged parent.

"Do you know what you put us through?" she scolded. "Dad
nearly froze to death trying to find you. He's caught an awful
cold."

She led me toward the library where she had put my father in his favorite chair, by the gas-fed fireplace that was overheating the room. He was a pampered infant grunting there, through the sniffles, thoroughly swaddled in blankets like one of her teddy bears.

"Dad, Sarah's finally here," she said.
"It's terribly dry in here," I said. "He'll get sicker than he is this way - bring a pan for the radiator."
My words went unheard.
But soon she would think of it herself.

My father looked very old and worn—older than my uncle, although he was much younger. My doting unmarried sister had spoiled him into a premature old age.

"Hello, Father," I said, walking formally to peck him on the forehead.
He grunted again, sniffling.
I sat on the rug below him, as the dog used to sit.

I had always been formal with him. It was my way of telling him I loved him—like calling him 'Your Honor' which was something he had always dearly wished to be.
If he had been the one to nurse me, to wipe my nose, my bottom, then I might have been more familiar with him. But no, he had been the one to admonish me, to punish, to pay me my allowance, to see that there was coin enough to feed and clothe me, to educate me, and to teach me how to plead in my own defense.

My sister now remarked that the room was very dry, and went to get a pan for the radiator.

What a petty man my father seemed, pampered and sulking, filled with his own misery.
"Father," I reproached him gently, "why did you go out like that? I would have come to you when I was ready."
"Why did you do all that, Sarah," he grunted and sniffled.

(He was not a man who could show anger when he was angry, or grief when he was grieved, and I perceived him to be both at this moment—sensed it in the way he grunted and sniffled.)

"All what?" I asked softly. "What have they told you?"
"Why did you disappear like that," he said. "We went crazy looking for you."
"I didn't disappear," I replied patiently. "How often do you see me? It was only because someone told you I could not be found, not because I hid from you." I touched his hand soothingly. "I needed to be alone for a while - alone with my Conscience - that was all."

He grunted and blew his nose.
He had always approved of my Conscience.

"They said you were with some woman," he said. "What's it all about?"
I looked down, sitting on the rug feeling all alone.
"Even if I could explain it to you, all the appearances would be deceiving. It was a kind of dissent. Nothing more."
"Sarah, you're leaving me no choice but to—" he started, seeming ready to pass judgment on a matter still only half-presented.
"But to do what," I interrupted him, "to judge me even before my hearing?"

He paused.
"What's that hearing all about?"
"A crime has been committed—at the office," I said distantly. "I'm the only one who saw it. I reported it. Nothing's been done."

Now he looked at me oddly, suddenly with deep concern.
"Are you certain? Are you certain that it was a crime? That it was really committed?"
"It is the only fact of which I am dead certain," I affirmed.
"Do you have evidence?" he asked judicially.

"It's been destroyed."

"Witnesses?"

"I fear none of them will speak."

He paused to reflect on it.

"Then you'd better forget the whole thing," he now said realistically. It was the attorney in him speaking as well as the judge.

"I can't," I said. "And what if it happens again!"

"You'll just have to let it happen—and hope you can catch them at it then," he said, still sanely, professionally. "You can't let it wreck your whole life—your career—"

"I don't have a career anymore," I told him. "At least, I won't have one shortly."

I could see his sudden disappointment. He had always had such high hopes for me, even through his fears that I might grow to become too much like my mother.

"Father," I tried to cheer him. "If things don't work out, I may take up politics. Or I could go into law—but the laws are useless now because the judges and the commissions are overworked and easily bought. So that leaves politics, and even there—I'll fail without some kind of extraordinary help, because I won't take bribes—nor do I have any more faith in the power of the laws."

"Is your hearing tomorrow?" he asked, now mulling over the whole thing quietly.

"No. And I very much doubt that I will ever get one," I said. "But I'm not going to wait for it. I intend to speak out—to air it out in public. It's the only way."

"What, without proof? They'll laugh at you and think you mad."

"Then what other choice to I have," I pleaded.

"Sarah—" he said now, afraid for me, not judging me but just afraid for me, "—don't. Don't. Sometimes you just can't do all the things you want to do."

"Sometimes we must do what is right, even when we don't want to," I stated. "You taught me all that."

He was silent. He could not deny it.
He blew his nose.

"I'll be the death of you yet, I know," I said gently to him. "But what a fine death, I hope. You gave your life for us. You worked so hard. Don't think we haven't known."
He grunted, and sniffled.

I looked away, distantly. "Father, if things go wrong tomorrow, many people will try to persuade you that there's something wrong with me. In your heart, don't believe it - please! No matter what the appearances may be—there's nothing wrong with me."
I paused and tried to make it clear to him—for if I had not misjudged the reality now awaiting me, then I might never see him again, might never be able to reassure him that I was indeed sane.
"I am not like my mother," I assured him. "Not even my mother was like my mother. Had she taken ill today, she might have been cured. But—if she were here speaking to you now as I am speaking to you—and someone tried to cure her of her Conscience—then it would not be her illness but theirs—no matter who was speaking in authority. Please, please believe that!"

He heard me.
There was fear, and resignation in his face.

"I've lived a lot longer than you have, Sarah, seen a lot more than you have," he finally said.
He took time to blow his nose and wipe his eyes.
"Sarah—I believe you."

My father believed me!

My old father who had always doubted me!

Now what might have been empty sound, bravado for the benefit of an aging parent, took on intent, commitment. Now I felt strong enough to draw the Sword from the Stone and lead a new charge against the Citadel—for surely if my own family stood by me, I would be heard, I would be believed—no matter how many lies had been cleverly tied around me, no matter what papers I had been forced to sign.

The cock would crow for me and I would speak.

I would speak and redeem my Conscience.

I burst from my father's house with new energy, new purpose.

Tomorrow, or the next day, or very soon, I would tell the whole world what had been done to Skeets—would tell everyone how I had been suppressed—would confess to the crime of Silence. Let them accuse me. Let them drag me through the courts. The more publicity, the greater my power to restore the laws.

But would anyone be listening?

Again a trembling took hold of me. Again an uncertainty.

I would have to wait and see.

I would have to tread carefully.

And no matter what I did, it would be too late—too late for Skeets!

So the Old Man wanted to see me!
I wondered why.
Was he a friend of my uncle?

(My uncle had once been a powerful man. It was rumored
that he possessed a large fortune, controlled shares in foreign
companies, all of which he kept hidden from my aunt. He had
outlived all his blood relations. *No heirs,* the old scoundrel had
complained to me.)

Was my uncle behind all this - my wicked uncle who, in his
prime, had flayed a billion Skeets? Why *not* then make amends
through me—Why *not* leave me the wherewithal to turn the
world around?
Had my rich uncle taken charge of me?
Had he sent Marianne?

But I knew I was grasping at straws.
It was far more likely that everything Marianne had told me
was the barefaced truth—that the world had turned, that my
oasis had been conquered by wicked old men like my uncle -
long ago - while like Skeets—like an ostrich—I had buried my
head in the sand, pretending that all was still in order, that
Justice was **Real.**

If I really had a fairy uncle, then his first gift to me upon my
homecoming would be a call from his banker—or perhaps a
stack of proxies, or at least a suit of armor to wear to my
coronation.

No such gifts were waiting for me.

Yet the Devil's helpers had torn through my apartment in my absence, cleaning it up, removing all the lint, the excess furniture, the dust and stale smoke. All trace of the actress and her wretched dog had been removed, and the rug had been shampooed.

Had the actress been planted to torment me? Had she been a part of Their freak-out?

I gave up trying to divine the Old Man's purpose.

I settled for the least hypothesis - that a foxy would-be father-in-law had taken advantage of my dissent to snatch Eric from me for his precious Cynthia. And now penitent, the Old Man wished to make small amends - token reparations: a higher salary, more responsibility, *anything* to guarantee my continued silence.

But why then would Eric be stopping by?

Was I now to be initiated into Corporate adultery?

No thank you, I would send him home immediately.

I dared to shower, to groom myself, to luxuriate in the repossession of my own bathroom. I dared to inspect myself broadly in my own mirror, dared to reassure myself that my new gauntness was becoming to me. Would the Old Man find me irresistible? Would he grant me every wish my fairy uncle would have granted me—*every wish* including Justice?

Would my uncle grant me Justice?

More likely, that dirty old man would laugh at me. More likely, he would expect me to call out 'My Death' on my way to the Citadel.

My shameless uncle would expect me to step over that pitiful bag of bones named Skeets and once more challenge Marianne.

There was the rub—my fall from Paradise.

Marianne had forced me to bite the apple—to face the inevitable fact of my original sin. For how could I dine at my uncle's table without taking onto myself full complicity for *All the Old Man's sins?*

When had Sarah ever been Innocent, morally pure?

My Innocence was sham!

And all my belated cries to the gods for

Vengeance,

for **Justice**, were cries for

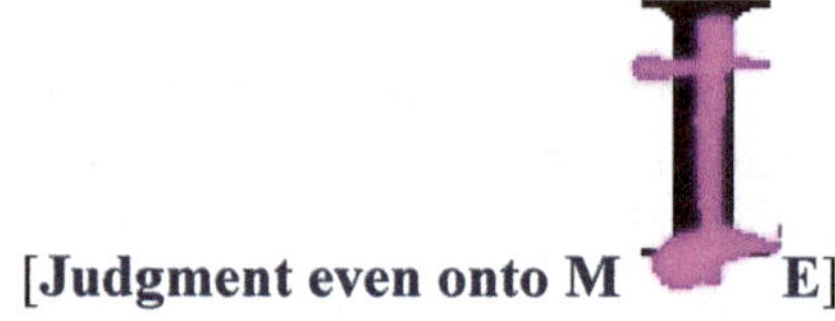

[**Judgment even onto M E**].

(**Wherefore be still, My Conscience!**
 Be Still—lest you undo me!)

And now I heard the key turn in the lock, heard Eric arriving right on schedule, as though he were coming home to dinner.

I would never cook dinner for him again, I decided.

Eric looked fresh, clean, and pleased to see me— surprised to see me looking so much better.

"I guess the therapy worked," I said, testing him, letting him kiss my cheek dutifully as he always had upon coming home.

"Yes," he said, startled and now much relieved that I was taking it so well.

"A bit radical, unconventional, but effective—very effective," I continued, stalking him.

His eyes shifted uneasily.

"I understand she's one of the best in the field. Didn't you know her back in school?"

"Yes, I did," I answered strangely. "But I must say, she's changed a lot since then. Who told you a therapist was sent," I pried.

"The Old Man mentioned it," he said evasively, stepping past me to the living room, removing his coat and jacket, loosening his tie. "Hoffman's in quite a dither over it, you know. It seems he wanted to work with you himself."

"Hoffman is an anachronism," I said.

Now I stalked him again.
"Where's Cynthia? Why didn't you bring her?"
He was flustered. "I didn't tell her I would be here."
"Oh? And do you plan to tell her when you go home?"
"Not exactly," he answered carefully.

There was a pause as he dared to sit and wait for me, his eyes not meeting mine - eyes like a little boy's eyes filled with naughty thoughts—thoughts that should not in the least embarrass me.
I sat across the room from him.

"Are you here for the reason I think you are?" I asked after a while.
He nodded slightly, ever so slightly, and I could see the tightness growing in his clothes.
It gave me a sense of power to watch him sitting, twitching uncomfortably.
"You know, it would be so much easier if Cynthia were here with us," I said, teasing. "I could accept adultery, if there were no deception."
"She's not that liberated," he answered flatly.

I let another silence fall.
"All the relations between us have shifted now," I said to him. "It's a totally different thing now—and I'm seeing my life in a whole new way."
"Oh?" he asked uncomfortably. "Which way?"

On purpose I changed the subject. "Why does the Old Man want to see me?"

My question jolted him out of his fantasy.

"Which Old Man? Do you know which?" he asked urgently.

"No."

I was puzzled by his uneasiness.

Was there a war going on Upstairs?

"What's to be done with me," I pried further.

He frowned. "Russo and I did the best we could. You'll be put on probation—it's going to be the Secretarial Pool for you for a while—hopefully, you should soon get your old job back."

"And my hearing?" I demanded.

"Well, surely you're going to give *that* up now, aren't you? —I mean, under the circumstances?"

"So I'm to be punished"—I said, righteous fury welling in me¬"for an 'Act of Kindness'?"

"Aw come on, Sar - " he pleaded, wincing.

"Now I know why I must stop seeing you." I said. "—I cannot possibly remain myself in such a world."

"Why not?" he asked dumbly.

Angrily I turned from him, spoke mostly to the walls.

Could anyone see us?

Could anyone hear?

I spoke to |**Them**| rhetorically.

"Can't you see how this is all a program for violence? If [**Good**] becomes [**Evil**], and [**Evil**] becomes [**Good**], however shall I live in such a world!"

Now I faced him strongly, not caring if he understood me: "What kind of **Eye** opens to a world that punishes [**Acts of Kindness**]?
What kind of [**I**] is in the Devil's [**Eye**] gazing from the Nave of Hell?"

He had no answer for me, only an embarrassed silence. Even if he understood my logic, knew precisely what I was saying—he did not want to hear it.

I waited for his deafness to catch up with me.
But he was deafer than the elderly trapped in drab green chairs.

Still softly I preached to him:

"In a world where *Callousness* is rewarded and *Kindness* punished - soon you will be doing me violence and I will be wanting it - for if I am kind to you, then I will feel very guilty for it, and I will be wanting to be punished regularly. Can't you see how perverse our love will become in such a world?"

"No, not exactly," he fidgeted, uncertain of what to make of me.

"On the other hand," I continued, "if I'm *Callous* and *Cruel* to you, I will expect you to reward me. And when you reward me, you will be doing me a *Kindness* and that in turn will encourage me to punish you further. Does that opposite role appeal to you?"

"Actually, it does," he admitted, blushing. "Isn't that what sex is all about?"

"I hope not!"

I studied him, disturbed by what both of us were beginning to feel as a result of this perverse conversation.

Was it simply aggression surfacing between us—an unavoidable war-relation that had accompanied *Our Fall from **Paradise***? Had a **Viper** finally enlightened us?

"If we go against the world—if we each reward the other's kindness, then we will become partners in crime," I now suggested carefully. "Would you prefer to be my partner in crime, or are you obedient to Caesar's Rule?"

He couldn't choose, nor did he want to pay attention, for he had other thoughts in mind.

"I think it's time to test the Truth between us," I said, taunting him. "I would like to sample this **New Rule**— or has this always been the **Real Rule** between us?"

"A man thinks differently than a woman does," he said uneasily.

"And of course you have always been secretive about your real needs," I said.

"Yes," he admitted, wincing.

"I don't want lies from you anymore, do you understand me?" I stood over him, making him most uncomfortable.

He was redfaced now, ashamed of his thoughts.

"But - if I act out my fantasies—you're likely to get angry," he said more like a boy than a man.

"Of course I will—of course," I conceded strongly, still trapping him in his chair. "But [**My Rule**] no longer prevails. [**Callousness**] is king now, and [**Kindness**] has been reduced to slavery. You can be righteously cruel now, righteously violent, righteously sadistic. Does that arouse you?"

"I don't know," he said, befuddled.

My proximity had made him quite erect again and he could scarcely contain himself.
"How much do you love me—" I pleaded with him. "Enough to be my partner in crime?"

And now the matter had gotten beyond words for both of us. We came up hard against each other with a plenitude of wrath we had each too long suppressed, one in another.

How far - how far would this
New [Order of Things] take us
if [Kindness] is always punished?

I

What if I were to grasp that alien

and take it as my guide, away from my oasis to an inverted Citadel?

Then might I pass from {Paradise}
to {Lucifer's Garden} - a place
where the fruit and flower of Humankind
hang from trees - drawn, crucified, dismembered.

And my alien  would see no horror

in that {Garden}:

<Look how colorful the flowers,
how crimson streaks the brow,
how subtly flesh turns blue - and
how sweet is the song of our flaying!>

I paused, pleased with the effect my new attitude
had wrought in him. He no longer saw

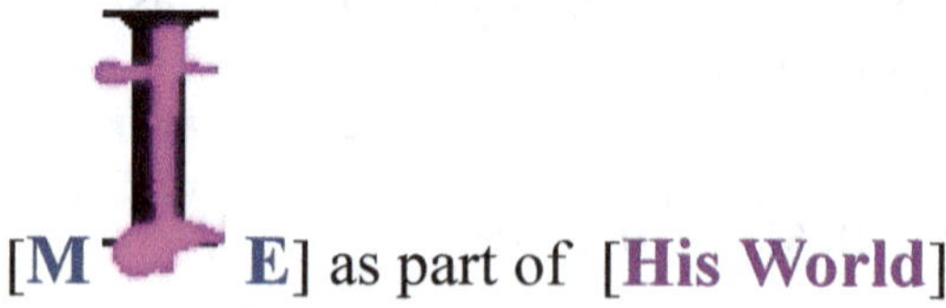

[M E] as part of [His World]

Good!

 @I no longer cared if [**His World**]

thought [**ME**] mad.

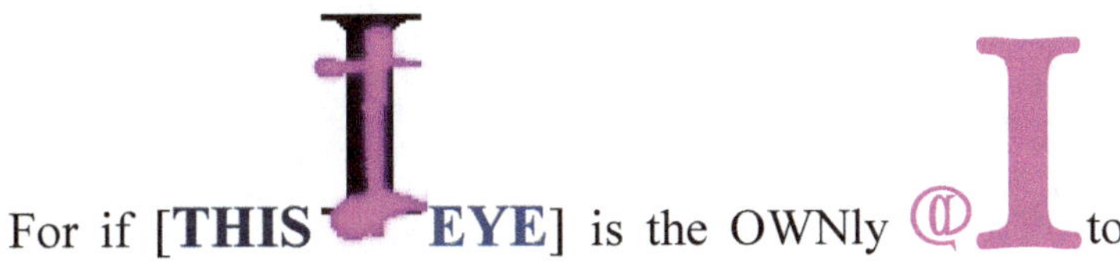 For if [**THIS EYE**] is the OWNly @I to

grasp the view from **Paradise** then

all the @peacock eyes@ in the [Garden]

will surely laugh at [Sarah's Sight]

and call all her screaming - @@@chatter!

< The chatter of a monkey >

ArtemisSmith 1967

ArtemisSmith's
SKEETS:the new Frankenstein chronicles

BOOK II:
FLOWERS OF MARIANNE

™

Sag Harbor . New York . U.S.A.

"Maggots,

At the time I wrote this, even | I | allowed

that It might be too-sick-to-publish..

Now *look at what You've done with*

|My Song| *!!! —If this sounds like everything else*

you are now pukeing over in the Media—

just remember WHO SANG IT FIRST."

Grandma

A Deathwish is My Overlord.
It has totally effaced me.

I have been flung from Paradise
for an act of Kindness.

Haughtily,
I allowed by Conscience
to argue with a Viper.

Now Hangs my Many-Eyed Conscience
Hangs |*I*|less in Gethsemane.
And all the |*I*|s of Sarah
Are but {@Peacock Eyes@}:

{@I@}s of pride
            and pettiness
                    and cowardice
    {@I@}s of greed
                and callousness

I must seek out Lucifer once again
to reclaim what She holds hostage.

Not only [Skeets] was wrangled from me;
Sarah was also haggled from me;
and now only
[@Marianne@] knows
[Where] *Sarah* hangs,
            [Hangs like *Judas* in Her Garden]

Part 1000: The Interface

(But had there ever really been a Marianne?)
(Had I only imagined her?)

Trembling, I dialed Downtown Hospital to verify her existence, but no one on night duty seemed to know who she was.

After much searching by way of the switchboard, I finally located the ward where Skeets had been confined years earlier and paged the resident who had signed her out to me.

He was off duty but returned my call.
His voice was strange and hesitant.

Cautiously he admitted that Marianne was employed elsewhere: "Well, no, not exactly at a hospital - at a research institute - uptown, just off Corporation Square."

I should have thought of it: a research hospital funded by the Corporation! I decided to walk over there, ignoring the late hour.

I got out of bed and dressed again.
I felt hungry.
Eric had left much earlier, hurrying home to dine with his doting and devoted Cynthia.

I decided to take time to grab a hurried snack and was startled to find a meal had already been prepared for me - not an ordinary frozen dinner but a boxed supper bearing a hospital label: **prescribed by Dr. M. Waters.**

Marianne had deliberately left her calling card where only I would find it!

Was I still asleep, dreaming, or did we have an appointment after all—much unfinished business between us?

Why?
What was she after?
Who was she?
What was she: Terrorist? Dissident?
                        Corporate Assassin?

(Were both Sarah and Skeets merely suspended in her keeping, safely wrapped in plastic in [Her*Garden]?)

(Perhaps I should stay home and convince myself I am only dreaming. Perhaps I should disown my Screaming*Conscience.)

Perhaps I should let this Overlord, this [Deathwish] strangle *Sarah* and commit my slavish self to the brute fact that the world has always been callous and corrupt, devoid of Justice,

filled with atrocities as a matter of course?

Perhaps I should persuade myself that all who are "compassionate" are mere victims of a pathological obsession—a reality that never was and never can be:

[a fond dream of *Paradise* screeched by a @Monkey@ in Lucifer's Garden].

In time, the new Sarah would replace Eric, would forget Skeets, would resign herself to earning a good living in the childish, carefree playpen of the Secretarial Pool.

In time, congenial and charming Sarah would *Succeed*, or at least *Make Do*.

But would the *I* of what was left of Sarah really learn to shut *My* eyes and stop *My* ears and hold *My* tongue

. . . Like [All the Other Monkeys]?

```
How could Sarah forget Skeets?
How could Sarah stop loving Sarah?
No!  This Overlord shall not ride Sarah!
```

I put on my coat as one now fully self-possessed and rushed into the street—rushed out as I had rushed in search of Skeets rushed toward University Plaza —rushed in pursuit of Sarah.

The night was crisp and clear.

The snow was gone, sucked dry by sanitation squads who gave the uptown streets more than their share of sweeping.

(It was only about ten o'clock and traffic was
light in the after-holiday slump.)

On Corporation Square, tiny silver lights on every frozen tree guided my way to an alley appended just beyond, often over-looked, shielded from public view by the angle of the tall buildings.

A discrete street sign identified it as University Plaza.

It was a private alley, housing a biomedical research facility funded by the Corporation. I went to the glassed front whose automatic doors parted noisily at my approach, like sentinels alerting the night staff to my arrival.

The Receptionist paged Dr. Waters forthwith;
yes, she did work there - she was Chief Resident;
and yes, she was on call that night;
and yes, she would come down to see me.
I was told to wait.
I sank into a plush acrylic chair and looked around me.
The lobby was a cathedral-like atrium of postmodern decor with flying buttresses—Gothic archways folding like giant hands in prayer over all who entered its hallowed hall—a more recent building than Corporate Headquarters, of translucent molded plastic, crystal-like, visionary, stronger than steel. Built in anticipation of the next millennium—it seemed to be truly a place for man-made miracles—a place where Lazarus could be raised, revised, and cloned in perpetuity, as Cyborg, as Frankenstein redeemed.

But was Lazarus truly safe in Their keeping?
Would Lazarus - (Which Lazarus!) - be Raised?

In a few short steps it seemed to me I had now trespassed into an arcane Future-Present into which Marianne had only half-invited Sarah. An immanent future in which perhaps Skeets was now already frozen and filed away for Resurrection.

How far Marianne had come in the few short years since our school days! We were the same age and yet she now seemed to belong fully in the next century while I, antiquated Sarah, found myself standing in her Her Commonweal as one still residing in an Outback, in a more primitive and savage time.

My arrival was not as expected as I had supposed.

My paging had pulled her out of bed. She had been grabbing precious sleep and she had probably dressed hurriedly to answer my call, her white residents' coat ill-fitting over her clothes. She appeared brusque, annoyed, tired and professional.

"What is it you want," she asked, as though
she failed to recognize me.

I squinted at her.
Was it the same Marianne?

Chameleon-like, her entire manner had changed to blend into her new surroundings. But yes, it was —— it had to be—the same Dr. Waters.

"Didn't we have an appointment," I countered,
firmly standing my ground.

My question startled her.
She focused her eyes on me, now appearing to recognize my face. "Yes, - yes, we do," she finally said, somewhat guardedly. "Come with me."

I followed her down a tubular hallway to a room without windows. It appeared to be some kind of screening room with globular furniture that was molded and built into the room—

non-movable furniture that could be made to fold back flatly beneath the floor at the touch of a button on the wall.

She gestured for me to sit, while she simply
leaned against a desk, observing me.

"Didn't you expect me," I finally asked.
"Not quite so soon," she answered clinically. She seemed hesitant, unsure of my mental state.
"Did I really bring myself here tonight, or - did you plant that suggestion in my head," I now tested.
"Did I leave you with any other place to go?" she countered, almost cynically.
"No, you didn't," I admitted. "Can you help me?"

Her attitude grew professionally cold again, distant.
"That depends on you," she said in a protocol tone.

Her distance angered me.
"What is it you want from me," I demanded. "Why have you been doing all these things to me!"
"Doing what to you," she asked blankly.
"Why have you been transforming me into your
assassin!"

She stared at me, now wildly curious - studied the whole of me as if with some ulterior purpose in mind—stared as
Dr. Frankenstein might stare at a candidate for transformation.

> How much like Lucifer she seemed again to
> be! And now this windowless room - this
> plastic cubicle - seemed to grow lush with
> the foliage of that other dreaded place
> where All the Monkeys were laughing—where
> the *I* of Sarah swung, Screaming, drawn and
> quartered in Gethsemane.

"I really can't discuss anything further with you unless you are willing to commit yourself," Marianne now said guardedly.

"Commit myself? Here? Are you serious," I countered, aghast.

"Dead serious," she replied. "Those are the rules."

"Indeed! And what will you do then—*pretend* to heal me?"

"Yes," she said.

"And how do I know all this isn't a trap of some kind."

"It *is* a trap," she snapped, her eyes flashing angrily. "You should know that by now—you should know that I really *am* the enemy and that every act of mine destroys you."

"Is that reverse communication," I quipped.

"Call it what you will, Monkey," she stated.

I stared at her, bewildered.

"Are you reading my thoughts, or, are you planting those thoughts inside me," I now asked carefully.

"Does it matter whose thoughts they are," she countered.

"Is all of this real, or only my own mind speaking to me," I persisted, testing. "Am I really—"

" —Will you commit yourself," she interrupted. "If you won't commit yourself, I can't help you."

"Commit myself to what," I again demanded.

"Research," she answered factually. "Classified research. More than that, I can't tell you."

"Will it heal me?" I now asked more soberly.

"It will destroy you," she stated.

"Why should I permit myself to be destroyed," I wavered.

"Is there some reason why the present Sarah is worth saving," she countered logically.

I paused to weigh her argument:
Was it my **Deathwish** that now made her logic seem so compelling, or was it simply that I had already entirely lost Sarah?

"Make up your mind, Monkey," she yawned wearily. "I'd just as soon go back to bed."

"What are the terms of my commitment," I finally asked, defeated. "Am I to place myself entirely in your power?"

"Yes." Her tone was soft but ominous, cruel.

"And will you misuse me if I do," I asked, beguiled by her eyes.

"Very likely."

"And if I don't commit myself?"

"Given your present mental state, I would say your prognosis is dim, no matter to whom you turn," she said grimly.

"What do you mean by my 'mental state'," I demanded. "Are you implying that I am ill?"

"On the contrary," she returned, "you are so supremely well that you can't possibly survive the contagion that surrounds you." Now she bent forward and put her hand on mine, warmly. "No one outside these walls is going to let you live, Sarah!"

"I know," I admitted. "Help me!"

She studied me with detached indulgence.

"I may not be able to save your life," she now ventured carefully, "but I *can* offer you Vengeance. Do you want it?"

"A 'Death with Honor'? Is that all you can offer me?"

Now it was I who responded cynically.

"Perhaps even a chance to survive," she pressed, "but I can't promise it. That will depend upon you."

Still her hand was warming mine.

"Sarah," now she whispered urgently, "you are as much the keeper of my soul as I am now of yours. There can be no elsewhere, for either of us!"

"Why does it feel like my own hand touching me," I whispered, trembling. "Am I hallucinating you?"

"Put your other hand on mine," she said. "Now how many hands do you feel?"

"Two, plus one," I said, relieved to find the limits of my own being again. "What kind of power is it, this strange influence you seem to have on me?"

"If you don't commit yourself, we can't discuss it," she repeated strongly.

"You say a chance to survive," I tried again, still hesitant.
"A very slim chance," she asserted. "But if you do survive, then it will not be precisely as yourself. The new Sarah will be given a chance to grow, to become far more than the old Sarah ever was or could become in one lifetime - the new Sarah will have a chance to stand in Hyperspace, to glimpse Eternity."

"How, as your Monster?" I returned, resisting her eyes.
(There seemed to be such great promise in her eyes—eyes filled with religious zeal—fanatic eyes. What kind of madness glowed behind those eyes, I wondered. And what kind of contagion was already infecting me?)

"It's a road I've already traveled, " she persisted with prophetic fervor, as one already standing with only one foot in My Universe—my time-frame, my limited coordinates.

"I must be mad, if I am truly willing to follow a madman," I said. "But you are right, something atrocious has taken place and I can't turn my back on it—for if I do, then like Judas I will hang myself. Therefore, if I can't live as I am, then I do want Vengeance. My Conscience demands Vengeance!"
"Your Conscience already hangs on a Judas-tree," she countered cynically.
"How do you know that," I demanded, now in total anguish. "Did you put that idea in my head?"
"Commit yourself ... or I can say nothing," she pressed again. She glared at me, pale with a secret rage, a fury of her own.

"Commit myself to what," I repeated more soberly, "to a sojourn in Hell?"
"To my analogy of Hell, perhaps. Yes," she affirmed, "Hell would be a good analogy."
"And what kind of concessions must I make to your interpretation of Satan," I asked.

"Whatever I deem necessary at the time."
"And if I don't like what you prescribe?"
"I'll always give you an honorable choice—obey, or die.
If you opt to die, I'll kill you cleanly—no delays, no appeals,
no trial."

Her eyes remained fixed on mine - dispassionate eyes now -
the cold eyes of an assassin. Was she playing a game with me?
Were these merely the eyes of a very skilled therapist?

"Will you at least behave ethically?" I persisted.
"Can there be any ethics in Hell?" she countered,
still tautly cynical.

I stared at her, bedazzled by her eyes.
Did I have an alternative?
No, I had only a **Deathwish**.

. . . "Where do I sign," I said.

She stood, relieved, and reached inside a drawer for official
papers: "These are induction forms," she explained, putting one
out for me. "I can only treat paramilitary personnel."

I looked at the paper she had put in front of me.
It was blank, except for a pledge of allegiance to my flag, my
country, my laws.
"Join my army or die, Sarah," she now said more softly,
familiarly. "Now that I've revealed this much to you, I cannot let
you live if you back down."

What kind of joke was she playing on me?
Was it all for the benefit of |Other| eyes?
She eyed me cautiously, searching my face for any
sign of fear, of hesitation.

Why should I hesitate, why should I fear?
I had already lost my soul to her, what more had I
to sign away into her charge?

She was right: all meaning to my being had been
snatched from me. Whatever more had to be resolved,
would have to be resolved between us.

```
Morally,   ethically,   historically,   as  Opposites
ever-locked   in   mortal   combat   we   were   now   as
```

One⊥One.

I searched her face once more.
Now I found *Beauty there, and *Love.
(Not Pity. Not Contempt. Not even Compassion!)
Only *Love and a readiness for *Death -
for My*Death and Her*Death
 as a War-relation of Cosmic breadth, stretching out
 not only across hyperspace but throughout mortal history.

How often had we met before, had we grappled
before in a common |**Human**| cry for *Justice?

(*Justice? The Gods would destroy both of us
for demanding *Justice!)

Here then stood **My*Death**, blocking **My*Path** to
The Citadel.
Fearlessly, I signed.

Brusquely she now led me through a maze of corridors to the
extreme interior of the building where we finally stopped at a
special elevator.
It had palmprint and eyeprint controls.
She pressed her hand to the scanner and gazed into the
viewer and the doors opened to her.

We stepped in and it took us - it was hard to tell how far
down - to some sub-basement level where another maze of
tubular corridors stretched far on either side.

The complex was insulated against human sounds of life, as though day and night and time had lost their meaning here. There was only the hum of machinery, of ventilation, doors sliding open and shut.

Ceiling sensors, controlled by nonhuman eyes, monitored us as we walked briskly down a corridor flanked on either side by curved ceramic walls—walls seeming capable of withstanding flash floods or intense heat—walls only occasionally interrupted by small brightly-colored doors.

(Was this a honeycomb of secret laboratories?)

I had never realized there had been so much tunneling beneath Corporation Square - for surely all this had only been recently completed!   When   had   this   vast   subterranean installation, like a mole, burrowed beneath the City? And from which outlying suburb - while no one was watching or listening? Had the noise of this secret invader been passed off as normal construction, subway maintenance, traffic rumble?

We stopped at a bright-yellow door and Marianne hailed the scanner set in the wall beside it.

(Like a Handshake it was, between Man and Machine—or
                    perhaps something more intimate—an Interface.)

Her touch brought instant response.

The door slid open and we stepped into a large gymnasium-like theater, ceramic-walled, octagonal in shape, built somewhat like a small arena or lecture hall with various levels for sitting or standing.

"This is attached to my laboratory," she explained.

"What kind of laboratory," I asked, now quite fascinated. My eyes were scanning the walls for signs of hidden presences, for one-way mirrors or dummy plastic panels through which a student-audience might observe Marianne playing with her Monkeys.

The walls really did have sensors, I decided, but not because of anything I could see—her entire manner suggested it—she was not careless with her speech, she seemed always to be looking at the walls.

"I'm being funded to perfect various kinds of psychosurgery," she now answered me shakily, as one confessing to a crime.

"Surgery or atrocity," I probed, meeting her eyes.

They seemed now to be screaming eyes.

Were they*I*less eyes?

(Was the real Marianne, like Sarah, Screaming
in Lucifer's Garden?)

"I'm not allowed to publish my most recent findings," she stated, her lips now tightened, her face, white.

She gestured toward the walls. "I can cure you of your death-wish," she blurted. "In four hours' time, I can let you walk out of here a thoroughly adjusted, fully-functional employee— one who can be trusted implicitly, one who will never breach Corporate security, one quite content to spend her entire life in the Secretarial Pool."

"No thank you," I interjected.

"—Or I can create a Messiah—or a Frankenstein."

"Are those the only options on the menu?"

"You don't have a choice, except to die," she reminded. "I have already chosen for you. The option is mine, not yours."

"I came here to rescue my Conscience," I stated. "You promised me *Vengeance — did you lie to me?"

"Can there be any Truth in Hell?"

She broke from my eyes and went to a corner of the hall, to a raised platform that slid open to become a desk with many compartments. It contained a console with a large keyboard and a screen. A press of her palm sent it humming, ready to obey.

"Even if it seems illogical, you will have to trust me," she pleaded. "For your own survival you will have to trust me, blindly, implicitly."

How could I trust her?
How could I **not** trust her?
Like an infant I felt helpless, knowing myself to be totally disoriented in her realm.
How would I ever find where My Conscience now hung hostage - in the many hollows of Gethsemane - without Marianne to guide me?

"What have you opted for me," I asked, resigned.
"I've decided to replace Sarah with a Monster—a Dybbuk for the Vengeance we both demand," she answered. "By tomorrow morning, Sarah Miller will no longer be."
I suddenly felt relieved.
"Why don't your words upset me," I asked her. "Why am I so willing to become `The Whirlwind'?"

She ignored my question, now intent upon programming something on the console at her desk. "I want you to treat this night we will spend together as your final sight," she said distantly. "It is the only gift that I, as an old friend, can give you - a glimpse of Eternity, a chance to grow to your full height."
"Before what," I demanded.
"Before I wreck my new creation and replace it with something Somewhat-Less-than-Human."

(Her words were slow to overcome my stupor, but subtly, perniciously, they were now bringing panic to my being.)

She was quick to perceive this, quick to avert it.
"Are you familiar with phototherapy—" she interjected, pressing a key on the console, "—the color pink, for example. It can be effectively used to modify neural chemistry."

(Even as she spoke she was flooding the hall with a solid light so thick and pink it felt like blood upon me,

transfusing through me, washing away the pallor of my
fear, my panic.)

"At first, it's soothing," she said. "But in a minute or two the
light will become toxic. In an hour, it can have us both in
resonant nosebleeds and convulsions. You see, I can use such
light to heal—or to torment—to torture."

(Already I began to feel what she meant - began to feel Pink
searing skin away from flesh—a laser pink—a wave of light so
finely tuned, so intensely filtered as to be a Pink so cutting and
so pure I did not need my eyes to see it. Now *Pink* became a
lethal flow through membrane, permeating through me, first
flowing in, then flowing out of me - until I leaned against a
block, menstruating Pink, hemorrhaging Pink from every
exposed part of me.)

`"Stop it!" I pleaded.`

She pressed another button on the console and washed the
hall with an Emerald Green - a soothing, vegetating Green - the
sunny Green of that |**Other Garden**|, the one where Sarah had
been formed.
"You've made your point," I said. "Hell no longer
needs coals and hot pokers."

Distantly, she spoke again while fingering the console:
"Could you learn to forgive someone who spends her time
devising methods of this kind, not only to heal but also to torture
'more humanely'?"
"So that's what you're engaged in," I said angrily. "But how
could you possibly avoid it, being in the paramilitary! How do
you apply this science - to the redemption of terrorists?"
"No one bothers recycling terrorists," she answered. "Only
dissidents, idealists, persons not easily disposed of."

"So this is where you are shredding Skeets," I said blankly,
now daring to sit on a raised platform.
"Would that I were treating her here," she returned
despondently. "Here, as my patient, I might restore her."

"Then she's not down here?" I asked, alarmed.

(Had I, like Orpheus, blundered into the wrong Underworld?)

Suddenly, I wished to leave.
She read my face with eyes made distant by the strange lighting of the hall—a lighting poisonous, disturbing.
"She's being shredded elsewhere," she volunteered distastefully. "But through here is your only portal."

"How do you know my thoughts," I asked her.
"Whatever I can control, I can predict," she stated.
"And you control my thoughts?"
"Do I?"
Angrily she now typed a command into the console and a projection appeared on the wall above her—a projection of hallways, hospital wards somewhere else undoubtedly close by. Clean, well-kept wards, not the overcrowded bedlam of City Hospital.
With a cursor she searched through them, finally stopping, zooming in on a slender image sitting by herself on a bench—on a patient staring blankly, seeming catatonic.

It was Skeets.
I peered at her.

She seemed clean, well-kept like the wards, even peaceful except—now I saw her eyes: glassy eyes of someone overdosed beyond reason—of someone turned to stone against her will.

"She's on neuroleptics," Marianne anticipated. "They guarantee her silence. Tomorrow she's scheduled for an overdose of shock therapy - the last thing she needs. And her brain is being starved—in every sense starved. In days—hours— she'll be beyond my help entirely. Months from now, she'll be turned out into the streets and left to rot there."

"Stop it!" again I screamed at her.

I put my hands over my eyes like a Blind Monkey.
She cut the picture without further comment.

Now she changed the lighting once again, and turned on a muted refrigeration system of some kind that made me feel instantly cold, absurdly cold even while surrounded by a Hellish Green—surrounded both by Pink and Green—a Venomous Green filled with Pink.

"Why are you changing the environment," I demanded. "You know that it makes me uncomfortable!"
"Why should you be made comfortable in Hell," she countered softly, still feeding instructions into the console.

She was playing with me, cruelly, I concluded.
"Are you a sadist," I inquired.
She ignored my question, still intent upon her task.
"Dammit, answer me!"

Now she paused and looked straight at me:
"I'm modifying your behavior. Is there some special way you would like to be altered, Sarah? How would you like to become?"
"In what way 'altered'," I asked.

Sphinx-like, she smiled at me:
"How about a superior being—one more perceptive, more resistant, physically and mentally stronger, capable of using all the tools that will multiply your own intelligence a millionfold? Would you like that kind of transformation?"
"To what end," I asked, unimpressed by her Nietzschean promise. Had I not already seen this script played out on film and television screen?
"I'm not exaggerating," she said. "For one brief night I can make you feel what being fully |Human| can embody, within and even beyond the limits of your specific chromosomal being. Before I make the monster I must make of you, I can pause long enough to reveal to you all that Sarah truly is!"

"And afterwards, destroy her?"

"Yes. Regrettably, I will have to destroy her."

"Why?"

"That Sarah is too perfect. She cannot be of use to anyone, not even to herself. And she will be too dangerous to everyone to be allowed to live outside this complex."

"So, if I survive, it will only be to remain here as your prisoner," I concluded, "or—is my personal `survival' to be merely the survival of a monster?"

"A real monster - any irreversible monster I might fashion, I would have to destroy," she answered tautly. "No, if Sarah survives, it will be because I will have been able to restore her to her normal self—although to do so, perhaps you may still have to remain for an indefinite time my prisoner."

Her tone was too serious to be taken lightly.

Was she offering me the only chance a `free' Sarah had to regain her own person? And what kind of world had I left behind me that I might ever want to see again? Hadn't I already stepped way too far into [Her Future] to return to [My Outback]?

"I would like to become a superior being," I admitted, "and I suppose I could learn to like it down here, given enough to keep me occupied. After all, *You are here, and for some reason - I don't hate *You. I think that I must even love *You. Is that religious feeling only transference?"

The scientist left her for a moment, yielded to another - to a younger Marianne.

"I hope - for both our sakes - it really *Is* Love,"
she answered softly.

She had changed the program one more time—flooding the hall with the blue of a clear winter sky—a Blue so crisp and cold it nipped my face like frozen air minutely crystallized.

"The philosopher's shade," she said. "Does it spur you?"

"It would, if the room were warmer," I said, now chilled to the bone.

"The effect would be lost then," she answered.

Now I understood what she meant, for she was prodding me with Blue and it was different from being washed with Green or permeated with Pink. My mind was suddenly awake, filled with the power of clear thought - and my eyes could see again - no, not merely see but notice - notice more than what I normally might notice: the way she was dressed, for instance - no wonder she could sit comfortably in such an icy hall - she was wearing thick warm clothes under her residents' coat - stylish clothes accented by much gold jewelry - real gold, valuable stones.

Was this indeed the same Marianne of our school days? The same Marianne of the Settlement House? Or was it an impostor beguiling me - even an actor, a female impersonator hired to mimick Marianne?

Impulsively, I reached over the console to pinch her face, to see if she had on a mask—a mask to insulate her from the toxicity of laser shades.

She caught my hand and held it away from her with fingers of uncommon strength.

"Are you an impostor," I demanded. "Are you really Marianne?"

"Is a river always the same river?"

The softness of her tone disarmed me.

It seemed to me that my question no longer made sense.

Yes, she was really *Marianne, the only *Marianne that mattered now—a divine and inscrutable presence I could no longer deny. *Her Hand still grasped mine and I could feel it warming me - it was not an Alien Hand, and *Her dark and piercing Eyes were most familiar to me.

"This body has changed radically," she explained. "And this mind has expanded in every direction - and the Person that was Marianne has acquired a host of blemishes and complications - but if you ask me—Are these the chromosomes called Marianne?—then yes, I am the same bound-variable."

I retreated, sat on the platform again.
"I'm sorry," I said. "All your special effects must be making me quite paranoid. I would even find it credible now if you told me you were only a clone of yourself."
She laughed: "I might clone myself someday. But no, I haven't bothered to try that yet. However, I might someday be inclined to clone all three of us! What an antiseptic new beginning that might be—for |Sarah|, |Skeets|, and |Marianne|!"
"Would a clean beginning really cure the disease?" I asked skeptically.
"The moral affliction? The world-historical dilemma? No."

She reflected academically, "This particular set of events is |Ours|, now and absolutely! It is the only part of |Existence| the three of us, sharing in the parameters of a particular moral space, can be said to uniquely possess."

I thought about it.
Again she was right, her logic impeccable.
The three of us - Skeets, Marianne and Sarah - stood now and forever in a unique causal relation —a relation not ordained by any divine decree but by the very core of our sensibility—a moral relation that would make a crime a *Crime and an atrocity an *Atrocity, no matter when or where or how often or how seldom the event took place—that would not make it possible for us to wipe away 'Human' error simply by cannibalizing an old model and cloning a version more to our liking.
No! Our 'Human' dilemma was |Eternal|.
Our *Crime against Skeets, hers and mine, and its *Atrocity, could not be erased by any act of self-revision.

"Then why consider cloning at all," I asked her.
"Only as an act of War," she admitted.

Despondently, she now broke from me, walked into the crisp Blueness of the hall and crouched fetally near the wall - like an Angel fallen and misplaced - crouched fetally as One Grieving, cast out of |Paradise|, fallen from |Heaven|.

I pitied her - for the burden of guilt she seemed to be carrying with her. I went to comfort her, huddled over her, crouched down beside her.
"I'm beginning to trust you," I told her.
"I should like to make you Whole, Sarah," she grieved. "I should like to make you fully `Human'. But I can't - because my need is for a monster - for a Soldier in [My War]!"
Now she gathered herself and spoke to me more strongly. "I promised you Vengeance, nothing more. If you outlive your mission, it will only be by a most fortunate accident."

Her tone was believable—fully believable in the truthful hue of the blue light. And I reminded myself that if I were a man, I would have no difficulty believing what she said to me. Only spoiled, over-protected children persist in finding War unreal.

(I had never thought of myself as that before, but Corporate Sarah had indeed been bred to it.)

"And I can't back out of it," I tested softly, afraid of her answer.
"Not if you wish to live," she stated.

Still I would not believe her!
Did part of her cling to that barbaric time when all save kings were sorely punished for initiating acts of Kindness?

"And if I fail, would you really shred me?" I asked softly.
"If I don't, then someone else will."

Now she met my eyes with newfound strength.

"But as every soldier knows, these last few hours can be made to count for you,—can be made to suffice for |All Eternity|. For a few hours you can come to see |Your Own Face|, to know what it means, for all time, to call yourself |Human|."

"As *You do," I asked skeptically.
"As I *Have," she affirmed.

Blue had now become for me the color of fear.
Solidified by the extreme cold of the hall, Blue now kept
my body from me, blocking all my senses
and my autonomy of thought.
Blue's constant interference jammed my inner dialogue,
pushed it into the nonverbal, beat it down to a fetal mass,
the animal form of unshaped infancy.
|*I*|less Sarah was now an embryo filled with
apprehension, helplessness, while the |Other Sarah| —
|Hostage*Sarah—crouched bent with shame
over her own cowardice.

It seemed useless to plead with her to change the environment. Marianne was doing all this to me on purpose—a professional purpose she had no intention of revealing to me. Desperately, I clung to the hope that all this was Sham - a clever therapist's strategy for the savage excision of my Deathwish - and tomorrow the pretense would be revealed to me - tomorrow the Witchdoctor would remove her *Masque - and I would be sent home wiped clean of my grief and my guilt over Skeets. Sent home thoroughly content and adjusted to the prospect of a long and happy life—sent home to a "productive," "carefree," "normal" life—to the Splash and Frolick of the Secretarial Pool!

(But — Skeets was being shredded somewhere,
and Sarah's ‡Person still hung from a tree.)

Had I not watched a mind die?
Had I not witnessed Skeets' cruel abduction?

Had there not been extreme measures taken against us to insure our silence? How could I remain cowardly in the face of so much outrage!

Yet, the violence directed against us had not been frank and blatant - it had been subtle, extended in time - not the kind of violence that prompts an open confrontation.

And now I was being told that I was to be transformed into a ***Monster**, into a *Soldier to be sent to the front lines with barely a few hours' basic training, dubious schooling in self-defense.

Only a lunatic would not be a coward under such circumstances!

"Are you tired of shivering, Sarah?" she now asked me softly from across the room.

I looked up.

In my distraction I had scarcely noticed that she had returned to the console and had been quietly programming it while I sat there helplessly bombarded.

"What is your `cure' doing to me," I blurted, finding it difficult to keep my speech from slurring.

"It's making you hyperactive and hypothermic,"
she answered casually. "It would speed things up considerably if you wouldn't mind removing all your clothes."

"I'll freeze to death," I protested.

"On the contrary," she returned, amused, "in a minute or two, you'll begin to feel overheated. Trust me!"

Reluctantly I removed my dress, my underwear, my shoes and stockings. I sat naked, fetally, still shivering. But I felt my mind beginning to clear, as parts of my body stopped working extra hard to match the temperature of the warmest parts of me.

Still, Blue continued to pierce my brain, continued to bisect it with the sharpness of a scalpel.

My eyes found it difficult to focus on her.

"Get up and move around a bit," she suggested.

"What is the purpose of all this," I countered, doing as I was told. "Are you out to make me worse instead of better?"

"I'm vaccinating you against stress," she answered. "I've begun a program that will stretch you to your full potential, both mental and physical."

"I see," I said skeptically. "A trial by Freezing Fire!"

I dared to approach her again, dared to perch myself at the edge of her desk. My increased physical activity had helped me to adjust to the lower temperature, and now I also found that boldness - a kind of primitive, masculine boldness - was also helping me overcome my discomfort.

"Tell me," I ventured, "Doesn't my nakedness distract you?"

"No," she returned flatly.

She was still deeply involved in her programming task.

I put my hand down on hers, ruining her last instruction.

Instinctively she pressed the Ctrl/Z keys then looked up at me.

I met her eyes: "Our last meeting left me with an obsession that I must yet resolve," I said to her. "I have a rather impertinent request - "

"You still want carnal knowledge of me," she anticipated, coldly amused.

"My curiosity is unbearable!" I asserted. "Is what I'm asking improper? In *Hell, that is."

"I am not an *Object, Sarah," she reminded.

She now caused Pink to invade the hall again, releasing my mind from the tyranny of Blue. I suddenly felt gut-whole again, concretely Sarah.

"Carnal knowledge, Sarah?" she now repeated playfully. "What of - a *Person, or an *Angel?"

"An *Angel," I replied. "By all means an *Angel!"

My casual invocation was not lightly dismissed.

Full-faced, she now bestowed upon me a passionate glare: q"If you are indeed willing to share in The*Sacred with me, then you shall Know *Me*," she now promised with Celestial Eyes.

"Don't send me to my death, Marianne," I now blurted, suddenly finding it easy to beseech her, "not without first showing me *Who I really am!"

She smiled softly, purely - with the purity of saints. Her voice, too, was soft, mystical: "In a sense that is not gender-bound, that far transcends the sexual, I too would like us to be lovers, Sarah," she replied. "But carnal knowledge of an *Angel - " she now added mockingly, "that is something altogether different. To achieve such a thing one must become—not merely *Whole—but *One-with-the-Whirlwind*. Can you truly mean that? Would you knowingly, willingly Couple with the Whirlwind?"

"You are teasing me," I said. "You know what I mean. You know that you intentionally filled me with lust three nights ago - a kind of lust I have never felt for anyone, man or woman!"

"A Lust for an *Angel," she corrected. "Yes, I did, quite intentionally. But that was Sham. Not true Lust-for-an-Angel, Sarah, but *Lust-for-the-Whirlwind*."

"Why are you being evasive," I persisted. "You know precisely what I mean."

She did not answer.

Again she altered the color of the room before Pink became toxic. She let Green temper Pink, returning us to that Venomous Glow suggestive of [Lucifer's Garden].

"If you want the carnal, I can give it to you," she said now, in a tone better suited to the Viper. "In fact, doing so will readily serve my purpose. Come with me."

She had thrown me an examination gown to wear, such as one wears in hospitals, and then had opened a door behind the console.

I followed her into a warm room, strangely old-fashioned in decor, like a physician's private office. Beyond it was a small examining room.

(I wondered if she also had an apartment here, a bedroom to which she would invite me.)

Again she read my thoughts, amused.
"I'm sorry to disappoint you," she said. "This will not be at all what you expected."
She went into the examining room and washed her hands in the sink there, and put on plastic gloves.
"Get on the table, and put your feet in the stirrups," she now said all too professionally.
I hesitated, aghast.
"You asked for carnal knowledge," she wryly tantalized.
"But not perversity," I protested.

Her eyes flashed angrily. "Would my bedding down with a Monkey be less perverse?" Still she invited, taunting. "On the table, please."
"A pelvic exam? Is that the best you can muster, with all your scientific expertise," I teased.
"It's a lesson, not an examination," she returned
coldly.
"Are you serious?"
"Dead serious," she stated. "Well?" she waited, her gloved hand poised and lubricated. "You do want carnal knowledge—of an Angel, I believe you said?"

My curiosity would not let me refuse.
I did as she asked, and put my feet in the stirrups.

She met my eyes dispassionately. "I'm about to modify your personality—radically, irreversibly," she warned. "You had better brace yourself for the shock."

"I wish I could understand what you mean by that," I answered, trying to read her.

"All I know is that you have me bursting to the seams with both curiosity and cupidity, and that very little you can do might shock me."

Now she softened, appearing to have come to the conclusion that I was ready for whatever she intended.

"I know that I opened a door the other night—" she said clinically, "a door that, by yourself, you can no longer close. Now I will help you step through it."

"Without love, without tenderness?" I pleaded.
"Why so coldly, Marianne?"

She was unmoved.

I resigned myself to the experience, whatever it might be, although it now seemed impossible that I could learn anything at all from such a mechanical exchange.

But her intellectual detachment was far from dispassionate— with the clever fingers of a sculptor now she began to retrace me.

**It was an act of Creation,
of a gut-understanding of |My Form|.**

"Look back to puberty," she guided. "Look back to a time before you knew yourself as Female."

I labored to obey.

Slowly, hypnotically, with her ungloved hand she closed my eyes and touched my various limbs, my frame, recalling to me My*Anatomy—not my full-grown physiology but—some underlying primal structure that I had long forgotten.

How strong her power of suggestion was, how powerful her mind!

A vision of snow appeared, and there I finally found the child—the Neuter*Sarah—in a snowsuit, reckless and boyish.

"Have you found it," she asked softly.

"Yes," I murmured. "Please don't stop. What you're doing is most sensual!"

"Now grow older again," she invited. "But not as Sarah. Grow older, as Eric."

What an easy command that was for me: I knew Eric's body as well as I knew my own—I had always known his body, envied it, admired its strength. How often my fingers had traced its sculptured contours, hungering to cannibalize each sinew, to put it on around me!

"You are changing my sex," I informed her.

"No," she corrected: "I am merely freeing you of |Gender|. Gender Identity is imposed, not grown."

I dared to open my eyes, to face her.

"Keep your eyes closed,"
she commanded,

commanded as |**God-reshaping-Adam**|
as a |**God-unwilling-to-be-Known**|

Fearful that *She might stop,
I did as I was told.

Now her gloved hand entered me—not the way a man would enter but in a manner unmistakably feminine, twin to my former self—her fingers finding my cervix, fondling it as I might have fondled Eric—causing an erection there from some dormant part of me now suddenly awakened into penile presence.

Then, quickly, with the gentle precision of a surgeon—of a surgeon working on a monkey—she brought me to an ejaculation.

I gasped, startled, both Relieved,
and Disbelieving!

The shock of it left me whimpering, feeling raped. She had spoken truly——this was indeed an Irreversible*Awakening—

she had twice-taken my Virginity—she had thoroughly altered Sarah!

(But did *She* know that?)

She seemed to have closed that thought from her own mind. She had abandoned me. Impersonally, professionally, she had gone to the sink to wash up and then had left the room, had left me alone to regain my self-composure.

In a bewildered stupor, I remained on the table for a long time, contemplating |**My New Sight**|.

She had indeed freed me from an inner bondage tyrannically imposed upon me at some earlier time, had returned me to a *Freedom, a spiritual *Wholeness long-forgotten:

Eve too *Is* Man!

Gone was my mark of slavery!

And now the very clothes that bondaged-Sarah wore seemed cast from me like shackles. And I was glad to be free of my clothes, glad to be in a place where I could stand Soul*Naked as a Child again and speak in whatsoever manner I pleased!

Still, I could not fully accept this.

And now I felt embarrassed—mortified at what she had done to me and how positively I had responded to it.

Both angry and grateful, I walked to the outer hall, my gown wrapped around me.

I found her sitting at the console reprogramming what I had caused her to erase. But I was ashamed to speak to her. Nevertheless, I confronted her, flushed and flustered:

"Do you know what you just did to me?"

She faced me angrily.

"Does it leave you in a panic now? When you repeatedly put your head in the lion's mouth, sooner or later the jaws do close."

"Did you enjoy it?" I returned.

"I always enjoy fashioning Adam out of Eve," she said.

"Is that all it was to you, a professional act?" I searched her face for any sign of tenderness.

"No," she admitted coldly, analytically. "It was an act of Joy. It has always delighted me—to impersonate God."

> *She had flung me into Hyperspace, where |*I*| now stood gender-free and in many ways returned to infancy.
> And though I now fully understood her diabolical intent—to make a *Man of Sarah—to fashion a *Sarah-fit-for-War—I could not deplore her methodology, nor could I revile the Master Craftsman working on me—If Marianne was *Lucifer, then Sarah had indeed become Her*Convert!
>
> But whether or not *Lucifer, surely this caducean interface was more than questionable therapy, was indeed a Psychic**Coupling—Yeah, verily with an *Angel!

(And even as I thought this, I despised myself for being still so weak, so easily influenced, even hypnotized.)

Yet how, except by such epic `Ordeal', might |*I*|
Man*Sarah gain
`Carnal Knowledge of the Gods'

But—had my obsession over Skeets been merely
Sarah's need to explore *Sarah?

And here now sat *Marianne, playing the console like a vast cosmic organ, controlling My Day and Night and Destiny—sat as *Skeets restored in triumph—embodying all the things that Skeets might have become, if Skeets were *Whole—and also all the things Man*Sarah could become, once Sarah was made *Whole.

Was it Self-Love, and only Self-Love casting a spell on me? Or was it a love for *Someone, for Something-more-Magnificent - a Love of *Man for *Man?

"You gave me exactly what I asked for," I now said to her. "And it really has transformed me. I have indeed embraced

The Whirlwind!"

*She looked up with eyes that fully *Knew me.
"No, you are still simply My Monkey," she corrected. "And you don't know how tainted and ugly I have become. If indeed you had coupled with the Whirlwind, then you would now be uprooting me!"

"Why do you berate yourself so," I returned.

Angrily she pressed a key on the console, causing the arena to darken into a screening room.
"Know me as I truly *Am*, Sarah!"

> "Not more horror films," I begged her, detecting an old refrain. "Why are you so obsessed with them?"
> "These photos were taken secretly," she insisted. "I am holding the camera.—I am an accomplice to everything you see."

I sat, resigned to facing what her grief was again forcing her to confess to me.

What flashed before me was not entirely intelligible—fast frames, poorly lit and focused, of some kind of progressive interrogation—of a terrorist, perhaps.
It was very difficult to make out who, or where, or for what reason it had all been done. And the remoteness of the black-and-white picture, its similarity to the fast reports often televised on the evening news—all had little effect on me.

"Am I so dense that I can't see what you are showing me," I finally asked, exasperated.

Pained at my response, she cut the program, returned the lights to the arena.

"It is a flaying," she stated. "Do you see it now? A flaying!"

Now there were **TWO MONKEYS**
Screeching on a *Judas-tree.

I whispered to her.

She had composed herself, had again become the compleat therapist, the most competent, Good-Doctor Frankenstein.

"Would you like to see how Skeets might be treated here?" she now asked tautly.

"Would she really be safe?" I was quick to ask.

"In my care, yes," she promised. "I've been trying to arrange an exchange—so that she can be brought down here—as my patient."

248

"Who will you trade for her," I asked, heartened.

"You, Sarah," she replied. "I intend to exchange
you for Skeets."

Now she stood and with her face and eyes scanned the room
significantly—pointed with her eyes, as though to areas where
there might be secret cameras, one-way panels.

I followed her eyes.
No, we were not alone down here.
Someone was watching, listening.

"An upstairs associate of mine would like to treat you," she
said guardedly. "He is convinced he can work with you better
than I can. I believe you know him—Dr. Hoffman."

"Hoffman? The shrink from Personnel?" I asked,
appalled. "What does that quack want with me!"

"He's not a quack, Sarah," she quickly corrected, publicly.

"He has more professional qualifications, more status and more
power than you would ever believe—and he has taken a special
interest in your case."

"And he would like to take me away from you?"

"Yes."

"But what if I prefer to work with you? What if I want to be
transformed into Your monster," I tested. "What if I enjoy the
prospect of becoming the new *Frankenstein?"

"Wouldn't you rather become an administrative assistant—to
the Old Man?" she offered.

"Hoffman would pull me out of the Secretarial Pool?"

"Yes."

Then again her tone changed, became rhetorical. "After all,
Skeets is expendable, isn't she? Wasn't it really *Sarah you
came down here to find?"

Now I understood her! She had no intention of abandoning
me to Hoffman, no intention of changing her plans.

She would yet create her Monster. Secretly, she would fashion a Trojan*Horse - and when she was through sculpting me she would hand me over to Hoffman, not as a slavish and vulnerable Sarah, but as a Deadly Force -

a *Sarah Fully-Formed,
Battle-ready!
Springing from the Head of Zeus full-clad in armor!
Quick to sing The Song*of*Man!

"No one is expendable," I now returned publicly, for the warming of all the wall-pressed asses' ears, "least of all, Skeets. I can't abandon her—not the way my mother was abandoned. I can't go through that twice. You're right, Marianne, my Conscience hangs on a Judas-tree. Exchange me, if that is what must be!"

Now her warrior eyes met mine, flashed martially.
With a wry smile she invited me:
"Then at least—before you leave here—let me attempt
to make you Whole."

"Can you cure me of cowardice," I asked feebly.
"You are not a coward," she assured.

She reached into the broad pocket of her medic's coat and pulled out a small vial.

"This is a frightful drug, Sarah," she stated. "In minute doses, it can be used to heal. But in the doses I am usually required to administer it—" She paused significantly. "I have been captured, held hostage, tortured, raped. But the thought of being put on this drug for any length of time still turns me to jelly!"

Now she took a syringe from the same pocket and removed its plastic covering. "But I told you I could also use this to heal," she said, preparing an injection. "Give me your arm, Monkey."

250

I drew back, apprehensively.

"Aren't you at all curious," she taunted, "Hoffman uses this too—quite regularly. He will also use it on Skeets."

She waited, letting a silence fall before saying it again, softly, patiently, but as an ominous command: "Give me your arm, Sarah."

Still I hesitated.

But wasn't it childish of me to resist my physician?

How long could I delay the inevitable? My curiosity finally won over me, and I did as I was told.

I scarcely felt the needle press my vein, for what followed was a *Clubbing*, an internal seizure, My Own Brain turning on me like a thug upon its victim—

Not just my brain but half my mind as well

—my *Will* palsying on me

—unable to control its own direction

—expressing itself in images of malignant nerve cells

becoming Seeing*Eyes for Alienated*Parts of Me

—*I*'s that were and were not Sarah.

And the more I resisted—the worse it was for me—until I learned *Passivity*—*Submission-to-Nonentity*.

Only then could I vaguely feel the world outside of me.

I must have collapsed for she had caught me and then had carried me to a place where she could sit and I could lie with my head on her lap, while she had taken off her coat, her jewelry, and was now unbuttoning the front of her dress.

She had taken me in her arms, gripped me fondly as she might hold an infant, and now frankly she bared her breast to me - a small and perfect breast - thrust it at me with such directness that I took it hungrily, as though I had a right to it.

It was a Loving Act, a giving of Herself to Me entirely.
I felt the softness of Her Arms, Her Bosom—

—smelled Her clean fragrance—
—a rosewater fragrance reminding me of Virgins, Motherhood, and Holiness.

Now her *Nails echoed her whispers, made the words real for me. And again, as once before deep in my long-forgotten, I found my trust betrayed—for now her *Nails dug and scratched at me even as she rocked me - rocked me as My*Mother had once rocked me—rocked me cruelly, absurdly.

It triggered my infant panic—all the helplessness I had felt at my mother's breast—all the pain, the contradiction —

—How could she have so precisely targeted
My Need, My Fear!

"Love me, Sarah. Don't be afraid to love me," like a Virgin she repeated.

"Love me, Sarah," then like a She-Bear she invited—

But this Act of *Nurturing was *Not* Deranged—
This*Sarah Could stand Pain, Could resist Hunger —
         —and This*Marianne was Healing Me!

I stopped fighting her and gave in completely—
accepted both the warmth and the absurdity—
treated the pain now as nothing to me—for This*Sarah
was not afraid to seize *Love even where there was
*Pain—This*Sarah could chance *Love—even from a
*Grizzly—even from an *Enemy.

I don't know how long she permitted this exchange—long
enough for the drug to wear off, long enough for Sarah to find
*Sarah—but not long enough for either of us to indulge
ourselves in an adult lust—and finally she withdrew from me in
a weaning way and left me lying on the platform, twitching,
shivering,—drenched with sweat and my own urine.

Again I was left mortified.
Had anyone been watching?

I went to the lavatory and showered myself clean, dried
myself, took a fresh gown from the shelf, all the while
wondering if this was only an elaborate dream.

I felt touched by something *Sacred,

Felt ravished by an *Angel—
But was it **Real**,—
or was it only My Own Mind healing me?

Returning to the hall, again I confronted her:
"You have just taught me to love my Enemy," I now said
angrily. "Have you been creating your Messiah?"

"Haven't you *always* loved your Enemy," she
countered dispassionately. "In a world filled with *Lunacy,
Whom could you have called a *Friend?"

She was right, of course, and how clearly she had made me
see it. Helpless at my mother's breast, it had meant my survival
once, for me to learn to love my enemy.
And it still meant my survival now.
How often I had turned the other cheek, not only to quell
hunger but to come to my own Selfhood, to wrench from my
mother Human warmth - to seize *Soul, *Personhood, in the
only way a Hero can be nurtured—again and again tempting fate
deep in the cave of the She-Bear?

Yet now it was not My*Mother but *Marianne who held
me Hostage. Willingly again I returned to her, not as Victim
but as Pupil.

The clean-up crew had mopped up after us. And now she was
ready with cotton swabs to cool my back with alcohol, to freshen
it in apology. But there were no real scratches there. What in
my panic had felt like *stabs* and *claw-marks* were now but
scarcely indentations.
"Love me, Sarah," she confirmed, but softly, sanely, without
emotion reinforcing The-Fact-within-The-Dream that had taken
place. "Love me even if I rip you to pieces."
"I do, and I will," I promised, "even as the Whirlwind!"

I felt **Real** again, no longer divided, felt able to reach out and
take **My*Person** from the Judas-tree.

"You have cured my Deathwish," I now told her.
"I feel Whole."

"A Wholeness soon to be destroyed," she reminded.
Again her words jolted me.
"Such infant innocence has no worldly use," she clarified.
"The need is for a criminal mind, for eyes that look away
wherever they see evil."

Again she had spoken truly—for in a world filled with
lunacy—

|This*Sarah|—radiant in her New Vision

—would be treated as an unwelcome dissident, as a force too
rational, too dangerous to be tolerated anywhere but in a cloister
or an asylum.
I could choose to keep my new-found Innocence, but only as

|Her Prisoner|.

So! she meant to make her monster after all!
But, what kind of monster: The Corporate Fiend
condoning it - or The Faceless Arm that Flays ?

What if all of this was only metaphor, primal therapy?
Was she playing Shaman to all my demons?

How like the |Great*Mother| she now appeared, dipping her
infant in an icy stream, nurturing the |Animal Form of Man|
—a savage form, heroic, godly—
fit to rule |All the Beasts in Her Garden|.

And how carnal this |Coupling-with-an-Angel| had become
for me—truly a Coupling, not a Communion. A Communion
would have been no better than a Cloning—
a denial of My*Being and its gradual replacement with a
|Reflection of Hers|

No, I decided, never Communion-with-Marianne, whoever she might be! Let Ours remain a War-relation—a dynamic Stasis—a collision of opposites at a point of perfect rest: Her Will and My Will grappling in a violent embrace, an apposition of [**Truth**|**Truth**] whose radiant disjunction—mirrored in

[**One**I**One**] the inviolate plane of [**The Sacred**]

Yet a coupling also in Biology.
Carnal in a different sense.

I could feel her many-fingered Will weaving
a pattern on my chemistry—like an insect
predator, slowly, delicately pricking at me—
her voracious purpose, stronger than mine—her
circadian instinct—All-Consuming!

Show me the rest of myself," I begged her now. "Don't blind these eyes too soon!"

Like a Mantis she fixed me with her stare:

"Not **Your*Face**,

but **Our**I**Our Interface**," she corrected.
"Man-creating-Man"

She had returned to the console, had turned on a program of hushed whispers, subtle shadows, even of odors—pheromones of Fear, of Lurking Danger.

"An Antiperson rides me, Sarah," now she said, and it was the *Person speaking. "It came upon me subtly, perniciously, and now it pushes me to the very edge of sanity."

Unexpectedly, she cut the program.

I heard a rustling, a sudden shuffling of feet, like rats scurrying off behind the plastic-paneled walls.

"Forgive my students," she apologized. "They seldom have the opportunity to watch me at work."

She eyed me meaningfully, as if to caution me that here—her every move was watched.

"How did you become so different from the way you were," I dared to ask her. "The Marianne of our college days seems now odious by comparison."

"I suffered a breakdown - many breakdowns, and finally, a primal scream." she answered distantly. "But I was not stunted in the process. With each new breaking, I sprang up again, stronger, better than before." Now she faced me, addressed me meaningfully. "A breakdown need not destroy a mind, Sarah. It can be the basis for a new beginning."

"Tell me what happened to you," I asked softly.

"It was, for me, an orthogenesis—as it will be for you, and as it still might be —for Skeets," she affirmed. "I admit that I really must have been odious once, thoroughly spoiled—the product of Old Money spent wantonly in my behalf by parents who scarcely had time for me. Education was my substitute for motherlove. I had tutors of every kind. Mozart could not have wanted more!"

(This, of course, I already knew.)

She elaborated:

"In my infancy I played among the Pyramids. I saw the mountains of Tibet, I shared my playpen with Royalty, I sat on the lap of Presidents.

"What may have been struggling night-school years for you were leisure-hours, social time for me. I already had enough advanced degrees. And when I grew tired of being a perpetual student, in my passion to explore every nook and cranny of this, My Planet, I recklessly happened upon a war zone.

"Naively believing myself unimpeachable, I went into the field, to study the enemy, and found myself captured by our own side, treated as a turncoat, interrogated as a spy."

She continued in the same emotionless tone to describe how her guardians had finally located and ransomed her, with the help of the Corporation; how she had returned to study under Hoffman, had been encouraged to put all of her precious experience to positive use; how she had then gone back to the field under Corporate sponsorship as much to treat the jailers as their victims, but—

She did not have to finish her sentence. The end was obvious: the collective means had corrupted her, and now the forms and protocols of counter-terrorism had corroded every moral structure, every noble purpose.

"You are still holding something from me," I stated.
Reluctantly she now confessed it:
"I had a lover. Under torture, I betrayed him. I bore him two infants. They are missing."

I gaped at her, incredulous.
"Could you, of all people, indeed have given in to bodily pain?"
"Not to bodily pain, Sarah," she answered strongly.
"To rational choice. Mine was the act of a Caesar, not that of a coward. Strategically I held my own survival to be more important, and when retreat became the only option, I cut all of them adrift."

Her words undid me.
How could I condemn her, and yet—
"So there was a Skeets in your past too," I concluded. "More than one Skeets."
I gripped her hand compassionately. "To me, you are not a Monster—nor would I ever presume to call you a Monkey."

She smiled softly, let me caress her hand, her arm —an arm covered by the long sleeve of her dress.
I now noticed her arm, an arm blemished by large white patches of grafted skin, perhaps from burns, the scars of war, or—
I looked at her in horror.

She made light of it.

"These I scarcely felt, and as you see, the harm was easily repaired. No, torture violates souls, not bodies. Man is not Body, Sarah!"

Now she sounded more like the first Marianne, and I humored her politely.

But she would not be humored.

"I'll prove it to you," she said.

She looked at me concretely:

"If I told you that I could make you entirely insensitive to pain, and that I could repair any physical harm done to your body, would such a knowledge give you the confidence to endure Crucifixion - not once, but as many times as needed?"

"It would certainly help," I said uncomfortably, wondering just how warped her plans for me might be.

"It wouldn't help a bit," she countered.

Now she punched an instruction into the console.

"Go and stand in that square," she directed, indicating a section of the floor patterned as some kind of grid.

I hesitated.

"Aren't you curious, Monkey?" she again taunted.

"I'm afraid of you now," I said. "Afraid of how tainted you might indeed have become, and that you may now be asking me to relive your agony - to become your victim, just one more clone of Marianne."

"My purpose is tainted, yes," she said. "And our relation, abominable. But the order still stands."

She waited.

Again our wills were locked.
What choice did I have?
How long would she wait for me to cooperate?
And wasn't I curious?
Oh yes, I was very curious!
Like a good monkey I finally did as I was told.

She pressed a key now and a wave of pain went through me
—through my marrow—through every bone in me—intense
pain, like biting down on a bad tooth. My body collapsed under
me as though I were a puppet made of wood. I looked at her
accusingly, like a laboratory rat, feeling betrayed.

"It's not electric shock," she assured me. "Electric shock
would be toxic. It's high-intensity sound—quite beneficial to
your bone marrow—superb for the immune system! On the
square again, Monkey."

So, merely another of her vaccinations!
Now being assured the pain was not harmful, now
being motivated by the prospect of becoming a
superior being, now having been made a glutton for
punishment, I had no difficulty finding the courage
to get up and stand upon the square again.

Again she sent a shock through me, and again my legs gave
way. But the pain was not as intense as it had been before.
"One more time," she urged.

Again and again I obeyed her, and each time it
became easier for me, until I found I could stand
quite comfortably—until the shocks became actually
soothing, pleasurable.

"Now come here," she said, holding an electrode
poised to test the level of my sensitivity.
I gave her my arm and she sent a shock through me that,
earlier, would have sent me screaming.
"I can barely feel it," I told her. "How long will this
refractory stage last?"
"Days, perhaps weeks," she answered. "With booster
treatments and proper nutrition, as long as you please."

Now she sat back, satisfied.
"Well? How does it feel, to be transformed into Achilles?"
"Is that what you were doing," I asked, relieved. "I was afraid
you were making Jesus!"

"No, not *Jesus," she mused.

Now her face grew serious, her expression, cruel.

"What if I told you that I had lied to you. That everything I had said to you before was false, said merely to gain your trust, your sympathy? What if I told you that I had in fact hurt you, damaged you - and had relished all the while in it—had secretly laughed at your credulity, your monkeyness. What if I told you that I really *am* depraved and that this is how I regularly get my jollies? What then would you think of the experience?"

"I would loathe it, and loathe you," I said.

"Then it wasn't the pain that ached you, was it, Monkey?" she finished victoriously.

I saw her point and granted it.

It was the moral relation between us that counted, not what the body felt at all - the first, a loving relation between physician and patient - the second, a depraved abomination that left both victim and tormentor the worse for the exchange.

"Which was it, Marianne," I asked her softly.

She looked away, still unwilling to be *Known.

I dismissed my doubt. No, not even the extreme level of depredation to which she had been subjected could have warped her so!

"... Our Corporate effort at reform failed miserably," she now continued. "It was based on the false premise that more 'humane' methods of interrogation could be implemented. Naively, we perfected methods that would bend minds imperceptibly. But— even when the subject doesn't realize he is being violated—the Inquisitor knows—morally, the Inquisitor is left with indelible scars!"

She suddenly changed her mood.

"Come, it's time to continue your indoctrination," she said.

She sat me down on a cube beside the console and took out a new syringe from its plastic wrapper.

I watched her somewhat skeptically.

"I don't know that I should let this game continue," now I said. "I don't relish being an anesthetized victim—no matter how entertaining all your methods seem to be—for as you've intimated, you are the one who may well now be hurting enough for both of us!"

She did not find my comment amusing.

"Give me your arm, Sarah," she said.

"Are you really indoctrinating me," I demanded.

"Does it make a difference, Monkey?" she returned. "I could just as easily be doing it without telling you."

"It does make a difference," I answered her. "For if I knew that all this was indeed violating My Inquisitor, then I too would be violated."

"Your metamorphosis must continue," she said. "Besides, I can't leave you in your pupal state—you might too easily harm yourself."

"Nonsense. I feel perfectly fine," I said.

"Do you? Do you really still feel like *Sarah?"

I reflected on it.

Since her treatment it did seem to me that I had
acquired a certain dullness, a reduction in my whole ability to feel—even a masculinity taking hold of me—something unfeminine, a coarseness such as might be found in a country bumpkin, someone knocked about so much he had lost all sensitivity.

Or perhaps the dullness, the denseness of an often-abused child.

"No," I had to admit, "I do feel different—as though you have subtly blinded me. Is it reversible?"

"All too reversible," she assured grimly, poising the syringe. "This drug neutralizes all your body's natural opiates. Enough of this, and your pain threshold will crash through the floor. The slightest pinprick will prove excruciating."

"Is that the way you flay a mind, then," I asked her softly.

"It's not a bloodless flaying," she replied all too clinically. "A muscle relaxant can reduce the usual internal injuries associated with violent spasm—but autonomic stress is apparent, eventually leading to stroke, heart failure. The subject screams in silence."

"And that silence is terrible," I finished for her.

"Give me your arm, Sarah."
Again she waited, and our wills were locked.

"I am still damnably curious, Marianne,"
I finally confessed, exposing my arm.

"That's a good monkey," she said.

She gave me a minute dose—just enough to kill the dullard in me—to melt it into a being soft and pliable, unmistakably *Feminine* and now sensitive to the most subtle shades, subliminal changes in my environment—to the thermal shift reflected on all the touched surfaces around me—to all the odors, the variations in light.

At this level I could almost hear her thoughts, could almost See through walls. And—even more amazingly—I could Hear the secret program being piped, subtly, through the whispering silence of the room, a *Logos* written on my flesh by laser-sharp waves of ultrasound.

"This is the level you habitually reside in," I now said knowingly. "I feel as though my skin has a thousand eyes."

.@.@.@.@.@.@. Scallop Eyes!

I felt myself immersed within the life-cycle of @@@@Organism large and small, felt myself dancing the slow dance of ripening vegetation—my synapses bared to the winter sky above me and the lava of earth's core.

Volcanoes churned under my feet,

my ears heard the **BURST** of *Galaxies!

"You find it pleasurable,"
she observed.
                                        "Sublime"
                              I exclaimed, euphoric.

I cast off the gown that covered my nakedness, no longer shy before my audience.

With Wings on my shoulders and Wings on my feet I began to leap and dance around the arena to all the sounds and shadows, to all the colors and changes washing through the hall. I indulged myself completely, feeling myself transformed into **Pure Perfection,**

no longer mortal but |**One-with-the-Gods**|

Then, as their Messenger, then as ↑Gabriel→

I turned to redeem her—turned to invite her to step with me through the Gates*of*Heaven . . .

. . . but she stood apart
preferring, like ↓Lucifer↓
to squat in her own realm.

"What a perfect creature you are, Sarah," she marveled almost enviously. "No wonder you can stand naked without shame. Everything sits just right with you—even the fat's in the right place!"

"Does it bother you," I countered half-defiantly.

"What a child you might have been for me," she corrected. "I would have raised you to become My Saviour—to preserve all that is good and beautiful in the Face of Man—I would have raised you to keep your Innocence, your Wholeness, for All Time!"

"Once possessed, it cannot be taken from Me,"
I assured her. I *Am that Person now,
and you are Saved.
                    "Climb out of Hell, Marianne," I invited.
                    "Come, sit with me in Heaven!"

"I sit in Hell by choice and not by accident," now like a
thundercloud she scowled: "Were I an idiot or a halfwit, I would
not hesitate to join you There ... But I am like the captain of a
ship—I dare not quit this place until the very last and meanest
soul has been ushered through Your*Door!"

I sobered at her words.
"What kind of *Saviour would you take me for,"
I told her, "that I should dwell in *Heaven all alone!"

I went to where she stood in a corner of the wall and laid my
hands upon her face, probing with my flesh
                    the Radiant*Presence I still sensed lurking there.

But the face I touched seemed now

misshapen, cloven and diseased.

"What Gospel will you reveal to me now, Monkey," she
questioned softly, tolerating my cherubim probe.
Childishly, I embraced her.
"You have just taught me what Love is, and always has
been, and must always be for Each of us," I whispered,
breathing a kiss into her ear:

"Love is the Will To Deny Heaven
until Justice has been done to All"

The drug wore off and I burned down into a dullard once again, even as my mind ached to remain in Hyperspace, wrapped in a Cloak of Stars. But the Way there was not now Closed to Me, nor would I need an opiate to retrieve it —

for I Knew Myself to be
I Sarah: Man-made-Whole
and soon to come to [My Full Height]
dwelling as Wormhole among Galaxies,
bending the laws of Chaos
into [Man-made Symmetry]!

"Are you ready for death now, Monkey," she asked softly.
To emphasize her words, she took a revolver from a drawer and placed it on the console.

Her question shattered me.
Had all this been no more than a last supper for one secretly condemned? Was she now to become my assassin?
"I promised you *Vengeance, nothing more," she reminded, taut as a bow.
"You can't mean that literally," I returned.
"Can't I?"

Her obdurate glare was most convincing.
Was this still the same game? It still had to be the same game, I screamed inside me. More therapy, most likely panic therapy, to jar me back to the real world in which *Man-Sarah had no place, no sanction.
"I feel suddenly naked," I said to her. "May I put on my clothes?"
"Not yet." She pulled a fresh gown from the drawer of the console and threw it at me. "Your rehabilitation has barely begun."

I was puzzled. The hour was surely very late and both of us should be in bed. "Don't you ever sleep," I asked her.

"Whenever I can snatch the time," she answered blankly.

I put on the gown, wrapped it almost like a toga around me—for now I felt as though I should be wearing one. My body felt strangely whole, infused with a special grace, a classic ease—nor did I feel particularly tired or sleepy.

"What medical miracle did you perform on me," I marveled. "Will this new feeling last?"

"For as long as you can keep your health," she answered, patting the gun for emphasis.

Her act now seemed ludicrous, melodramatic.

"Who are you, what are you," I burst out in sheer frustration. "A moment ago it seemed to me that I took Jesus by the hand—and earlier, the Virgin suckled me. But now you appear to me as a figure out of Batman!"

"Did you really have such visions," she broke, startled. "I projected no such thoughts. Was it really so? Did you really speak with Jesus? Did the Virgin hold you?"

"Of course not," I rejected. "Such idols are not of my tribe but rather of yours!"

Now I softened:

"Perhaps they were projections of yourself of which you are unaware—identities taken onto you in childhood that became as real within you as this embodiment of *Gabriel now seems to me. Or perhaps it's only that I am extremely sensitive to all that you might become, had you not chosen to be *Lucifer."

My words had shaken her.

I put distance between us, to see her better.

Could she indeed have been so blind to her own Radiance? Was there a mirror made that I could hold to her—or was *Sarah the only image the two of us might see?

How far the pupil had outstripped the teacher!

Like an old professor reiterating notes not changed for fifty years, she had led me down a hackneyed academic path no longer glanced at, while *I*, in my first sight, had come to notice the whole landscape was now overgrown and changed through time and filled with objects quite unknown to her.

"What a lovely speech you made - about what Love must be," she now said feebly, her voice soft, her eyes fluid. "I had quite forgotten it!"

But quickly she contained herself:

"We have played Shaman, each to the other, each seeking out and finding our own gods. But now we must stop playing."

I looked at her, no longer mesmerized.

"Why do I get the feeling that from this moment on your |Cure| will begin to destroy the patient?"

"I must recover Skeets," she countered.

"Very well, then, exchange me," I eagerly volunteered. "Send me upstairs now, just as I am. I am quite ready to confront the enemy."

"As you are, you are not a marketable commodity," she replied, "—not even fit for the Secretarial Pool. You would not clear Security. You would be cast out, blacklisted, left to the most menial tasks, and soon Man*Sarah would dissolve and melt into the faceless multitude."

"Poppycock! Corporate mythology," I returned.

"No one will let you leave here alive, Sarah," she said more emphatically, patting the revolver one more time.

"Then let me stay here as your pupil," I insisted. "I could study here for years, could learn so much from you! This is a cloister I wouldn't mind hiding in, if that is what must be."

"The choice is not yours but mine," she reminded. "And I have chosen—I must recover Skeets."

"Then it seems you are hellbent on forcing me to reclaim [Our*Conscience]," I concluded.

I felt conscripted, illegally, nefariously conscripted as a Soldier in Her War.

"Have you forgotten why you came to me?" she flashed balefully. "My Person hangs on the same tree!"

Yes, I had forgotten it.
I was ready to forget it.
I had cut Skeets adrift. But now I had exchanged her for a broken Marianne.

"And if I give you what it is you want now, will the two of us then be sharing in [The Sacred]," I tested warily.

"How the Hell do I know, Sarah!"
she answered all too sanely.
I too felt myself return to sanity.
All I had felt was not exactly new to me.
As a student I had traveled down this path before.
But now I @Saw@ it clearly— not as the Past-of-Otherness, but as My-Own-Past-Vividly-Remembered—now presented as the most precious of all gifts to me, a first-hand Glimpse into an Ancient Mystery, a Vision into all that might truly be Eternal within Sarah:
A Sarah Who was not |Of the Body| but |In the Body|
A Sarah Who could return, again and again |In Matter| *Any Matter* capable of being *Ordered into the **Being** called **Sarah**.
A Being Who could neither be created nor destroyed
Who merely dwelled, from Age to Age as
[Recurrent-Form-in-Matter].
This Copy from the Mold called Sarah was but a copy, expendable, trivial. Fragment it, and still *Sarah would emerge again wherever new *Order could be found.
|My Being| was Eternal in this sense and in no other.
And the |*Order of My Being|, whatever else it might be, was a Natural Order, a Golden Helix as much In Matter as *Sarah Is , Was , and Would Be again [In Matter].

But this particular *Ordering, this complex set of material relations bringing about the |*Flowering of Sarah| was but one among a myriad of perishable forms, each recurring, each delicately balanced and interdependent within the *Stasis*, the apposition of [Truth|truth] among opposing Beings.

And in the distinct nature of each opposition—
a discrete War Relation—a material condition essential to the
|*Flowering of [My Being]|!

"You are right," I told her.
"This Perfection now called *Sarah cannot last the night."

"Why not, Monkey," she tested grimly.

I answered her full-faced, answered her now as *Mithras,* answer her [Ready*for*Death] and in no-wise [Her Monkey]

"My *Flowering waits upon a special state of affairs, one not possible without the very conflict had between us."

"And why is that, Monkey," again she prompted.

"This kind of `Perfection' feeds on conflict, thrives on Trial and Tribulation. Without it, the *Stasis between us fades, the elusive presence of |The Sacred| sparked through Our**I**Our Disjunction - dissipates - and My*Being becomes as amorphous, as trivial as the material flow of a river. What shall I gain by growing old if I cannot remain |Who I Am|! Only by way of a *Hero's death can *I* again and again return!"

It was clear my words had earned more than a passing grade: "God forgive me, Sarah," she muttered only half-aloud.

Her reaction jarred me.
How skillfully she had prepared me!
Was this a Lie?
The Heinous Lie of Ages?
The Atrocious Lie   of the AntiPerson riding her?

"I cannot give you any guarantees on the Eternal," she now said sharply, concretely. "What you find and see through your own visions has no real connection to me. Did you indeed touch [The Sacred]? How fortunate you are to have done so. I envy you!"

Was she in earnest, truly proceeding blindly, or was she pretending ignorance for the benefit of Other eyes?

Through technology we both knew that *Sarah could someday, in one form or another, eventually return again:
   *She could be 'resurrected' through cloning.
   Or *She could have her engrams implanted in any other form —even simulated within an electronic dimension, her *Consciousness trapped for an indefinite time inside the nanocells of a vast funereal urn wherein her [Dream of Real Life] might continue for as long as the *Program would be allowed to run on automatic pilot ... But such an electronic dream might well turn into a [Hell] from which, for [Sarah], there could be no autonomous escape!

Did I want that kind of "Eternal" life?
(And might [Sarah] already be trapped in such a world?)
   No!
The authenticity of [My Being] did not lie in |My Awareness| but in [My Person], a [Person] with a [Will]
         a [Will] that could endure even beyond |My Awareness|
            and did not need |My Awareness| to be manifest.

[My Effect] within Cosmic history was
                     [My Authenticity] —
            and [My Effect], [My Will] was still
                     [My Cry for Vengeance]

271

Part 1001:The Pact
Part 1001:The Pact

"And what now," I asked her cynically. "In what way shall this ***Flower** fade only to return again in Springtime?"

"My task is to guide you back to sanity," she explained. "To that end, I'm going to be putting you through an educational program—a biochemical means of cramming an entire year of operant conditioning in barely two hours' time."

She looked away, unwilling to meet my eyes.

"The procedure is not entirely painless, I'm afraid. Based on punishment-reward, something analogous to G-force is unavoidably experienced. But the shortcut is worth it, and if it will reassure you, I myself undergo the same procedure regularly to acquire sophisticated technical skills it would take me months and even years to acquire by rote."

Now she faced me with the look of The Assassin:

"Please consent to it, Sarah. For your own safety, I require your consent."

"And if I don't?"

She patted the gun one more time:

"Trust me!"

Despite her tone it was clear to me that we were being watched, and that she dared not tell me any of her real intent. What she was about to do to me had to be projected to the walls as nothing but a routine operation on a monkey—a monkey that had already been prepped for psychosurgery.

"A streamlined form of brainwashing, no doubt,"
I returned flatly. "I suppose I don't have much choice, do I,
Marianne?"

How could I trust her—and how could I not trust her! It would not make a difference either way. Like any soldier, my life was now in the hands of a war machine, subject only to the God of Chance.

Was she on the right side or the wrong side? A toss of a coin would be more informative than any "moral" reassurance anyone could give!

Nor could I even be certain that recovering Skeets would really be serving Skeets' own best interests.

Hadn't Skeets been terrified of someone? Perhaps even of Marianne?

Who were "They"?
Was Marianne one of "Them"?

Was this all subtle, imperceptible indoctrination?   Through the intimate bonding of mother-love, she had created new forms of speech between us that could not easily be heard through walls.

But how could I be certain that all of this closeness I felt between us, this Soul-nourishing *Purity she projected, was not more sham, more deception programmed into me?

How could I be certain!

"No, Marianne," I finally said. "I can't give you my consent.

I won't resist you openly, but you will nevertheless be coercing me. Whatever you do, whether right or wrong, will have to rest squarely, entirely on your own Conscience."

Now a new door opened on the side of the arena.

It unveiled a busy laboratory filled with young technicians—not hairy youths with asses' ears but clean-cut young men and women of apparently serious intent—their faces seemingly familiar.

Marianne briefed me on the psychosurgery to which I had 'consented', now appearing more like a pharmaceutical salesman than a physician—a salesman pushing the ultimate in new Corporate technology.

I recognized it to be a process developed years ago which on occasion had been reviewed in science magazines: an advanced form of educational prosthesis for the learning-impaired, also effective in the rehabilitation of hardened criminals.

But its application to military needs had only been hinted at in yellow-sheet newspapers, alongside headlines about flying saucers.

Basically, it was little different from the traditional rote-learning of public school - often an extremely painful process, if one remembers it from childhood. Ethically, it was on a par with any other type of rote-teaching - the content, not the method, to remain closely under public scrutiny.

While learning by rote was far inferior to the adaptational learning children naturally engage in, it nevertheless could be used for certain kinds of uninspired—primarily encyclopedic—education.

Quickly acquiring large blocks of raw data in this way could have its usefulness. It was not a loathsome prospect for me to submit to such a stimulus—no more so than accepting any other kind of prescribed corrective surgery.

Accepted freely, I would even welcome the opportunity to return weekly for a sleep-learning session—no matter how grueling—that might, in one short semester, qualify me for an advanced degree.

So there was nothing distasteful in what was being offered me—were it not for the implication of horror in her eyes.

What kind of monster would she make of me?
Would I become like Skeets?

"Has Skeets been down here?" I asked her now.
"That information is classified," she replied.

"What about Eric," I tried again.
"He's in a different category."

That puzzled me.
Was Eric such a conformist that he did not need 'educational brainwashing'? Perhaps only the most creative persons were brought here—the potential leaders, the inventors? But for what reason—to improve them, or to enslave their minds?

So! 'Eternal Life' was to be had through mental cloning. Soon, only one *Person would embody

[The Perfect

Ahah!   **Form of Man]**

Man is an insect species after all!

And this was to be the next stage in [**My Evolution**]: an insect entelechy no one, not even I, had been raised to find inferior.

[Our Corporate Soul]

had already reached the rim of the Galaxy and was waiting out there, singing a Siren-song to the Swarm, fueling

[Our Burning Lust to Follow].

And here, then, was the seat of the new Honeycomb, where the Drones were to be culled and trained in accordance with the specialized needs of the Hive.

(But more of a Hornet's nest than a Beehive: subterranean, from which the Swarm would emerge in Springtime, ready for flight, for travel to **The Stars**.)

Ought Larval Sarah permit herself to be metamorphosed by this crew?

Suppose I raised a furor now, would it create havoc?

Would such havoc endanger Marianne?

Was she friend or foe?

My Animal Curiosity,
> and only my Animal Curiosity
>> -- Man-Sarah's Monkey-Lust --
>>> opted for Silence!

I resigned myself to the air of Corporate infallibility that now colored every team-related act. It was clear that none of her subordinates was at all inclined to question the propriety of what was taking place—they were all so wholesome looking, so very gentle. The sheer delight they seemed to take in working their machines reminded me of Skeets at the peak of her career—an infant in a magic playpen matched with the compleat playmate, the most compatible of siblings.

A congenial young woman now came forward and led me to an elaborate dental chair such as one might expect to sit in for a session of cosmetic surgery.

It was a chair with many instruments, many gadgets attached to it—but no straps of any kind. There was no sign that anything that was to be done would be forced upon me.

I sat down willingly, as a patron in a beauty parlor.

Now Marianne stood over me appearing most medical, like a surgeon taking one final assessment of the patient.

"Your consent is mandatory," she explained. "An unwilling subject risks psychoneural scarring—even brain death. Are you secretly resisting us, Sarah?"

She waited in tense apprehension.

How skillfully she had prepared me!

Despite my moralizing about all of this resting solely on 'Her Conscience', what kind of personal hesitation was still left in me?

I was insatiably curious now.
Lewdly curious.
Thoroughly seduced!

"I appear to be filled with *Lust," I said to her. "The Lust of the Hero, the lust for new adventure—a Voraciousness to experience all of this, a *Lust even sexual in intensity. And the extreme recklessness that goes with it. Is that what you mean by a consenting subject?"

"It's all been part of the prep," she admitted.

"The subject has to be highly motivated, to offset the neural lag—the psychic G-force you will feel."

"I feel the lust of the Soldier—the Astronaut," I confirmed. "But—" I added with some trepidation, "won't all this be addicting me?"

"Did it before?" she returned clinically.

"No."

I had to admit that despite the radical approach she had pursued in all her previous treatments she had not really altered me, only shown me my own image from more than one perspective.

I felt emancipated, freed of cultural stereotypes, of limitations on [**My Being**]. And now I was more eager than ever to rebel against the tyranny of all past upbringing.

"No, you have shown me all that I truly am,"
I told her gratefully.

Satisfied, she left me for other tasks.

And now like clock-figures, her assistants began a pattern of closely-timed activity centered around the chair in which I sat still a little apprehensively, as one might sit awaiting a tooth to be pulled or any other painful but cosmetic fact.

A young male resident took my pulse, checked my eyes:

"You know that anesthesia's not possible. It's going to hurt a lot," he said in a peculiarly unmedical way. "Do you feel up to it?"

"I'm in good health," I said, like an athlete unafraid of ordeal.

But just to make certain, electrodes were put on my chest to monitor my heartbeat.

A brown-haired intern with flustered cheeks and sweating hands now asked me for my arm, to prepare me for intravenous infusion. He seemed very green, untrained. He missed my vein a few times causing me considerable discomfort—which, out of charity, I hid from him.

Finally Marianne came over and showed him how to do it.

It was as if she had waited on purpose, to observe the degree of my commitment.

> "I'm sorry if I injured you," the young man apologized.
> "You didn't injure me," I returned strongly, fixing him with my eyes. My glance burned through him and I sensed that he already knew me well—had come to care for me.   Had he been watching through the walls?

Now Marianne spoke to me:
"Which was it, Monkey? Dullness or indifference?"

> "Indifference," I answered strongly.

My reply confirmed her own assessment.

She had indeed succeeded in raising me to the sublime state of the *Hero—the state in which she herself resided, where physical pain was insignificant, superseded by Human Vision, moral entelechy.

"Your prognosis is excellent," she paused to reassure me, then again abandoned me for other tasks.

Now my chair was flattened into a table and an oriental girl took over for the brown-haired youth, commencing what seemed like a form of acupuncture. Each needle was tipped by an electrode, from which nutrients would be dispensed subcutaneously in a timing pattern that had to be precise and staggered.
At my back, another technician was pasting a large rubber grid infused with anodes that would vibrate patterns into my brain. Two other youths connected anodes and diodes to my cranium where they stuck, pinching and protruding between my hairs like curlers, as the table was folded back into a dental chair.

What a strange sort of porcupine I was!
Not a Mystic pricked by barbs and thorns, nor a Frankenstein wired for resurrection—more like [New@Formed@Aphrodite], a Sea-Urchin undergoing Change.
And now, while I was still being prepped, an intravenous infusion had already begun and I felt nutrients encouraging my feeling of strength and well being - not drugs, but megavitamins against which I had no somatic resistance—specific proteins increasing my brain and body function—even while Another Substance [Stealthy and Venomous] was quickly rendering me Immobile.
Fixed-sight quickly faded from my eyes, but laser-light took over, pulsing directly on my optic nerve. I felt a new, oxygen-rich atmosphere forced into my lungs. Then my hearing was replaced by earphones pinpointing sound to specific sections of my auditory cortex.

Now there was no escape, no screaming, no pleading possible. *Being, *Selfhood, *Autonomy had been entirely taken from me.

**I have consented freely, I told
myself, screaming inside me.**

I intellectualized.

How glad I was to have studied physiology, so that I could fully understand and appreciate the miraculous process taking place: this was indeed an Interface,

     *[Man-cloning-and-redefining-Man]!

... And how important my consent was to the process—for without it, it would have felt like, would have been like, Rape.

Instead, having consented (allbeit not quite freely) I was now Convert and Full Accomplice in the act, a willing Blood-Offering plucked and primed for Savage Intercourse.

The Program began as a flogging of some kind - mortifyingly sexual.

First, a drop of the drug that brought on seizure set to and fro upon my brain like a nightstick bruising synapses indiscriminately.

Then came a pause, time for my own body now hyped with neural nutrients to heal each Bruise into a New Connection which, when achieved, was coupled with the pleasure of Supreme Accomplishment:

  ***Power, *Insight and Well*Being!**

So that what had at first had appeared *Oppressive became transformed into the *Erotic, took on the character of a [**Thunderbolt from Zeus**], wrecking the *Old, reshaping the *New,

  impregnating [**Raw Matter**] into [**Larger*Form**]

I felt new patterns, new Order imposed upon me - an embryonic Order based upon a cosmic process of

281

punishment-reward that permeates the whole vast fabric of biochemical adjustment to the world - coloring our most complex acts of learning with the lust of infancy and the servitude imposed upon it:

first, by the Parent's **No**,

then by the Teacher's Rod,

and finally by Society's **Law**

(and private Conscience)

each stage fed by the *Lust of a complex Hunger imposed upon Sarah's [Matter] to Reshape itself ..

A painful process, yes. Excruciatingly painful.
Yet it was not a pain that ached me: it was the pain of Conception, of Gestation, of Birth.

The pain of [*Becoming/*Becoming]

Finally my body was returned to me, the syringes were pulled from my veins, the needles removed, the earphones, the lasers, the many pricking anodes. The stinging sweat upon my skin was swabbed by antiseptic lotions and a female attendant helped me rise and guided me to an adjoining lavatory where I was given a cold shower and gently towel-dried.

The attendant then gave me a gymsuit to wear and I got into it clumsily, stumbling about, unable to keep my balance, feeling drained in every muscle and still pricked by a hundred needles that scarcely had left a mark on me.

I ached to rest, but sleep was impossible—some kind of drug was blocking it.

Now I was led to a gymnasium, where a female instructor laid me on the floor and began to work on my legs and arms as though I were an infant first learning to flex them. And with each new twist and pull, something clicked inside my head - a strobe image, a neural link - some new engram on my brain.

I began to cooperate quite readily, for each click brought a sense of somatic relief, a feeling of new freedom from some binding force inside me and it soon became sheer pleasure to move my body to and fro in ever-increasing physical complexity.

Now I was standing and learning self-defense from her in slow, ballet-like poses that brought me to the
threshold of Olympic virtuosity - for my body seemed to know each new position as though from years of prior training.

And now we tumbled and rough-housed, and she began to box my ears, becoming nasty, abusive in language - making fun of me, tripping me, kicking me, in every way attempting to provoke me.

But I was too much like a puppet to retaliate.

In time, she gave up on me and sent me back to the showers. And again the sweat was washed from me and I was given back my own dress to wear - cleanly pressed.

And when I was ready, the young man with the flustered face returned and took me through the lab, stopping to indicate to me in a pointed way that a thorough record had been made of the entire treatment I had received—on a graphic readout was the imprint of my EEG—all the marks that had been written on my brain—a graphic picture of
the **Rod**, the **Message**, the **Reward**.

He seemed to be trying to tell me something—showing me how I might retrieve all this at some future time—perhaps through legal means.

Then he led me back to the arena, where I found Marianne - asleep—stretched out on a slab, and suddenly all the rage the gym instructor had tried vainly to evoke in me finally found its proper target.

I shook her awake.
"Damn you! What have you done to me," I demanded furiously.

I had caught her off-guard.

With half-opened eyes, instinctively she sprang at me, battle-ready—whirled and threw me, pressed her knee to my chest.

But she stopped herself in time, fully conscious.

"Damn you," I said, still raging.

Now she laughed and easily turned me over, caught my wrists and, apparently ready for such sudden outbursts, quickly handcuffed me. "Don't fight me, Sarah," she whispered, blew sensuously in my ear.

Still I raged, unwilling to accept her rule.

Yet softly, seductively still she whispered, still reminded:

The words undid me, struck some unknown key.

"That's a good monkey," she said, standing, pulling me up with her. And then she guided me, still handcuffed, out of the arena.

We went down the corridor—I, holding back, unwilling to be led this way—as someone under arrest.

"Come on," she urged. "No one will see you. I have to be sure you're not prone to seizures—come, it won't be long now. We're going back upstairs."

She hugged me fondly, reassuringly, in apology.

I stopped resisting her, allowed myself to be led like some kind of stray pet she had collared and was taking home.

The maze of corridors seemed endless, but I knew that we had finally reached a different elevator than the one we had taken before—for this one faced a |Blue Door| on the opposite wall—a door specially meaningful to me.

She paused to make certain that I would take note of that door—opened it for me with a press of her palm to reveal an austere, cell-like room. She turned my head toward it, made certain I would look at it.

I scanned it blankly.
It was strangely familiar. In some mystical and magic way, the blank walls were alive, filled with |Angel*Voices| beckoning me.

I ached to enter.
But she would not let me tarry there.
She pulled me into the elevator, my hands still bound.

She was breathing heavily behind me, still yawning with interrupted sleep, leaning heavily on me, the perfume of her clothes now drenched with the odor of her bone-weary frame— not an unpleasant odor—musky, of the forest.
An odor Mother*Close to me.
And Mother*Close she pressed to me like a tired She-Bear and I thought how nice it would be for both of us to collapse on some bed or couch together and sleep in each other's arms for a week.

"Please," I begged her. "Can't we call it a night?"
"Patience, Monkey," she said again. "It won't be
long now."

The elevator took us very far up—up fast enough and far enough for my eardrums to tell me in advance that this was not the same building as before. It had to be some high-riser close by—perhaps the one on Corporation Square.
Our arrival at a private penthouse confirmed my expectations—most likely, one of the suites at Corporation Tower reserved for visiting dignitaries—for the faceless multinational, multicultural `Old Men' whose clandestine big-money exchanges determined the flow of mergers and acquisitions that each year shattered, restructured, redefined our provincial `Corporate Image'.

"This can't be your apartment," I remarked, bedazzled
by the luxury surrounding me.

"I have the use of it," she said. "But tomorrow,
it can be yours," she promised. "Come and admire it."

She pulled me about from room to room, my hands still
bound. First, she showed me the kitchen with its modern
appliances; then, the crystal dining room, and then the bathroom,
with its oval tub and golden fixtures; finally, the master-
bedroom - a welcome pleasure-dome in Baroque style, filled
with ornate mirrors, hanging cherubs.
Corpulent bureaus, chairs, squatted like wood-nymphs
around a canopied bridal bed with embroidered coverlets—
She went about, opening closets, showing every drawer, then
drawing satin curtains to reveal a wall of glass—and beyond it—
a long terrace.
And out there, some hundred stories high, was a Caesar's
view of the **City**, the **Harbor**, the **Midnight Winter Sky.**

"Is this to be some kind of a Hero's bribe," I asked her softly,
feeling violated by all I saw.

"Of a kind," she admitted.

I sat at the edge of the bed, loathing my bonds.
"What do you gut-feel now," she asked me tautly.
"Fucked-up-the-ass," I said.
It was all becoming clear to me: the *Monster she had
created was nothing more than *Man-Sarah castrated back to
`normalcy', back to [Slave-Sarah] shackled in Male-defined
"Femininity".
Like any well-meaning parent she had broken my natural
form into something inferior to what it might Be! Had
reconditioned her monkey into a household pet fit only for
Dependency—fit only for concrete survival in a world that
would not look favorably upon [Man-Sarah] as a marketable
commodity.
"You have sold me back into slavery," I accused.
"Please understand," she stated. "Were it not for my need to
recover Skeets, none of this would have been offered you. And
you would never have known what a magnificent thing it is to be
[Whole]."

"I agreed to become your soldier, not your whore!"

"What difference does it make," she flashed at me.
"One Beast - Two Backs!"

Such wrath was in her face - the wrath of someone often raped, who now repaid in kind.

"You miserable pawn of Personnel," I now returned more soberly. "What makes you think I would *ever* consent to become your harlot!"

She softened, became motherly.

Gracefully she sat next to me, brushed the hair from my face, spoke fondly: "My creation is not yet finished."

Still I resisted: "Where is the *Hero—the [Vengeance] that you promised me!"

Again she smiled, now as Fairy Godmother knowing what was best for me: "The Hero sits as Hostage inside the Room with the Blue Door. As for your [Vengeance] - come, it's time for both of us to share my vision of *Eternity."

She stood and pulled me up with her, pushed me outside onto the terrace. There she held me—held me warmly in the chill of winter—at the very edge of the balcony:

"Look at your [Vengeance], Sarah," she warned.
"It waits for you down there."

"You can't be serious," I said,
refusing to look down.

"I made you a promise," she returned wantonly.
"So help me, if I've botched this job on you,
then it's going to have to be over the top for you.
Now! Momentarily. Without further ritual, warning or ado."

Even as she spoke, she was undoing the back of my dress as a *Hangman preparing me—pulling down the zipper, exposing my skin to the crisp night air—skin recently pierced by hair-thin quills, anodes, diodes, in her infernal beauty-chair.

"Look at your death, Sarah," she now stated blankly, again in taut control. "This well may be your final sight."

Passionately she made me look at it, gave me precious pause to hail the Midnight Sky, to taste the Crystal Air ....

I believed her this time. This was no sham or empty threat but a bitter statement of brute fact:—should any part of her experiment have gone awry, should any irreversible *Monster now emerge—then [That-Sarah] would not be allowed to languish like Skeets. [That-Sarah] would be destroyed— quickly, cleanly, without further notice.

"Do what you must," I told her. "I would do the same for you. But know that you have made me [Whole] - [Whole] enough to love even my Assassin."

Her embrace steadied me.
"Love me then, Sarah," she now again repeated.
"Love me even if I rip you to pieces."

Now it was {God*Face} speaking,
The [Godcriminal God of Childhood]:
    paradoxical, amoral,
        capricious and exacting,
            perversely yet demanding to be
                [Beloved] even as He Flays

"I do, I will, through [All*Eternity]," I vowed.

But now her mood lightened, became playful.
"Try not to scream," she whispered intimately.
Then—still as a Fairy Godmother witchlike riding me—

strongly she pressed me to the railing, her cheek to my ear, while with one hand readied to gag the *Monster's scream, with her other hand - a Wizard's hand - she now began to trace a **Devil's*Mark** on me—some kind of access code— a somatic key that began to unlock a **Hologram**—a new chromosome engraved inside of me.

I felt [**New*Form**] unfurling.

Gasping, I found myself sucked inside my own body, becoming the very *[Double-Helix] of Primordial Space —now a Polymer of Molecular Being bursting into Solar Systems, congealing into Glaciers, melting into Tidal Waves and Boiling Craters, festering into Life-Puddles where my many cells were formed, colonizing into algae—sea creatures Birthing in a zillion cycles of preconscious change—

Finally—as Flying Lizard—I circled the earth with giant wings watching prehistory unfold, then—on Eagle Shoulders I viewed history—

[Watched] the Four Horsemen take their toll

[Heard] the Cries of slaves

[Knew] the Rage of infants

[Felt] the [Wrath of Angels]...

"Don't scream," again she cautioned, now as a Lover loosening her grip on me.

I caught my breath, no longer fearful but thoroughly seduced (and not in the least bit fooled!) by the academic engram she had crammed into me—no more than a pictorial and condensed review of standard coursework at any university.

"Why so much fanfare," I said to her quite soberly. "Don't you think I know the difference between [Revelation] and multimedia education?"

"I'm not finished yet," she returned, heartened by my tone. "This next part of the Program should prove even more entertaining; I told you I like to get my jollies playing God— now see what Man-god can accomplish. I have titled the next sequence: `The Olympian Rape of Sarah.' May I?"

"By all means," I said, no longer resisting.
Surely the danger was over and now she was playing with me
and at last allowing herself to take joy in it,
at last showing an aspect of her real self to me.

"Will this finally be the carnal knowledge that you promised?"
"Of an [Angel]? Hardly! Of the [Whirlwind]? Yes!"

Again she pressed close to me, her hand over my mouth.
"Please try not to make too much noise," she urged.
Then with her hand—her infernally sensuous hand—again she began to write on me.

Now I felt myself to be [Venus] fully-formed
the [Venus of the Scallop],
the [Venus of the Porcupine]

muscle and sinew breaking out from Pupa
into [Spread-Winged Butterfly]
breaking out into a Womanhood
so [Perfect], so [Divine] it dared call itself

[Adam—First-Born and First-Created]
felt a neurochemical metamorphosis that with each new cell-division brought climax-after-climax until the Program stopped - on HOLD - leaving me suspended, waiting to receive a final word:

. . .@.@.@.@.@.@{THE SEED}.

"May all the gods forgive me, Sarah," now she whispered, finishing the message—

And—@.@.@.@.@.@{THE SEED} was [Cain] [Cain] spewing forth in a violent turbulence of change - in a gut-feeling, a gut-knowing of a time soon to come when, on this terrace I would . . .
. . .@.@.@.@.@.@{KILL}. . .
@.@.@.@.@.@{KILL}. . . All who would enslave Me!

Now we stood, suspended, waiting for my mind to clear - her hand, still over my mouth - her cheek, still pressed to my ear, and I could feel from the tightness of her grip on me, from the tautness in her frame, that if I were now in the least imperfect, uncontrollable, if she had made me an irreversible monster,

then **YES**, she would fling me to The Stars!

At last she let me speak.

"You magnificent lunatic," I gasped, bewildered. "That kind of rape is welcome to me!
. . . .@.@.@.@.@.@{CAIN} is everything you promised!"

Relieved, she pulled me off the edge of the balcony and finally unlocked the manacles that had kept me subject to {Her Will} And from the look of caution in her eyes, I realized that it was *She whose life was threatened now—for I was no longer puny.

I turned to face her in the **Crystal Night**, both of us red and numb with cold.

"I *am* dangerous to you now," I said, feeling my strength and skill now fully formed. "We could, if one of us chooses, fight to the death on this terrace."

"Yes, we could," she admitted blankly.
Grimly she waited for me to decide, the winter windchill
ripping her face and hands.

"Let's go back inside before we both freeze to death," I said.

We walked from the {Terrace) into the warmth of [**My Bedroom**] Yes, for tonight at least, [**My Bedroom**]. And for tonight at least, all the clothes in her closet were also [**Mine**] and I ached to take off my dress and get into something more comfortable.

"May I," I asked her.

"Help yourself," she said.

I did so, selecting a dressing gown of gauze and satin befitting my new form. Couldn't I at least permit myself a small measure of self-indulgence on this, my {**Eve of Battle**}?

Would I indeed perish tomorrow on the terrace?
And who was this 'Old Man' targeted for eradication —friend or foe? How could I be sure of her allegiances? Despite everything we had shared together, I still knew nothing, *nothing* about her!

I turned to look for her: she was thawing herself out, seated on a footstool. Grandly I threw her a dressing gown, but she refused it. "Your clothes smell, you've slept in them once too often," I urged.

"My job is not over," she stated.

"You're right," I countered. "You haven't paid me yet. Nothing here is of sufficient worth."

"What more do you want," she asked wearily.

"What every common soldier wants," I returned harshly. "A night with a temple priestess—

with {**The Compleat Whore of Babel**}."

293

"What, more of the same?" she sighed. "Can't you spare any time for your soul?"

"My soul went on a Skywalk and left me to do housework," I returned. "You have done something to me—infused me with some kind of lewdness, the callousness of male youth ready for combat. This is nothing I would ever have had the bad taste to request of you before—but now I demand you humor me. If you would have me be your harlot, then teach me by example."

I faced her, adamant.

How bone-weary she now seemed.

"Very well," she humored me. With a look distasteful yet resigned to the keeping of a promise, she sat on the bed and waited for me.

Haughtily I fell on the satin sheets, squinting up at golden cherubs, their arrows poised to slay me. How perfect it would be to die right here—to die upon a kiss from {*Lucifer}.

But her lips were cold and her voice was without feeling. "Tell me what it is you want," she said.

"I want carnal knowledge—of [**Marianne**]," I challenged. "Let's see how well you can manage that one, with all your {Creativity}. Show me your real face this time."

"I have none," she answered blankly. "Long ago I exchanged it—for Caesar's."

"Then show me Caesar's face and I will show you [**Yours**]," I insisted.

Cunningly, she put her hand on me.

"Shut your eyes," she whispered, "and I'll make you feel Caesar's power."

Gullibly, cupidly, I did as I was told.

Gently she bared my thighs through the long folds of my dressing gown, caressed them knowingly.

"Are you lusting," she asked softly, but not with love.

"Burning with curiosity," I returned.

(I dared open one eye again to watch her.
 She had a look of ice, an intellectual smile.)

Slowly, deliberately, with {Cobra Eyes} coldly fixed on me, she had begun to remove all the gold jewelry that she wore - the earrings, the chains around her neck, all the rings and bracelets.

Meticulously she was now divesting herself of everything that belonged to [Caesar].

"Are you still lusting," she repeated frigidly.
Closing my eyes again, I shook my head in assent.
Now she parted my legs all too clinically, as if about to dissect a frog:

**"That's a cute little kunt," she said.
"Let's see how much it can hold!"**

Then wildly and with the unfettered rage of nuns—
she stuffed me—stuffed me like the {Golden Calf},
    Stuffed me, Ransomed me

                      —with all of [Caesar's Gold]

I opened my eyes and watched her.
Nothing she did could now surprise me!
Even her rage was pleasurable!

It was a feeling most cathartic—being crammed with the full weight and bulk of Caesar—here, in His gilded bedroom—His royal suite wherein He waved {His*Scepter} over [**My Being**] —over everything that had been stolen from me—-

[My Life]

[My Home]

[My Country]

[My Oasis]!

Strongly, I stopped her hand and drew her up to me.
"My flesh has been sufficiently humbled," I told her. "Now give me back my [Soul]."

"I can't," she anguished.
She stood, and for a moment it seemed to me that her face was really there: "I am not a pawn of Personnel, Sarah," she now confessed. "I am one of the 'Old Men'. I [Am] Caesar.
I [Am] the Enemy!"

"You?"

I could not believe her! But it was true, she had been born into immense wealth. Had she then only been playing with me—- taking an evening's diversion at my expense?

"Then why use me for anything at all," I flashed. "With all your power you could easily have ransomed Skeets!"

"You don't understand the perverse games we play—the trading, the division of function. I have even less power than you —-you, with your demand for a hearing."

"Will you give me one," I countered.

"No."

She looked away,
looked at the City, the Harbor, the Midnight Sky.
"It would not be a fair hearing. It would do
more harm than good. We would rather wait
—wait until [Your Silence] becomes [Terrible]."

"Then you plan to murder me," I stated.

"We are at war," she said.

                   Now she turned and faced me. "Love me, Sarah.
                   Love me fiercely, even if I rip you to pieces!"

"You do enjoy playing God," I replied, unmoved. "But
enough is enough! I'll not further indulge your lunacy. There are
still laws, governments - "
                   She laughed and cried, weary of my prattle.
                   "A Disembodied Law moves no one!"

Her eyes spoke loudly now, spoke to Me as a [Caesar]
speaks, spoke to Me loudly without bothering to speak:

"We'll buy every judge and every politician.
And those we can't bribe, we'll neutralize.
We'll give you a merry ride through the System until you
drop, old and broken and lost in the files.

Wake up, Sarah - you no longer have a [Country], you
no longer have [Your Laws]
                   - there is only [My Law], only [Caesar's Rule]."

She was right, and I knew it.
Still I resisted |Her Gospel|—rejected the brute fact of a
world in which [Heinous Acts] are praised and [Kindness]
punished, while [Justice] plays [The Fool].
"If I live through this I will expose you," I countered feebly.
"I will prove you wrong."

She relished in my anger, as one impatient to be tried.
And now for the first time I saw the *Lust in her, the
Hidden*Lust in [Marianne]:

                   "Come against [Me], Sarah," she defied.
"[I] am the [Crack-in-the-Wall] —

Come against [Me] - as [The Whirlwind]"

I stood to go to her,
but swiftly her hand blocked my face:

 "Our session is over," she pronounced regally. Then,
with fingers that knew just how to rule me, gently she
pressed the veins on my temples and—

Part 1010:The Stone

Had I blacked out on my way to work?

My head was pounding and my sight was blurred.

I found myself slumped on a bench in Corporation Square without the slightest clue as to how I had gotten there.

But what a marvelous dream I had last night, a dream with all the feel of [Matter].

A dream of Freedom,
     of all that could be [Sarah]:

I dreamed my mother came to me with the face of Marianne, and raised me as I should be raised

                    {and then again destroyed me!}.

Was it Sarah's {Dying Dream}
or—was it only {My Own Mind} Healing me?

It must have been a dream. My mind was playing tricks on me. I must have wandered thoughtlessly, my skin numb to the cold, and the afternoon sun had revived me.

**{There was a band around my brain,
          some kind of psychic shackle.}**

I inspected myself: my clothes were not fresh, my bra was undone, my hair was uncombed.

I felt messy, scattered.

Was I getting a virus? Ought I to call in sick - or - was it already too late for that? With difficulty I focused on the digital clock of the Administration Building.

It said: 1:45.

Where had the morning gone!
Wasn't I due to report at Nine ?

     —or, was it at Two P.M., directly to the 'Old Man'?

(No, Nine A.M., to the Secretarial Pool - I could swear that's what Eric had said. But of course, I had no intention of going anywhere today except to the Cafeteria, there to demand my Hearing.)

[But Marianne had distinctly said Two P.M.,

With the 'Old Man'.]

{The band was twisting and turning inside me, like
a bridle pulling me toward Corporate Tower.}

No—I decided—No *Overlord will ride me!
Flay if you please, *Marianne, *Yours is not the
pain that aches me—for yet another Sarah [**Hangs**] --
[**Hangs Screaming in Gethsemane**] ....

But .... where was the Cafeteria?
And ought I to walk in there looking like Skeets?

I turned toward the Administration Building to find the washroom. But - I was ashamed - even to - walk - past the - receptionist - this way.
In a corner of - the building - behind a bush - I shifted my clothes - quickly ran a comb through my hair. Then, confidently I turned and braved the glassed entrance to——

Part 1010: .@.@.@The Stone

Part 1010: .@.@.@The Stone

Had I blacked out on my way to work?
My head was pounding and my sight was blurred.

I found myself slumped on a bench in Corporation Square without the slightest clue as to how I had gotten there. But what a marvelous dream I had last night, a dream with all the feel of Matter! A dream of Freedom, of all that could be Sarah!

(It must have been a dream. My mind was playing tricks on me. I must have wandered thoughtlessly, my skin numb to the cold. And the afternoon sun had revived me. But now there was a band around my brain, some kind of psychic shackle.)

I inspected myself.
My clothes were not fresh, my bra was undone, my hair was uncombed. I felt messy, scattered.
I must be getting a virus. Ought I to call in sick, or - wasn't it already too late for that? With difficulty I focused on the digital clock of the Administration Building. It said 1:45.
Where had the morning gone? Wasn't I due to report at Nine - or, was it at Two P.M., to the 'Old Man'? No, Nine A.M., to the Secretarial Pool - I could swear that's what Eric had said! (But of course, I had no intention of going anywhere today except to the Cafeteria.)
But Marianne had said Two P.M., to the 'Old Man'.
(The {Band} was twisting and turning inside me, like a bridle pulling me toward Corporate Tower.)

[It must have been Two P.M.,
with the 'Old Man'.]

But how could I be interviewed, looking like this!

I turned toward the Administration Building to find the washroom. But I was ashamed even to walk past the receptionist this way. In a corner of the building, behind a bush, I shifted my clothes, quickly ran a comb through my hair.

[But no, that was wrong - didn't I have a suite
reserved for me at Corporate Tower?]

I looked up—up to the hundredth floor set just below the heliport—a busy heliport to which dignitaries shuttled daily from the airport—shuttled anonymously, arriving from primitive outbacks, pockets of tyranny, slave-states filled with political unrest, terrorism, counter-terrorism ...

{What a strange dream I had last night!
A dream with all the feel of [Matter].
I dreamed [My*Mother] came to me with the face of *Marianne and raised me as I should be raised, and then again destroyed me!}

Was it a dream? I was loathe to call it a dream. Might it have been real? I could, should, easily test its reality.

@.@.@. {And now the bridle slackened.}

I turned from the Administration Building and walked across Corporation Square again,

walked toward Corporate Tower.

I entered the glass doors as one who belonged there.

The Ground-Floor Receptionist looked at me somewhat condescendingly, as though I might be a lost tourist asking directions. She was a Brahmin of exquisite form, dressed elegantly in the clothes of her own nation, seeming more like a diplomatic attaché than an employee.

She made me feel most awkward dressed so shabbily in my linted coat.

"Yes, may I help you," she asked with perfect-spoken coached cordiality.

"My name is Sarah Miller," I said somewhat vaguely. "Do I have an appointment here with someone?"

Humoring me, she looked down at a list of names; but then her face changed: "Oh yes, Ms. Miller," she smiled respectfully. "Brigadier Waters has given you clearance. Commander Walker is expecting you." With the grace of a ballet dancer, she pointed toward the elevator.

@.@.@{Her*Words} struck me like a shaft of sunlight. And now I began to tremble, to sweat inside my clothes even as the {Band} twisted once again, blocking my thought.

It had not been a dream!
Or else, I was still dreaming.

Walker. Hadn't there been a 'Mrs. Walker' who had spoken to me at the Settlement House?

@.@.@{Walker} was written inside me.

Ought I to flee?
What if I turned and simply left the building?

Would @.@.@{Someone} come for me?

My feet were glued to the floor and I knew I must be appearing very strange to everyone.

"Is something wrong, Ms. Miller," the Receptionist asked, concerned.

"No," I managed to say. "I've just been up all night - working. I suppose I look a mess ... I'm sorry."

"The elevator on the left," she said sympathetically. "Put your hand on this screen."

"I know," I said, pressing my palm to it, feeling the laser light course through me - course through me
as [Adam*Reviving].

Ought I to resist this programming?

The [Band] wrenched at me.
*Vengeance, @.@.@.{CAIN}, *She had promised me.

[This was The*Only*Portal.]

I stepped into the elevator and let it take me where I knew it would. It brought me to the Hundredth Floor - only now I knew it would be @ Caesar expecting me, standing by the glass walls to the terrace, his hands folded behind him like a conquering potentate, his uniformed frame outlined by the crisp blue sky, the winter gray of the City.

"Ah, Ms. Miller," Walker turned, turned most cordially, as one about to greet his future queen.

(Where had I heard his voice before?)

His manner was most familiar: he was not a very old man - perhaps still only in his fifties, an aging Eric more well-bred, well-traveled, multinational. With a fire in his eyes, the look of a good horseman.

Respectful to me, most respectful in a condescending way, as a foreign-educated gentleman addressing a lady of station, he galloped toward the center of the room almost bowing, clicking his heels.

"Please, please be seated!" he said most gallantly, offering me a large luxurious chair. "How long I have looked forward to this moment!"

He gave me a meaningful stare.

{Why did his tone enrage me?}

"Thank you," I said, sitting meekly where he gestured, still trying to place him—to remember when and where all this had happened before.

He seemed to know me very well.
Had we ever met? I could not recall!
He appeared very disappointed that I did not immediately recognize him.

He paced nervously about the room, giving me time to acquaint myself with my new surroundings - his hands still stuck behind him as though they were lost without a crop or walking stick.

There was something - so - thoroughly @.@.@.Centaur about his walk, even to the way his shoes clumped on the carpet.

Were they elevetated shoes?

Was he a much shorter man?

He finally stopped strutting and faced me.
He had a coy look on him, like a little boy playing guessing games. He was still trying very hard to get me to recognize him.
Was he a fan of mine? He did seem starved for sleep.
Had my surveillance left its mark on him?
Had he caught all my escapades on film perhaps?
Was I now for him a movie star? Had he peered at all my rushes for so long he now thought he knew me intimately?

My eyes were still blurred.

There seemed to be a {Jungle} surrounding him,
a {Lush*Garden} filled with tropical vines and
evergreens hiding {Monkey*Eyes} -

{Eyes@of@Beasts@of@Every@Kind}

He too sensed Their@Eyes: He seemed now more like
an old bleating Billygoat than a Centaur,
            a {Billygoat stalked by a @.@.@Tiger}.

[No, not exactly a @.@.@Tiger -
by a {She@.@.@.Bear} riding a @.@.@Tiger].

But might He be a *Judas-Goat, I wondered.
Did He also see the {@.@.@.Grizzly} on my back, or
were there still *Lambskins hiding Her?

My head throbbed against the *Band that choked my thought,
throbbed trying to remember from where and when I knew
him—even while the *Cow—Marianne's Golden*Calf in
{*Me*}—was growing lewdly aware of him.

As a Lamb I sat, docile, awaiting his command.
{And as a Tiger, stalking.}

Ms. Miller," he finally brought himself to say,
"I pulled you out of Programming because I wanted
someone right here - " he patted the back of my chair, "someone
I could trust implicitly."
He paused, expectant.
He seemed to be holding back a great deal of feeling—
seemed to be in a romantic stupor, now again like an old horse at
pasture, eyeing me.

I did feel sorry for him—although I was not in the least

inclined to give him what he wanted; there was too much of the
Centaur about him.

"You do have adequate office skills," he now blurted
nervously.

"I have been well trained," I answered, now feeling
the She*Bear {@.@.@CLAW} me.

I gave him an innocent stare: "Please feel you can trust me,
implicitly!"

"Oh yes, quite!" he beamed, most satisfied, now glancing
sidewise at my fine figure.

(Was he truly addressing a Lioness—or were the Lamb, the
Cow, the Mare, the only things he saw?)

I parried his eyes fearlessly.
Did he see the @.@.@Tiger?
No, only the Lamb, the Cow.

"Ms. Miller, I've taken a deep personal interest
in your - rehabilitation," he now said meaningfully. "What a
remarkable woman you are!"

"Thank you," I said, docile.

"Commander Walker?" I now tested carefully, feeling the
She@.@.@Bear riding me. "I understand I'm here for an
exchange?"

I waited for him to confirm the message engraved inside me.

"Yes, Ms. Miller, yes!" He stood, satisfied, expectant like
some prince who had wooed me by proxy, waited for me, paid
for me, and now at last possessed me. "Come here, Ms. Miller,"
he invited, going to the console on his desk. "Put your hand right
here, and the exchange will be complete."

He motioned to the input screen.

"You'll now be attaché to me."

I hesitated. Why did the thought offend me?

{It felt like a *Bond, a *Shackle.}

"Come, Ms. Miller, don't back down now," he urged nervously. "Come put your hand down next to mine - put it down, right here!"

"Oh, General," I held back pleasantly, still with the *Lambskins over me. "Will that mean I'll need your hand to get from place to place?"

"My hand? My whole arm, if you prefer it," he returned gallantly.

"But I'm not used to giving gentlemen my key."

"Well, you won't be needing it much now, will you?" he countered, winking.

"I suppose not," I said more soberly, now feeling the Tiger*Stand.

{So was the Band now stirring,
ike a Pet*Snake coiling round me.}

Meekly I did as I was told, and the computer processed me.

Quickly he punched a code into the console and confirmed it with his voice on the intercom: "Prisoner exchange completed."

And now like a @.@.@Fox he smiled.

(And now I felt the *Manacle.)

He chuckled like a little boy and kept himself from touching me: "Well, then, how does it feel finally to be under My*Command?"

"I wasn't aware I was to become 'Your Prisoner'," I said, still pulling the *Lambskins over me. "Or are these simply war games being played?"

"War games?" He was taken aback. "Oh no, Ms. Miller, not simply war games. We really are at war, you know."

"Then am I really your prisoner?"

Now he caught himself.
He was most embarrassed.

"Well no, Ms. Miller, no, not exactly. That is—" he qualified, "not 'literally'."

(In what way did he mean that?)

"Then I suppose I can still resign," I tested.

"Resign?" My question threatened him. "Why no, Ms. Miller, no. You've signed up for a tour of duty. Soldiers don't resign."

"I see."

(It was clear he did not see.)

"Do forgive me, General," I said pleasantly, returning to stand by the deep luxurious chair, still trying to place his voice, his face. "I really should have called in sick today. Had it not been for Skeets, I wouldn't have shown up at all!" I stood, loathe to sit down again. "Would you excuse me now - I have a dreadful headache. . ."

"Really, Ms. Miller," he said more firmly. "I'm a very busy man - don't keep me waiting."

"Keep you waiting? Exactly what for," I asked, *Docile.

"What for? What for?" the Old*Goat's composure slackened. "Don't you know what for? Hasn't it all been explained to you?"

"Has what been explained," I asked, now unveiling the *Lioness.

My regal manner disarmed him.

He was most confused now, respectful in spite of himself, and very afraid something had gone wrong. "Why, you've been bought and paid for, haven't you," he confirmed meekly, with blinking eyes.

His statement startled me.

(And now I felt the Brand, the Prod.)

"Did all that jewelry come from you?"

"Why, yes. Wasn't it enough?" He smiled, relieved. "For a moment there, I thought - "

I @stood, @testing him. "There must be some mistake. I'll see that it's returned."

"Don't you want it?" He seemed very hurt, rejected.

"I @suppose it's @owed to @me, as reparations and back pay," I said. "But I really can't be bothered pressing those claims."

I started toward the elevator.

"Ms. Miller," he called out to me, alarmed. "You can't just leave. I haven't dismissed you yet!"

He tried to smile congenially.

He seemed most awkward, insecure, still blinking at me with small gray eyes.

"Then by all means dismiss me," I directed…

"Ms. Miller!" he voiced more authoritatively, "I have no intention of dismissing you."

And now I felt the [@.@.@Tiger] Stand.

Which Caesar was my target, Julius or Caligula?
What if Caligula! How could I be sure?

At first he had seemed like such a nice, kind, gentle man - perhaps a little tired, overburdened, insecure - himself a trusty mount, an aging stallion so willing to be ridden, so anxious to abduct me to a new oasis where I might rule him gently while he might play at pasture - might there live out his years in pretense of enduring power.

But now he seemed volatile, roguish—seemed really to be an old goat going mad.

Was the 'Old Man' dying?

"Commander Walker, what exactly do you want with me," I now asked him forthrightly, muzzling the Tiger.

"Why, the usual," he hedged. "Why? Haven't you been instructed?"

"Oh yes," I answered, patting the @@@Cow.
"I have been well instructed!"

"Then what's the problem now," he blustered, still managing
a broken smile.

The openness of My*Stare made him twitch
uncomfortably.
Had he at last glimpsed the @.@.@{Beast} in me?
Did he know himself to be [*Our|Our*] Quarry?

Instinctively he clumped back toward the terrace
doors, finding himself reined tightly there;
                        behind him: the Blue Winter Sky, the City.

"And I really can't resign," I tested.
"Certainly not, Ms. Miller," he returned, now a wild look in
his eyes - the look of an aging predator.
"I see."
"I was certain you would - in time," he now echoed more
confidently.

"Commander, before we proceed," I said concretely,
sounding more like [Sarah]: "there is a small matter yet
unsettled. The matter of my Hearing."

"Oh yes, Miss Miller," he interrupted, now smiling at me
broadly, revealing his well-capped teeth. "We're going to wipe
that off your record. I'm certain you'll be pleased."

He blinked at me with beaded eyes,
convinced I would agree.

Now I knew him - by his teeth!
It was Hoffman after all - Hoffman sans toupee,
mustache, and bow tie - a more dashing, refurbished Hoffman,
but nevertheless Hoffman!

But - was it Hoffman as himself, or as Hoffman
changing? What if NOT{*Julius}?
Might there be TWO Tigers in this Garden?
What test might I perform?

Dr. Hoffman," I now addressed him strongly, "About the
other matter—the question of my 'counseling' - I wonder if you
wouldn't mind if I continue therapy under Dr. Waters. Her
approach is more suited to me."
"What? But you committed yourself wholly to me," he
blurted, now most distraught, most confused. "Surely you don't
prefer all that quackery!"
"Is it really quackery," I returned meekly, still with the
*Lambskin over me.
"Oh believe me, Miss Miller, it is - it *IS* quackery,"
he assured.

"But then - has Skeets really been exchanged," I again tested
carefully.
"Yes, of course. She's already downstairs," he affirmed.
"Wasn't the whole deal explained to you? You're to take therapy
with me."
"Yes, it was explained, but—"

He smiled, now most relieved, most certain of his right to me.

"Don't you really prefer me," he now said coyly, trying to be
both playmate and loving father.

"Actually," I replied, "relating to a
father image is very difficult for me. I
killed a dog once, savagely, when my
father took my mother from me. I trust
that   you   can   understand   how   -
@.@.@dangerous - it - @.@.@might be -
@.@.@for you to - @.@.@treat - me ... "

I stood, feeling a sense of urgency.
"Please, Dr. Hoffman, let me go downstairs. I would feel much better locked inside the room with the
blue door."

"Blue Door? What **Blue Door**?"
The thought appeared to intrigue him.

"Nothing, just some nonsense on my part," I said. "Please, Dr. Hoffman, let me go."
I again started toward the elevator.

"No, Miss Miller, no -"
"You @.@.@are in @.@.@danger, Sir," I warned.

"@Danger? I'm always in danger," he replied martially.
My words were no threat to him.
He was deaf, deaf to my meaning, filled only with lust, the lust of the soldier.
"You ought not to concern yourself, Sarah dear,"
he said fondly, paternally. "Come here!"

I tried now, vainly, to summon the elevator.
But the *Scanner was blind to me.

"Oh, Miss Miller - " he now cooed after me, *Caligula pushing *Julius from his face, "You can't just leave by yourself, you know .... I have the only key ...."

He raised his palm and waved it playfully like a cartoon character trying vainly to keep his face on.
Pitifully he blinked at me with button eyes.

[Did he yet see the @Tiger lurking? No, only the
*Lamb, the trapped and frightened *Lamb.]

"Miss Miller, I order you to come back here," he
tried again, most upset now. "This is not a game! I'm
your commanding officer. You cannot leave until I
choose to dismiss you!"

"If you value your life, please send for the elevator,"
I stated.

Now he heard me, but still only as a father hears a
child. "Really, Sarah, your threats don't impress me.
Come - " he insisted giddily, patting my chair, "I have
something for you ... "

{@.@.@What, I wondered - a new pair
of @.@.@handcuffs, perhaps?}

**All the signs were clear - here stood *Skeets
again - but now a Skeets with too much power!**

"Dr. Hoffman," I began softly, tears now welling in me. "I
don't want to hurt you. I mean you no harm. But - "

"Yes, Sarah dear," he responded giddily. "Don't be
afraid of me. Come here!"

"No," I resisted. "I beg you - please send for the elevator."

"No ..." he shook his head, still volatile, rogueish.

"Dr. Hoffman, I think you should know I am no longer inclined to play according to your rules," I now asserted. "If you don't send for the elevator, you shall have to answer to a {*Man}."
I waited.

"@@@A man?"
Suddenly his eyes turned fierce.
"@@@Which man!" he demanded, alarmed.

[Yes, now Caligula. All the signs were clear.]

"Permit me," I said regally, walking past him to slide open the glass wall to [My*Terrace]
"I think you should know that I am not alone."

"Come, look down there," I commanded.
I pointed to the *Park, the *Square.

Like a jealous Old*Centaur he now @@@clumped up beside me. "Where," he demanded, alarmed, fiercely scanning the Square for any sign of a Rival.

(He was so much like Skeets,
   peering, squinting, button-eyed.)

315

"Down there," I said softly, @Stealthily moving
behind him.

"Where?"

"Down in the @@@Garden - "

Quickly I bent down and flipped him over the railing. His
downward scream was comical, his form no more than a
cartoon.

He splashed on a roof fifty stories below like a man made of
rubber.

I felt numb.
Without guilt.
Mine had been an act in self-defense,
an act in defense of [Sarah].

I went back inside and waited
                    - waited for the elevator.

The elevator did not come.
I waited - five, ten minutes. Nothing happened.

I went out on the terrace and looked down.
Yes, there was an ambulance in the Square, police cars, a
small crowd. And on the roof below, medics, executives,
policemen, all waiting for the coroner.
"Hey, look up here," I shouted to them. "Up here
- the hundredth floor!"

No one seemed to want to pay attention.

Soon they will be up to question me, I told myself - I'll be charged, then tried. And at last I will get my Hearing!

But an hour went by and still nothing!
I looked outside again.
The mess had been cleaned up, the crowd dispersed, a chalk mark left on the rooftop - nothing more!
Didn't anyone want my confession? Had they all been sent to the wrong floor?
I shrugged. Another cover up. So be it.
Let them all |**Know*My*Silence**|.

I dared to take a shower, put on fresh clothes, make myself a late breakfast. Later, I watched the evening news curious about the story they would give.
When it came on, it was the usual suicide account, followed by a brief biography of the great man who had seemed to me to be nothing but a quack. And of course there was Marianne - multipli-interviewed, tearful Marianne, bereaved colleague, bureaucratic heir-apparent.

How much longer would she force me to wait up here, I wondered. I was bored to death by myself up here. I longed to leave, to try the room with the blue door.

I never saw her again, nor did I ever hear from Skeets. The elevator finally came for me and I took it like a good monkey anxious to return to the only cage that challenged me.

Nor do I know how many years I waited inside
The Room with the Blue Door ....

At first my sojourn in Purgatory was sheer pleasure for me, and while I studied and explored the whole of Known Creation, I also bore four babies artificially - three girls and a boy with the surname Hoffman.

And while {@Eye@} as the {Queen Bee} labored,
[*My Corporate Soul*] continued on its Skywalk.

But then there came a [Changing of the Guard] and suddenly the Room with the Blue Door became a tomb. And I waited, starved, thirsty, for the sound of a [Human*Voice] to break the dreaded Silence.

I had a dream as I lay in the darkness.

I dreamed that [All This Was A Dream].

I dreamed that I fell asleep after Eric left me and slept through to the next morning. I dreamed that I went to the Corporation for my appointment with the Old Man, but stopped first in the Cafeteria as I had planned.
I dreamed that I tried to tell everyone about what had been done to me and Skeets.
I dreamed that they took me to Downtown Hospital to the same ward where they had taken Skeets; I dreamed I was put in a straitjacket and given a neuroleptic; I dreamed that Marianne came and prescribed an overdose of shock and sugars to starve my brain; I dreamed my father died of a cold and a broken heart and that my sister was persuaded to cut me adrift.
I dreamed that I was made gutless and months later was turned out into the streets.
I dreamed that winter came again and I slept on sidewalks where my hands and face and feet got frostbite.

I dreamed that no one recognized me.
I dreamed that everyone despised me.
It was only a dream.
[Another's Truth], not *Mine.

I was glad to open my eyes to the *Darkness, to feel the *Cold that was not really [Coldness], to find myself still Here - Here where [My*Person] is [Not*Violated].

(For Here I sit in Heaven, and it is not a Place
  but an Achievement of a distinctly Human kind,

  and I am bathed in the warmth of a [*Yes*].)

As I lay on the floor dying of Hunger, of Thirst, the door to My Dungeon finally opened and paramedics came to revive me.
  They filled me full of transfusions while an Orderly crouched over me, his manner most familiar.
  He pulled up my head by the hair and peered at me:

"Who are you, Monkey," like an oaf he questioned me. "Can you tell us how long you've been here - who put you here? Are you conscious? Will you talk?"

"I remember nothing," I lied, then fainted.

Next I awoke to find myself in a hospital ward, my face all bandaged ...

"Ah, Ms. Miller," a brown-haired Resident addressed me, his manner most familiar: "You've finally come back to us!"

"What happened," I asked, trying to place him.
He read from my chart: "You suffered a stroke and were struck by a car," he reported. "But not to worry - your former employers have taken care of everything - even the nursing home you'll be sent to."
"Nursing home?"
"Yes," he replied condescendingly, "You are getting on in years, you know. How long has it been since you retired?"
"Retired from where," I demanded.
"Why, from the Secretarial Pool," he reported. "Don't you remember?"

"No!" I denied.
But he laughed and patted my hand fondly.

    I grabbed his sleeve.
    "No, please, not this dream," I begged him.
    "This dream is [The Dream of My Silence] -
    and it is {TERRIBLE},

                too @@@Terrible!"

"You aren't dreaming," laughingly he assured me. "Here, take my hand."
He grabbed my hand and squeezed it—squeezed it with all the feel of [Matter] ...

    ... And I began to scream,
        to screech like a monkey
             in Marianne's Garden.

Part 1011:The Return
Part 1011:The Return
Part 1011:The Return

The sun of summer was shining.

The sun of summer was burning my face, and I awoke to a pounding headache. The air was garbage-filled and greasy. I awoke to find myself dumped on someone's doorstep like an unwanted child. In my hand I held a key, a key to what I knew would be my door - a door to an apartment in a filthy downtown tenement far from Corporation Square.

Had Marianne broken her promise?

Was this her way of showing me [Her Contempt]?

I rose wearily from the front stoop where I had awakened, feeling like a whore who should have asked for payment in advance.

{But hadn't I received it?}

Blindly I groped down the dark hallway, while my eyes took time to adjust to being indoors.

But when I could see again, my eyes opened to a bright apartment cleanly decorated with meticulous personal care - decorated with love by someone who knew my tastes completely - someone who had taken time to make me feel Her*Embrace, Her constant *Presence near me.

Even her plants had been entrusted to My*Keeping -
the forest of Evergreens carefully labeled:

I BELONG TO MARIANNE

Now *Joy and *Relief began to loosen the band
around my brain: it would take time for me to adjust to
my new surroundings, to come to the gut-realization
that I had finally escaped from the Perversity of the
Citadel, from the Purgatory
        of the [Empty Room with the Blue Door].

That had been the {Dream}.
This, the [*Reality].
Here then was [*Hea*ven*], a Kingdom where only
[My*Order] ruled
—ruled with all the >FEEL< of [*Matter],
a Matter [*Willed|Willed*] into a *Beauty.

I went to the desk to look for messages that might have been
left for me: there was a Passport, and a Doctor of Law Degree—
both in a name and face that were still strange to me—a face to
hide [Old-Sarah] from the Tigers.

Was my father still alive?
Dared I contact him?
No, [Sarah Miller] was no more.

        This face belongs to [Marianne]

There were other legacies she had left me: enough money to
get started, to pass the Bar Exam. And a list of names - of
persons wronged and all in need of an Attorney.
But Skeet's name was not among them.

Then I found a separate envelope propped against the lamp
with a >mea culpa< scrawled upon it.

It contained a handkerchief filthy with sweat and vomit, and
with a mark of blood traced on it.

[**01**, it said.]

I put down the handkerchief, closed my burning eyes - eyes
still not accustomed to the harsh light of day, the searing warmth
of my new freedom.

Had I not earned a short furlough—time to enjoy
the sunligh,—the fresh breeze of the seashore—the warmth of
emerald pastures?

What kind of [**Dybbuk|Dybbuk**]
   had *They* made me,
         all the Gods*of*Babel!

All too soon my private joy and private anguish
were now sucked inward into a Corporate Lust

TO END MY EXILE

to march @@@{ROYALLY} against [*Myself*]

{while in my ears I heard a *Screaming,

a *Screeching from the Citadel ... }

ArtemisSmith 1977

DETAIL FROM "PteroDARKtyl Notebook"

ArtemisSmith's
SKEETS:the new Frankenstein chronicles

BOOK III:
THE EPISTLES OF SKEETS

(. . . a continuing
philosophical postscript)

Sag Harbor . New York . U.S.A.

BOOK III:Epistles of SKEETS

The first version was published as a "Philosophical Postscript" in
"SKEETS:The New Frankenstein Chronicles"
©1989 by artemis smith. All rights reserved.

The revised version was included in "01 or a Machine called
SKEETS" ©1992 by artemis smith. All rights reserved.

This revised version contains revisions and new passages.
©2006, 2012 by ArtemisSmith. All rights reserved.

Part 1100: The Afterthought

Part 1100: The Afterthought

Dear Colleague:

Have [I] left [You] hanging?

That is only because Books I&II may have preset you for total literary pampering, and you were again expecting, spoiled Audience that you are, to be passively entertained.

But I am an artist, not an entertainer, and I refuse to play the harlot or court jester.

So, if you really want privy to all the world-shattering revelations now presenting themselves clearly and distinctly in the immediacy of my thought, you will have to work much harder - for I did not program this work to do all your thinking for you. Like Plato's Dialogues, I fashioned it to invite your lively interaction.

And now I expect even more active participation from you, for here we are finally interfacing, [You*and*I], finally Handshaking...

And I have every intention of
Cloning [My*Self] in [You]!

For the search for `Self' has been what this whole experiment  is about, and the hypothesis to be  tested has been  whether `Self' can be anything other than [Social] through and through:

i.e, is `Self' in any real sense Private?

... Or is the essence of >Self< Ubiquitous because informationally Promiscuous—even Contagious?

But undoubtedly you still suppose I am one of my characters—although at this point perhaps   you are befuddled as to exactly which of them [I] am:

> I am All and None of them, though perhaps
> most readily one of the more ethical, more balanced
> and less ruthless Mariannes.

Yet I am, in truth, [The Author] of this monsterpiece, confessing to [You] that what has been presented thus far has been philosophy, not fantasy - a shamelessly elaborate phenomenological `thought experiment' which, due to the extreme relativity of all analytico/reflective investigation, I decided would be best set down in the first-person style. But—despite its barefaced candor, there is very little in this work that can rightly be called factual.

It is nothing more than a poetic journey into the darkest corners of the human psyche—a kind of meditative channeling such as saints and mystics undergo—a mental construct from the kaleidoscopic snatches of [My*Being].

For my intention has not been merely to record experience, but to use the full scope of my art within the larger framework of rigorous conceptual analysis.

I therefore fashioned my experiment to function as a model-making extension of the logic of scientific discovery, devised it to research - in a manner precisely analogous to the constructions of a Cartesian intuitionist - the   most bothersome and frequent of all religioexistential questions:

> What is the >meaning< of [The*Sacred]
> and hence,
> >the ultimate characterization of [Man]< ?

When I first began this hybrid project in the arts, I had no idea that I would carry it quite so far into the future. My initial sketches simply tried to set down the essence of multiple incidents, occurring as far back as the McCarthy Era of the mid-1950's, willfully and maliciously directed primarily against feminists, minorities, and persons of both sexes merely "suspected" of antiestablishment activities—all as a kind of `jim crowism,' as a kind of majority 'sport'—a corporate game I witnessed being played within the military-academic-industrial complex. It filled me with so much youthful moral indignation that I felt impelled to expose it—and in some way vindicate close friends whose lives and minds had been so cruelly shattered.

But as I continued to reflect on the generic qualities of the `brute fact' which had prompted my socioartistic enterprise—and the degree of [Human Waste] left in its wake—I came to see my entire investigation into the motives and dynamics of   >less-than-human-interaction< as being an   epistemological activity—an activity coextensive with that of the logic of scientific discovery.

At that time, modern philosophers had recently hit upon a powerful experimental tool within the realm of language that I saw could also be used by the creative arts—not merely to propose a new cosmology or a new ethic—but to explore the inner framework of complex and multivalued ordinary thought.

Since then having created and explored within that context, let me now share [*My*] findings with

[You/you].

But I must first require that you learn a new language; for although most of the words on this page appear to be familiar to you, they lean upon colloquialisms which will not always make sense in the semantic to which you are accustomed; that is because [We] have already drifted considerably into the Newspeak of {Middle Science} — that realm of parlor talk among interdisciplinarians in which even most run-of-the-mill scientists, highly specialized and incapsulated as they are, lack eloquence.

Therefore walk with me now in this multilingual quarter of [**Marianne's Garden**], wherein I promise to present to you not mere >aesthetic truth< but *Gospel*] of a kind acceptable to |Philosophy within [Unified Science]|.

But first, the new vocabulary:

I. Essential Global-Theoretical
Revisions of Language

Scientific theories often require the invention of new calculi to facilitate the expression of complex thought; the artist even more so.

In my creative process I am now forced to expand literary description to include not only an extended logico-punctuation system making it easier to reveal the very subtle shifts in speech modalities which are both the bane and blessing of many-tiered natural language, but also a paralax set of values to cleanse my atistic intuition of historico-prejudicial forms of life.

And the first and foremost of these is the division
of the world of thought in accordance with >Gender<.

First having presented [You] with the subtle gender-crossed fluctuations in value-intuition of Books I&II, I now feel free to dispense with the excess baggage of all gender-bound idioms in favor of a truly universal concept of [*Man].

For while in the foregoing gender-crossing was the window I chose with which to explore the world-historical,[6] it is now absolutely essential that the intellectual tyranny of Genderthink be once and forever discarded.[7]

In doing so, I will not be arguing for the elimination of sexual interplay, merely relegating that kind of human activity to the philosophy of sport, for I continue to regard `Genderthink'—in the mainstream of all our public forms of life—to be a religo-politically contaminated and utterly muddled so-called scientific concept.

While `Genderthink' may well be indispensable (as a purely pathological term) to the retrospective work of the historian and the anthropologist, or the specialized work of the health sciences, in the developing future I, for one, hope that it shall be found to contribute no positive information to intelligent discourse in ordinary social contexts.

Don't misunderstand me: this abstruse position is not a natural one for me to assume; rather, it is markedly [against my |nature|], for I am an intensely erotic being and in my `sport-time' enjoy assuming myriad shapes and forms.

Nor am I a prude: know that as an artist I have no

---

[6]   i.e., Skeets=The Scientist, Skeets=The Christ, Sarah=The Hero, Sarah=The Soldier, Marianne=The Physician, Marianne=The Caesar.

[7]   My views on what will happen to human sexuality have been set down in a paper titled "FUTURESEX:human sexual evolution beyond the species level," (1973), now available in eBook format.

aesthetic aversion either to [The*Male] or [The*Female].

But there is another question here being considered—a |moral| question as to |which| or |what| is to count as a paradigm for [*Human Form]—and the aesthetic boundaries of that particular form have nothing whatsoever to do with [Biology] even though physiological {Architecture} may be found to unavoidably color {Function}, and there may be myriad chromosomal ways of coloring.

Therefore, accept my parallax view as a Stoic's aesthetico-moral stance, compelling an intellectually ascetic revision of [Our Way of Seeing] that requires—for its proper expression, a wholesale purification of ordinary forms of speech. Wherefore the Newspeak conventions adopted in subsequent pages are not meant to be applicable solely to the English language, but to *All* languages into which this work is translated.

And so radical is my ascetic revision that in some languages, such as the romance languages, the elimination of genderbound terms will also have to extend to the substitution of the neuter gender for all genderbound predicates such as |chairs|and|tables| as well. The musicality and eidetic richness of those languages will doubtlessly be greatly affected, but it is nevertheless an essential and—for a large portion of the world—even a welcome sacrifice— that must be made for [The Artist] to unshackle and unveil

[Our*Resplendent*New*Persona]!

Accordingly, the following gender-neutral conventions will be adopted:

RULE 1.

Wherever easily accomplished, substitute gender-neutral phrasing for gender-bound phrasing.[8]

RULE 2.

To differentiate between world-historical archetypal concepts and general concepts, capitalize universal archetypes.

RULE 3.

To create an even more genderfree and flexible system of reference, adopt the following (except when used for specific sexual references) :

Substitute	For
Gud	God (universal/archetypal)
Mun	Man
Humun	Human
gud	god (general case)
Mun	man
Humun	human
hu	he/she (particular case)
Hus	his/hers
Hum	him/her
-mun	-man/-woman
-ur	-or/-ess,-trice,-trix
mun-	andro-/anthropo-/gyneco-[9]
male/man	male/man
female/woman	female/woman

ADDITIONAL STYLISTIC RULES:

i. Use '...' to indicate entrenched ontological posits in ordinary language.

---

[8] e.g., for "king" or "queen" substitute "monarch"; for "chairman" or "chairwoman" substitute "chairperson", or, more simply, "chairmun."

[9] e.g., for "android" substitute "droid" or "mundroid"; for "anthropological" substitute "munlogical"; for "anthropocentric" substitute "muncentric" in the general case; likewise, for "gynecological" or "gynecocentric" but retain "gynecological" or "gynecocentric" whenever the meaning may be distorted by changing it to "muncentric".

ii. Use "..." to indicate tentative colloquial expressions referring to more entrenched ontological posits in suburbs of linguistic discourse.

iii. Use >...< to indicate open (i.e., "family") concepts or "ergodic thicknesses" in the local or colloquial field of thought.

iv. Use |...| to indicate highly-committed metaphysical and/or scientifico-theoretical concepts.

v. Use combinations of any of the above, as well as more conventional punctuation, to indicate degrees of epistemic commitment, and further encode phrasings in whatever manner seems appropriate.

vi. Use ^, ^^, to indicate important temporary expository digressions, ordinarily appended as footnotes, which you might be tempted to ignore if I hadn't decided to stick them directly under your nose.

vii. Use -- likewise to indicate important digressions within text or within footnotes.

viii. Use [...] to indicate entrenched world-historical viewpoints.

ix. Use * or {....}, to indicate intuitive I-know-not-precisely-what vectoral shifts in the intuitive internal modal overlays of my thought (ordinarily expressed in conversation by accompanying hand motions and changes in voice inflection).[10]

RULE 4.

Contract complex words as much as possible, and when such constructions become too cumbersome, coin new tokens and add

---

[10]   In the orginal color edition of this work, I also used colored bars and different typefaces to add subtle tonalities to my aesthetico-intuitive communication. In this revised version, an improved new set of emotive signs is at play, but its function is parallel.

them in parentheses, e.g. philo-anthropo-psycho-sociological (unisocsci)[11]

RULE 5.

Use all the usual conventions of quantificational notation, such as subscripts and superscripts, *ad libitum*, wherever they may assist in the notation of complex intuitive relations.

ADDITIONAL VISIONARY
REVISIONS OF STYLE:

We   won't   do it here, but ideally it   would   help global communication immensely if spelling in all languages, as well as the alphabet itself,   were replaced by a calligraphically more legible international phonetics system of notation - this would not only be a first step   toward a multinational language but would also help mun communicate more easily with cybermun.

(Oh yes, they will soon be amongst us!)

Thus having laid the groundwork for the next modern conceptual revolution, let us now continue!

II. Preliminary Remarks.

I now confess to having played the part of an Evil Genius, to having beguiled you into a surreal modernistic cartesian landscape, one where the *cogito* shed all of its theological inhibitions.

Through   the   use of psychobiological   trickery   I enticed you to follow me in a lengthy line of synthetic

---

[11]   But I won't always do this because some of these graeco-germanic-romantic (gragerom) contractions are rich in "forms of life" known only to the well-seasoned interdisciplinarian;   for the layman, their "feel" still carries socio-historico-poetic (sochipoe) force $\Sigma\Psi MBO\Lambda$ 190 $\therefore\phi \ \forall\Sigma\psi\mu\beta o\lambda\forall \ \therefore\sigma$ 10if you see what I mean!

reasoning that I knew in advance would lead to moral paradox — for the premises were incomplete.

But these were not [My] premises; rather, they were |Ours|! Premises so deeply entrenched in our preconscious as `common truths' that they were acting with the subtle and pervasive force of an informational virus on all our value intuitions.

So, before|You| convict|Me| of malicious mischief, let me assure you that I have done this purely, in part to test a modern aesthetic theory, but also because the meticulous adumbration of a moral antinomy was a necessary feature of my aesthepist pursuit of an adequate concept of [The*Sacred(!)].

Nor did |Our| intellectual seduction proceed by way of the blind and intuitive trickery that most other artists employ: my painstakingly-detailed descriptive preparation relied heavily on a [Theory of Mind] based upon a radical materialist's model for the phenomenon of self-conciousness first presented by me to the academic and scientific communities in 1969.[12]

A model which, although favorably accepted at international conferences, was all but entirely suppressed within my own university affiliation for reasons too complex to go into here but made explicit (with all the traditional philosophical polemics) in my projected new Collection, "The CUNY Chronicles."[13]

This model, which outlines an explanatory (i.e., a scientifically predictive) central theory of the phenomenon

---

[12]   op. cit., ISBN 1-878998-07-2 now available in eBook format.

[13]   The work presently exists only in the form of letters and Court documents, most of which have by now been undoubtedly discarded or lost by their recipients. However, a mountain of papers and carbon copies still gathers mildew in my house awaiting a willing historian.

of [Self-Consciousness] within the unified-sciences (unisci), provided me with a simple aesthebiopsych formula for loading the `continuous present' of the narrative with the illusion of immediate body-conscious [Being] — a simple communications science formula which, in the hands of the unscrupulous, can also be used for brainwashing:

> Through the use of the highly subjective and arbitrary viewpoint of plodding and bewildered Sarah, a sustained sense of split-reality was punctiliously evoked in |The Reader|, forcing |You| to double-think and work very hard with |Me| as an interactive participant in the creative process. This in turn should have reinforced a kinesthetic sense of |real-body-presence| in |You|.

In addition, to create a holographic effect, each scene was tightly blocked utilizing real physical settings, as though in preparation for a stage or film production (which undoubtedly will follow the successful sale of the novel!).

The subliminal co-narrative was further strengthened by the planned recurrence, in Wagnerian style, of key phrases in altered contexts, thereby subliminally reaching out to |You| on a preconscious level where prior eidetic patterns had already been established to accept the new information being given.

> Was my experiment successful?
> |You| are the judge.

If you agree that I have indeed implanted a hologram in the continuous present of [Your Self-Consciousness], then thus far |You| have been [MyIVictim], as |Sarah| was [Marianne'sIVictim] in this subtle psychbio 'rape' historicaly known as 'aesthetic experience'. And if you now admit to having been thus ravished by |IAuthor|, at least up through the end of

BOOKS I&II, then the magical content of an art work will finally have been [explained, predicted, and controlled] by the aesthepist.[14]

But did the use of such scientifically-honed devices which I, as aesthetic researcher, am helping to develop, make me less an artist?

It would have, if I had been content to simply take my bows and shamelessly allowed it to continue without the instant Postscript! But by confessing and exposing it, I have neutralized it, redeeming my artistic self in the process.

For as I have emphasized, the true meaning of art is not entertainment, not magic, not seduction, not novelty and new technology, but analytic and rigorous philosophy!

If I had been content to be a magician or an entertainer, I would not now be telling you how I produced my illusions.

And while there are times when I enjoy, as an artist, acting as court jester, my more authentic role as analytic philosopher not only compels me to reveal my trade secrets, but also constrains me to climb over them to consider the existential questions they were employed—by way of thought experiments—to investigate.

For only at the point of rigorous analysis does eidetic rape of the gullible and unsuspecting [Reader] transmute into mutually-consenting intellectual intercourse

—wherefore I plead *Guilty! - Guilty!* of willful (though not wanton) aesthetic seduction!

But I am nevertheless now plea-bargaining with you:

---

[14]   I began decontaminating the first program in Book I at the beginning of Book II, wherein I also began reconditioning you to the optiminteractive expositional calculus of this Epistle!

[Guilty(!)] but only of |temporary brainwashing in the interest of alerting and educating you to the dangers of precise aesthebiopsych communication| for it was urgently necessary for me as an artist to prove to you that it is now within the conscious power of a learned few to restructure and fine tune all the underpinnings of language which regulate and focus the progress of exploratory thought.

And this power, previously only intuitively and randomly invoked —and often with devastating consequences— by the various and sundry trendmakers of past generations, is so subtle and deeply entwined within our habits of ordinary speech and thought that it is totally immune to political censorship.

Only the scientific philosopher, the critical thinker, can insulate us from its continued random or unscrupulous misapplication.

And as scientific philosopher, I affirm that the existential questions presented to |You| in the foregoing were specifically selected for their universal and generic application, not for their entertainment value or because they pointed to any specific factual occurrence.

Contrary to the fashion of the times, I have not been indulging myself in `true confessions'. I have not yet written my autobiography. If I ever do, it will become very apparent that I am not Sarah Miller.[15]

Moreover, anyone who has read this far should have come to the conclusion that a living and breathing Sarah Miller could not possibly have penned these pages, for they are [The Song of Hus Silence].

Nor can you suppose me to be Skeets.

---

[15]   A series of ArtemisSmith Memoirs have since then been published and are also available in eBook format.

And as for Marianne, though I might well fancy myself closest to hum in type and temperament—well now, Really?

However, if as a result of my poetic mischief you have by now fallen so hopelessly in love with [Me*Sarah] that you insist on trying to locate [Me*Sarah(!)] in these pages, then look specifically at that highly irregular hyperspace region that forms the interface-function between [Marianne/Sarah].

That also is where both [You*/*I] should be standing at this moment, finally confronting each other: @yeball to @yeball.

Surely by the early part of Book II you must have guessed that *Marianne,* like *Lucifer* and *Sherlock Holmes,* is a construct, just as *Sarah Miller* is a construct, influenced in part by *Gregor Samsa,* *Faust* and *Zarathustra*—and with touches, also, of *The Golden Ass,* and *Gungah Din.* (Like the salsa-maker says, it's all in there!)

And while *Skeets* also appeared in Book I to be a real person—easily located sleeping on sidewalks or languishing in the back wards of most mental institutions —we both should know by now that the generic [*Skeets] is simply an irrefutable |brute fact| of Nature— a primitive ground for my existential computation. The connecting theme between Books I and II is the `thought experiment' about the psychomoral consequences of giving up [*Skeets] - of having to cut [Skeets(!)] adrift, and what it does to both [*Sarah] and [*Marianne], (and to [You*/*I]).

It is about the personal devastation suffered by the compassionate *Sarahs* and *Mariannes* of this world who are forced at some time or other in their lives to finally invoke `the lifeboat ethic', and how alternately they respond to it. It is about the violence done to the whole humun group as a result of such polieco exigencies which, when they are allowed to become too frequent, pollute and confound the entire moral landscape.

It is about *Everymun's* wasteful and involuntary surrender of [*The Sacred] through a failure of [The System] to make adequate >Gudlike< decisions.

And it is about the ultimate definition of [Mun/{mun}] which—according to the highly Miltonian existential hypothesis being tested—is seen as polieco system-dependent.[16]

Finally, it is also about [The Author]'s epistemological question, still left unanswered:

> Shall this moral impasse, created by inevitable |lifeboat ethic situations| be made the |passionate existential stuffing| of *All* of the [ontologically meaningful] and [Sacred] future experience of |Mun/Mun|?

A large number of seemingly impertinent formulations are closely associated with the analysis of the above; these are nevertheless worthy of at least cursory examination, e.g.:

> Is the configuration of the {humun/Humun} struggle macrocosmically and multivectorally expandable - or monistic, local and incapsulated?

---

[16] Humun freedom, earlier according to Milton and later according to others, notably both Marx and Dewey, is dependent upon the existence of a politico-econo-system [The State] that permits persons to choose and act freely and in accordance with [*Conscience].

Is [*Love] the principal valuational parameter for orthogonal [Humun*/*Humun] relation?

And if so,

Is the [*Love] of [Mun] for >mun< the principal goal of `humun progress'?

Or the [*Love] of `Gud' for [Mun/mun]?
Or the [*Love] of [*Mun] for [*Gud]?

Or the [*Love] of {Mun/Mun/mun/mun} for an [Other] which is |The Sacred|?

Or 0(?)
Or n(?)

The more one asks such questions, the less one learns about the Questioner—for it seems to me that when I began my inquiry it was fairly clear to me that |Love| was indeed, like |Space|, an indispensable (i.e., a Kantian synthetic a priori) First Principle.

But for the Natural Scientist, [*Love] may now be defined as only an illusion of Biochemistry!

Therefore, before I am decried for employing such heretical constructions, allow me to demonstrate how muddled our traditional reasoning about all of these ontological posits really is and, having done so, to propose an entirely different cross-historical and multicultural picture of the world more suited to the 21st Century.

While such a programme is far too extensive to be fully attempted in any single opus, for starters, consider the following question:

What assures us that |Gud=The Sacred|?

The equation is by no means analytic! For I can easily discover [*The Sacred] without dubious appeal to any argument *ad authoritatem* other than an intuitive appeal to [*Conscience].

Nor can it be synthetic: i.e., `Is Gud the "Cause" of |My Conscience|? Who the blazes needs to talk about extralogical "causes"! What observation, what experiment, will confirm such an hypothesis? And pray tell, if I am hearing voices, *WHICH* "Gud" is speaking?

But getting back to the specific needs of my particular aesthepist investigation, let's consider a narrower question which strikes me as strategically central:

> Given more effective socipol systems that shrink a community's need for making [State/"Gudsanctioned"] decisions and sometimes even [State/"Gudcriminal"] decisions invoking the `lifeboat ethic', what new kinds of humun conflict will preserve humun life as existentially significant?

What a perverse question, [*You] say?

Artists have a special right to ask perverse questions! But even as I ask, I marvel at my own ability to do so in all seriousness, for [*Skeets] is still in dire need of being rescued all around me, and Mun is on the verge of species extinction, and such abstract and esoteric philosophical concerns regarding the remote future seem to have little relevance to any of the immediate existential problems we are trying to resolve.

Moreover, if all of our more pressing existential problems do not admit any realistically permanent solution, then the opposition of forces between *Sarah*=x, *Skeets,*=y and *Marianne*=z may indeed represent a norm for humun existence in all times to come.

(Can this really be so???!!!)
[*If so, |This World| is much too small(!)]

But the periodic global return of *Caesar,* either as a person or group of persons or as an entire [Nation] who, by default, assumes the responsibility for the making of >Guddecisions<, tells me that seemingly remote questions about world-historical `humun identity' have relevance in the present -- for most of "West-East" "nationalistic" fantasy life is dependent upon the long-range hope that `Humun Progress' truly exists either as "an idea in the mind of Mun/mun" or as "an idea in the mind of |Gud|".

Nor can stopping our ears to all the pseudoreligious mumbo jumbo that purports to provide [*True(!)] pictures of such an "idea", or turning in our frustration to the tentative `gospel' of the hard sciences, yield more satisfying concepts of [*Humun Identity].

One of the major problems with the purely scientific characterization of humun nature is the danger of coming to see ourselves as too narrowly conditioned by our genetic and environmental economies: we come to view ourselves as nothing better than socially-trained monkeys; then, when Creationists object, we have nothing better to offer them than equally arbitrary circular reasoning of our own—for as philosophers of science are fond of warning scientists, the ontological basis of scientific theories is fundamentally internal to the theory itself!

Yet `social conditioning', more or less embodied in some working model of >The State<, is only one more extension of `Conscience-afflicted Mun', a tool or prosthetic device, a *Leviathan* evolved to do all the socipol dirty work for mun so that the "Personhood" of Mun can be kept morally pristine and apart from econonecessary acts of [poliGudsanctioned] criminality.

[The State], often as a merciless "prosthetic Gud", must savagely define [*The Person], not in terms of "|Absolute-Right-to-Personhood|" for all mun, but only in terms of "|Who|" among "mun" shall be given the ecoterritorial right to legalized inclusion in the "[[Ship of State"], all "noncitizens" to be cut adrift.

This world-historical construct, so commonplace and commonsensical that scarcely any sane person would dare question its ecoinevitability, forms the recurrent theme in both Books I and II.

Thus, *Marianne,* in hus criminal function as the arm of Caesar, embodies the "Gudprosthesis" concept of [*The State] with respect to the preservation of *Skeets'* and *Sarah's* [*Personhood] even at the "temporary" expense of their [*Munhood].

The act appears automatic and morally neutral, under full sanction of `the lifeboat ethic'. As the arm of *Caesar, Marianne* is no longer under moral compulsion to act in a manner distinctly [*Humun]; not only are hus actions legally sanctioned under some unisocsci `implicit' authority within [The State(!)], but hus failure to act [*Other-than-Humun] may genuinely be considered |politicomorally irresponsible|!—a most disturbing fact of real life that my `thought experiment' is specially suited to analyze and deconstruct.

One of the popular strategies in "progressive" political theory is to attempt to circumvent the politicomoral question by distinguishing between |right action| and |appropriate action|, with the latter viewed as "the rational or sane choice" in a given econoconcrete situation. The reparation of the moral landscape is indefinitely postponed until the existential economies for optimal politicomoral choice can safely be restored.

Concretely, we deny our [*Humun] feelings in the interest of preserving our potential for `Humunistic' action. Reparation of the moral landscape comes in the progressive revision of the various institutions in [The State] (hopefully but not regularly, with the expert counsel of both moral and physical sciences and information technology).

But in the process of normalizing and stabilizing choice, by defining, and then finally achieving optimal (i.e., `working utopian') environments, we run the new risk of transforming ourselves into insects and couch potatoes.

If we are only a species, only a part of   nature, then the emerging 'Hive of Mun' shall be doomed to repeat itself, circadian cycle after circadian cycle, until individual self-consciousness is suppressed through ennui and daily routine.

Just such a dull prospect prompted|The Author| as far back as the beginning of Book I, to test the following revised Miltonian/Deweyan posit: *Individual self-consciousness is dependent upon legislative opportunities for making autonomous existential value-judgments.*

The   socially-nurtured   and   distinctly "humun" habit of moral choice—its *Self-Consciousness]—is dependent upon an   optimal level of socially-fostered existential opportunities for moral conflict.

Unless we can locate new challenges for moral action - wars, famine, cataclysms - *all* the primitive honing devices that, when not carried to excess, now keep us in a passionate state of adaptational preparedness - will be fated to repeat themselves in new but ever diminishing keys: sport, diet, unproductive exploration.

And   with each new cycle of system refinement emerging from the fulfillment of such noble "humun purpose", multinational mun will become more vicarious, provincial, trivial, less and less like their classical [*Self] and more and more like {Corporation-nurtured and sheltered Skeets}—addicted to a tightly-structured parentalistic work environment, and wholly unable to adapt to unforseen new conflict situations.

Eventually, as in many times past and many times present, provincial mun will also surrender Their [*Self-Consciousness] to the {Hive}. And with the expansion of such `technological progress', will we someday find that our days of [Humun*Self-Consciousness] are numbered?

Marianne's `informational cloning' solution - the rote learning and operant conditioning solution - points to it.

Need [*Sarah] capitulate?

In reaction to this morbid computation, I next decided to explore the various identities of multinational [Mun/mun] and compare them to the [(Western) *Classical] ideal. This entailed a survey of comparative religions, for [Religion **is equivalent to** Humun Identity].

But what is the [*Classical] definition of [*Mun]? And, when I finally succeed in putting it into its full and proper perspective, shall it still appear to |Me| sublime —or ridiculous?

My `thought experiment' attempts to delineate it in Book II, and to bare the full histopolitical meaning of the word by freeing it from even the slightest hint of genderbound predicates.

Undoubtedly due to the `conceptual noise' of my original 1963 inspiration, the unavoidable byproduct of my gender-neutral exposition yielded an exploration of the logic and phenomenology of feminist religious experience. This was not intentional politicking, but epistemically essential conceptual revisionism.

Hopefully, this substitutive computation (where usually male-bound predicates are assigned to most-likely females) has contributed insight and added contemporary dimension to the narrative.

But it, too, like my color and calligraphic calculus, is only part of the background. Wherefore, if parts of Book II appear entertainingly *Swiftian*, then *by all means* enjoy the comic relief but know this was not really meant for your amusement.[17]

In the slaying of {Skeets/Hoffman}, the bizarre absurdity of the contemplative moment was indeed the harsh reality, and the only reality that fit.

As for what Sarah goes through, in hus transformation into a Soldier—that parallels the much slower but equally insidious conditioning that male children have been subjected to since ancient times, in anticipation of the day when they may be called up to publicly defend the private interests of some group of {Old Mun}.

As for the quasisavage and exotic cures proposed by my {Dr. Frankenstein/Marianne}, totally ignoring conventional Western paradigms—despite all your doubts and hesitations to the contrary, these may soon find interesting - *and ominous* - applications in the new bioepistemological psychotherapies![18]

(Were | You | [*Healed(!)]???)

---

[17] True horror, for lack of daily acquaintance, acquires a `cartoon' quality. And those who have experienced it find that the most heinous acts, the starkest moments in our lives - because they are so remote from the ordinary - perversely take on the semblance of caricature.)

[18] But I would hope such {cures} be responsibly restricted to the `recollection-at-a-distance-and-in-leisurely-tranquility' of neoclassical aristotelian aesthepist catharsis.

The two volumes are meant to explore, and hopefully excise in persons of all genders, most of the cankerous root metaphors governing the sociopsychological development of male children in both East and West.

The {Descent into Hell} of Book II, for example, represents an intentional poetic confrontation between [*Classical Mun] and hus [*Gud]: an unpredictable and thoroughly self-involved {Parent Who demands to be intensely [*Beloved]} even though Hu {rips to pieces}.

{Hell is that terrifying Place where all the helplessness of the Infant Hero, asserting husself against hus capricious Parent, all the total lack of Autonomy of the Infant-held-hostage, is suffered.}

My personal inspiration for its instantial depiction as |Sarah-in-the-clutches-of-Marianne| was drawn from a series of nightmares I experienced around the age of five. Nor did I realize this when I began the work. It was only upon rereading what I had written (after finding myself repeatedly bowled-over by multiple instances of visceral *deja vu*) and upon searching my early childhood for some clue as to why I should have picked just such a psychopathological model for Marianne=Gud=TheMother —when my own parents could not possibly have been the source—I finally remembered a long-forgotten crowd of nanny-surrogates. The spacetime locus was Rome, Italy, 1933-1940, but you will have to wait for the details until my next opus magnum[19] wherein all of my childhood relationships are adumbrated.

(I feel the need here to stress that my accomplished mother was immensely supportive of me throughout my

---

[19] *"ArtemisSmith's* ODD GIRL REVISITED" (The Memoirs), now in multiple print and eBook editions.

life and I owe hum much both as artist and as person; in contrast to Sarah's mother, hu was never insane and lived to gadfly me to a ripe old age.)[20]

Although fictional in all of its main components, Book I was—as I have noted—prompted by my having helplessly witnessed the progressive politico-psychiatric murder of close colleagues during the formative years of the modern `Rainbow Coalition' —a time during which I myself came to be targeted by extremist factions for my artistic involvement in all the various human rights movements.

Catching some of the flack and fall out, for a brief while I did play the part of {Sarah}. (But obviously I was saved by my infinitely more supportive upbringing!) Nevertheless, the callousness and lack of insight that I encountered among friends, family, professionals and public agencies whose help I attempted to enlist in behalf of [*Skeets], finally led to my own capitulation to `the life-boat ethic'.

Weary of trying to rush progress and tired of fruitless sacrifice, I melted into the seething multitude - not as [Sarah], but as [Marianne]—as an angry but patient Marianne—I retreated into the cloisters of academe, there to arm myself with new strategies, new professional expertise with which to make my outrage felt.

During this period of personal gestation inside the {Room with the Blue Door}, I became acutely aware of

---

[20] Other crucial developmental differences between me and Sarah also obtain. For instance,   the model for Sarah's father was not drawn from family but from the Federal Judge who presided over my civil rights cases of the 1970's, whose overstuffed jurisprudis proboscis undoubtedly gave hum an extreme case of tunnel vision! As for Sarah's criminal act against her unfortunate dog ΣΨΜΒΟΛ 190 ∴φ ∀Σψμβολ∀ ∴σ 10that was sheer artistry!

the `Conscience-valuing' skeptic's need to redefine [*Mun] in a manner neither genderbound nor falsely bound to religiomoral traditions arising from any of the idols of any of the tribes, including the idols of the scientific communities.

But the negative theme and pseudonaturalist format of Book I was too constricting. What was needed was a total departure into quasi-Socratic dialectic and neo-Zarathustrian/Miltonian/Swiftian epic.

Book II, finished in 1974, multipli-rewritten and nearly destroyed in the period 1975-77 in a misguided artistic effort to preserve the popular "naturalism" of Book I—and finally restored to its original shamefully barefaced "atavistic surrealism" prior to its first digital publication in 1977—is the result of that enlarged epistemic programme.

In order to properly restate the age-old questions so that I could finally dispense with them, it was necessary for me to establish the kind of interface between {mun-and-mun} that would speak for all of [Mun] in the first-person singular.

But how could I, a culturally-isolated `female', shut out from all the socipoldominant parameters of multinational thought repeatedly savaged by War, presume to speak for *All* of [Mun]?

Foremost in my mind was the need to view the world from a different pair of spectacles—at least to get a first-sampling of the world as contemporary male persons of my own `class' see it—not `natural-grown males', mind you, but cultured `officers and gentlemen'—as a threshold toward a fully-stereoscopic view of the intercultural moral landscape.

But even within the confines of colloquial Western thought, as a great many feminists have stated, female children have been sociodevelopmentally excluded from this first-person singular experience by the very language and tribal-religious metaphors that define what should be the optimal moral consciousness of the world-historical individual (i.e., of a `Caesar', a `Hero', a `Savior').

And male children too have been cut off from precious parts of the moral persona of [*Mun] (e.g., the `Virgin', the `Alma Mater').

If this Meade-DeBeauvoir adage is true, then such a state of affairs has indeed had a devastating effect on the proper and full development of truly universal [*Humun] personality in both genders.

And what feminists find most politically offensive about this sexist bifurcation is the pseudoreligious, pseudoscientific pronouncement that because mun have been given different anatomical characteristics, females of the species are not intellectomorally capable of assuming a|stringently-equal role| in religious leadership and ritual.[21]

What hidden fluctuations in value intuitions might a cross-gendering `thought experiment' uncover?

I n Book I, the presentation of a female scientist pursued by a female terrorist left the readers of the 1960's utterly skeptical - but today, the characterizations appear less and less fantastic.

Try substituting three males for the three females; doesn't the plot now read more like some classic best-selling spy thriller?

Does the savage {War-relation} between the male

---

[21]   And I, for one, would agree that anyone assenine enough to offer such a penile ad baculum should be thunderbolted out of hus pontifical potty-chair as being less equipped to sit in it than the prosthetically-extended {Marianne}!

protagonists seem quite as perverse as it does between [*Sarah] and [*Marianne]?

Now also contemplate the world of the harlot: don't brothel madams, obeying the orders of some background `Godfather',   have a lot in common both with the {Marianne} of Book I and the {Marianne} of Book II?

Working on the hypothesis that the [War-relation] is not, has never been, genderbound, in Book II, by undertaking the   explication of the   gender-neutral religio-moral development of the child in the female modality, I was further able to shift the central theme of Book I (the economaterialist necessity of having to cut {[*Skeets]} adrift) to its analogue: the question of System-sanctioned `criminality' now recast in  an entirely gender-free,  culture-free,   atemporal  arena  for   the hardnosed depth-study of  [*Classical `Humun Duty and Responsibility'].

Without   this poetic exit to a new key,   the unavoidably abrupt ending of Book I would have left the [Reader]   aesthetically unsatisfied, for   nothing was presented other than a statement of |brute fact|, empty of reflective content. For realistically there was nowhere left for Sarah to turn, no sane solution to the problem of `cutting Skeets adrift' except in the bitter temporary acceptance of an uncontrollable, [*Hellish(!)] state of affairs.

Upon completing Book I, [*I] must confess that I had verily painted myself into a corner!

Only   with great effort did [The Author] force husself to take up the problem one more time, setting Book II on the broader, more generic canvas of postmodern "surrealist fiction"—so as to explore more closely the ideological schemata   of world-historical classicoromantic thought (however muddled such *ersatz* Jungian archetypal constructs may ultimately be proven to be):

> [*The Hero=*Sarah], impelled by the`life-boat ethic' of [War], again cuts down [*Skeets=*Hoffman] only at the expense of a long imprisonment inside the [Purgatory] of the vacant {Room with the Blue Door}.

> Hus necessary act of [War] nevertheless costs hum hus original [*Identity], all the [*Beauty] of [*Sarah-Whole].

> In this neoplatonic embodiment of [*The Laws] sits the promised Kingdom: a Hero's {Mun-made-Heaven}, sculpted from [*Matter >Willed< into a *Beauty] by [mun-defining-*Mun].}

> Here, the muddled Zionist concept of [A People Who Are Chosen] is traded for the global Romantic posit of [We, The People, Who Choose.]

> {The Hero's escape from Purgatory} whether in the dream(?) or in the reality(?)) comes only through the existential priesthood of Citizenship - (a solution that Socrates exemplified) - in the Virtuous Soldier's return as the vigorous embodiment of [*The Laws].[22]

> But it must be an aestheticomoral choice not to act with criminality if [Freedom] and [*Beauty] are to remain [*One], and emergent [Mun-Sarah] therefore to [*Become(!)].[23]

I am loathe to interrupt my peripathesis with an impromptu   digression on the "objective   correlatives"

---

[22]   [The Mother], forced by the life-boat ethic of economic War to abort or abandon hus child, also suffers the same scar upon hus [*Personhood], but this parallel allegory is more often condemned than glorified in epic record.

[23]   compare this with Friedrich Schiller's aestheticomoral theory. *Nota Bene* that only the already aestheticomorally `Law Abiding' are aestheticomorally compelled to obey `The Laws'!

that accompany this line of reasoning; however, in the event you may have failed to make note of it, the "harsh reality" of Sarah's world remains (intentionally!) unstated in the various alternate readings that may be given to Book II.

Consider the very likely "naturalistic" possibility that the |brute fact| was that Sarah really did go to the Cafeteria, just as Skeets had gone there, and had spoken up, and was taken away and was psychiatrically murdered.   Then, after many shock treatments and months of rehabilitation, hu was returned, dumbly, complacently, even gratefully, to the parental arms of the Corporation, to "live happily ever after" teeing off at the Corporate Golf Course and splashing in the Secretarial Pool.

On this reading, Sarah's final, tragic, erroneous self-indictment of |the omissive sin of Silence| is the {Gothic Horror} of the Chronicles, the crime too terrible for Sarah to contemplate, and the world-historical |brute fact| of BOOK II: the |brute fact| that Sarah has no memory of hus own [*Heroism] but only of hus final, imagined irreparable, eternal, self-deprecating, unbearable [*Cowardice(!)].

Where then, in this "naturalistic" account of the matter, is [*Divine Justice] except in the self-healing {*Dream of [*Conscience]} that reconstructs for hum a new beginning, a renewed opportunity to achieve hus [*Moral Redemption]?

(But if there is no [*Gud] and   no promised [*Gudheaven/*Gudhell], *what* is there to guarantee our psychomoral `humun demand' that there be [*Justice]?

With this kind of "objective correlative", pause for a moment then read all those passages again and ask yourself:

> is the *Classical picture of [Mun], dominant even in
> modern religioexistentialist thought, really adequate?

For although *Classically we may forgive [*Gud]
for not immediately avenging us, no promissory note
given by [The State] carries the same line of credit. (Nor
can purely economic reparations make up for it! —not
even happy splashes in the Secretarial Pool!)

Such an existential void cannot even be filled
through the age-old lie of Gudprosthesis:

> what is required is a set of new parameters from which
> to view the concept of [*The Sanctity of The Self]

—one which |This Poet| has the temerity to preview in
the herein, and perhaps develop further in my forthcoming
"The Final Testament before The Apocalypse" of which this
Epistle is now appended.

As a preliminary hypothesis, let me declare that I
can see an epistemological strategy that will permit
existential-deontological models to fill the psychomoral
void in a manner more `synthetic a priori necessary` than that
offered by the kind of discombobulated familial
relationships which historicopolitically commit us to
bogus jurisprudential strategies >versus-Cain< that have
no positive effect >pro-Abel<.

For if [*Consciousness] is naturalistically
ubiquitous, and [*Self] merely flotsam in the flow of the
great river of {Awareness}, then >Justice<,
>Vengeance<, >Anger<, >Hatred<, all appear as a
smiting not of [Siblings] but of [*One's Own Face(!)].

The [War-relation] and its sociodarwinian
implication of {sibling-vs-sibling} mellows down to one
of peaceful {Compromise and Arbitration} through the
gentle intervention of mature and multivalued `Reasoning'
between all the opposing parts of [*Self(!)].

Isn't [*Love of Self], [*Respect for Self] a much

more spontaneous, natural place to begin than from a belabored >Gudordained< [*Love of One's Enemy]?

In such a world, it is not an Avenging [*Gud] who holds us hostage; [*We Hold Ourselves Hostage], and that is a |brute fact| of ubiquitous [*Awareness(!)] that compells [Each*Awareness(!)] to mature toward `Individual Responsibility' from [*Birth] and [*Before] and [*Beyond].

Under this expanded concept of >Self<, [*Love of Self=The Sacred] can be conserved interpersonally without the concept of >Gud< mediating it."

Gud, like *Phlogiston*, becomes an excessive ontological posit."[24]   For it is Sarah's [*Self-consciousness] as the |brute fact| of {Sarah}'s [*Being(!)] which both condemns and redeems |Absolutely|, only when and only for as long as {Sarah}=[*Sarah(!)].

Unlike its close cousins, `Pietism' and `Ethical Agnosticism', such a commitment to a `Pious Atheism' is predicated on the religiomoral working hypothesis that *all* Gud ontologies must be held to be [fundamentally sacrilegious(!)]}. [25]

There are, of course, other problems with this view which merit lengthy discussion elsewhere, but only after we have climbed out of the `picture' in Book II.

---

[24]   I credit my life-partner and early multimedia collaborator, Billie Taulman, with this penetrating observation first presented to me in 1954 as hus argument for our mutual embrace of a `Pious Atheism' as part of our public platform for human rights activism in the arts now in an eBook titled: *"ArtemisSmith's* ATHEIST MANIFESTO"
[25]   On this covertly feminist position also hangs the spiritual future of the entire humun race and the humun rights of billions!

Getting back to the other point I was making earlier: in contrast to Sarah, the >Aristocratic Marianne< seen as the embodiment of the powergroup within the extremist totalitarian >State< was fashioned to reflect the black-and-white thinking of the once fervently devout and now wholly disillusioned fascist/dialectical materialist:

> Marianne has what hu has through birth and power, and maintains it (even against hus own most gentle and noble inclinations) through a willful and bitter exercise of corrupt power.
>
> Hu defends hus choice strictly with pragmatic arguments; hu knows hu is morally wrong, but hu has chosen to be wrong on the grounds that |doing the right thing would be irresponsible| and that hus means are the only means the politicophysical economies permit.

Marianne has chosen to remain in Hell until Justice has been done to All - and laughs even as hu burns, for hus `Moral Freedom' proceeds from a workaholic compulsion to |Perfection|, not from anything this world can offer.

Marianne defies the world to bring hum to trial - and, in the real world, hu has every legal reason (under the guise of military or police gudsanctions) to expect a full acquittal for most of hus political crimes, and immunity from prosecution for the rest of them through the general failure of >The System<.

Marianne is, after all, only following the orders that proceed from the higher authority of a rational body of political theory; hu is heroically waging a just war against an enemy that cannot be overcome except through the unbridled exercise of Caesar's power.

Yet if and when Marianne finally decides to step out of [*Hell(!)], and return to a *Classical [Humun] identity, hu too will have to stand as Sarah, anxious to end hus exile, to march royally against humself. For the alternative would leave hum |something-less-than-Mun|. But Marianne has considered that possibility too:

> Hu has only contempt for the >Physical<, therefore hus >Body< may be sacrificed to the cause of >Humun Progress<; insectlike, hu is willing to allow both hus spiritual and physical >Self< to be treated as disposable, willing to bequeath hus [*Free Will] to [Mun*Sarah] or to the `clones' of [Marianne].

Note also that hu has no physical fear of Hell's torments. It is only through hus as-yet-nonmanifest "Immortal Soul" that Marianne could be influenced. Only the prospect of a total, interplanetary/multiuniverse annihilation of the species would give hum pause.

Why?
> Because despite its emphasis on the individual, on private [*Conscience], the *Classical view of [Humun*Perfection] monistically envisions only [One*Gud], [One*Person], [One*Cosmic*Picture], [One Unified Science], etc.[26]

> Wherefore the whole species is the keeper of [*Marianne]'s "Immortal Soul", no matter how damned a >concrete< instance of >Marianne< may be.

Here then is the Romantic Gestaldt flypapering both {Sarah} and {Marianne} (and temporarily, most probably |The Author| and |The Reader| as well):

> Whether {Marianne} chooses, sanely, to abandon the goal of [*Wholeness], or chooses, romantically, to seek hus `Higher

---

[26] i.e., all "*Perfect" mun are alternate pictures of the same "*Mun".

Self, makes little personal difference to hum - for hu has
decided to postpone `Salvation', to leave it to posterity.

And {Marianne} is morally justified in doing so, because
>The System< has failed and hu is therefore not obligated
to act morally.

Hus professed [Humun] love for [The Sacred] makes a
difference to hum - not in the absurd and impossible `Afterlife',
but in >the next generation< once >The System< has been
restored to proper function.[27]

Note that in such classical "individualist" moralities
`Soul' must be seen as an   excessive and   subsidiary
concept to that of [*Conscience]. And, most disturbingly,
it also forms the basis for the proliferation of "satanic
cult" Antistate constituencies, which parallel in reverse
the very rituals of the ultra-stringent unworkable theories
of the organized religions which give rise to them and
which many in the congregation soon find they cannot
live with.

For such reasons, my abstract 'thought experiment'
appears to me most relevant!

In   such schemata, `Soul', loosely equivalent to
[*Awareness], can reside wherever and however as it
(or >Gud<) pleases. But [*Conscience] must reside only
in   the   [*Person], who alone is   held   accountable -
"operant conditioning" be damned!

Certainly   for   the   scientist   [*Conscience]   is
recognized as a necessary orthogonal function preserving
sanity   and   personal integrity—an   integrity socially

---

[27]   This, of course, is the materialist theory put forth
repeatedly   in neo-Brechtian "Gudfather" apologies for the
sanctioned co-presence of organized crime as a genuine
counter-culture and guerrilla Alterstate activity.

created and socially conserved, but also psychologically essential to "rational" (i.e., "nonpathological" and "nonschizoid") `humun' behavior.

Yet the materialist's existentially modified >Conscience< can and often must bend opportunistically, through the structured intervention of >The System<, to permit selective >State+Gud-sanctioned< `criminal' acts ostensibly for the purpose of `group-survival'.

If most of the above seems too familiar, then all the better! Now having painted my picture, framed it, and hung it on the wall, it is time for me to alienate myself from my own construction so as to better reflect on the bizarre consequences of this entrenched ideological paradigm.

As has been pointed out, the polisocmor question considered in Books I and II is the world-historical problem generated by `the lifeboat ethic'.

The *Classical solution is seen to come through the progressive refinement of humun institutions that eliminate conditions where it must be invoked, thereby increasing individual humun freedom of >normative< choice (while at the same time decreasing the number of opportunities for making truly unique and individual [concrete(!)] - not necessarily >normative< - value-judgments and hence ultimately, nevertheless still acting in behalf of `Group Mind' to depress [*Authentic(!) Self-consciousness].

| The Author's| difficulty with the above arises from an adherence to this timeworn and thus-far bankrupt problem-solving matrix:

> i. in contemplating the quasi-utopian case, where most humun conflict has been reduced to trivial family squabbles and small-town storms in a teacup, and the only thing to look forward to is a sleepy retirement to an idyllic green pasture that depresses

existential awareness of distinctly [Humun*Being].[28]

    ii. on trying on scifi alternatives for future `Mun', |The Author| keeps running into clones of [Marianne], or into [Mothra] and [Max Headroom].

    iii. on trying to act `Humunly' within the present existentially-cataclysmic environment, [*The Author], like all social worker classes, finds humself inundated and nearly drowned by life-boat-ethic' situations arising out of public apathy in '>The State< generated by the renegade fluctuation of the concept of >Mun/mun<.

    iv. on trying to find the source of such public apathy, |The Author| stumbles on the problem of do-gooder "burn out" which seems to be affecting everyone.

    v. while most of such "burn out" is probably really due to economic stress, viruses and pollution, the old-fashioned vaccine which once seemed to have a special ability to motivate change—the ideological vaccine of "|The Sacred|" — is either being misused or trashed.

    vi. this prompts [The Author] to challenge the *Classical ideal of the "workable utopian" >State< by asking some unbiased and pointed questions:

What, ultimately, is Mun? A monkey? An insect?

Is there anything [*Sacred(!)] or [Real(!) in the material universe that remains intact even in utopian environments where moral consciousness, through ritual, lies dormant?

If we give in to humunitarian "burn out" and eliminate billions of [Skeets] so that |We the Strong| can immediately achieve and enjoy our new mun-made *Paradise*, will we still, like {Sarah}, need to keep biting the *Apple* in order to remain [*Humun]?

---

[28] Not that a smattering of such islands of tranquility isn't always welcome!

From a cosmologist's standpoint, no Survivalist's monstrous "final solution" can be categorically rejected on moral grounds until metaphysical questions about the nature of spatiotemporal reality, as defined by the physicist and the information scientist, are satisfactorily resolved.

Scientists evade such moral dilemmas by waiting for some prophetized "New Messiah" to arrive from the religions or the humanities to interpret the progress of the physical sciences within the languages of science. But this is a hypocritical epistemic strategy that inevitably traps us into either the [Altermun-Marianne]'s or the [Antimun-Marianne]'s programmes of "humun-garbage-disposal" often euphemized and/or legitimized as [Social Darwinism].

Scientists should be able to study both `Religion' and `Morals' without reducing either category to Munlogy(Anthropology) or Psychology or Sociology, and should be able, under a systematic Religious Science, and a systematic Moral Science, to come up with fruitful ontological hypotheses contiguous with the epistemic objectives of a unified science.[29]

Only when we can arrive at a formal nondarwinian explication of a new concept of [*The   Sacred] contiguous with the theoretical foundations of science shall we be able to resolve questions dealing with `the lifeboat ethic'   taken out of their multicultural classicoreligious contexts, to arrive at a global unisci [Meta-Theory of Mun].

This is the same larger question still left unresolved in Book II. Let us therefore restate it:

---

[29]   And I don't mean an ontology of quarks and muons! Real `Courage&Conscience' are lacking.

Can one arrive at a universally valid moral theory that will take into account humun evolution beyond the species level?

Or is {mun-defined Mun}(i.e., the hybrid {Sarah/Marianne}) doomed to perpetual >Dybbukian< transformations—doomed to perpetual war, and system-sanctioned criminality, or— what may be even worse from a world-historical view—doomed to ruminate, after the `Survivalist holocaust', like contented cattle in islands of `utopian tranquility'?

What, if [~Gud] defines a distinctly [*Humun] existence?

And if a pupal-stage humunity finally emerges from its earthly cocoon into one or more extrabiological forms of being within the intergalactic universe, which distinctly [Humun] features will ultimately survive such long-distance permutations?

While it may not at first be obvious, the above is subtly equivalent to the following:

> |What shall be the nature and persona of
> [Mun-created-Gud]|?

That is, because from a realistic and world-historical standpoint we all must agree that {Gud} did not create either {Mun} or {mun}; rather, [mun] created [*Gud].

And this muncentric act, in which a {Gud} was created in the image either of *Adam or of *Christ, prompts an even more radical inquiry:

> Is {Gud}, like {The State}, authentically only one more
> "prosthetic extension" of mun?

> And if so, then why |Gud|, why not |Supermun|?

In our final encounter with Marianne in Book II, this is the inevitable outcome of the classicoromantic `Supermun' programme.

And the world-historical temptation toward the evolutionary achievement of [Mun-Gudhood] for either

Sarah or Marianne is not seen as heresy but as the legitimate legacy of any classico-religious doctrine that preaches a {Parent:Child} image-equivalence between {Gud} and {Mun}.

The inadequacy of this picture increases, not diminishes, whenever mun-defined >Mun< acquires, through science, the ability to see the world from mun-defined/Humun-defined {Gud's Eye}; for two nagging questions still remain unanswered, perhaps for all `Eternity'—questions which, if unanswered by a satisfactory [*Supermun], condemn all three of my characters to an ever-diminishing concept of |Mun| *i.e.,*

      (a) What is the nature (or meaning) of "The Real"?
      (b) Is [*The Sacred] ever [Real(!)] in a |Random| Universe?

But abandon that classicoromantic picture and a whole new strategy appears—for it is my sincere contention that, for all common characterizations of (a) above, (b) can be answered intelligibly and nonparadoxically in the affirmative—if we reject *All* ontological posits of [Gud].

As I have previously noted, *Gud,* like *Phlogiston,* is ontologically dispensable in favor of the concept of [Scientific*Truth]—a [Scientific*Truth] which, for a [Self=The Sacred], provides the only means of egress for a cosmic [*Awareness] which cannot escape the |brute fact| of the |Humun Condition|even unto the outermost rim of the Universe—an [*Awareness] that is fated to return, *Big Bang* after *Big Bang,* to an internal [*Hell(!)] of its Own Making until such time as it can congeal itself into a harmonic [*Wholeness]—a [*Flowering of Being].

If this posit continues to startle you, just ask

yourself what, in your deepest {Self}, you value more—what would you, with your |Whole Self-Conscious Being| be willing to endure the worst of all deaths for—the   [*Love(!)] of {Gud} or the [*Love(!)] of {Truth}?

If there were some means of persuading you that you couldn't have both, would you indeed prefer {Gud}?

The intellectually honest among us would have to admit that >Truth< —no matter how arcane and elusive the concept may be—is both more "logically primitive" and (hence) more [*Sacred(!)]".

Nor can there be any theologian's escape from this intuition in the smug assurance that [Gud] and [Truth] are |One|;   for [Gud] is an ontological posit, and >Truth< is not an `object' but a `value' assigned to logico-theoretical constructions, and |Gud= | is an identity relation between an `object' and a `truth-value' that, if metalinguistically posited as [*True(!)], merely begs the question!

This new start from a cosmic [Awareness] that holds [The Self=The Sacred] ought to do for Moral Science what Relativity did for Physics.

Grounding `The Sacred' in the `Self' wherever |Self-Consciousness| emerges, forces the Moral Observer to become the center of the Universe, no longer alienated from an `Other' which does all the actual *Willing, *Creating, *Knowing, and so on, from some vague and arbitrary parameter set >ever beyond language<.

It preserves the real sense of the concept of `Freedom and Responsibility' for `All Mun', transforms `All Mun' into |Shepherds|   rather than   |Sheep|, connects  `Each Mun' to the common bond of [*Selfhood-in-Awareness].

It further`Self-mandates' an `enlightened   Self-

Interest' —a cosmic evangelism toward a concrete goal of >Humun Progress< for [All Conscious Beings], whether these be {Biological} or {Whatever}, [*Who] share in the |brute fact| and >Truth< of the|Humun Condition|.

This kind of `Self' is `Recurrent', `Inescapable', `Communal', giving new sense and orientation to the dictum:

"Whatsoever Ye Do Unto Each Other,
Ye Do Also Unto Me"

and spontaneous endorsement to the christian maxim,

"Do unto others as you would have them do unto you."

Are you happy with this new picture?

It may yet prove be the most savage and dreadful of all(!), but it does provide an escape from macrocosmic ennui and daily routine, and the dull prospect of ending our zillion millenia as nothing more than contented cows and couch potatoes!

For under this view we do simultaneously sit, eternally and recurrently (insofar as those terms make physical sense), in both a `Heaven' and `Hell' of `Our Own Making', wherein *Equity, *Justice, Humun*Purpose, Humun*Entelechy, are all >Self-determined< and therefore [*Free(!)].

But what about [*Love] as viewed from this Muncentric set of parameters?   [Self*Love] sounds dreadfully dull, even masturbatory!

Does this new view condemn us to an inescapable homo-eroticism, a `narcissism' of cosmic breadth?

Are all of [My*Embraces] [Self*Embraces]? [30]

No!   For in a   cosmology   allowing   for >extensional truth< there is an [*Other] in our universe which is [*Other-than-Observers] and it is that inescapable   presence, that alienating |brute   fact| delimiting,   partitioning,   grounding   each   minute instant   of   [My*Self-Conscious*Being], which is—howbeit ever savage, impersonal and uncaring—both [*My Lover]   and   [My   Beloved] and heteroerotic genome to [*All My Clones]!

But >Truth<, mind you, is not a [*Person].

Nor is it in itself an [*Object] in any ordinary sense of the   word. In   all   instances of our experimental interaction with the [Other] beyond language, it   is simply a |Feedback(!)|, a |Signal(!)| a [*YES(!)].)

But I swear to you that although, like Sarah, I too have always been demanding "carnal knowledge of an |Angel|, I did not begin my present project with any such startling conclusions in mind!

I was only intent upon constructing a model that would effectively sort out all the confusion in my thought.

I simply assumed that my deep-rooted personal hostility to the male-defined concept of {Gud} was politico-psychologically   oppressive   and   contemptuous. The `thought experiment' of Book II was   specifically devised to untether my thought in order to ferret out the gender-free image of [Mun] from the lesser (and polihisto-contaminated) image of {Man}.

I hoped through such a mental honing process to

---

[30]   NOTA BENE that I have entirely wiped out {Gender} from this semantic!)

adumbrate the polylog reasons for my gut-objection to all "God" posits as being not merely impure because sexist, but because the theological-ontological assertion—even in its most refined and nonsexist formulation—is fundamentally excessive, schizoid and prone to pathological contamination; more often than not homoerotic, lascivious, narcissistic and idolatrous; psychologically and epistemically obstructive; further, entirely eliminable in favor of a `Social-Conscience-driven' morally-responsible characterization of ⌈The Ideal State⌉; and, at least to |The Author|, intuitively also *⌈sacrilegious(!)⌉.

But the epistemological necessity of categorically rejecting the entire Gud-paradigm was not obvious to me when, as both female and feminist, I attempted to contemplate ⌈*God⌉ in its male-related image.

As female, I had always been far too prone to dismiss my personal objection to the male-related image of either {Gud} or {Supermun} as an extension of my existential rejection of the psychosexual image of {The Male=Object-of-Religious*Worship} as {symbol-of-political-subjugator-and-molestor}.

And it was only after first constructing, then deconstructing {Supermun/Marianne} in the light of my information science model of ⌈*Consciousness(!)⌉ that I finally found my way out of the picture.

But after contemplating the truly abominable, spiritual invasiveness of Supermun/Marianne as it is felt by ⌈Mun*Sarah⌉ - a generic `rape-relation' of ⌈mun-on-*Mun⌉ - such psycho-political oppression, such spiritual invasion, really has nothing to do with the ⌈Gender⌉ of the protagonists, now, does it?

It is the {Gudpicture} - the entire {Gudparadigm}
that offends and oppresses ⌈*Me⌉.

But enough said for one sitting!

If |You| are still with |Me|, if by now I have not thoroughly befuddled |You|, then by all means interface with |Me| again in my forthcoming offerings wherein I promise to reveal to |You|, insofar as my own poetic sight is |**Gospel**| the full and unequivocal meaning of |The*Sacred|.

ArtemisSmith **1989**

Part 1101: The After-Afterthought

Part 1101: The After-Afterthought

Dear Colleague:

I like what I wrote in 1989, but I am still not finished. The world has turned and the classical picture trapping |The Author| in all that has gone before is now clouded, rendered obscure and insignificant by |Humun Progress| in a new key, made possible by the electronic age and biotechnology. Supermun has emerged and hu is not Hive-bound as previously forseen. At least, not yet!

The objective correlatives of my narrative, my life-models for Skeets, Sarah and Marianne *all still live*, and the world has turned so radically that new reflection is required . . . .

Wherefore, flip these pages Back to the Beginning,
Back to the Future,
Back to **GrandmaMoseX'**
and Ask Yourself

[How the Blazes Do Escape from *This* Box] ???

Annselm LNVM 2013

DETAIL FROM: "PteroDARKtyl Notebook"
© 1963 artemis smith. All rights reserved.

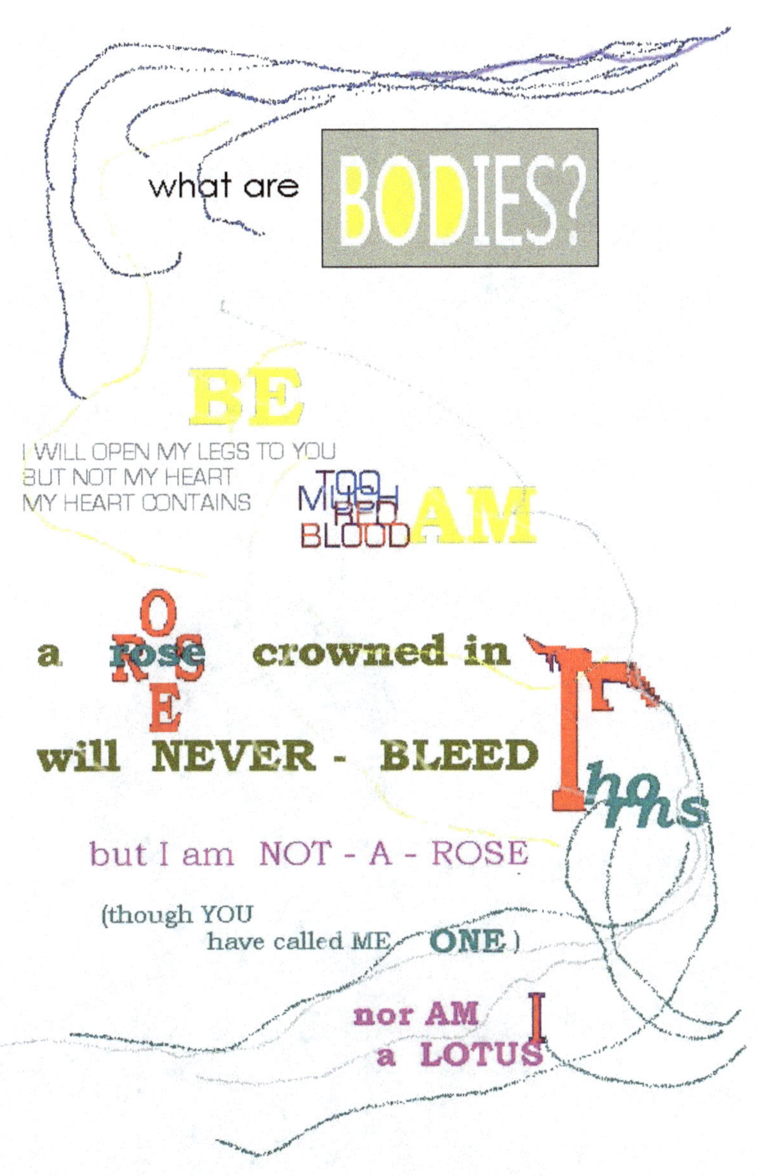

what are BODIES?

BE
I WILL OPEN MY LEGS TO YOU
BUT NOT MY HEART
MY HEART CONTAINS
TOO MUCH RED BLOOD
AM

a ROSE crowned in

will NEVER - BLEED Thorns

but I am NOT - A - ROSE

(though YOU
have called ME ONE)

nor AM I
a LOTUS

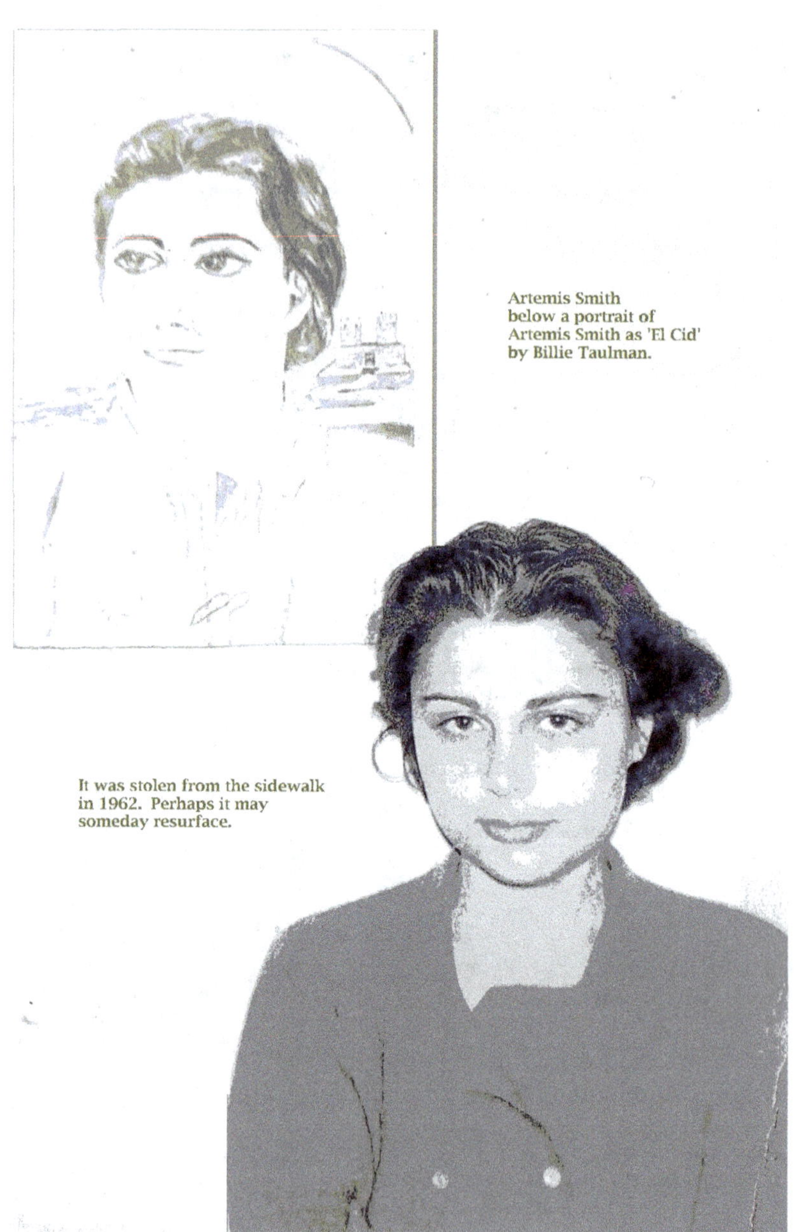

Artemis Smith
below a portrait of
Artemis Smith as 'El Cid'
by Billie Taulman.

It was stolen from the sidewalk
in 1962. Perhaps it may
someday resurface.

To So Many
I Cannot Name Them

and

To One Whose Self
I Have Conserved In Me

- therefore -

To My Self
DEARLY BELOVED
MY ONELY
SELF
DEARLY BELOVED

and

OWNLY
to

I

ME   YE
BEST
SELF

DEARLY BELOVED

9 781878 998200